Remembering Dixie

Remembering DIXIE

A NOVEL

BUDDY
IGNATIUS D'AQUILA

HOT AUGUST NIGHTS

1 9 9 7

I would like to thank The TIMES-PICAYUNE Publishing Company for permission to use the DIXIE logo.

FIRST EDITION, 1000 Copies

LIBRARY OF CONGRESS CATALOG CARD NUMBER 97-94103

ISBN 0-9659156-0-3

Cover and text illustrations copyright © 1997
by Michael Ledet

Designed by MICHAEL LEDET art & design, New Orleans

Edited by Mimi Byrnes Pelton

Typography production by Marlene Bernard

Published by
Hot August Nights, New Orleans

PRINTED IN THE UNITED STATES OF AMERICA

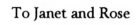

To Janet and Rose

You may remember that I have written that myths get thought in man unbeknownst to him.

-----Claude Lévi-Strauss

Even when someone we know tells a story straight out, the myth may hide itself, moving along behind the details of what happened just yesterday, right next door, and could just as well have happened to us.

-----Dennis Tetlock

Part One

Chapter 1

*I*n 1934, when I was five, Mama Gomez took me home with her on Marais Street. Thereafter, I was known as Bobby Gomez. We lived in a little shot-gun single--one would have to say modestly--even by Depression standards, suffering through cold winters huddled around portable kerosene heaters and through torrid summers without air conditioning or even fans. The windows and doors were shuttered with louvered blinds, which for some reason Mama Gomez kept closed even when the windows were raised. On summer mornings I would awake early and walk up through the darkened, single-filed rooms to Mama Gomez's little parlor and reach up blindly for the little chain switch on the light--a single bulb enclosed in a frosted-glass shade. Mama's few pieces of furniture would glow with oily brightness in the barely adequate light and exude the smarting, resinous odor of O-Cedar polish which she applied generously every Saturday. I would peek out of the window through the blinds at our narrow street with its bumpy brick banquettes, slate-lined gutters and oyster-shell bedding--usually deserted at this early hour--and be reminded of another street in a similar house and another window that I remembered looking out of at a earlier time in my life. This house, according to Mama Gomez--no willing purveyor of information--was somewhere near Bayou St. John. I only dimly recall being there, sitting by a greasy window on an old battered armchair whose stuffings littered the floor--small, comforting cotton fibers I must have pulled out myself. In other rooms were the odors of things rotting in corners, a mattress without linen that gave off an itchy, damp smell I can still recreate and the ineradicable memory of a fermenting orange, fuzzy with green mold, rolling over the rocky grooves of a worn-through linoleum floor. And roaches, giant flying roaches, more frightening creatures than anything found in the jungle. I was left for hours I think, and perhaps days, looking out of the window at boys running, playing football in the narrow street, women on their front steps conversing with their arms swinging out in excited flourishes, children on bicycles speeding across my limited field of vision. Surely I was beyond the mere physical effects of hunger, beyond feeling abandoned and lonely--a small child feels no real loneliness perhaps but rather a primitive, all-consuming solitude. I felt no pain, but instead, an acuity of vision, strangely fascinated by whatever was framed within the purview of my window, simply because it moved. Hunger and sheer isolation had rendered me rapt, I was, no doubt, in a delirium.

I was rescued by Mrs. Cusimano, who has been an indelible presence for me. I cannot possibly forget her raspy voice, calling me.

"Open the door, honey, open the door for Miss Cusimano," she said, rattling the blinds with her banging. She seemed at first simply another radiant fragment of life, until she reached up and knocked on the window panes, startling me out of my precious seclusion. She had brought a pot of soup and a pint of milk. I smiled at her, understanding somehow that she was there to help me. Only then did I realize what great effort I was exerting to sustain myself, and only then did I let down, nearly collapsing with weakness. I got up slowly and unlocked the door and she led me half stumbling through the shut-up, darkened house back into the kitchen, where she began opening windows and pushing out blinds. The light nearly blinded me. She fed me hot soup and I knew suddenly with the first sip how hungry I was.

Mrs. Cusimano and her husband ran the corner grocery store and I spent a few days with them in their quarters behind the store. I clung the entire time to the poor lady. She allowed me to do so, knowing my extreme insecurity. Not even Theresa, her daughter, could lure me away from her mother. Theresa was a year or so older than I and a head taller.

"See, Robert," Theresa exclaimed, "a ball." She bounced the ball furiously and when I buried my face in Mrs. Cusimano's long dress, Theresa would put her face right up to mine, fluttering my cheeks with her long lashes, nearly kissing me with her wet, open mouth. I wanted to play with her, but could not, for it meant leaving her mother where I had at last felt safe.

2

After that I was taken to an orphanage, where Mama Gomez, then recently a widow, worked as a cook and cleaning lady. I was there for only a month, I believe, when Mama Gomez took me home with her on Marais Street.

Just how this Filipino widow qualified to adopt me is a mystery, since she was poor, illiterate and partially crippled with great varicose veins, and obviously not of my fair lineage. The nuns who ran the orphanage were guided, no doubt, by a kind of old-world wisdom; they were as dark-skinned as Mama herself, and just as bold, willing to cast aside legal procedures if it suited their purposes. And so, by whatever kind of criminality and arcane Latin intuition, it was done. A winning combination, it was to be, I might add, this ponderous dark mother and her frail, fair son.

This much I remember--but I've been told I was born somewhere else, where, presumably, I had another name. In this and other ways, I am a stranger to myself. My life before Mama Gomez was a blur, a few fleeting glimpses of uncertain order, like bright pieces tumbled in a memory box, or album snapshots found in a stranger's attic. And yet none of this uncertainty had scarred me; in fact, I have considered myself fortunate, and have hoarded the contentment and success that should not have been possible for me. Not even my abandonment by my parents, who were mere teenagers, carries any accusatory rage. Their departure, attested to by Sister Catherine at the orphanage, was simply a fact, rehearsed only in the realm of my imagination--I don't remember the event. But I have witnessed it over and over; not that I remember any parting words, even if they spoke such words to me, or the sight of them waving good-bye, or an embrace and parting kiss: I see them, rather, turned away, the backs of their heads visible in some middle-distance, where they were not striding but fading away.

Have I crossed them out of my consciousness completely and forever? If I did, I am not aware of it, and if I did, would I not be pent up with anger and plagued with nightmares from which I would awaken trembling and frightened, or at the very least, permanently embittered by the kind of invincible paranoia that cripples feral children? Shouldn't I have been neurotic or insane, or given to drink or drugs or violent crime? But this is not what happened, because as far as I can remember I have always been normal.

3

Chapter 2

_P_ hilip Rotolo was my best friend; he lived just down the block from me, in a camel-back house behind his family's laundry shop. The Rotolos were considered well-off with space heaters and oscillating fans in every room. At that time, for the most part, Philip and I made nothing of the difference between our families, nor did we think one way or another about the quality of life in the ninth ward. It seemed as good a place as any. I can't speak for our friend Ronnie Hingle, who lived on Poland Avenue, in the lower ward. I don't think Ronnie ever considered growing up downtown a good thing.

Of course, we didn't meet Ronnie until after the war, and might never have known him if Philip hadn't run into him in Munich when they were stationed together in Occupied Germany--a bit of international irony--fellow ninth-warders meeting in a foreign land as perfect strangers, one of the anomalies of finishing a global war.

The war had changed everything for us and the ninth ward, sweeping away the last remnants of the Depression--that cozy era of poverty so fondly remembered today; in the meantime, the ninth ward became a piece of forgotten history.

Actually, we had all missed the war--wars I should say--because we served our tour of duty between 1945 and 1950--the Peace as we like to call it, that scintillating interlude between the Japanese surrender and the Korean Conflict. Although it wasn't really exciting since the war was over, I enjoyed military life very much; it provided the kind of detachment and anonymity that suited me very well. The guys who had actually fought the war were already home going to college and offering their GI diplomas on the job market.

Our years in the service seem to pass very quickly and almost before we realized it, by 1950 the Cold War had set in and we were back home, ready to begin college on our GI Bill. I arrived home from Fort Polk in July, having spent my entire tour of duty in the desolate hills near Kileen in central Texas, a few days after Philip had gotten back from Munich, as I later learned. I found myself in a strange exalted state, standing in the middle of the Southern Railway terminal on Canal Street, next to my duffel bag, like Adam, set down afresh in a new world with barely enough gravity to plant my feet. No one, not even Mama Gomez, my sole relative, knew of my return. It presented the possibility of simply getting back on the train. I don't know where I would have gone--California maybe. I felt myself floating free in the vast universe. As long as I stood there in my infantry khakis, nudging my duffel bag, the world seemed completely my oyster. My real options were to jump a streetcar on Canal Street or hail a taxi. What I really had in mind, however, was to call Philip, hoping he was already home.

I remember hesitating right before I picked up the receiver with the odd thought that Philip and I might now be strangers. How happy I was to hear him roar his elation into the phone--a matter of perfect timing; he had gotten back a few days earlier.

"Stay right where you are champ, I'm on my way!" he yelled, and hung up before I could tell him to inform Mama Gomez of my arrival, she didn't have a phone--I had to call him back.

All of a sudden, I became nervous with new anticipation and started pacing in the front of the station with my bag, anxiously counting the minutes, waiting for the Rotolo Pontiac to appear down Canal Street. He finally arrived, of course, to find me staring off into the distance, lost in a day dream. I looked up, momentarily shocked because he seemed both familiar and strange with his GI haircut, army tan and civilian clothes, banging the sides of the Pontiac.

"Well, don't just stand there, ace," he fired out, "Get in and let's go." When Philip smiled he reminded you of Victor Mature.

He kept yelling and punching me on the arm, calling me a son of a bitch; he was really beside himself and so was I, unable to speak from smiling so much or protect myself from his murderous blows; Philip didn't know his strength.

On Marais Street, I could hear oyster shell fragments kicking up under the Pontiac's fenders; even with my eyes closed I would have known exactly where I was. We bounced in and out of holes big as craters, and in that first somewhat shocking but objective moment, the shot-gun houses looked cramped and hoary, as did Impastato's corner grocery with its pre-war Dutch cleanser decal and vintage Coca-Cola sign. Mama Gomez was sitting on our tiny front steps with her huge legs spread out to balance her great bulk; her hand was cupped over her eyes, shading them from the sun. I hadn't seen her in six months and she seemed a lot darker than I remembered. Her black hair shone with a blue sheen and her brown cheeks were as sparkling as Hattie MacDaniels'. I can't say I knew what to make of her in her sleeveless cotton print and bulging slippers--she was all the family I had. A little spasm of pure happiness fluttered my heart when I dumped my duffel bag on the banquette and decided to embrace her--to lose myself in her great wealth of flesh, not our usual manner of greeting--in fact, I had never given her more than a one-armed tentative hug. But I did then, and she seemed temporarily overwhelmed, and although she hesitated to hug back, tears were streaming from her eyes. She had to break loose from me to wipe her nose. She led me back into the kitchen, fried a chop, and sat down to watch me eat it. I told her about going to college on my GI Bill, she smiled, not because she understood but because she could serve me the kind of food we could never afford. I was too excited to be hungry, but I ate all of it, more for her pleasure than mine.

The kitchen was hot, but I didn't mind, I couldn't get enough of looking at everything. Out of the back door, which was wide open for maximum ventilation, I surveyed the backyard overrun now with tall summer weeds. Two oleander trees with their daggered leaves and scarlet blossoms exuded their heavy perfume which carried into the kitchen over the piquant odor of the fried chop. Along the back fence, an ancient, twisted fig tree and a Japanese plum bore sticky, late summer fruit. Althea scrubs thick with purple blossoms and their protruding golden stamens stood next to the open-fronted back shed, harboring savage alley cats scratching and clawing among stacks of old newspaper and rusting hardware collected over long years. I was soaking wet after eating and peeled off my khaki shirt before stepping out onto the little back porch. Small yellow butterflies and bumble bees hovered about the oleanders and altheas; I caught flashes of big, golden mosquito hawks darting about after gnats and mosquitoes that buzzed in the weeds. The sun bore down and made me think of the narrow alleyway that ran along side of the house, that cool corridor, protected as it is from the scorching heat by the flanking houses and a high board fence, collecting moisture in the sodden earth between the porous bricks, out of which sprouted tiny wild succulents and iridescent ground moss. It was here, as a child, among all the crawling insects that I would have spent most of my days had Mama Gomez not dragged me out. As I stood there daydreaming, clouds built cathedral heights; above in the blue expanses a lost gull made his way crazily across the sky. When I dropped my eyes, the granddaddy of all mosquitoes was plunging his hypodermic into my arm. I watched with great interest as his abdomen swelled to crimson with my blood. I was home.

Things settled down very briefly for Philip and me after the excitement of coming home, until a week or so later, when Philip came over in the Pontiac to tell me that Ronnie Hingle was back from Munich. He was worked up about driving down to Poland Avenue to welcome Ronnie back, jamming the Pontiac's brakes and spraying oyster shells from the street onto the brick banquette at my feet. I was sitting on the steps in front of my shot-gun.

"Ronnie's out, champ. Hop in!" He ordered. I got in--it was impossible to resist Philip--only to have him deliver one of his brutal arm punches, smiling that big exasperating grin of his. It was the dog days of summer, and sweat was soon soaking us down to our GI T-shirts. In spite of Philip's joy, I was leery about meeting Ronnie, not only because he lived in the lower ward--bad news in itself--but because Philip told me he had enrolled at Tulane on his GI Bill, which smelled like real trouble. Ninth-warders, especially lower ninth-warders, would do well to avoid Tulane--a good example of the strange effect the war 's invigorating aftermath was having on us.

The Pontiac gave us no relief from the heat, AC for cars was not available in 1950, if it had been, the Rotolos with their thriving cleaning business, would have had it. Philip headed the Pontiac downriver on St. Claude Avenue, the ninth ward's principal artery, with its swaying, milling old streetcar, a street I had considered fairly modern before the war, but now seemed a dingy, outdated strip--a jumble of shops and small businesses, everything from Gulf stations to funeral parlors. As we crossed Desire Street, entering the lower ward, Philip finally settled back into his seat. Heavy black clouds gathered over the marshes, darkening the sky, and for the briefest moment, the sun disappeared and a cool breeze blew into my window. The smell of rain was in the air, but it didn't matter, nor did my concerns about Ronnie, even if he was one of those bone-headed, incorrigible graduates from Francis T. Nicholls High School down on Alva Street, who had gotten his diploma only because his teachers couldn't stand him anymore. Nothing could quell this strange unguarded feeling of ringing excitement. It was going to be a glorious gathering.

Ronnie's street, Poland Avenue, as I remembered, was no grand avenue, though it might have been once; it was just another oyster-shell street lined with shot-gun houses. Beyond Poland Avenue, a draw bridge rose over the Industrial Canal where St. Claude Avenue begins to twist and turn with the river, past Pakenham Oaks and the old Chalmette battleground, on and on, trailing away, far out of the city boundaries into the swamps and marsh lakes of St. Bernard Parish where reside alligators, muskrats, nutria, yellow-fever mosquitoes and God knows what else--that is boogalees as natives of St. Bernard are known, who according to legend have webbing between their toes. (This I've never observed but am inclined to believe. We refer to St. Bernard as *down-below* for the same reason that Australians call the desolate middle of their country *outback*, both interesting places to visit but neither fit for human habitation.) In the old days we would jump a streetcar on St. Claude to the end of the line and go slouching through the palmetto swamps, keeping one eye peeled for water moccasins and the other for the little red flags we marked our crawfish nets with. It was possible to lose your way and never be found.

The sun blazed away, blistering the St. Claude pavements. I sat up expectantly, waiting for the clouds to collide in the brilliant stillness and for the distant sound of thunder to come rolling up from the river delta.

We had turned down Poland Avenue and Philip broke out with a chorus of *It's Been a Long, Long Time*, sinking his chin into his chest in the style of Bing Crosby, giving it everything he had:

> *"Kiss me once, and kiss me twice,*
> *And kiss me once again,*
> *It's been a long, long time."*

A perfect song for returning war heroes. Just down the street someone wearing summer khakis was leaning far down into the motor of a gray '49 Plymouth. It was Ronnie, but all I could see of him was the seat of his pants. The Plymouth's intricate parts were set out like jewelry on a neatly spread cloth on the brick banquette. The lady sitting on the low cypress steps, I learned, was his mother, Miss Thelma. Her side of the street was shaded and she sat there as cool as you pleased, sipping an RC Cola.

Philip eased the Pontiac up behind the Plymouth but neither Ronnie nor Miss Thelma stirred, transfixed, it appeared, by the sulfurous heat. Philip hailed Miss Thelma as if he was an old friend of the family. Actually he had met her only once, but nobody was a stranger to Philip very long.

Ronnie rose out of the Plymouth, wrench in hand, rangy and graceful; he smiled at us and struck the willowly hip-shot pose of Polyclitus. He seemed shy and altogether charming with his close-cropped curly hair and natural smile. I liked him immediately. Perhaps, I thought, it wasn't cockiness or thuggish insensitivity that had driven him to Tulane, but, more probably, a vagrant ambition-- not usual in lower ninth-warders--an innocent need to climb out of the dreary backwardness he was born into.

They had not seen each other in months and Philip was exuberant, roughing him up. But Ronnie was nimble and covered up neatly, bobbing and weaving. There they went, laughing and asking a million questions about their buddies, hardly stopping for answers, Ronnie quickly side-stepping Philip's punches, and Philip laughing uproariously when Ronnie, suddenly shedding his boyish self-consciousness, did a quick little mime of their company C.O.

Miss Thelma was smiling and sipping. She seemed to flush a bit like a young girl as she gestured toward Ronnie with the RC.

"How you think m'boy looks, Philip?"

Philip scanned Ronnie up and down as a tailor would and sidled up to Miss Thelma bending down slightly as if to noodle her.

"He ain't half as pretty as you, Miss Thelma." She made a face of mock indignation and slapped at Philip's shoulder.

"You go on boy--I know I ain't pretty no more."

"C'mon, Miss Thelma," Philip said moving close again, "Aren't you my sweetheart?"

She drew up her toothless mouth into a vehement humph and rolled her eyes. She was having none of it. Her gray hair was chopped off and pulled back with bobbie pins and she had long since lost her waistline, but her unconcern for her vanished beauty had settled into a sweetness which glimmered in her faded green eyes and somehow her toothless wrinkles and lumpiness had not canceled her girlishness. One suspected that she had sailed through menopause without a hitch.

She sipped more RC working her lips and gums elaborately as she swallowed and gestured once more toward Ronnie.

"M'boy has been accepted at Tulane. He got a letter in the mail." She raised the bottle of RC seeming to toast Ronnie and Tulane again. Ronnie just stood there smiling, wiping grease from his hands, accepting the fact that his mother was talking about him as if he was not present to speak for himself. "He's gonna major in business," she boasted.

"That's right, Miss Thelma," Philip teased, "and what are you going to do when he graduates and starts making all that money?"

"Don't worry, honey," she replied lifting her chin in good natured indignation again. What does she need with money--will the price of RC go up?

I didn't think that Philip should have been joking about Ronnie graduating from Tulane as if it wasn't a big enough joke that Tulane accepted him. But what the hell did I know. I was an alarmist, I should be more like Miss Thelma--take it easy, drink RC, and take letters that come in the mail for good news.

Then, without warning, and just as I feared, Philip and Ronnie got down into the Plymouth's motor and started craning and speaking in serious whispers. Miss Thelma and I were left to smile uneasily at one another. Well, she wasn't uneasy, she was doing fine: beating the heat with a cold RC, perched upon her front steps ready to talk to anyone who passed or came visiting as we did. She probably approved of me, not knowing what kind of idler I was. I smiled at her and she smiled back. "You was in the army with Ronnie, honey?" "No, ma'am." Just then as I was trying to decide if I should tell Miss Thelma that I was in the army, lest she think I was a reject, I thought I caught a whiff of swamp rank: a mosquito lit on my arm and I looked up to see if a wind was blowing up from the St. Bernard swamps. But it was perfectly calm.

What I was smelling came walking out of the alley gate: a scowling, knotty, close knit little man with lank mousy hair falling down from his narrow head. He was barefooted and shirtless, wearing a knitted, vested Fruit of the Loom undershirt. It was Mr. Charlie, Ronnie's father. He looked at me, seemingly, but somehow right past me as if I was transparent or simply not there at all. I nearly popped out of my skin and backed away immediately, jumping into the gutter to join Philip and Ronnie down in the Plymouth's motor. I know this man's pedigree, I was thinking, he's a boogalee, a swamp man who has migrated up from the mucky lowlands. I saw it as an awkward maybe even a desperate situation, for he continued to scowl and greeted no one. What in the hell does he want? I asked myself and began to nervously hum *It's Been a Long, Long Time*, hardly conscious of what I was doing. I nudged Philip who rose up, spotted Mr. Charlie and to my amazement yelled out to him immediately as if he was not the mean little sour man I was looking at but--for Christ's sake--a center fielder for the Pelicans. "Hey, Mr. Charlie, what's ya problem, old man?" Philip roared, jumping up onto the banquette and poking him on the arm. Philip pulled the punch and I was happy for that. But Mr. Charlie didn't give up his scowl and still would not deem to look at anyone, certainly not me. I would have broken out running if he had. I knew, however, that it was only a matter of time before Philip would bring him around. Even then Philip would bubble with joy over the sight of such men as Mr. Charlie. Being a populist as was Huey Long before him, Philip knew that although Mr. Charlie had endured the Depression and other embittering hardships, a dirty joke and a few beers would fix him up.

Sure enough, Philip put his arm around Mr. Charlie's shoulder and whispered something in his ear and he finally smiled.

My own guess was that Mr. Charlie was from Toca, down in St. Bernard. His father was probably a trapper and they lived in a shack among gliding water moccasins, ate nothing but pould'eau and crawfish. Some parts of Toca are quite lovely, with majestic live oaks, graceful pecan orchards, a land interlaced with fecund bayous rippling with black bass and goggle-eyes. Either he lived in Toca or in Arabi and his old man worked at the Sugar Refinery, sweeping up sugar.

While I was speculating, Philip was really getting close to Mr. Charlie, working on that scowl. He had in mind that we could walk up the street to Steckmann's Bar and have a few cold beers.

11

He folded his arms like a sultan and put the proposition squarely to Mr. Charlie.

"C'mon, old man, let's walk over to Steckmann's and get a cold one."

"A-a-a-a-u-g-h," scowled Mr. Charlie in disgust, "What makes you think I drink wid dagos?"

"I'm buying," rejoined Philip, holding his ground.

Mr. Charlie went into a half crouch and did a little stutter step, grinning wryly, "Dat's different. I'll go put my shoes on."

The clouds over the marshes turned nearly black, and the sun beamed torridly, twinkling the oyster shells in the street, like so many rhinestones. We needed to be on our way to Steckmann's.

Miss Thelma looked at the last of the RC and drained it off. She got up to go inside. Philip hadn't invited her for beer out of respect since she was a lady. Chances are she had better things to do anyway.

But why was I still apprehensive? I had just acquired a new comfortable friend: Ronnie walked along ahead of me with Philip, smiling brightly. Was it because I was walking beside Mr. Charlie at whom I furtively and anxiously shot quick glances? I observed that with his shoes on, he and I were about the same height. What, after all, did I have to fear from this man, who was no bigger than myself? Shouldn't I jolly up to him with a nice dirty joke and poke him on his arm? The very thought of it caused me to shy toward the gutter and sent my heart thumping. Philip liked him, why shouldn't I? Shouldn't I strike up a companionship with any random boogalee, and be at my ease as I walked along to a good ninth-ward bar to drink beer with my friends? I should, of course, as I should stop making blind speculations about where my friend's father may be from, and take an interest in my friend's car, instead of making up stories about St. Bernard migrations.

Steckmann's was empty except for three rednecks sitting at a back table. That meant trouble, it was too early for rednecks. Rednecks were always drifting through, nobody ever knew where they came from or where they went afterwards. They were laughing and talking very loud and drinking whiskey. Who but rednecks would be drinking whiskey on such a hot day?

Sterling Steckmann, the proprietor, rolled his eyes ominously at Mr. Charlie as we got seated on the bar stools. He was concerned all right, he leaned over the bar and whispered that we shouldn't worry because he had a .38 in the cash register. The .38 was probably not loaded and was only for show. Sterl was old and consumptive and had no business fooling with a gun anyway. Just then Miss Gladys, Sterl's wife, appeared in the back doorway at the end of the bar. She had evidently heard the noise and came in from the back. Miss Gladys had the girt and upper arms of a wrestler and was in no mood to put up with rowdy rednecks. She started yelling, telling them that this was a nice, quiet neighborhood bar and they were making too much noise, so they would have to drink up and get out, and that they had better hurry because the wagon was on its way.

One of the rednecks snickered but seemed immediately sorry, because Miss Gladys started to yell even louder. He realized that her rage knew no limit, that short of challenging her to a fight he was helpless. Miss Gladys was now beyond herself. The rednecks began to sulk and squirm, looking at each other, trying to decide what to do, and finally their snickering leader grinned, got up and led the others out. Miss Gladys grabbed up their glasses and slammed them on the bar. She could handle a dozen rednecks, with or without a loaded .38. Old Sterl who had been wiping the bar the whole time suddenly wheezed out a crooked smile. "Hicks," he said, drawing himself up to catch his breath. His friend, Mr. Charlie, congratulated him for throwing them out and ordered up a round of beer, which Philip paid for. Of course, the rednecks were not really dangerous, and there was certainly no reason to call the cops. It was just that a neighborhood bar should be nice and peaceful. That's the way Sterl ran his business.

The sun had passed behind another cloud for suddenly it grew dark again.

The beer was icy and good and we settled comfortably under the strumming of the ceiling fans that whipped soft little curling wind currents all around us. The only thing wrong then was the seating arrangement; I was on the end with Mr. Charlie between me and my friends who were talking away, probably about the Plymouth or maybe Tulane. I didn't know what I could talk to Mr. Charlie about, especially since he didn't seem interested in conversation. He just sat there with his scowl drinking his beer as if it was poison, making me more nervous than the rednecks. But, of course, I didn't want to change stools and hurt his feelings. I got up to use the bathroom and on the way back I stopped to play the jukebox. By then Mr. Charlie was wound up, going on to Sterl about something. I really wanted to play *Sentimental Journey* by Doris Day, but I knew that this was not Mr. Charlie's taste. Being from St. Bernard, he probably preferred country music, but like all youngsters in the fifties, I hated country music. I settled for *The South Rampart Street Parade* by Sharkey, a Dixieland number.

When I sat down, I got no indication from Mr. Charlie about the music, in all likelihood he thought Dixieland was nigger music. He had no time for music anyway. Today his concern was for his hard times. He did sheet metal work and Augie was cutting him short on his hours. Sterl was trying to listen as best he could, looking over every once in a while, but it was pretty hard to follow, especially while he was busy tidying up, with the music blaring (Sharkey was cutting out with a cornet solo) and with only one lung to keep him going. When Sterl drifted down to the end of the bar, Mr. Charlie, in order not to lose momentum, turned to me, grabbed my arm with his vise-like grip, fixed my wandering eyes and demanded approval: "Am I right? Can a man support a family widout work!" I knew that no answer was required, but just to be sure I nodded my head. When Sterl returned he turned away from me again. After all, I was nothing but a kid--what did I know about anything. And yet when Sterl disappeared for a short time again he seized my arm, looked me directly in the eyes and called Augie a rotten, cheap bastard. "You're damn right," I blurted out before I realized it. But I could tell he didn't hear me. My poor arm, still bruised from Philip, was taking a beating and I was drenched with Mr. Charlie's spit, but it was worth it. The spit didn't really worry me, I knew from the strength of his grip that he was without disease. He was really a fine physical specimen for a man of fifty-odd, compact and wiry like his son Ronnie, but with none of Ronnie's lanky easiness.

Philip now turned away from Ronnie and started to egg Mr. Charlie on. Sterl had set us up with another beer, our third, and Mr. Charlie was suddenly in a good mood. The scowl gave way to earsplitting laughter. He almost fell off his stool telling us about the time Joe Trepagnier's wife threw his ass out of the house. It seemed Joe lost his weekly salary down in one of the gambling houses in St. Bernard.

But Mr. Charlie's moods changed as fast as the weather. The fourth beer turned him sour again and he began to lecture us.

"Ya see dese hands?" He began extending his hands, palms up. "Ya see dose corns?" They were indeed heavily callused and bunioned. "Dat m'boys is hard work. When ya worked as hard as dat ya can say ya done somethin'. It took thirty-five years to get hands like dis." I couldn't take my eyes off his hands. In fact, we all for a few moments stared transfixed at his calluses, even his son Ronnie looked impressed. It seemed a solemn moment which I think unnerved Mr. Charlie and sent him into a spell of sour mutterings. "...... don't tell me about hard work, ya won't learn dat in college."

The fact that we were going to college must have bothered him. "Don't tell me about college boys," he went on, and probably nobody had. It was a safe bet that outside of a doctor or a lawyer Mr. Charlie didn't know anybody who went to college. He complained under his breath for a while and looked up to confront Sterl who had come up just then with four more beers. "Tell 'em Sterl, do I know what I'm talkin' about?" Sterl, of course, didn't know what he was talking about and Philip filled him in.

"Mr. Charlie here thinks that we should get a job instead of going to college." And although Philip was laughing, Sterl took the question seriously. I thought his eyes became wistful as he stood there. Perhaps he was thinking of some lost opportunity in his own life.

"Education is a wonderful thing," said Sterl with quiet sincerity. "Oh yeah!" said Mr. Charlie, "What the hell do you know, Sterl, look at you--you're half dead."

"Maybe so," replied Sterl and wiped the bar.

Mr. Charlie put his elbows on the bar and shook his head as if we were hopeless. "College," he said and trailed off into inaudible profanities.

Philip started to really chuckle and put his arm around Mr. Charlie's shoulders drawing him close. "You know something, old man," he said, "I'll bet you would like to come to college with us, and you know why, huh?" Philip was talking directly into his ear.

15

"Because you'd like to get some of that cute college stuff--am I right? Tell me?"

There was no way that Mr. Charlie could deny it. He pushed Philip off of him and slumped over his beer, laughing lasciviously. Philip laughed along with him, poking him a few sporting jabs on the chin.

"Dago bastard!" muttered Mr. Charlie. Philip really had his number all right.

I noticed that Ronnie was really smiling. It's great when your best friend gets along with your old man.

Thunder rolled off in the distance and a few hard drops of rain rattled on Sterl's little banquette shed. It became dark; the rain started up again and grew quickly to a heavy downpour. Sterl set us up with a fresh beer and we settled onto our stools to listen to the sweet music of a summer shower. We had no where to go anyway.

Sterl turned the bar over to Ernie Schnexnayder and shuffled off to the back. He had lost the good reflexes of his ball playing years and deferred to Ernie when business got heavy.

When the rain stopped, the regulars began arriving and in no time the place was packed, which made Mr. Charlie happy since three or four of his friends were offering to buy him a beer. I knew we would be there on into the night and why not. I had a good buzz and not even the fact that Mr. Charlie and his friend Joe Rooney were speaking across me bothered me that much. Rooney was a big red-faced Irishman who evidently also worked for Augie.

The place was crowded and noisy, the jukebox blasting away with country songs. I was waiting for *A Prisoner of Love* by Perry Como. I was jammed in and was about to sink into a drunken reverie when I spotted my friend Cats leaning on the jukebox. I checked quickly to see if Ernie had spotted him; Cats was not always welcome--in fact, almost never unless he had funds which was never. Cats, who was very familiar to me, was not really my friend or anybody else's friend; he was an old wino who roamed the length and breadth of the ninth ward mooching drinks. I thought it was appropriate that Cats showed up on this particular evening. There was a tale about him that I had heard many times and always wanted to check out. What better time than now I figured.

Cats was a tall, skinny guy whose pants always seemed too big for him. He had a lean, stern jaw which he jutted when he talked. It was impossible to know if he was drunk or not for he was always weaving. I had never actually talked to Cats and didn't really know if he was available for conversation.

"Whatsay, Cats," I ventured, as I walked up, but he continued to weave, staring right past me. "How 'bout a wine, Cats?" I persisted. At this he made several shifts in position and found me in his sights.

"You gon buy Cats a wine, Little Henry?" He called all of us youngsters Little Henry, maybe that was his name, his real name. "Sure, Cats, what are you drinking, red or white?"

"It don't matter, Little Henry, Cats drinks any color." He swayed toward me, stuck out his jaw and narrowed his eyes which made him look like a demented John Brown. Cats always seemed angry. His hair looked kinky and I wondered if he had colored blood. But I knew I should be careful or I could start a rumor and cause trouble. I happened to have known that Cats was Jewish--Katz, Katzmann or Katzenheimer. And there was this story about him that I wanted to check out.

I went over to the end of the bar and got a wine for Cats and a beer for me. Ernie raised his eyebrows, but was too busy to object.

Cats staggered toward me as I approached, eyes gleaming, tongue licking.

"Thank you, Little Henry, Cats is very grateful." He took half of it down and gazed at the rest, admiring it.

"Say, Cats," I ventured. "Is it true you studied law at Tulane?" I was almost sorry I asked for he suddenly arched back on his heels lifting his eyes up to the ceiling as though he had been stabbed.

"Are you all right, Cats?" I entreated, but he straightened up and drained off the rest of the wine. I didn't know whether his little seizure was caused by some painful memory about Tulane (if he really had been a student there) or was some quirky alcoholic reflex. He was measuring me now and I wondered if he had even heard my question. I knew, of course, that he needed another wine.

"Another wine, Cats?"

"If you please, Little Henry," How many wines was my research going to cost me?

When I ordered the wine Ernie leaned over the bar and told me that he didn't appreciate my buying wine for Cats and encouraging him to stick around.

"He's telling me a story, Ernie," I offered, but Ernie only looked disgusted; I guess he had heard too many stories from winos.

This time Cats went all the way down with the wine and a tremor shook the entire length of his lanky frame. He then seemed to recover, and drew himself up with renewed composure. I could only guess that it took two wines to fix him up, for his eyes now seemed to flash with alertness.

"Well what about it, Cats, did you ever go to Tulane?"

"Are you making fun of Cats, Little Henry?"

"Me, I bought you two wines!"

"I did go to Tulane, Little Henry, I went to Tulane in nineteen and twenty-eight."

This was it I thought, at last I would find out. I had heard the story so many times: how Cats was so brilliant and sensitive, so borderline between genius and madness that his fine mind broke, and how he was tragically driven to drink when he was far and away at the head of his class, headed for a Fulbright scholarship and the attorney-generalship of the U.S.A. The story came straight from the unwritten chronicles of ninth-ward lore, I didn't make it up.

As a matter of fact, Cats was the only college man I knew. His family had a furniture store on Franklin Avenue where they lived above the store, or so I had heard. Actual ninth-ward residents who sent their son uptown to Tulane. Now at last I would be able to confirm the story from Cats himself.

"Well, what happened at Tulane, Cats?"

"What happened, Little Henry?" he said abstractly, his gaze was fixed on his wine glass which he had handed to me as he worked his lips and tongue.

"Okay, Cats, I'll get you one more wine if you tell me what happened at Tulane."

He looked up from the glass and measured me through his slits. It was hard to tell if he understood the bargain.

"At Tulane, Little Henry, I dropped out."

"You dropped out and what then--what happened then?"

"I dropped out, Little Henry, and I never went back."

"Is that it, Cats?"

"That's it, Little Henry, I dropped out and never went back. In nineteen and twenty-eight I dropped out and never went back." He said this with sweeping finality.

Poor Cats, I thought, your brilliant brain is too wine-soaked, there is no one to tell your tragic story. I felt myself tear up as I drained off my beer.

"Cats, let's have one more drink. Come over here and meet my friends and have a drink with us." He seemed not to comprehend and I took his arm and led him over to where Ronnie and Philip were sitting at the bar. "Philip Rotolo and Ronnie Hingle," I said stumbling forward, "this is my friend, Cats." I was holding the two empty glasses and noticed that I was weaving as much as Cats. Philip took the glasses from me and chuckled, leading me to the bar for support.

"Okay, Champ." He and Ronnie were grinning from ear to ear.

"Cats here is an old Tulane man, and I thought that we college men could have a drink together." I was holding onto the bar with one hand and onto Cats' arm with the other while Philip and Ronnie steadied both of us.

"Sure, Champ; but to tell the truth, I didn't know Cats was a Tulane man."

"Well, he was. He was at Tulane in nineteen and twenty-eight, and Ronnie is going to be there in nineteen and fifty." I turned to Cats, "Ronnie here is going to Tulane, Cats."

Cats shook his head from side to side but did not speak. I knew what he meant and I agreed. People from this part of town shouldn't go to Tulane. (Would Tulane drive Ronnie to alcoholism? I didn't think so; Ronnie, while not brainy like Cats, was easy and steady, so he wouldn't break as Cats did.) Still Cats was shaking his head for good reason. What chance did a son of a boogalee and a graduate of a downtown Confederate high school (Francis T. Nicholls High School, first school erected in the ninth ward in 1939) have at Tulane.

Philip got Ernie over for the drinks. Ernie looked at Cats and then at me, wagging his head in disgust. He appealed to Philip.

"After this drink, can I run him out of here, he's stinking up the place?"

"Okay, Ernie, I'll take care of it." As Philip said this I noticed that Mr. Charlie, one stool down, was holding his nose and cursing.

"Here's to Tulane and college days," I toasted as we all lifted our drinks.

I tried to chugalug the beer but it was a mistake. I spilled most of it on my shirt and was overcome with vertigo, falling into Philip's arms. By the time he got me upright, I remembered that Cats was behind me, but when I turned, he was gone. I looked up just in time to see him tight-leg it out of the door. Poor Cats, not even enough ass to stir his baggy pants. He was not welcome and that made me mad: boogalees (latent Marxists) can squeeze arms and raise hell, but poor bedeviled Jewish intellectuals must go thirsty. I tried to follow him out, but Philip held me firm.

"Take it easy, tiger."

"Cats really did go to Tulane, Philip. I asked him myself. He was there in nineteen and twenty-eight."

Philip lifted me up onto a stool and as I lowered my head to the bar I heard Perry Como's sweet, supplicating voice wailing away. At last: *Prisoner of Love*! But I was too far gone for a heartrending song. I was thinking instead of Ronnie at Tulane. Maybe he would make it, a lot had happened since nineteen and twenty-eight. Nevertheless, Philip and I had better prospects at Loyola. Loyola was a good school for local downtown kids like us, especially Catholics. Rumor had it that Tulane was shot through with heathenism and atheism. Should I warn Ronnie about this? I didn't think so. He was a non-practicing Lutheran and planned to major in Business Administration.

I woke up the next morning in my little single bed, having no idea how I got there. It was late morning and already hot; sun rays streamed through the louvered blinds on my window, printing parallel bars of light on the darkened wall. I could barely see my sturdy chiffarobe, the only other piece of furniture in my room. I was sweaty but surprisingly relaxed, no hangover. It occurred to me in my dreamy state that last night might have been my farewell to downtown neighborhood life. What will happen to old Bobby Gomez, I wondered?

Later that week, Philip took Ronnie and me shopping for civilian clothes on Canal Street. Afterwards, in the spirit of our new freedom, we wandered into the French Quarter down Bourbon Street, gawking at the strippers on the billboards and sneering at the low-life who were busy cleaning the clubs for the late evening business, hosing banquettes, dumping out broken glasses, cocktail napkins and other debris. Ordinarily downtowners steer clear of Bourbon Street, even during the day; Bourbon Street is strictly for tourists. We lunched at Galatoire's, the first time for Ronnie and me at a fancy restaurant. Philip, an old hand at fine dining, ordered Trout Meuniere for us, which I ate in very small bites, sipping wine between bites. Philip insisted on paying the bill, peeling off a two dollar tip for the waiter, who had not spoken more than a dozen or so whispered words; I imagined him from Marseilles or Paris, but when he opened the door for us, Philip socked him an up-close, elegant punch on his arm.

"See you next time, tiger," Philip said, and it suddenly hit me.

"That's Harold Chauvin."

"That's right, champ."

Harold Chauvin lived down on Urquhart Street and drank beer on his nights off at Ralph's bar.

What other surprising discoveries would I make, I wondered, shaking my head. The day swirled gloriously around us, stretching out endlessly. We took in a movie at the Saenger, an F.B.I. movie which we sat through silently and seriously, taking heart, since the Red Menace now threatened us from within.

When we emerged it was dark, Canal Street was all lit up with neon. We walked over to a little jazz club called the Brass Rail and sat perched upon cushioned bar stools, drinking something called Vodka Gimlets, listening to bebop jazz; reality seemed slipped into another gear. I sipped the bitter drink, wondering from where such music came, swaying with the sax player whose eyes were squeezed tight. The music was bright, frantic and plaintive, sparkling the chromium-studded lounge. I looked at Ronnie and Philip bobbing their heads and found I was bobbing mine, too. We were looking in the mirror behind the bar, smiling at each other, knowing somehow that we were at some fortunate moment in history, lucky to be exactly who we were and where we were. We were served another gimlet and the drummer's arms flew out in all directions, hitting cymbals and drums, unlocking hidden sources of our energy.

I thought of the new civilian clothes I had bought and of going to college; the mirror suddenly loomed as the one magical world in which we existed, opening out to unlimited space.

After six gimlets everything became brilliantly blurred and I grew so light of head I couldn't move. Ronnie and Philip helped me off my stool and guided me back to the Pontiac, as I raved and gestured among all of the neon glitter, exclaiming our glorious future. Marais Street seemed very far behind like a dusty ghost town.

Chapter 3

*I*t came time for Philip, Ronnie and I to venture up among the mansions on St. Charles Avenue, where Tulane and Loyola universities stand curiously next door to each other, a treacherous proximity in 1950, but not for the reasons one would suspect, since Loyola is a Jesuit school and Tulane is secular. Religions in New Orleans were solidly established, no one dared proselytize, conversions which are common today, were nonexistent in 1950. The real danger was social scandal, Loyola was for downtowners, Tulane for the upper-registers. Adding to the confusion, Sophie Newcomb College for highly placed girls lay indistinguishably within the very embraces of the Tulane campus. One had to be very careful about boundaries.

For Philip and me, it was an easy adjustment. Loyola was a small, noisy, friendly school, the Jesuit fathers were satisfied to turn out graduates with practical careers to serve the local community: pharmacists, dentists, probate lawyers, politicians, radio announcers, TV sports casters. There were never more than a few sour intellectuals and, whether lay or clerical, they usually moved on after a year. Freshmen carried on loud, vicious discussions on the proofs for God's existence, but it was pure gamesmanship--there were no atheists at Loyola. The campus was a happy mix of red brick Tudor Gothic, asbestos barracks from the war years, and several old uptown homes where the campus spilled over onto the neighborhood. Behind the complex of gothic buildings on the Avenue, everything was set down randomly, connected by informal footpaths and a few paved walkways. Social life flourished while library carrels gathered dust, most of the students were local Catholics like Philip and me. We had the good feeling that the Jesuit fathers cared more for our souls than for our minds. (At what other university would a philosophy teacher jocularly cast aside Emmanuel Kant as just another confused skeptic?) The cafeteria was housed in one of the surplus barracks buildings, where the lay faculty and students enjoyed their meals; the atmosphere was decidedly jolly and easy-going.

We didn't see Ronnie during those first few weeks and I wondered how he was doing over at Tulane. From one side of the cafeteria you could peek out of the window, over the jumble of barracks huts, up at the great stone edifices of Tulane. One day, out of sheer curiosity, I wandered over. I walked among the stone buildings as an early September wind blew through the tall trees with a throaty whistle, subsuming the quiet voices of the students I passed; I could barely hear the muffled social din from Loyola. Had I known of such places, I would have thought the Tulane campus to be a transplanted piece of Amherst, Massachusetts. I hurried back to the Loyola cafeteria where I was greeted by the clatter of coffee cups and pie saucers mingling with giggles and shouts of happy Catholic kids.

Of course Philip was soon in the thick of things on the campus; we were very quickly settled in, and things went nicely--I got on as a cub reporter with the Maroon, and, before the semester was over, Philip was elected president of the freshman class, a terrific coup for a downtowner. We were very busy, there was no time even for a few beers in the evening. My life seemed complete, or nearly complete. Once or twice I took a break from my studies to accompany Philip and his girlfriend Mary Ann to the movies.

Then one Friday afternoon, I walked over to Doucet's Drug Store to use their phone to call Gloria Schwartz, whom I had been meaning to get in touch with ever since I had gotten home. Gloria and I had gone out a few times before I was drafted: twice to be exact, if you counted our meeting at the popcorn concession in the Famous Theater where we were introduced by Jerry Ragusa. I don't think we said more than a few words to each other then. The second time was officially a blind date since Gloria didn't remember meeting me at the Famous. We had gone that night to the Best Ice Cream Parlor on St. Claude for a sundae. The place was packed and we somehow got separated and I found out later that my friend Jerry Ragusa walked Gloria home. One of the reasons I hadn't called Gloria was because I had heard that Jerry Ragusa was walking her home on a regular basis. I wondered if Gloria remembered the kiss she gave me that night on the way to the ice cream parlor.

Gloria's father answered and seemed angry when I ask to speak to Gloria. I heard he and Gloria yelling at each other. He had mistaken me for Jerry Ragusa, which didn't please a college man like myself, because Jerry's speech was very ungrammatical. She was speaking very loud, trying to convince her father that I was not Jerry. Jerry had fallen from Mr. Schwartz's grace. She won the argument evidently because she finally came to the phone.

"Hello Gloria." I said, not knowing if it was safe for her to talk to me.

"Hello, Bobby, how've you been?" I was surprised that she recognized my voice.

"Fine, Gloria, and what about you? I'm sorry I didn't call you sooner. I've been very busy going to Loyola and all."

"Oh, I didn't know you were going to college."

"Yeah, Philip and I started this semester." ▸

"That's nice." I could hear a clicking sound which I recognized as gum popping. I was beset by contradictory urges at that moment. I wanted to raise my voice to her, to tell her that going to Loyola was not a trivial matter: it wasn't nice. I didn't, of course, because in spite of what I considered her commonness I had been in love with her ever since she kissed me, and therefore thought myself pitiful since I was sure Gloria had forgotten the kiss I so treasured.

"Well, Gloria," I said in a hollow, unleavened tone, "I thought you might like to go to a movie with me tonight or tomorrow night--whenever you are free." The clicking sound stopped and I waited for her to answer. It seemed forever. I cleared my throat to fill in the emptiness.

"It's nice of you to ask me, Bobby, but I'm busy this weekend."

When I left the drug store there was the faintest smell of the coming fall in the air, the late afternoon light seemed a shade mellower, which could have been my imagination for it was still very hot even though it was October. I took a long unscheduled ride on the Frenchmen bus up Elysian Fields Avenue to Lake Pontchartrain. The lake stretched out peacefully in the distance; a few shrimpers down the sea wall were lighting their lanterns, tossing cracked clams into the water and untangling their caste nets. The sun was slowly dipping into the water, lighting up the clouds, a very spectacular sight that for some reason made me sad. I lay down on the broad top step and waited for the darkness, losing myself in the soft lapping sound of little waves spilling upon the slimy bottom steps. I must have fallen asleep. I awoke to a black moonless night. The shrimpers were all gone. I walked to the bus stop where I had to wait almost an hour for the bus.

Chapter 4

*P*hillip and I thought often about Ronnie over at Tulane during that first semester. Tulane was right next door, but could just have well been in Casmir. Except for Ronnie, we seldom thought about it. And yet, everyone, uptown and downtown, rooted for the Green Wave. We thought Tulane was like those colleges in Jack Oakie movies, with kids in sweaters and beanies cheering their hearts out for the team, and old grads singing their alma mater with brimming eyes, hands pressed to their bosoms. The old Olive and Blue, really classy colors, so all-American but also a bastion of Jewish intellectualism. (Did Cats have relatives on the board of directors? Should I ask him--no, he's too sensitive about whatever happened to him there.)

Tulane was also the quietest place in town, silence clung to the great granite walls, filled the Romanesque arches. Academic solemnity reigned in those hallowed halls, built in the great revival style of Henry Hobson Richardson and set down unbelievably with all of that grand display of rock, upon the swampy bottom of a rain-soaked Latin city. Time seemed in some way to have stalled there. The campus with its malls and tall trees was lovely by any standard, but it was a fading loveliness where one sensed a lingering Victorian sweetness, a mirthless, immemorializing whiff of sequestration. Little wonder that a rumor persisted that Walter Pater lectured there in 1885, and although unconfirmed, would not Walter have been entirely at his ease at Tulane? One could imagine that many Oxfordians passed that way.

Today along the long pathways in the mall, barefooted boys and girls stroll in cut-offs, their long hair flowing softly, their eyes sober and serious. The wind twines among the thick branches of the tall trees and whistles over their speech.

It is a new day, but once and again, a tall, broad-shouldered youth comes with his old-fashioned sweater emblazoned with a great green "T", and whether he is white or black (as he is apt to be these days), he is likely to be accompanied by a coed who cocks her head in a certain way, swings her arms happily and throws a playful hip at her companion; her eyes roll around and her mouth forms sounds which one can imagine to be lines from a popular song, and off they go down the winding pathway. To see them is to imagine that it is 1936 or 1880. One may hear, if one is still and quiet enough, the very flutter and heart-throb of old Sophie Newcomb herself. How was Ronnie Hingle, fresh out of the lower ninth ward, supposed to find his way there?

Chapter 5

*R*onnie had arrived at Tulane on the day of registration with his usual straight-forwardness, carrying his papers along the winding pathways, not having the slightest notion which of the great stone buildings was Gibson Hall. He stopped once or twice and listened intently, not at all sure that he was hearing what he seemed to be hearing: a murmuring sound, so sad and tender as to almost bring tears to his eyes. Were his ears playing tricks on him? Was it the wind?

Satisfied that it was indeed the wind he walked along again, confident that the pathway would lead him to Gibson Hall, when three girls striding abreast forced him over. They were Tulane girls as new to the campus as Ronnie himself, ex-WACs who knew how to stand up for their rights, Tulane's first female students. They wore their hair close-cropped, and their skirts were as severe as their discarded uniforms. They pumped along almost in formation, but Ronnie hardly noticed. His attention was elsewhere, craning to see another girl far ahead of him. Strong sunlight showered dappled shade through the canopy of tall trees, and he strained to see the girl in the flickering distance. Unlike the WACs this girl sauntered along, her plaid skirt swinging, highlights flashing from her honey-colored hair which hung down around her shoulders in thick curls. Ronnie pulled up almost breathless beside one of the tall trees, and waited for the girl to blur out of his vision. It took a few seconds for him to come back to himself. He blinked and to his startlement another sauntering girl appeared along one of the branching pathways--this one coming towards him. (Were she and the other one twins?)

These were Newcomb girls, but how could Ronnie have known; no one had told him of Newcomb's proximity to Tulane.

The girl floated by him and her trailing scent filled his nostrils. Something in his head spun; it was very slight, but he was forced to swallow hard in order to restore his natural rhythm. A little further ahead he broke stride to avoid a trio of professors, each clad in a tweed jacket, who had stopped along the path to converse. As he swung by them, bending an ear inadvertently, a phrase rose out of the group like a word balloon: ". . . a re-emerging barbarism . . ." It was English but could just as well have been Russian. He wondered admiringly what it could mean, and thought suddenly of his college education as a journey that would return him after four years to this exact spot where he would converse with these same professors about ". . . a re-emerging barbarism." Ronnie could have been right, but he didn't know that the meaning of this phrase was as close as a dictionary in the library.

He saw another girl with the same shade of honey-blonde hair walking with a football player in a green sweater and actually stopped in his tracks at the sight of what he saw her do: she had thrown her head back, exactly like an actress and laughed. Her windpipe and sinews glided so smoothly beneath her milky skin that he shivered. The wonderment of it propelled him mindlessly along the path, his ears straining to hear a distant fluctuating hum that sounded almost like music.

He found himself at Freret Street which cuts through the campus, dividing it in half. Light traffic was passing, students in their sport coupes. Ahead of him a wide green space stretched out, sparsely landscaped with young pin oaks. Two flanking multi-story dormitories stood starkly in the middle distance behind a row of slender date palms. In the far distance loomed the football stadium. He had walked too far.

He scratched his head and turned around two full times in his confusion.

He started back, suddenly feeling fatigued. One of the benches along the path invited him and he sat down. He was not really tired but disoriented. He gazed off in the distance at the lovely green mall with its winding random paths, tall trees and wooden benches. Several couples dotted the walkways. The word that Ronnie required was "classy".

He sat there wishing somehow he could forget that he lived down on Poland Avenue. Soft breezes floated through the trees. He smelled the leaves and recalled the scent of the girl. He compared it with the dank, musty odor of the banquette bricks on Poland Avenue after a rain. He drew in a deep breath, fascinated all at once with his olfactory powers. His nostrils filled with the dark briny odor of Joe Impastato's grocery store. (Could he at will smell whatever he chose?) But the odor left as quickly as it had come, and the scent of the girl returned. He sat up with a start: something strange was happening to him--odors born from invisible sources. His practical sense questioned the oddness of it, and he sniffed again, determined to smell the real things around him. He was tempted to press his nostrils to the wooden bench he sat on, but then he saw the girl. How had she gotten so close without him seeing her?

Consoled that he was again smelling reality, he got up and shook his legs, and his papers slipped out of his hands, floating down to the ground. As he stooped to gather them up a voice behind him spoke, "You missed this one." He turned to face a young man wearing a blue and green beanie--a freshman like himself--holding one of his papers. "You must be looking for the Office of Admissions," said the young man.

"Huh--well, yes, I guess I am," he said, trying to avoid the young man's insistent gaze.

The young man stepped right up to him and handed him the paper and stuck out his other hand, "I'm Foster Sutherland."

Ronnie was thrown into confusion by Foster's aggressive friendliness, fumbling the paper and just barely getting his right hand out for his companion to shake. "Oh, Ronnie, uh, Ronnie Hingle."

"I am going to Admissions myself, Ronnie; shall we walk along together?"

"Huh?--oh--yeah; thank you." As they walked along Foster complained about administrative red tape and Ronnie nodded his head and smiled. He was struck by Foster's glib speech and was suddenly frightened to say a word in return, realizing that all of his life he had used speech which was vulgarly ethnic and ungrammatical. But Foster seemed content to have someone to listen to him--he was a real talker, and Ronnie thanked the luck as he kept up his rhythmical nodding, smiling also for the pleasure of being directed to the right place.

And so, with Foster's help, he got himself registered in the College of Business Administration. Foster was pre-legal, but Ronnie had not the vaguest notion of what pre-legal meant.

Before long Foster left him to join a crowd of freshmen who all seemed to know each other.

As Ronnie stood there, Foster, walking rapidly in the midst of his friends, turned and waved to him.

He was alone again and a strange feeling came over him. It was loneliness but Ronnie didn't recognize it.

He walked along, conscious again of the wind murmuring through the tall trees. He smelled the leaves, and to his amazement he began to sense the unmistakable, peculiar stale odor of his own room on Poland Avenue. He hurried along to Freret Street where he had parked the Plymouth.

Later as he pulled up in front of his shotgun he was surprised to find that everything on Poland Avenue was as strange to him as it was at Tulane. He sat behind the steering wheel staring vacantly down the street. A few people were sitting out on their front steps at this late hour enjoying respite from the torrid sun which was descending behind the houses. The air seemed dense and fetid. As he looked, Mrs. Cusimano, one of his neighbors, slapped at her leg and held her hand up to examine a mosquito's smashed carcass. Mr. Cusimano sitting beside her drank deeply from a bottle of beer. Mr. Myer marched briskly by in his fireman's uniform. From the corner came the sound of Joe Impastato's screen door slamming. This sound somehow sunk Ronnie down into himself; it was as if a prison door had slammed shut. He felt trapped. The lives of his neighbors seemed to him at this moment pitifully meager. He wondered how they could go on living such hopeless lives, slapping mosquitoes, hustling overtime for a few groceries and a six-pack, having to gaze blearily out on the world through the thick humidity, irrigating their clogged ears, and straining for a clear thought with a brain that soaked up water faster than sphagnum moss.

He looked anxiously over at the front door of his shotgun, fearing suddenly that his mother would emerge. The sight of her at this moment he knew would have been unbearably painful. He bravely forced himself to think of what he had accomplished at Tulane; he was now registered and launched; and yet, whatever pleasant anticipations he entertained seemed sham beside the strange anxiety that had drained him and left him exhausted. What had he done that made him so tired?

It was dark and he could not remember falling asleep. But he could not deny it; he was slumped over in the front seat of the Plymouth. He dragged himself out, not knowing what time it was, made his way up the steps, through the small rooms, found his bed and lay down with no thought to the sticky air, nor to his father and mother snoring in the next room.

He fell immediately into a fitful sleep, alternately dreaming and waking in strange trances. He dreamed finally toward morning of himself and Foster Sutherland walking across the Tulane campus wearing beanies. In this dream he spoke intelligently of administrative red tape, using words that he did not understand. This dream woke him up.

He lay there blinking his eyes for several minutes. He heard the rustle of a page of newspaper being turned from the kitchen. Seconds later the toilet flushed. (The bathroom was wedged between his room and the kitchen.) It was his father. As Ronnie listened, his father walked through the kitchen, out the back door and up the alley.

He checked his watch; it was nearly six. He got up and slipped into the bathroom. His mother was sitting at the kitchen table reading the paper. He bathed hurriedly, wrapped a towel around his waist and went silently into his room to dress. When he was finished he stood in the doorway watching his mother. She was absorbed in the paper, humming absently as her eyes moved back and forth. She dipped a slice of buttered French bread into her *cafe au lait*. A drop of coffee rolled down her chin.

There was no time to tell her of his dreams of happiness and success or of his nagging anxieties. She buttered another slice of bread. Something about her absorption in the paper saddened him. He desired to touch her with a tenderness he had never felt before. She was reading the obituaries, every morning she found the name of an old friend. "Goodbye, Ma." "Goodbye, son."

She hadn't looked up from her paper.

He had an eight o'clock class at Gibson Hall. Where was Gibson Hall?

He went to his first class in Gibson Hall, Economics 101. The teacher wrote his name and the name of the textbook on the board: Dr. Saul Fleishmann; *The Basic Principles of Economic Theory*.

Halfway through the lecture, Ronnie's eyes drooped. He hadn't understood anything Dr. Fleishmann had said. The other students scribbled furiously in their notebooks. The page in his own notebook contained, besides the names on the board, a tiny drawing of a spark plug.

When the class was over he couldn't wait to get outside and stretch his legs. In fact, he struck out for Audubon Park which was across the Avenue from the campus.

In minutes he was walking rapidly along the banks of quiet lagoons. The park was deserted. He passed under gigantic live oaks and lush camphor trees, circled around a great granite rotunda of a bandstand and crossed over a little cement oriental bridge. He seemed to catch his stride near the botanical gardens and sped along the path. He was following a bridle path, in disuse at this hour of the morning.

He pulled up finally, winded and sweating, at the zoo, which was spread out peacefully under the shade of giant live oaks. It was not much of a zoo--all of the cages and enclosures were tucked away among the shrubbery and low trees or hidden in the shadows of the oaks. It smelled pleasantly of manure. A few mothers escorted their children around. One of the mothers coming upon Ronnie shot him a frightened look and grabbed her little girl's hand protectively. She hurried by him. Ronnie did not understand the meaning of her apparent fear; wasn't this a public place? Little wonder, though, that the mother was startled; had he reflected on his appearance, he would not have wondered. His face and neck were glistening with perspiration, ringlets of his wavy hair had fallen down on his forehead, and his chest heaved noticeably. Only the notebook which he had rolled up and shoved in his back pocket could have identified him as a student, but why would a student at his leisure be sweaty and out of breath? He had been running away all right but not from the police, and he could not have explained why he was visiting the zoo between classes.

He checked the back page of his notebook where he had written his schedule. His next class was at ten. His watch showed 9:46. These two bits of information caused him to remember his determination to be successful at Tulane and he turned and broke out running.

He forgot to eat lunch, but he stuck around the campus between his afternoon classes. He now had the names of all his teachers and the titles of the textbooks they had assigned, but, as yet, no notes. Beside the tiny spark plug, he made a detailed drawing of a carburetor, sectioned to reveal its internal parts.

Things would get better, he told himself, but they got worse. It became difficult for him to keep his mind on a lecture for more than thirty seconds, and he developed the irritating habit of scratching his head. He would sit on a campus bench and scratch and scratch, until his scalp was raw; little flaky scabs popped out when he combed his hair. The other thing was not a nervous habit like scratching his head, but it was even more disturbing. It was the illusion that the wind sounded like music when it passed through the leaves; sometimes it sounded like a woman singing. This would happen when his mind would drift out of the window during class or when he sat alone on a campus bench. He noticed also that very few students sat on these benches.

The only slight glimmer of hope occurred in the library, of all places, where he usually fell asleep. He was reading a chapter in the autobiography of John Stuart Mill which Dr. Fleishmann had assigned along with three chapters in Mill's *Principles of Political Economy*. His eyes were drifting over one of the pages lighting on a word here and there, his head becoming heavier by the second. He was dropping off when he read: "I felt that he was a poet and that I was not; that he was a man of intuition which I was not; and that as such he not only saw many things before me, but that it was highly probable he could see many things which were not visible to me even after they were pointed out." This struck a chord. Here at Tulane his teachers spoke of things that everyone seemed to understand but himself. He suddenly felt a kinship with Mill, whom Dr. Fleishmann had described as a practical man, and a utilitarian, but Ronnie didn't know what "utilitarian" meant.

Sometimes he looked very hard at a strange word like "utilitarian" thinking that perhaps words were after all like carburetors and he could by scrutinizing them, see how they work. His most serious problem, however, had to do with his social life. He felt blocked off. He did not have a single friend, not even an acquaintance. The students were friendly and he had many opportunities. His classmates told him hello and invited him to sit down with them for coffee or lunch, and he did a few times, but always with the same uncomfortable results. Everyone talked as glibly as Foster. He would sit there nodding and smiling, straining to follow the flow, fearing that someone would turn to him with a question or for a comment. When they did, it was disastrous. He would show a pleasant, interested expression while his stomach contorted, and try as he may, he could not speak. He ended up each time shrugging helplessly and flashing to his quick smile. No one pressured him or even seemed to find his muteness unusual. Nevertheless, his fear of being exposed developed into a full blown phobia and he began to hide out between classes in secluded places on the campus. This might have been convenient for a meditative person, but for Ronnie it was torturous. He had also lost contact with his Poland Avenue friends. Actually, though, he didn't understand why, he had been avoiding them.

One day he came upon a short little trellised arcade connecting the back entrances of two nearby buildings. It was a deserted spot. A Rose of Montana vine grew up the trellis, enveloping it. The vine spilled over, trailing down off the lattice nearly to the ground, and was thick with bushy pink blossoms, exuding their perfume. Honey bees swarmed over the flowers.

Peering through the hanging vine, he noticed a small cloister garden of camellias hidden away between the two buildings. By parting the vine like a curtain, he stepped into the garden and found an intricately carved marble bench facing a defunct little fountain and sat down.

The garden which seemed absolutely private was actually on the Newcomb campus, but Ronnie didn't know this. Almost all of the camellia bushes were dead: one or two retained a few leaves, but no blossoms. Weeds sprang up everywhere else. It was possible perhaps that no one had sat on the marble bench in many years, since 1935 or 1924--who could tell? The garden was clearly an afterthought, a remnant of space originally unaccounted for and then, as with so many orphaned things, given very special attention. The fountain, like the bench, was carved marble and supported a small bronze representation of Diana, the Huntress. It was undoubtedly a gift.

(An inscription noting the dedication surely could have been found somewhere under the weeds which had grown up around the base.)

It was not for Ronnie to speculate about any of this, nor did he wonder why he would sit in such an unlikely place. He was merely thankful that for the moment he could rest without fear of being accosted.

Numberless bees swarmed around the Rose of Montana blossoms and their buzzing seemed to fill up the tiny space, creating in Ronnie the odd feeling that he was at liberty to look very carefully and closely at the smallest things. He focused on a spiraling tendril, noting how it wrapped itself around a piece of lattice, and then upon a bee, crawling slowly over a blossom; the bee's wing caught a single ray of sunlight, causing it to wink luminously, as though it were transmitting a coded message.

Time stopped, and when he came back after he didn't know how long, he heard someone speaking down the arcade. It was the voice of a young girl talking privately to someone. The flow of her words resembled the slow trickle of water, but would not yield their meaning. A moment later, he detected the soft, tentative shuffle of footsteps coming his way. It was the girl whose voice he heard and someone else. They stopped on the other side of the Rose of Montana. They were silent. Ronnie became keenly alert and yet calm, shifting his eyes about for an identifying detail. Just below the trailing vine he made out a pair of brown saddle oxfords; he followed them up along a pair of shapely calves until the vine intruded. Moving his head very slightly in several directions, he found the right slit of open space. It was barely enough but he could see the girl's face. She was more than he had even hoped for. (Why was it so important to him that she be beautiful--was it that the shapely calves gave such promise, or that Ronnie's very being at this point was starved for some unimpeachable affirmation of life's essential worth?)

His heart leapt at the sight of her.

She and her companion were so motionless that Ronnie soon realized that they were silently choking on bitter words. They were having a quiet lovers' disagreement. For these precious seconds he saw her perfectly through the slit of open space. The smoothness of her skin sent a shudder along his back; his left leg jerked. He seemed to be able to see with amazing accuracy. She cast her head downward in the slightest degree, blinked her eyes twice and, most astonishingly, pushed out her bottom lip into a pout. Ronnie went nearly limp. Was it possible that he had fallen in love in the space of no more than ten or fifteen seconds with a girl he had never seen before and indeed could see now only partially?

She spoke again, startling him: "I don't care," she said, pouting and twisting her head as if this quiet complaint were her final word. Her companion changed his stance, heaving a wearisome sigh, and Ronnie caught a glimpse of his oxblood, wing-tip shoes. Ronnie looked up quickly, but the girl's head had moved out of the frame of the slit. "Let's go," the companion said roughly, and they walked away--heavy-footed.

It came to Ronnie then that the bench he sat on was made for two. It was in fact a love-seat had he known of such things, and it occurred to him also that the garden was a perfect place to sit with a girl--a tryst, but without the right words his mind steered a desultory course through all of these realizations.

Shadows fell in the garden and Ronnie was amazed at how quickly darkness came. As he parted the Rose of Montana and stepped out, the campus was unrecognizable to him: flood lights along the random paths showered soft yellow circles at long intervals; more light spilled into the darkness from the windows of the stone buildings. Trickles of night students could be seen entering and leaving. In the distance he heard the rumble of the St. Charles streetcar, grinding and squeaking its way along.

The strange enchantment of the darkened campus drove out the memory of the girl's face as he walked along. He felt comfortable if somewhat somber on the campus at this hour, and it crossed his mind briefly that he could attend night classes, if worse came to worst; but such was the abiding strength of his determination that he dismissed the thought peremptorily. He walked to the Plymouth and drove home.

On Poland Avenue he saw his mother standing under the street light, talking to Mrs. Impastato in front of the Impastato grocery store. No one was at the house; his father, he knew, was at Steckmann's bar. He thought of dropping in himself, but he discovered that his day at school had exhausted him. Some of his neighbors sat on their steps enjoying the cool night.

He sat on the front steps himself; it was still early. The still night carried sound back and forth along the street; loud laughter came down from Steckmann's and from over the houses he heard a dog barking incessantly. He was very tired; a sense of extreme weariness came over him. Something gave way in him, a sudden and almost desperate need for release. A lump rose in his throat and the face of the girl he'd seen from his secret garden loomed before him. The thought that he might see her again made him tremble.

He saw his mother coming and he quickly escaped into the house. Shedding his clothes hurriedly, he crawled into bed. As he turned over, and right before he drifted off into sleep, he made a note to call his friend Philip in the morning.

The next morning when he awoke, he heard his mother talking to Mrs. Cugliata in the kitchen. Mrs. Cugliata was distraught. Her husband had come home drunk and broken the kitchen table. She was close to tears. "I don't know what I'm gonna do with that man," she sobbed.

"Saints preserve us" his mother said, an expression she learned from her Catholic friends.

His bedroom was next to the kitchen and he couldn't help overhearing. He looked around his room, thinking how bare it was; there was no desk or desk lamp. It was not a suitable place for study.

His mother was offering Mrs. Cugliata more coffee. "Thank you, honey," the poor, bereaved woman said through her tearful sniffing.

He told himself that he had to get up, but his body would not respond. It seemed almost impossible for him to move even a finger; only his mind was awake, and his ears. Ordinary sounds seemed amplified: the kitchen floor creaking as his mother walked over to the stove; the coffee gurgling from pot to cup; Mrs. Cugliata's moanful slurping.

Helplessly he slid back into deep slumber and didn't wake up until almost two o'clock in the afternoon. It was the first time he missed any of his classes. He had dreamed of being married to Rosemary Lopacola; in the dream she had grown fat and lost her teeth. They had a terrible argument and he beat her up. It was a nightmare or a daymare.

He went back to sleep and had another unsettling dream but could not remember anything about it. It was dark and cold in his room. He wondered what would become of him. It was the first time Ronnie had such a thought.

Chapter 6

*W*e had been in school for nearly a month when Ronnie came over to Loyola. We were assembled in the barracks cafeteria having coffee. Ronnie's face had become drawn and haggard. He sat grimacing amid all the happy noise around him, he seemed distracted and present in body only. Philip, whom he had really come over to see, was busy as usual with well-wishers who continuously stopped to talk. I was watching Ronnie closely, thinking that, unfortunately, I had been right in fearing the worst. His distracted grimace was beginning to disfigure his good looks: an unexpected ghoulishness collected about the bony forehead, the slightly lantern jaw, and the strangely dimpled chin. And his lips, very unmistakably, were curling up into Mr. Charlie's scowl. It was no good. It was not an ugly face, but it needed the easiness, the spark of the quick smile, the merriment in the little round eyes, and some of that *bon vivant* RC drinking innocence.

The cafeteria was too crowded and noisy to really talk and Ronnie seemed to grow more and more forlorn. Philip was too much in demand, and the other person at our table--a certain Sheila Rosenberg--had already asked Ronnie several embarrassing questions about his choice of major, implying strongly that business majors were crassly ambitious and dull. I think, fortunately, that her snide attitude went by Ronnie; I hoped so, at least. Sheila had been elected vice-president of the freshman class with Philip so we saw a lot of her. It was our good luck, however, on this morning that she had to leave to attend a meeting with one of the many clubs she belonged to. This was Philip's cue evidently. He gave Ronnie and me the high sign and led us out of the cafeteria. He drove us to a quiet neighborhood bar on Magazine Street and bought us three quick beers during which he kept the conversation very light. When the fourth beer was set up,

Philip punched Ronnie on his arm with affection. "So, what's your problem, Champ?" he said.

Ronnie smiled weakly; Philip had this way of bringing us back to ourselves. Ronnie scratched his head. "There's just so much of this stuff to study," he said.

"Listen, man," Philip counseled, sliding his chair closer to Ronnie, "most of that stuff is just plain bullshit. You learn a few names, a couple of big words and for the rest you shoot the bull. As long as you shoot the same kind of crap the teacher shoots you got it made. Just remember to throw in a few big words."

It was good advice all right, but the words were exactly Ronnie's problem. He didn't tell Philip this, of course, nor did he speak of his kinship with John Stuart Mill, the Utilitarian; in fact, he must have reached some unprecedented point of mental frustration trying to read Mill's *Principles of Political Economy*, for he shook his head and laughed with bitterness--a cackle that was so out of character for Ronnie. "I just don't know why you have to know all of that shit. I mean, Jesus Christ, who in the fuck gives a shit about John Fucking Stuart Mill?"

Mill's name meant nothing to Philip and me. Had I known he was a philosopher, I would have told Ronnie of the dangers of studying philosophy at Tulane. Father Kirkland, our logic teacher, was right; it is far better and safer to study philosophy at Loyola. The philosophers were Thomistic and slow-footed, but at least you would not be led astray. This was good advice, even for Lutherans. (Was Ronnie going to end up like Cats--another victim of Tulane's predatory atheism?)

We had another beer and Philip told Ronnie that all he had to do was hold on to the end of the semester. The rest, said Philip, would be a breeze. There was such a strand of classicism about Philip in those days, the way he thought that each phase of our lives needed a proper end, as if our tragedies could be tidied up by simply rounding them off. It took an idler like me to know that false starts, fooling around and compulsive daydreaming were all signs of a life pulling itself together on a deeper, richer level. I didn't say so, of course. Ronnie liked me, but he knew by how low my glasses sometimes hung on my nose that I was immature.

Philip punched Ronnie on his arm one more time to reassure him, and Ronnie finally flashed that wonderful smile of his. He rubbed his arm briskly, it was quite a blow he took, but it was exactly what he needed. He seemed considerably brightened as we left.

The next day Ronnie went to the library, wondering if Philip could be right. Just stick it out, he told himself, keep plugging and everything will end up okay. Stacking his books up in order of size, from the largest to the smallest, he gave *Principles of Political Economy* one more great effort and fell asleep.

The following two weeks were the most discouraging. He began to cut more of his classes and sought refuge when his thoughts were blackest in the secret garden behind the Rose of Montana vine. But the season was changing: the heart-shaped leaves turned yellow and curled up; the pink blossoms shriveled to a lusty brown; the bees left, their buzzing ceased, and new winds blowing through the withering vine made a rasping music.

The vine could no longer conceal him and he stopped sitting in the garden, realizing how bizarre it might appear. He noticed, however, that no one paid him the least bit of attention even when he sat on a bench in the mall. His old companion Foster passed by several times with his friends, but didn't even say hello. Ronnie was happy for this: his despondency had settled into a torpid invincibility. He could not have spoken to anyone of its depth, not even to Philip, perhaps especially not to Philip.

He sat on a bench cutting his accounting class on one of these days. It was a mild amber October afternoon. The first chill of autumn was in the air. Dappled shade was all about his feet. The Newcomb coeds passed by, they were excited by the turn of the weather. The Green Wave was scheduled to play Auburn on Saturday afternoon. The coeds wore woolly sweaters, their cheeks were rosy, bitten lightly and sweetly by the October wind.

A little zephyr scurried across the mall and gave him a chill. He hugged his arms. He looked up suddenly and a dark shape passed cross his field of vision. He focused his eyes, revealing the shape as a horde of blackbirds which he at first took to be a storm cloud, but when he lowered his eyes he was not prepared for what he saw. It was the girl he had seen through the slit in the camellia garden. He had been waiting for her to appear, though, to be truthful, he had reached the conclusion that she was some kind of vision. Many of the coeds had a general resemblance to her, but none of them were--how could he say what it was about her? He had begun to distrust his memory of her, but there could be no mistake now. She was walking down the pathway and would pass close enough for him to touch. Everything in his life, it seemed, became nothing to this moment.

She passed, and fearing that he would lose her again--perhaps forever--he followed. She walked to the building which housed the School of Law. When she entered, he sat on a nearby bench, prepared to wait till nightfall if necessary.

Who could explain the next few weeks in Ronnie Hingle's life? He, the most straightforward of men, began to entertain a constant fantasy about this girl.

He imagined them sitting in the stadium cheering for the Green Wave against Auburn. Touchdown! Everyone rose to cheer, and she pressed herself against him. Her woolly sweater stirred him to the marrow of his bones, warm-cool, cool-warm. The fight song struck up, and, as he kissed her cheek, her peachy skin was surprisingly warm.

He teased her about her pouty mouth, and she looked up lovingly at him, "Ronnie, you're a devil; I can't help the way my mouth is."

"It's a lovely mouth, I was only teasing." The fight song excited him, but he heard from a far distance a haunting October rhapsody: oboes, if he knew of such instruments, and falling scalloped leaves from a mottled sycamore, canting like small kites. The leaves scraped along the ground; it made him feel both happy and sad. Where had such images come from? He was breathing regularly and felt serene.

He followed her around all week, discreetly of course, using clever maneuvers to disguise the tail, walking on parallel pathways, keeping her in view through his peripheral vision; sometimes walking ahead of her and stopping to tie his shoelaces until she passed again.

He learned her weekly routine and worked out an elaborate schedule of chance encounters (not really encounters, for he would have keeled over had she spoken to him). He arranged to be sitting on certain benches at those certain times of the day when she would be passing.

In the meantime, of course, he stopped attending his classes. Eventually, he received a notice in the mail from the dean. His mother, thinking that the letter was good news, handed him the envelope happily.

She had told everyone on the block that he was studying business at Tulane. In fact, the neighbors grew weary of hearing of Ronnie's success at school and began to avoid her when they saw her sitting on her steps. They would cross the street and give her only curt little nods of greeting.

He opened the envelope and discovered that he was being dismissed from school. He made an appointment with the dean, and surprised himself by convincing the dean that he had been ill. He explained to the dean that he was under the care of a psychiatrist because of certain emotional problems he had developed in the service. This was absolutely amazing for Ronnie knew nothing of psychiatrists or emotional problems. He did know, however, of Richard Mayeaux who was collecting full disability for emotional problems and was, in fact, seeing a psychiatrist. Fortunately, the dean did not check out his story.

The dean was unexpectedly sympathetic. He told Ronnie that he would be allowed to register for the spring semester, and that in the meantime he should try to go to his classes during the remainder of the semester.

He started attending class again and even tried reading *Principles of Political Economy*, but with the same lack of success. Still, he could not help feeling almost ecstatic and took his reprieve as a good omen in other matters. He was still in love. Wasn't anything possible now?

Through November and December he split his time between his classes (in which he had officially been given withdrawals) and his secretive encounters with the coed, and talked to no one. He had no idea of how bizarre his life had become.

The leaves fell down from the tall trees and the sky turned a dull yellow. The blackbirds passed overhead in greater numbers.

One cold December morning after a rain, it occurred to him that he should speak to the girl; but, as she came along the pathway huddled in a heavy tweed coat, its wide collar turned up around her golden hair, the blood seemed to drain from his body, sweat broke out on his palms and his throat closed. It was impossible; he could never speak to her. The gloomy wet campus seemed to close in on her as she hurried along. The wind knifed fiercely across the trees, shaking loose a horde of leaves which scurried about her diminishing figure like attacking birds. He ached with desire for her and hugged himself with all his strength. A misty rain began to fall, and Ronnie got up to leave.

During the Christmas break, Ronnie worked on the Plymouth. He completely rebuilt the engine, put in a new universal joint, and replaced all four shock-absorbers. It rode like silk when he test drove it. He looked on the coming semester as a fresh beginning. With the Plymouth running smoothly, he figured he had a better chance.

The day of registration for the new semester showed signs of an early spring. The sun was bright all day. Ronnie was full of confidence; he went through the complicated process of registering without any difficulty. His schedule was the same, he had to repeat all the courses of the first semester, and he was on academic probation. He decided also not to look for the girl. Actually, he knew nothing at all about her--not even her name.

During the first week of class, Dr. Fleishmann again assigned readings in Mill's *Principles of Political Economy*. Ronnie carried his brown copy of Mill's treatise to the library that very afternoon. He had high hopes of sailing right through it.

After reading the first page three times he grew drowsy. He still could not make heads or tails of it. Rage built up within him. He wanted to rip the volume apart, but simply closed it instead. He left the library and crossed the campus to the park, walking around with his hands in his pockets, kicking leaves. He tried to concentrate on why he could not understand what he read, but his mind went quickly blank. He stared down at the leaves without seeing them. Unwillingly, he began thinking of Rosemary Lopocola. In fact, he had been thinking of Rosemary all week. He had seen Rosemary in Impastato's grocery. She was there buying beer for her father. She told Ronnie that she had seen him working on the Plymouth. Her eyes were full of a flirtatious glow, subtle, but definite. She had on a pink satiny blouse, which gave a motherly quality to her bosom, and a tight grey skirt. The skirt defined everything perfectly, but it was her eyes that had aroused him. They walked out of the store together and talked on the corner. He asked her if he could call her sometime.

Sure, she said, but what did he want to tell her that he couldn't tell her now--here? Her eyes were big and shameless in the way they looked directly into his. He got flustered and said something stupid like, nothing, really. She stood so close that he felt her breath on his neck.

"Well," she finally said, "I have to get this beer home before it gets hot; do you want to tell me something or not." Like an ass he said no. He could still see her lovely rear rotating as she walked away carrying beer to her daddy. He could kick himself now; he kicked the leaves. He couldn't understand John Stuart Mill, but he could understand Rosemary Lopocola. A harsh grin parted his lips. What the hell was it up here at Tulane that he pursued? Whatever it was, he did want it, though--and he knew that he would not call Rosemary, and this realization coming so clearly made him viciously kick at the leaves.

The weeks passed and he went to class, but he was doing no better than he did the first semester. He didn't know what else he could do. The cold wet days of February brought him again to his former discouragement. He suffered through the soggy weather, grimly attending every class.

The leaves rotted and turned into a tobacco-colored loam. Ronnie walked in the park more and more. It was the time in the semester when he had to turn in his accounting project and his report on *Principles of Political Economy*. In the face of this reality he reckoned with the farce of his faithful attendance of class.

It was hopeless, and he started to cut class again. March came, and the sun began to shine brightly. The wind whipped through the tall trees and seemed to punish them. Ronnie sat idly on the mall benches as due dates for term papers came and went.

He received a letter summoning him to the dean's office--he was expecting it. He went, hoping somehow that the dean, who seemed like a kind man, might give him another chance.

As soon as he sat down he sensed that the dean was embarrassed. The dean kept his eyes down on his desk in front of him. "Mr. Hingle, I have received reports from your teachers that you are no longer attending class." The dean wiped his mouth nervously after he said this. His tone of voice was objective rather than stern.

Ronnie hung his head, "I'm sorry," he said. They were now both looking down. The silence became unbearable.

The dean opened his desk drawer as if to get something out of it, but closed it immediately. He moved some papers on his desk and cleared his throat. "Perhaps, Mr. Hingle, the strain of school--I mean there are pressures. Perhaps, Mr. Hingle, you should not attempt to complete your education now. I am prepared to give you a leave of absence."

"Thank you," Ronnie said, but he didn't know what a leave of absence was.

The dean seemed relieved and became talkative. He explained to Ronnie that emotional problems were nothing to be ashamed of, that when Ronnie and his psychiatrist got everything worked out he would be welcomed back at Tulane. Ronnie nodded his head during all of this. "Then it's settled," concluded the dean, rising to offer his hand to Ronnie. Ronnie shook his hand and left, not knowing exactly what his new status was. Was he still in school or not? The only thing he was sure of was that the dean thought he was crazy. He regretted lying about having emotional problems. I am *not* crazy, he told himself.

It was a brilliant March day. He sat on a bench in the dappled shade. Robins were feeding nearby. The campus azaleas were blooming in the chilled air.

Ronnie attempted to ponder his predicament, but the flailing March wind would not allow him his thoughts. It cut into his thick wavy hair, blowing it into a chaos of springy coils. A brown paper bag, notebook paper, and smaller bits of debris tumbled by. The coeds had to hold down their skirts which flapped crazily around their legs. The strongest gusts hummed through the leafless branches. The trees seemed to lean against the strong force. Everything threatened to become airborne. Ronnie looked up and saw a trio of jets streaming across the sky, and down lower over the park, two kites with long snaky tails were rising aloft. As he watched, the kites danced gracefully; he absently raised his hand from the stack of books which he had been holding down next to him, and a new gust spun the pages of a notebook, lifting it off the stack, sending it rolling along the pathway. Snatching up the other books, Ronnie chased after it. He caught up to it some fifteen or so yards down the pathway and was trying clumsily with his free hand to turn the pages back in order when he saw her coming. What else, he could have asked himself, would this demon wind bring next?

It was the girl. She was striding as briskly as the wind itself, pointing her nose to the sky and giving no heed to her flapping skirt. He was stunned momentarily and backed away awkwardly off the pathway out of her way; by a strange coincidence the wind died down just as she went by and their eyes met in a brief calm moment. As she passed, Ronnie unthinkingly followed her as naturally as one fallen leaf follows another in a sudden rush of wind.

He hastened his stride, nearly catching up with her, but then slowed down immediately--what the hell was he doing? He could not talk to her! But it was too late, she had already spun around to confront him, causing him to drop his books. As he pounced on them before they flew away, he thought frantically that he had been mistaken for a rapist when all he really was was an idling, harmless voyeur.

She loomed over him hissing as he did this W. C. Fields number with his books, trying helplessly to stack them up. "Oh, God," he sighed.

"That's good for you," she spat out, shooting her eyes at him.

"I wasn't following you, lady," he moaned.

"The hell you weren't," she snapped, hiking her small fists up into her waist.

"I was just walking in the same direction, going to my class. My God, lady, I'm sorry," he pleaded, gaining temporary control of his books and standing up.

What was she going to do? Fire came out of her eyes, and his books spilled out of his arms again. Oh, God!

"The same direction, huh? And getting an eyeful at the same time. Very convenient," she fired out, bending over him again.

"Jesus Christ, lady--I swear to you." He was getting an eyeful all right, but he was not going to do what she thought he was going to do.

He looked up at her angry eyes, and thought that she would start screaming any second, and the campus police would descend upon him from all directions.

48

In a frenzy he thought of running and leaving his books. He could outrun those old tubby campus cops. A plan came to him in a flash: jump a Greyhound; hide out in Baton Rouge; sleep in parks; stick it out for a month, until things cooled off.

But all he did was stack up his books and wonder how much more miserably hurt and terrified he could feel under the flash and power of those angry, twitching eyes.

"Please, lady, I . . . . ," he begged as he stood up, but broke off when he noticed that her eyes were twitching erratically. She dropped her arms limply to her sides, and as he looked on, tears welled up in her hazel eyes, her lips trembled. The knuckle of her curled forefinger shot up to meet her teeth. She was trying to stifle the rush of tears but could not, and finally she lowered her broken face into her cupped hands and sobbed freely.

A few passing students slowed down to see what was going on. They shot hostile expressions at Ronnie, but he no longer felt a need to justify himself. This poor girl crying so pitifully in her hands had not been angry, he realized, but hurt. Something had happened to her; she needed help. He took her gently by her arm and guided her over to a bench and softly urged her to sit.

"Is something wrong?" he asked. He touched her lightly on her shoulder. "Are you sick--can I help you?"

Her sobbing subsided as he asked these questions, and she finally lifted her head and looked at him with swollen eyes. Her lashes were soaked, her mascara smeared and dripping. One can only imagine the pang of love Ronnie must have felt as he looked upon this lovely, tearful girl, crumbled into helplessness by some secret tragedy; and, no doubt, embarrassed to reveal this before a perfect stranger like himself.

"Yes," she said at long last, "there *is* something wrong. I don't feel well." she said, throwing her head back and shaking her honey-colored hair, as if to throw off the last pieces of her distress. "I think I need a drink.

She suddenly smiled, "Would you care to come with me to get a drink?" she asked with a strangely calculated expression of appeal.

Her new manner registered somewhere in the back of Ronnie's mind, but he accepted it at face value. His mouth had fallen open as he gazed upon her with obvious awe.

"Well," she urged with tender insistence, "Will you come with me?"

"Oh--yeah--sure, I'll be glad to go with you," he responded, still puzzled by her new appealing manner. But there was no time to ruminate, she had stood up and was leading him away. As he walked beside her, he thought to pinch himself. What was happening was beyond his wildest imaginings. Her fragrance drifted up to him and his mind careened. Sweet spring was in the air, the wind was singing through the trees; it was all too utterly perfect.

They walked to a small campus parking area, and she stopped beside a gleaming white Cadillac. His mouth fell open again as she dug in her handbag. "Here," she said, holding up a set of keys. "Would you mind driving? I still feel shaky." She cocked her head and smiled again in her strange manner, but Ronnie was beyond puzzlement.

"Sure," he replied. "I'll drive."

The Cadillac powered up with marvelous silent force, here was no mere motor with metal part striking metal part, but the powerful cosmic drift of solemn clouds. It turned corners like rolling over ice cream. The pressing of brakes was like the pushing of thumbs into chocolate fudge, and the door clicked closed with the effort of a single finger--to the touch: like snapping your fingers in velvet!

"Where would you like to go?" he asked, noticing that his voice sounded mellow. Was it rapturous transport, the lubricity of sounds cushioned by the Cadillac's plush interior? Was it, in fact, his own voice?

She had told him where she wanted to be taken, but had he heard what she said? Ched's?

"Ched's?"

"You know, down St. Charles at Napoleon."

"Oh, yeah, that's great."

He drove to Ched's not knowing what kind of place it was. It was a brand new cocktail lounge brightly decorated with blue and orange neon tracery; its logo, a whipping, cursive modern scrawl. The entrance was a split pointed arch, grilled with polished chrome. He opened the door for her with his right hand, lightly touching her waist with his left.

Inside, the lounge was dark. It smelled new: new and modern. An attractive hostess with copper-colored hair appeared and escorted them to a booth. The seats were soft with high backs for privacy. When his eyes adjusted he became aware of couples sitting in other booths, whispering to each other. They were, he could tell, the Tulane crowd, like he and--he still didn't know her name.

The waitress came. She wore a red tailored skirt, a modish silky white blouse and to his mild astonishment: a red bow-tie. She smiled: what is the pleasure of the lady and gentleman?

Ronnie's companion flashed her eyes over at him and up at the waitress. "I need something strong, I'll have bourbon, straight up. What do you want--what's your name?"

"Huh? Oh, Ronnie, I'll have--let's see. Make it two. What's your name?" he ventured, encouraged by her sudden request for his name.

"Cheryl Remison--but call me Cher," she replied, smiling languorously and running her fingers through her hair. What to make of her? Ronnie fidgeted with his hands folded in front of him. Cher seemed to become distracted, staring off into the semi-darkness, and her features suddenly grew stoney. Ronnie read this as her sorrow and thought she would begin crying again. But she came back to him with one of her appealing smiles.

The bourbons arrived, and Cher took hold of hers, turning it slowly clockwise. Ronnie watched her carefully, as though she were performing a ritual.

"You like bourbon, Ronnie?" she asked, stirring the drink with her finger. She licked her finger, closing her eyes with abandoned pleasure, "M-m-m-m-." Lifting the glass, she gulped too fast and gagged. Her eyes watered, but she quickly recovered.

"You know, Ronnie--that's your name, right? I'm an alcoholic." She searched his eyes for his response to this confession.

Ronnie laughed, "You're joking." But she sat up immediately and stuck out her bottom lip, "No, I'm not! That was my first drink in three months," she said, throwing off her Shirley Temple pout and smiling a smile that was tinged with hostility.

Ronnie sipped his bourbon, feeling relaxed for the first time. She is so cute, he thought, to be joking about such a thing. "I drink a lot myself," he confessed, wishing to enter into her little charade, but it was a mistake.

"Listen, you," she snapped, jerking her glass so roughly that the bourbon splashed on her wrist. "Ronnie--whoever, I'm telling you the *truth*, you don't think I asked you to take me here for something casual. I needed that drink!" She was tiffed all right, lowering her voice to a vehement whisper--a hiss. "I don't just drink a lot, I have to drink a lot. If I don't, I get suicidal. And the drinking destroys me; not just hangovers, but terrible depressions--it's awful!"

Ronnie was confused, but he had no choice but to believe her.

"I believe you," he said, "I'm sorry I joked about it." But he did think it strange that she could have such vibrant, honey-colored hair, peachy skin, white teeth, and yet inexplicably to be ravaged within.

She sipped more bourbon, shivering as it went down and seemed to draw into herself, looking down into the glass. What did she see, Ronnie wondered--the pit of her tortured soul? He allowed her her silence.

He sipped his bourbon wondering if he really knew what an alcoholic was. A wino? Surely she wasn't that. The bourbon left a sweet aftertaste and brought him to a state of relaxation he hadn't known in weeks. He swallowed the rest of it and felt a buzz come on. Her fingernails glowed, they were so beautifully manicured--pink.

"Let's have another drink," he offered. She looked up sharply, putting her elbows on the table. "That's right, mister, get me drunk. When I drink, boys take advantage of me. But I don't care, you won't be the first and you won't be the last."

He was shocked, this was not at all what he wanted to happen. "I'll take you home safe and sound," he said defensively, "You don't have to worry about me."

"Wait 'til I'm drunk, mister. It doesn't take long."

"You got me wrong, lady; I wouldn't do nothing to you, I swear," he said, thinking how ironic it was that he'd got in trouble by offering to buy an alcoholic a drink. She is so mysterious: an alcoholic at her leisure between bourbons; and here he was upset and actually dying for another drink. "I mean, take your time, lady. When you're ready, I'll drive you home safe and sound."

"A gentleman, huh? I'll bet." She was so hostile, and he couldn't understand why. Was the alcoholism overtaking her--and, if so, why no hurry to get the next bourbon on its way?

"Please, lady, if you need another drink, don't worry. I won't touch you."

"Look, Mr. Gentleman," she said in a huffy whisper, looking, it seemed, not directly at him but past him as if she spoke to someone else beyond him. I'm very familiar with gentlemen who offer to help me. For one thing, you're drooling all over your chin."

"My God, lady--I swear to you--please. . . ." he importuned desperately. Why did she say such things? Were they not young and together in a fresh-smelling, soft-lit cocktail lounge in the quietest hour of a beautiful March afternoon; how could he or she do evil? But she continued gazing fiercely from under her brows, curling her lip. Although by a strange illusion she appeared not to be looking at him but somewhere behind him, as if she were cross-eyed.

"I know all about gentlemen," she said with her smoldering eyes definitely on him now. "And I'll tell you something about gentlemen. I had three psychiatrists, all gentlemen, just like you, but that didn't stop them from sleeping with me, and begging me to marry them. They were willing to divorce their wives." She smiled grimly. "I haven't had a lover since I stopped drinking three months ago. So relax, friend, we're going to have a good time, just don't try to reform me and don't beat me up. Get the picture?"

Poor Ronnie. He sat there speechless. Could he have spoken, he would have said that the *picture* was all out of focus. For it was beyond him how a sweety like Cher could be saying such terrible things. All he wanted was to speak tenderly and sweetly to her of his love, certainly not to exploit her afflictions.

Chapter 7

*E*ventually Ronnie drifted over to Loyola again. I remember seeing him and Philip walking around the little quarter-mile cinder track in the rear of the campus. Hardly anybody went back there, so it was very deserted. I could tell even from a distance that Ronnie was despondent. He walked with his hands folded behind him and his head down beside Philip who seemed to be listening intently to his story. Once or twice Philip gave him his customary punch on the arm, but Ronnie didn't even look up or rub his arm. It must be very bad this time, I thought. I was sitting in the makeshift wooden stands beside the tennis courts, partially hidden by a lagustrum hedge. The tennis courts, like the cinder track, were also deserted. Philip had asked me to wait for him. This was the only quiet part of the campus, and I was beginning to enjoy the solitude when Sheila Rosenberg showed up.

I can't say that Sheila was my favorite person on the campus, although she wasn't a bad looking girl, as well as being very intelligent. But she knew it. She was constantly correcting my grammar or analyzing my motives--actually, she would analyze anything, being Loyola's resident Freudian. She was the first girl I met who talked openly about sex, and I confess that it took a few times before I got used to it. Sex, she told us, was at the root of everything, even religion; but, of course, I couldn't buy that. I didn't say so because she told us the first time we met her that people were always subconsciously suppressing the truth to protect their illusions about the world. So no matter how good your arguments were, she would only claim that you were subconsciously resisting. She was really a big hypocrite, because I discovered that she was a good Catholic who went to Mass and Communion every Sunday. So she couldn't have known half as much about sex as she claimed she knew. She was looking for Philip that day and not for me, as usual.

"Hello, Sheila," I said as she walked up.

"Where's Philip?" she asked.

"He's having a private talk with Ronnie on the cinder track about his problems."

"Whose problems?"

"Ronnie's."

"That boy Ronnie is very neurotic," she said, shaking her head.

"Ronnie's normal, he's just having problems at Tulane," I said a bit too shrill.

We were looking over at Philip and Ronnie as they walked around the track. Ronnie had stopped and stood facing Philip, speaking, it appeared, very earnestly, his face drawn up very close. Sheila had sat down next to me on the stands. She miscalculated, I thought, because she was very close, touching, in fact. I could smell her.

"How long have they been talking?" she asked.

"About twenty minutes, I guess." When I turned to answer, our noses almost collided. For once she wasn't showing off what she knew about human psychology. I started to feel funny. I had never been with Sheila when she wasn't talking her head off. It was a beautiful spring day. From where we sat we could see the Tulane campus across Freret Street, the azaleas were in full bloom. Here beside the tennis courts a few dandelions had sprung up.

"Have you had lunch yet?" Sheila asked.

"No, I was waiting for Philip."

"Who needs to eat in weather like this." she said, smiling at the blue sky and then at me. I was surprised by the smile and forgot to smile back.

"Yeah," I said, recovering, "March is my favorite month."

"And April is the cruelest," she said mysteriously.

"It is?"

"So said T. S. Eliot," she cooed, smiling at the sky again.

"Who?" I asked, knowing that I would likely get a lecture. But I noticed just then that Ronnie and Philip must be concluding their talk, for Ronnie was rubbing his arm and seemed to be bravely smiling. Philip drew back one more time, but Ronnie backed away, and they parted waving to each other.

Sheila and I were straining our eyes to see. She had forgotten about T. S. Eliot, whoever he was.

Philip came over to us shaking his head. We went to the cafeteria, where Philip told us of Ronnie's meeting with Cher, and then swore us to secrecy.

I don't think he meant to betray a confidence, I was after all Ronnie's friend, and Sheila he felt could be helpful, since she seemed to know so much about psychology.

Sheila said that Cher's behavior was *bizarre*, a technical term. This is what Philip wanted, an analysis. He seemed more concerned than usual, and said he offered to make an appointment for Ronnie with Father Rodriguez, the campus chaplain. It was portentous, I thought, when a Catholic sent his Lutheran friend to a priest for advice on his love life.

In the meantime, however, Sheila's eyes were glowing in a way I was becoming familiar with. She couldn't wait to analyze Cher, who, of course, she hadn't even met, and Philip couldn't wait to hear what she was going to come up with. Personally, I wouldn't have given you two cents for any of Sheila's analyses. She delighted in saying shocking things, such as making fun of downtowners for what she mockingly called the "Jude Cult". St. Jude had a devoted following in the ninth ward; novenas were held every Thursday night. He was the patron saint of hopeless cases and was credited with many local miracles. "Belief in miracles," Sheila had told us, "is an opiate for backward people." She meant my downtown Sicilian and Slavic friends. Philip and I, she said one day to me privately, were exceptions. But I wasn't flattered. In fact, I thought she was a hypocrite for saying so. I had attended a St. Jude Novena myself once.

Sheila thought she was very progressive. It was not really her fault, though. This was what happened when liberal parents sent their precocious daughter to a free-swinging uptown school like Newman. Besides, she was the product of a mixed marriage. Only in this uptown part of town would a Jewish sociologist and a Creole belle be foolish enough to marry. And no one to tell them not to plan a family. Sheila was the result.

But what other person here at Loyola could have told us that Cher was suffering from nymphomania as well as alcoholism.

"What's nymphomania?" Philip asked, settling himself seriously on his chair. Here it comes, I thought. There was no way to stop Sheila, especially when Philip, who should have known better, was encouraging her. Here at Loyola Freud was never spoken of (indeed, that Viennese Gnostic was held anathema)--just Sheila and one or two young Ph.D.'s in the English Department, snide, cocky guys who spent most of their spare time seeking positions at schools like Brown or Bennington.

Sheila hiked up and folded one leg under her, and a parted-mouth eagerness came over her countenance. A sure sign that one of her off-colored, Freudian explanations was on its way.

"That girl is a text book case," she said, shaking her head as if she were a real psychiatrist consulting with her colleagues. "I mean," she began again, biting her lip thoughtfully, "it's one of those classic examples. She's obviously a victim of an unresolved oedipal attachment to her father, and that's why she cannot deal effectively with her primitive lust."

She gripped the edge of the table and sought my eyes. "Don't you see?" I didn't see, and I didn't want her to go into any more detail. "She projects," she continued, her voice rising to an almost gleeful register, "she projects this lust onto men, especially men like Ronnie, and is swept along by unbridled infant sexuality." The word sexuality coming from a girl, I have to admit, had a shocking effect on me. I think that I lowered my eyes and started to leaf through my Apologetics text. "Love and sex are one and the same thing to her," Sheila concluded.

I got a picture as she did of her parents, who I hadn't met yet, discussing sex in their living room with little Sheila hanging on every word.

I was avoiding her eyes and desperately wanted her to stop, but Philip was really leaning in, hoping, I suppose, to pick up words like oedipal and nymphomania for his expanding vocabulary. There were so many hot items that the ninth ward had no words for.

"It's so obvious," Sheila declared, chuckling a bit derisively, "that's why she radiates sex, and, incidentally, why men are so attracted to her."

"She is also," I put in, "a very gorgeous broad and I know that's not Freudian, but men always go for fine broads. It's the law of nature."

She looked at me as if I were a hopelessly confused adolescent.

"Sheila," I insisted, "beautiful girls attract a lot of men, what's so complicated about that--besides, she's rich." But it went by her, earthy facts simply didn't matter to her.

"Bobby," she said, making her eyes tender like a very patient mother's, "things are not as simple as you apparently think they are."

"Look, Sheila," I said, "you don't even know this girl. She's just another one of those promiscuous rich bitches. Newcomb is full of them." Trust a ninth-warder to give you the straight dope on an uptown college for daughters of socially prominent families.

Actually I kept my best theory about Cher to myself, knowing what ridicule it would have gotten from Sheila. If Philip got the story right, it was just another instance of a smartass girl picking up a cute routine from Barbara Stanwick or maybe Susan Hayworth: beautiful, tough girl, exiled into loneliness by her own accursed beauty. Classic Stanwyck. In the ninth ward we picked up many things from the movies--social graces, interior decor and routines (looking over the flaming match into the eyes of your sweetheart as she lights your cigarette). Lou Macaluso owed his success with women to the master, Clark Gable, and Lou had a million. But you see how Sheila could have used this against me.

But, in truth, neither Sheila nor myself could be trusted to deal with a real problem, so it is a good thing that Ronnie confided in Philip. Sheila was abstract and long-winded, and I, as a rookie reporter for the *Maroon*, was too quick to angle for human interest of the topical variety: DOWNTOWN HOOD MEETS UPTOWN DEB. It was hard to flesh out character when meeting deadlines for a college weekly.

Chapter 8

*I*n the first week of April grass sprouted between the bricks of Marais Street. At Loyola we were in the middle of Lent with mid-semester coming on. The sky was cloudless and we sighed, as we did yearly, with relief. For a few precious weeks we would have moderate temperatures and clear visibility. And yet here in New Orleans we really distrusted spring, as we did all ephemera. Spring was the season for solitary walks in the park and for moping, and New Orleanians as a rule cannot stand solitude. Since we are hemmed in by swamps, lakes and the river and are aware of how easily the very land we walk on can slip out from under us, we find it necessary at all times to entrench ourselves, and await natural catastrophes. What use is this sunny, breezy weather of April when everything is so gentle when our voices become muffled and our limbs bewitched.

We are much more trustful of the elements during the vibrant, unstable days of September when we wait expectantly from day to day for a hurricane to rocket in from the Gulf, when that tiny symbol appears on the weatherman's map. (A fat little circle with spiraling wings, one curving up, the other down, designed for momentous wheeling like the gyre of Mr. Yeats, who knew better than most of us that life is ceaseless and cyclical.) How is it at such times, when gales sweep in from the Gulf tearing the clouds and thrashing the summer leaves, that we neighbors who are so dreary and perfunctory in our daily salutations suddenly become heralders to one another, the force of the wind becoming our force and the weakest among us a dynamo. At last, the sadness of our slow, inevitable decline is proven false. Here, at last, is a force that will destroy the tired old structures which imprison us. We will rebuild the world. Even as we board up windows and curse the luck, we laugh and shout across at one another, brothers and sisters of the wild wind and driven rain.

Here I was in the Loyola library so benumbed by the new spring that I was writing down such nonsense about the weather just to stay awake. Whether it was Yeats or Milton, whose epic poem I was trying to read, that prompted my meditation I don't know. But it didn't work. My pupils went out of focus, dilating freely and for their own pleasure. Not even *Paradise Lost*, in which the very heavens were in upheaval with dark, unleashed forces, could keep me awake. The words on the page shifted and willowed, and Milton's sonorities gave way to the sweet concern of a librarian's whispers. I lifted my eyes to the emerald brightness of new foliage that showed through the gothic niches. I was hopelessly lost--fevered and restless. The last thing I needed was a poem about moral rectitude.

I decided that I had to leave. My eyes could not hold a focus for more than two lines.

Outside, as I descended the granite steps to the quadrangle (Loyola's little patch of green space), I stopped to draw in a deep breath. A lonely, scraggly little crepe-myrtle tree shook as a mockingbird hopped around among its few limbs. The bird began to sing, as only a mockingbird could when it cared to, silvery tones today instead of its usual squawking. Overhead the sky had turned a smooth porcelain blue. Students were sprawled all over the lawn, sunning themselves.

The book beneath my arm seemed unduly burdensome, and my legs were strangely uncooperative. I headed for the Avenue, reasoning as I moved along at this snail's pace, that I would find a peaceful spot in Audubon Park and read *Paradise Lost*. It didn't bother me in the least that this plan was wholly unrealistic.

I waited on the curb for the cars to pass. They seemed to only float along. Beyond the Avenue, the park was simply too gorgeous to be believed, moss laden oaks, blazing azaleas and pearly camellias. A perfect place to read poetry. (Lies, lies--doesn't Spring always lie to us.)

On the parkway I had to pull up for the streetcar. It went past, humming, swaying, lurching, a truly ridiculous old machine.

In the park I followed a little footpath through the swings and slides to a grassy spot along the edge of the water hidden by a hedge of fuschia azaleas. It seemed to me, in my enchantment, a fabled place, where ground moss crept along the water's edge and where, I imagined, salamanders slept on the muddy bottom of the lagoon.

I lay down in the grass and propped the book up on a rounded knoll. The water was as still as glass, and I peered into its depth. There I saw again the porcelain sky and the mossy limbs of the oaks. Two swans swam by rippling the surface, and, as I looked up into the oaks, little winds touched and lifted the tasseled moss. My eyes went their own mosaic way again, and, as I turned helplessly to the open book, among my drifting thoughts was the sudden and brief realization of my wretched loneliness and blatant horniness, just before my head began to lower onto the book to sleep.

A ninth-warder in Audubon Park in springtime was definitely in trouble. Fevered, resting on a poem of heavenly revolt, eyes to put Claude Monet to shame, and a quivering at my crotch.

Such was my predicament that first spring at Loyola when Sheila Rosenberg walked up seemingly out of nowhere.

"Hi, Bobby," she said, smiling down at me.

"Hello," I returned, struggling to a sitting position, trying to smooth my mussed hair.

"What are you doing out here?" she asked, as she sat down beside me.

"I'm reading *Paradise Lost*. We have a quiz tomorrow, remember? Aren't you going to read it?"

"Oh," she said dreamily, "I've already read it."

"The whole thing?" I asked incredulously.

"Of course, it's not that long. Milton was a great poet, but his imagery is hopelessly passé."

"His what?"

"His imagery--you know, his word pictures."

"Passé-what do you mean, is that going to be on the quiz?" I asked anxiously.

"No, of course not, passé means irrelevant to our times. Milton's angels are anthropomorphic and therefore inappropriate to our Einsteinian vision of the universe."

It was strange, ordinarily I would have been annoyed at her for talking like this. But on this particular day I could not take my eyes off of her lips, and when I lifted my gaze I noticed that her soft brown eyes were fixed on mine.

"Did you say anthro--anthro....?"

"Anthropomorphic."

"What's it mean?" I asked, not letting her eyes leave mine.

"It means using man as a model. Milton's angels are men with wings." She explained, looking at my eyes one at a time.

"Sheila, you're very smart."

"Oh," she said, dropping her eyes, "I'm not very smart."

"And you're pretty, too." I said as I put my hand on top of hers. My heart was thumping.

"Really?" she replied, looking up again.

"Yes, really."

We reached each others lips for a brief, breathy kiss.

"I'm sorry, Sheila."

"Why are you sorry?"

We kissed again, and I put my hand on her shoulder. She lay down on her back, and I came over her.

"Sheila, I think I'm in love with you."

"Don't say things that you don't mean."

"I mean it--really."

I kissed her again, lowering myself over her.

And there we lay, kissing and looking into each others' eyes for endless minutes, hours perhaps. It was a day of such color and soft languor as to be enrapturing, and there fell across us as we entwined the crosswork lyricism of long, springtime shadows, cast by the ancient oaks.

I tried to explain to her the irony of our attraction. "I guess we were falling in love, and that's why we argued so much. We were resisting the inevitable." She smiled very sweetly when I said this.

"That's right, Bobby, we were resisting."

"That makes us very Freudian, doesn't it?"

"Very," she said, pulling me down to kiss her.

It was here that I made a mistake. I guess the idea of us being Freudian excited me, and I grabbed one of her breasts. But she broke immediately and shook her head reproachfully. I apologized and loved her all the more for stopping me.

Sheila was a perfect springtime sweetheart, soft and wanton in the kiss, but tough and virginal when the hand began to roam.

Chapter 9

*B*efore long Ronnie was back over at Loyola's cafeteria telling Philip his troubles. Sheila and I sat far away at a separate table, but we could not resist looking over every few minutes. Ronnie kept wringing his hands and scratching his head, he seemed beside himself with anxiety. Philip would reach over now and again with soft little push-punches, trying to coax a smile from Ronnie, but it seemed hopeless. Sheila said she feared a crackup.

"It is common," she explained, "for female alcoholics to turn to nymphomania. Ronnie should try to forget her."

Of course, we hadn't met Cher, so Sheila was still speculating blindly.

"Very wasteful," she deprecated, as she rose to leave.

"Where are you going?" I asked worriedly.

"To my meeting."

"To your meeting--can't you skip it? Don't you want to know what happened to Ronnie?"

"It's the Philosophy Club and I'm president. I would be very irresponsible. Besides, it's none of my business."

"Ronnie's our friend, isn't he?"

"He's your friend, I hardly know him." and off she went. I guessed she was right, maybe I didn't know Ronnie as well as I thought, either.

A few minutes later Philip led Ronnie out of the cafeteria. As they passed my table, Philip leaned over and asked me to wait for him.

About twenty minutes later he returned alone and sat down to tell me the rest of Ronnie's story. None of us could have guessed what really happened that afternoon at Ched's.

It was not like Ronnie, who was usually so straightforward, to tell his friend Philip such a fragmentary, misleading version of the

63

story. It was his pride, no doubt, and his hope that the story could have a different, happier ending.

Cher, of course, was as big a phony as I expected. Her strange alcoholism, endured so contradictorily in the full flush of her glowing health and beauty, was merely a clever act, as was almost everything about her behavior. One bourbon was all Cher had that afternoon, and it was more than enough. Another would have brought on nausea or a spell of giggling. Her real addictions, as Ronnie learned, were more commonplace, Krystal hamburgers and vicious female craftiness. In short, she was no exiled goddess or hardened alky, and this business of bartering her favors to lure her psychiatrists from their happy, settled marriages was pure invention.

Her performance was calculated to provoke a certain person who just happened to be sitting one booth over. And her little scheme worked very well. No sooner had the waitress returned to ask if Ronnie and Cher needed another drink than this certain person suddenly loomed before them.

"What the hell do you think you're doing?" the strange young man snapped at Cher.

"It's none of your damn business what I am doing." Cher fired back.

"C'mon," he said, angrily, "I'm taking you home."

"Like hell you are, you bastard," shouted Cher. Ronnie's heart sank to hear such language coming from her.

This, of course, was Cher's boyfriend, and, as Ronnie later learned, he had witnessed Ronnie's eye-twitching confrontation with Cher and had followed them to Ched's in his Oldsmobile, a shadowy, betrayed figure slipping into the quiet, darkened lounge to seat himself in view of Cher. There had been an argument, and this was Cher's way of wreaking revenge. Ronnie was completely fooled by her tough repartee and her little routine with the glass of bourbon, but her boyfriend was livid. He sputtered with embarrassment and jealousy and tried to pull her out of the booth by her wrist. Ronnie was too stunned to react. (What was his duty--to protect her from physical harm?) The waitress ran off to get the copper-haired hostess, who had already heard the commotion and was on her way.

"Please," entreated the hostess, "you must keep your voices down. Please, I'll have to call the police."

Before Ronnie could decide what he should do, Cher broke the boyfriend's grip and banged him on the head with her handbag. "Let's go, Ronnie," she said, grabbing him by the collar; and out they went--Cher, swift and angry as a hornet, and Ronnie, a smitten dupe, being dragged from behind. The boyfriend just stood there for the moment, grinding his teeth, trying to ignore the hostess' insistence that he leave, too.

One can just imagine what great issue was at stake between Cher and Whatshisname. She was the type that would fly off just because her boyfriend didn't jump around exactly like she wanted him to. Only her tears had been real, and these were shed merely to quell the anger of a spoiled uptown deb.

We never did learn the boyfriend's name. Who knows what kind of names uptown people have? It was probably something like Reginald or Clive or Milbrook. I remember making a joke about it to Philip.

"What'd you think his name is, Philip? Monroe? What about Preston or Billingham? Wait, I got it--Rollo, right?" I thought this was very funny. Philip laughed, too, but he told me that the rest of the story was not so funny. In fact, he had taken Ronnie over to Thomas Hall, the Jesuit Rectory, and made an appointment for him with Father Rodriguez, the campus chaplain.

As soon as Ronnie had pulled off in the Cadillac with Cher fuming and cursing beside him, he noticed in the rear-view mirror that the boyfriend was struggling to get into his Olds. Somewhere around Louisiana Avenue the Olds caught up to them. Ronnie didn't know what to do. What if this guy tried to run them off the road?

"What's he going to do?" he asked nervously.

"Who?"

"Your friend, he's following us."

"Who cares?" she said, folding her arms.

At Jackson Avenue Ronnie decided that Rollo, or whatever his name was, seemed content to just follow. Ronnie was relieved that there would be no smash up, but was still very uncomfortable about the whole situation. The worst of it was his feeling of helplessness. He should have simply left Cher in her Cadillac right there in the middle of St. Charles Avenue. But he couldn't, the smallest, most remote possibility of Cher really caring for him was enough to make him endure whatever indignity he was being submitted to.

And so ensued the most bizarre week in Ronnie Hingle's life. Off they went, all that week, like the Keystone Kops, the Cadillac in the lead and the Olds in hot pursuit.

Each evening at dusk Ronnie would park the Plymouth on Freret Street and walk over to Tulane where he would meet Cher in the parking area by the Cadillac. Ronnie would spot the boyfriend sulking around his Olds, kicking the tires. And here would come Cher, flouncing her skirt, flinging her arms around Ronnie's neck as if he were Heathcliff. Her very touch was more than Ronnie could bear, even if he knew these brief embraces were for Rollo's benefit. Her need for retaliation seemed to know no bounds, and Ronnie wondered what had the guy done that made her so violently angry. Still, he longed to linger with her arms around his neck, but she would soon break with what he knew to be a bogus smile and then, it was into the Cadillac and on with the chase.

"Let's go somewhere and get drunk." Cher would command, but they didn't get drunk, they didn't even stop. On and on Ronnie would drive, aimlessly it seemed, the Cadillac's white hood gleaming in the violet light. He developed an almost ritual route for these nights, cruising along Carrollton Avenue past General Beauregard's equestrian monument at the entrance of City Park and then along Bayou St. John to Lake Pontchartrain where they would arrive each evening it seemed only moments after the sun had disappeared in the murky water.

And then as darkness descended he would guide the Cadillac along the seawall, on and on into the starlit night. Spring winds swept across the brackish water into his hair and he would breathe deeply of the air's faintly salted tang and of Cher's fragrance. It seemed to him on these nights as he looked up into the sky over the wide water where Venus glowed so near to a thin sliver of a moon that perhaps in some way and by some means he could win Cher's heart. He would suffer poignant palpitations as the little lapping waves would suddenly light up as if by some magical means. He would then realize that they were catching the beam from some pivoting searchlight on a distant humming motor launch. It was a strange loneliness he felt sitting as he was, so near to the one he loved on these lovely nights. He thought that he could be satisfied with so little, with her hand on his arm--some contact with her, anything.

But always when he came back to himself, he would check the rear view mirror and there would be the Olds; and beside him he would catch sight of Cher turning to check, her eyes flashing with spiteful delight. Her brazen presumptuousness at these times would make him so heartsick that he would try desperately to gather the courage to give it up.

Only once, as they sped past the amusement park at the very moment the zephyr was plummeting down amid the delighted screams of its passengers, did he momentarily come to his senses.

He turned to Cher then and asked, "Do you think he's had enough?"

"Who? Who's had enough, Ronnie?" she replied, and leaned closer to him in her pretended ingenuousness. He thrilled and blushed to hear her call his name. But then, of course, as she moved back away from him, he had to choke down the hurt.

That Friday at sunset, as Ronnie waited for Cher in the parking area near Gibson Hall, he thought he might have been early, for the Olds and boyfriend were nowhere in sight. The late light was burnishing the sides of the great stone buildings.

Ronnie felt empty. His eyelids tweaked, and he rubbed his eyes thinking that tiny leaf fragments had blown into them, but it was spring, and all the leaf fragments had already blown away. He felt a strange restlessness and wandered aimlessly to a nearby building. It was the Law School. As he stood in the entrance, he noticed what a more brooding person would have recognized as a spiritual glow showering in from three lancet stained glass windows. These three windows were designed by the great Art Nouveau glass master, Louis Tiffany, but no one had told Ronnie this. (That had been Ronnie's trouble at Tulane; nobody told him anything. Foster Sutherland had shown him where the office of admissions was, and that was the last bit of real information he'd gotten. His mother, as sweet and trusting as she was, couldn't have told him what he needed to know; she knew nothing of phantom specks or Tiffany windows, and, even if Ronnie knew to seek information, he knew his father wasn't the person to ask.)

He stood in the glowing light rubbing his eyes, determined to remove what he still supposed were irritating specks. He had every reason to cry, but nobody had told him that, either. He did, instead, the one thing he knew to do. He set himself more determinedly to win Cher's heart.

Later that night on the lakefront, the chase was on again. He saw Rollo's Olds through the rear-view mirror; the headlights reminded him of the Tiffany glow, and he fought back his mounting sorrow. A light from a motor launch sent a rippling, lucent path across the water, stars spangled the sky, the utter beauty of the night hurt Ronnie more than he could bear, and suddenly he could no longer sit next to the girl he loved so deeply, and without warning he pulled the Cadillac over to a deserted parking area.

Cher sat up, startled, "What are you doing?" she exclaimed. Before he could explain, they heard a loud screeching of tires and saw the Olds swerving past them, nearly out of control. "Oh," cried Cher, "look at that stupid bastard, he's going to kill himself."

The Olds finally found traction and stopped, and out of the darkness came the angry grinding of gears and back came the Olds twisting crazily, coming finally to a halt just beyond the Cadillac.

"My God!" yelled Cher.

Ronnie hardly noticed any of this as he had turned his full attention on Cher, who was turned around and literally bouncing on the seat. He came over to her, his arms circling like great hooks, trying to bring her into an embrace, moving his head around to get it in the right position to force a kiss. "Cher, please, you are so beautiful," he pleaded desperately.

But she squirmed to get loose, "Ronnie, stop! Don't!--My makeup!" As she wiggled and fought him off, Ronnie suddenly came to his senses and stopped fighting her.

"What got into you?" Cher asked, still holding him off, but at the same time turning back to see where the Olds was. But Ronnie, unable to endure any more, suddenly turned on her with fiery words.

"What about those psychiatrists? Did he follow you around with them?" he shouted.

"Psychiatrists?" she replied, "what psychiatrists--what are you talking about?"

He realized only then that she had lied to him about everything. What a mess, there was Rollo over there with his busted up transmission, an uptown fool, and here he was with the heel of Cher's hand forcing his chin back, a downtown fool. It was the bitter end, they had all three had enough.

"Look," Ronnie said, feeling perfectly miserable, "Why don't you go over there and make up with your boyfriend."

"Who said he's my boyfriend?"

"Well, he is, isn't he?"

"He's a friend, not my *boy*friend."

"Are you sure?" Ronnie asked, his hope rising in spite of himself.

"Of course, you don't think I'd go out with you if he was my boyfriend," she said, smiling at him, and then added, "but maybe you're right, I should go over and see if he's all right."

She got out of the Cadillac and walked over to the Olds, leaving Ronnie sitting behind the steering wheel more confused than ever. He sat there staring out across the water into the night. He felt numb.

He didn't know how much time had passed before he heard the Olds rev up and pull off. He turned around, and saw Cher yelling and waving. He got out and stood in the middle of the street, just in time to see the Oldsmobile's tail lights disappear into the darkness. Never did the sky look so vast or the night so black.

He drove the Cadillac to the campus and walked to the Plymouth on Freret Street, where he suffered his final humiliation. He had hardly checked the Plymouth's oil and water these past few weeks, and now, at nearly three o'clock in the morning, he discovered that the battery was dead. He had no choice but to leave it on Freret Street and walk home.

For the next three days he took the streetcars up to Freret Street to work on the Plymouth, but sulked around the campus instead in vain hope of seeing Cher. He searched in all the usual place, but couldn't find her.

On the third day, when he could no longer bear the pain of separation, he decided to call her.

A lady who identified herself as Cher's mother answered and seemed to dismiss him.

"I'm sorry, Ronnie, Cheryl hasn't been in all day."

The next day he called again. This time the lady seemed irritated.

"Is this Ronnie again? I must be frank with you, young man. My daughter simply doesn't want to talk to you." There was an odd slurring quality in her voice, incongruous with rich white ladies. He wondered: Could it be...? But he knew it was hopeless and promised himself that he would not call again.

The next day, however, he was more miserable than ever. He had to try one more time.

This time the lady was very angry and downright rude. "Who? Ronnie? My dear boy, I have been patient enough. Will it be necessary for my husband to speak to you?" This time, however, although the lady used no ethnic slang, there was no mistaking the tell-tale chromatic richness of her voice. She sounded like Ethel Waters. He was stunned and confused, but in his straightforwardness, he felt only vaguely insulted.

No one of Ronnie's background would consider this treatment condescending, certainly not Ronnie, who was at this point in his life very foggy about social decorum. Uptown maids were superbly trained and by necessity endowed with autonomous authority. Cher's parents, Mr. and Mrs. C. Anderson Remison, were seldom at home--he in Nicaragua on business, she, in New York shopping for the new season's wardrobe. They came home only to bury their dead or for Mr. C. Anderson Remison to rule as Comus during the Carnival season. Dealing with uptown maids carried no disrespect. These *cafe au lait* denizens of the city's silk-stocking wards were veritable powerhouses, appearing on porches and verandahs against intruders in their white-clad smocks, arms akimbo.

And now, to make matters even worst, Ronnie suddenly remembered Cher happily calling out to him on that last night on Lake Pontchartrain right before the Oldsmobile pulled off. "Perry and I are engaged!" She had blown him a kiss, the only one he got from her. Why had he forgotten this?

Yes, he remembered but refused to accept defeat and began to numbly hang around the entrance of the Tulane cafeteria, hoping against hope.

There was no show all week. His old teachers said hello to him. They didn't know that he had been dismissed from school. They were so pleasant that he was sure they didn't remember that they'd flunked him. A week was all he could stand; his disappointment became abstract and numbing, and he lost even the relevance and fire of his own pain. By the fourth day, no one seemed to even see him, as if he and the wooden bench beneath the tall tree had become the same kind of embedded fixture.

He remembered the appointment Philip made for him with Father Rodriguez and went out of some vague loyalty to his friend, but with great reluctance. The good Jesuit practically pleaded with him to speak freely with any language he felt necessary to express his problem. (Was this priest asking him to use vulgarity? He wasn't a Catholic. Did this holy man want him to express his simple, earthy desire for Cher? He imagined how really ridiculous he would have sounded. "Yeah, Father, you should have seen this broad. Tits and ass you would give your soul for.")

"Is she pregnant, Ronnie? Don't be afraid to tell me. There are ways to handle these situations." The priest asked, looking at Ronnie with his dark solemn eyes.

"No, Father, really." My god! Why did he say that? It forced Ronnie to recognize his lust, and, without warning, he also became aware of his corruption. He had an uncontrollable urge to tell this priest how horrible he had been. You don't know, Father. If I had gotten what I really wanted, I wouldn't be here in this dark room with its narrow windows, embossing my back on this funny old medieval chair. I'd be in that sweet-smelling Cadillac. My God!

He jumped up and started to shake his legs, gave a nervous half-stretch and a silly giggle trickled out of his easy smile. Every part of his body seemed to want to move all at the same time.

"Thanks, Father, you really helped me," he said, having the uncanny feeling that the priest knew exactly why he was practically doing a tap-dance on the cream and white marble floor.

He grabbed the hand of the priest, shook it twice and was out of the door before the good father could get to his feet.

Ronnie was reeling. Ordinarily he did not dwell on things. It was as if there was a swinging door at the entrance of his consciousness so that thoughts could easily come and go. Now, however, the swinging door was more like a revolving door, swinging out of control; and here he was walking at a break-neck clip down St. Charles Avenue. Where was he going? The Plymouth was parked back in the other direction. (But never mind the Plymouth, it was dirty and had a dead battery.)

He flew along, past great mansions of every variety, Greek-Revival, Spanish Baroque, Neo-Romanesque--what have you. Had Ronnie been reflecting instead of flying along he might have noticed how locked up and silent all of these great houses seemed, as Ethel Waters sound-alikes labored within, dusting and arranging.

Ronnie walked all the way to Napoleon Avenue. When he finally stopped, his legs were quivering and drenched with sweat. The Katz & Bestoff Drugs Store and the Esso Service Station should have reminded him of the commercial blight which for years had been creeping up the Avenue. But it reminded him instead of his friend, Philip Rotolo, who was across town on this Friday morning having a beer at Sam Giglio's corner grocery.

Poor Ronnie, He wanted to call Philip and come clean--to tell him everything, how his life had come apart. But could Philip help him now?--It was too late. He had to go it alone.

Chapter 10

*R*onnie stood there at the corner of Napoleon Avenue and St. Charles Avenue catching his breath and sweating profusely, still haunted by the memory of the evening light streaming through the Tiffany windows in the Law School building. It pervaded his mood; he could not cast it from his inner eye. Not that Ronnie consciously thought of his inner eye. He knew no more of his inner eye than he knew of Tiffany glass. He had flown pell-mell out of Thomas Hall seeking to forget how the priest--Father Rodriguez--had made him look into his heart and see his lust and corruption. He had loved Cher for her body, and worst--for that damn white Cadillac--when all the while he thought his love pure and innocent. But who would blame him? The illusion of innocent love was a persistent fantasy of many young men in the fifties.

A cool breeze blew over him, causing evaporation. The Drugs Store was sided with mirroring panels of purple plastic, a material much admired in these modern times. He thought well of Katz & Bestoff to adorn their drugs store so brilliantly and handsomely. The panels reflected his dishevelled image, and he began grooming himself, combing his hair, tucking in his shirt, pulling up his pants, brushing away dust particles from his shoes with his handkerchief. "There," he told himself, "that's better, maybe everything will be all right."

But he was in the wrong strategic position. He was headed for another calamity. The drug store was just up the street from Sacred Heart Academy, an exclusive school for the daughters of prominent Creole families, and Katz & Bestoff was the favorite haunt of the Sacred Heart girls. Ronnie knew nothing of this, or of Sacred Heart Academy itself. From the Avenue, the Academy gave the appearance of colonial elegance, that unique blend of French and West Indian elements, a rambling U-shaped building, with verandahs all around, an atrium, opened to the Avenue, formally landscaped with palms, tulips and velvety pansies. The girls were uniformed and instructed daily by the nuns, trained to be both spiritual and felicitous. A lovely *fin de siècle* spirit pervaded the academy. But in the after-hours the girls sought refuge from this colonial propriety at Katz and Bestoff, lacing themselves with fountain Cokes, trashy rumors from movie mags and group hysterics. One could hardly blame them, hadn't even Marie Antoinette costumed herself as a shepherdess and frolicked with her ladies in waiting in the garden of the Tuileries.

A small herd of Academy girls was about to come rushing out of the drug store, and Ronnie was in their path.

Look out! They came loping and squealing, ragging their white blouses, rippling their pleated skirts, pounding their saddle oxfords, and overran the poor, defenseless, heartbroken Lutheran.

"Watch where you're going, mister."

"Eek, look out! My God, is he drunk?"

"He kicked me!"

"Did he, Millie?"

"I think so, he's a wino."

They covered their mouths, giggled and screamed, and pointed daggered fingers, not of serious accusation, but of high spirited mockery. But Ronnie was no wino, he was only a ninth-ward dupe, out of his neck of the woods. He was not so much hurt or insulted, but, more simply, kicked down.

From the viewpoint of the girls, it was mostly innocent excitement. Had they not on this very day paraded in a chain, symbolic of a living rosary, praying and evoking the mysteries of the Virgin May amid tulips, pansies and sago-sago palms? And did they not pray to purify their spirits before each class? They would grow up handsome, chestnut-haired and matronly toward the arts. For now, however they are strapped with the strictures of a tradition which gave them the youthful privilege to kick down any trash who hung out at the entrance of their favorite Katz and Bestoff Drug Store.

But for Ronnie, it was the last straw. He was going home. He knew exactly where the Plymouth was parked, and set out striding, the blocks falling away behind his singing heels.

As he walked, he was assailed by odors and visions which he fought against in his practical, direct way. From Thomas Hall came a peculiar blended odor of incense smoke, Johnson's Floor Wax and the perspiration of men who wore black robes even during summer days--strange to Lutherans. Ronnie made nothing complex of his sensory responses, he sniffed, looked, listened and judged the results as either pleasant or unpleasant. He liked the smell of Ched's and Cher's Cadillac. He liked the dazzling surface of the purple reflecting plastic of Katz & Bestoff. He liked everything about the modern world. He sensed new global changes--old, spoiling, musty aromas of natural things giving way to the bracing tang of chemicals and man-made fibers. Many natural smells had already disappeared, if that's what odors do. Was there not a worldwide crusade afoot to eliminate all of the rotting, fermenting smells: refrigeration, air-conditioning, homogenization, plastics: all of the ersatz, synthetic inventions of World War II? Was all of this done out of mere necessity? Shouldn't the new, modern world smell fresh and clean?

The sight of the old brown volume of Mill's *Principles of Political Economy* made him nauseous, and the glow from the Tiffany windows filled him with an unsettling moodiness. And what of Miss Thelma's kitchen? Or Mr. Charlie's sweat-cured denim caps? He was not prepared to say.

The whole city stank, especially when a southerly wind blew in from the ninth ward and down-below in St. Bernard, reeking of the rotting, fermenting swamps. Some day the sun's rays and the flying pollen of fall might be eliminated.

That he could be a principal agent in this miraculous transformation did not occur to Ronnie; he was thinking of how soiled the Plymouth must be, of how rancid its insides smelled. He had neglected it for so long. He soon found himself on the Tulane campus, on Freret Street, standing beside his ailing Plymouth.

It was early spring in the Crescent City and the season's northwesterly winds blew furiously, punishing the leafy trees; long, streaking clouds race across the sky, gulls spun helplessly like cartwheeling boomerangs. But none of this meant anything to Ronnie. There was nothing to be done about the wind. But who was better equipped than Ronnie to deal with a Plymouth's dead battery?

The jump cable looped and draped on his shoulder could reach from here to yonder. His white dress shirt was opened, three buttons down, revealing the arched curve of his vested undershirt. The sleeves were rolled to the elbows. Out of the left front pocket the pink knitted tie hung like a goat's tongue. There was the smart contrast between the narrow white belt and the dark blue trousers, its monogrammed buckle of costume gold read: R. H., rode on the point of his pelvis, in the style of Poland Avenue.

No hurry. Just stand there with the hood up for a minute or two and one of those smiling, yellow-haired Tulane guys would come along in his '50 Chevy and offer to help.

And as if Ronnie had conjured him up, one did. Yellow hair and smiling face, but in a Dodge instead of a Chevy, a slight miscalculation. But Ronnie was not mystified by his premonition; Tulane guys were always driving up and down Freret Street.

This one was quick-minded. Spotting the jump cable, he jockeyed the Dodge to the curb, grill to grill with the Plymouth. And as he emerged and walked up, Ronnie knew that he was to suffer that odd style of formal friendliness practiced at Tulane.

"Roger Caulfield," the student said, smiling and shaking Ronnie's hand with such vigor that Ronnie, in order to avoid dislocation of an elbow or shoulder, was forced to shake back with equal force.

"Ronnie Hingle," he said, anticlimactically.

Roger was both breezy and serious, like all Tulane guys, a college man at his leisure. What now? Did he want to know Ronnie's major and prospects for the future? Or could they get on with the business of juicing up the Plymouth?

"A little battery trouble, right?" Good guess, Roger.

"Right." Ronnie was smiling, too, in spite of himself. But how long could he and Roger go on smiling at each other? Should there be such joy over a dead battery? Roger stepped over and looked at the battery. Did he want an explanation?

"It's dry--in this hot sun, all day." Ronnie explained. Roger shaded his eyes and looked up at the sun. Was he testing Ronnie's theory, or did he think that Ronnie was lying?

"O.K., Ronnie," said Roger, rubbing his hands together. "Let's see if we can crank it up." Yea, Green Wave!

Roger lifted his hood; Ronnie clamped on the cable, Dodge to Plymouth, and in the next minute the Plymouth was purring.

As Ronnie removed the cable and closed down both hoods, Roger was winking and smiling through the windshield. That's right,

Roger old boy, we did it. But now I am leaving Tulane and going home to Poland Avenue.

Ronnie waited for the signal light to turn green where Freret Street meets the central mall of the Tulane campus. For the moment, the wind had died down, the tall trees seemed still and lifeless. Dappled patterns of shade floated through the distance. He saw a Newcomb coed lilting her skirt. He sucked in his breath and bit his salty bottom lip. A flash of green caught his eye and he gunned the Plymouth, screeching off.

The winds of April were random and various; blowing high and low, north and south. The season was changing. There were sprawled in the blue sky, fleecy, wandering clouds, which, when caught by high northerly winds, pushed southward toward the Gulf. Not this, nor the little flipping sound of leaves, caught by the occasional rush of light eddies of lower winds distracted Ronnie from pumping the accelerator when he was forced to stop for a stop sign or a red light.

At Carrollton Avenue he should have turned right onto Esplanade Avenue. This would have headed him home; but he didn't turn and there was no simple explanation why he didn't.

He was headed for Lake Pontchartrain. It was a fine day for a lakeshore drive, especially for a practical man who had never allowed himself such excess and had never asked his faithful Plymouth to do extra duty on a dead battery and an almost empty tank of gas.

On his left were the rolling golf links of City Park; on his right, Bayou St. John, an early, connecting waterway between the river and the lake. Its surface was calm. Only now and again did it register the glitter of circular ripples, sent off by mullets nibbling at floating morsels.

The Plymouth droned and was like all things else, distant to Ronnie's ear. The world had never been so far away.

He parked on the Point, a nubbed finger of land near the Marina, and sat watching the sail boats and motor launches slip out and diminish into the green expanses of the lake. Miles away, at the horizon, the murky, brackish water turned translucent blue, like the sky itself. A merging of blue with blue. The tiny sails floated in this blue current of air, like pale kites. Ronnie patted the gas pedal; the motor growled with each pat and purred between them

How long did he stay there, thinking of nothing? The last brightness of the day was vanishing when he rolled up in front of his shot-gun. The gas gauge needle was quivering at empty. He killed the motor and, when he tried to start it up again, it wouldn't. He called Philip, and he went to bed.

When he awoke, it was as if he had closed his eyes the moment before. He had slept twelve hours of dreamless sleep. From the kitchen next to his room, he heard Miss Thelma's sweet croon of resignation, and what she always said afterwards.

"Well, whatcha gonna do?" And the slap she gave to her thigh he thought he heard, too, picturing her mouth set so and the little roll of her eyes. Someone was having coffee with her and unburdening. It was Mrs. Montegut having more trouble with Leo. Leo was her only child, her affliction, being forty-odd and moronic. It was the usual problem, Leo was giving the grocery money to the children. 'The children' were the little dark ones who waylaid Leo on his errands to Impastato's Grocery. Mrs. Montegut told it as though Leo was too generous and loved 'the children'. In reality, they snatched the little bundle of change wrapped in a paper note from his hands and led him in a merry chase. The fun of it was what they told him to do, if he wanted the money back. Piss in the gutter, Leo. Leo would piss in the gutter, but didn't get his money back. But Leo loved those children, said Mrs. Montegut. Miss Thelma crooned and slapped her thigh. "Whatcha gonna do?"

Ronnie smiled to himself, thinking: I am home. The pain of his broken heart stabbed him and brought him to another level of wakefulness. There was something interesting about what happened to him uptown at Tulane, and what happened to Leo on his errands. But Ronnie was not interested in what was interesting; he had one and only one way to go at things. He looked and moved, and grabbed hold of the tail of the bull, wanting to see what kind of ride he'd get. At Tulane he missed the tail of the bull. His hands were clenched and empty, his eyes, watery and bleary, the tassel swished about his face, leaving little stings on his cheeks and the tip of his nose.

Could he manage as Mrs. Montegut did unburdening to Miss Thelma in the kitchen? They took my money, threw away the note, made me piss in the gutter, Ma. Then to hear her croon, and see her slap her thigh, and know that his Mama understood. That's right, Ma, we suffer indignities when we reach too high. The promise of beauty, wealth and social prominence will always elude us. We must be resigned. Whatcha gonna do?

Should he ask Augie to put him on, he wondered? He imagined the knuckles of Mr. Charlie's open hand strike his breastbone, scowling and reassuring Augie. "You put him on, I'll teach him right. You'll get an honest day's work out of him, or I'll have his ass."

It took Ronnie a minute to slip into his army khakis and tuck in the tail of his white T-shirt. He uncustomarily slipped out through the front door. No one but rednecks entered and exited their shotguns by the front door, natives used the alley.

Mr. Lapara was sitting on his front steps enjoying the morning shade.

Ronnie felt like a bank robber trying to make a getaway. He remembered his dead battery. Mr. Lapara's Ford was parked next to the Plymouth, grill to grill. Lucky, but could he rouse the old man out of his leisure?

"Mr. Lapara, I've got a dead battery. Could you give me a jump-off?"

"What's wrong with your battery?" said Mr. Lapara, looking suspiciously at the Plymouth with its two weeks of traffic scum. The Ford glistened with a recent Simonize.

"It's just old and worn out. I need a new one," Ronnie explained.

"They last a long time, if you take care of them," Mr. Lapara counseled. Ronnie nodded in agreement, smiling to appear thankful for an older man's advice.

"You gotta check the water every week. Keep those terminals cleaned up," the old man continued.

"Yes, sir," replied Ronnie, lowering his head and kicking the oyster shells.

"I'll get my keys. We'll see if we can get it started for you. Then you better drive it over to Larry's and have him check it for you." He talked like a man of action, but his elbows were still resting on his knees, looking cool and relaxed in his undershirt.

"Yessir. I'll have Larry check it."

Mr. Lapara pulled himself erect. "O.K., but if you let those cells go dry you got a gone battery." He disappeared inside of the door, leaving Ronnie scratching his head and wondering why he had to make a getaway. He fetched the jump cable from his trunk and lifted the hood of the Plymouth. O.K., old man Lapara, let's go.

Old man Lapara came down the steps cautiously, mumbling something to himself: If a sixty year old man with diabetes can Simonize his Ford, a young man in the prime of his life. . .

Ronnie almost reached out to give him support as he stepped over the gutter. Come on you old diabetic fart. What's he doing now. Adjusting his sun visor and wiping a film of dust off his dash. He held his keys up before his failing eyes, carefully picking out the right one and bent over searching for the slot. The Ford kicked off, humming smoothly and Ronnie waited for him to rev it. He waited an endless minute while the old man let his motor warm up.

"You got it in neutral?" Mr. Lapara barked to him.

"Yes, sir," replied Ronnie, and as the old man revved it, Ronnie turned the ignition, and the Plymouth turned over and purred.

Ronnie got out, unclamped the cable, shut down the hoods of both cars, brought his hand up to his brow and gave Mr. Lapara a curt little salute. The old man received this sourly, but Ronnie did not wait for his final words of advice. The Plymouth's rear wheels churned into the oyster shells, and he was off on his getaway. But where to?

Ronnie drove aimlessly, nor did he wonder why he was drawn yesterday to Lake Pontchartrain and seemed today to be headed for the river. Neither did he reflect that in this city water is our destiny, seeping constantly beneath us, binding and governing our very spirit, whether we dream in the blue-green provinces of the lake or find at every turn the inevitable river.

Had he not sunk so low, he would have noticed that the day was exquisite. Misty, shapeless clouds drifted south to the Gulf and on the light air was born the scent of honeysuckle and oleanders promising the drenching vapors of the coming summer, when hot, southern winds would blow over the festering swamps, bringing mosquitoes and crawfish, the worst and best of Mother Water.

The Plymouth droned, no motor answered it. The River Road was seldom traveled on spring mornings, except by those who were lost and broken-hearted. Clover and buttercups congregated, climbing the green slope of the levee which wound ahead, guiding the road.

Easy, short rotations of the steering wheel, and the Plymouth wound with the road.

Here were endless relics of a former life, falling down in a thriving wilderness. An ancient oak, deleaved, spread grandly in its naked lifelessness. Silvered fences were clutched by brambles. The old houses they encompassed, also silvered and clutched. The Realtors said this land was undeveloped, applying for rezoning in order to sell it. The owners, having moved out, paid their taxes and said no to the Realtors. "It belongs to the family, mostly dead, we have no authority." It belongs to Old Man River, who may reclaim it, save the levee. But you never know, there are seepages every spring. Everything lived here by seasons and generations, destroyed by the slow catastrophe of natural growth. What disappeared was replaced and never missed--a fine meeting place for lovers who seek ageless enchantment like love itself, for those who dreamed, and for those who were broken and dreamless.

The great river bridge tortured the Plymouth's broken motor, but there was no choice; on a getaway one goes where one is led. The loftiness was an intrusion, and the great distances harrowing, just when Ronnie wanted to be low near the bosom of the earth. The river was wide and brown, greenish in the distance. The freighters and tugs shoving long trains of barges seemed motionless, their white wake trailing behind like kite tails. The soft, green mattress of trees all but hid a man-made city. Water towers loomed as white temples, the irony of the functional appearing sacred.

Ronnie knew Algiers not at all. But the River Road was the same as on the other side. The Plymouth wound along an identical road, guided by an identical levee. The same splashes of clover and buttercups climbed the green slope. The same clutched fences, tumbled houses, the same majesty of cottonwoods, oaks, pecans, and just beyond the levee the same banks of feathery willows. The same, the getaway endless and unvarying.

Where he was, Ronnie did not know. He pulled the Plymouth over to the wide white-shelled shoulder and stopped the motor, waiting afterwards, it would seem, for the songs of birds to replace the drone, and for the seated girl on the levee beyond to move: an intruder? A statue wearing a real dress, its hem momentarily rippled by a breeze? Who was she? Companion in his getaway? Goddess of the springtime earth? Did she hear the Plymouth pull over and stop? She did not turn to look his way as he climbed the levee. Her stillness lured him on. That he might again appear as a rapist flashed and vanished in his mind. He felt akin to her as part of a picture. He would walk past her, cocooned in his own private thoughts. What could she do? Scream and run? Gee, lady. I didn't mean to scare you. I was only walking and thinking, taking in the view. Don't go, please. As he came up to her, (her flesh and hair becoming real) he stopped and heard his real voice say, "Hello."

She looked up with brown, unalarmed eyes, catching a strand of chestnut hair, fluttered by a breeze, and pulled it behind her ear.

"Hello." She looked at him like a tired, nighttime waitress, awaiting his order. He flashed his quick, natural smile.

"Can I help you?" she asked. Was she a waitress?

"I'm just walking. Do you like that house?" He caught sight of the big ante-bellum house at that moment.

"I used to live in that house. Are you trying to pick me up?"

"No, I'm sorry, I was just walking."

"You live nearby, then?"

"No, I was driving. I live on the other side."

"Why did you stop? Because you saw me sitting here?"

"No. I wanted to walk on the levee. I'm sorry."

"You're sorry for what?"

"You think I want to pick you up."

"Do you?"

"No, really."

"You wanted to talk to me, then?"

"You were just here where I was walking."

"I believe you. Do you want to talk to me?"

"I guess so. I was just passing."

"Then you will be going on with your walk?"

"Yes, I guess so."

"If you're undecided, why don't you sit down for a while. I don't want to be picked up, but I will talk to you. How's that? You can rest, and I won't get a crick in my neck."

"If you don't mind."

"Sit down, please."

He did, a few feet away and slightly behind her. He looked at the house, as she did.

"Did you really live in that house? It looks old."

"I did, a long time ago, until I was eight."

"Where do you live now?"

"New York."

"New York. . . ."

"What am I doing here in Algiers looking at my old house, huh?"

He didn't answer. She would go on and tell him why, he thought. She did.

"I want to buy it, and move back to Algiers and live in it again."

She was beginning to tell him a story, and he listened.

"When I was eight my father died in that house. His name was Maurice Duplantier. He was a very successful lawyer here in New Orleans. He was only thirty-two when he died. The house was beautiful. It had crystal chandeliers, Oriental carpets, beautiful Victorian furniture. The grounds were lovely: Azaleas, camellias, a vining sweetheart rose growing up its piers. Fruit orchard in the back, figs, pears, plums and peaches. They bore all summer, beautiful fruit. In the spring everything was covered with blossoms. My father's friends would come over for a barbecue, he always entertained. He..."

Her hand dropped in the grass between them, groping. Ronnie saw the cigarettes and Zippo lighter. He got a cigarette and put it in her hand. She turned, her eyes distant, lost in the phantasm of her words. He flicked the Zippo, sparking its little hell of flames. She leaned into the flames, lighting up. (His first act of homage, Knight of the Torch.) She turned back to the house, inhaled, blew out the smoke which drifted off, like the fleecy clouds. A mockingbird sang, the notes forming perfect shapes in the calm air. The bird, they assumed, was perched in the cottonwood behind the house. A purling cascade came rippling from the cottonwood, its leaves on their long stems, flashing a slow pointillist pattern. All was clear, perfect in shape.

They looked at the house, past and present, when it was white and stately, an ideal foil for the flaming azaleas; and today, among its brambles and honeysuckle, a noble ruin, paint peeling from its columns, the slate roof tiles loosened and in random array.

"The party . . ." his voice husky, succumbed by the natural stillness.

She shook her chestnut hair, inhaled again, "I would call them soirees. The barbecues, you mean?"

He listened knowing she had started again.

John Stuart Mill, you old atheist, begone. The moaning trees of Tulane, shallow artifice beside the purling cottonwood. Peace in his mind and heart.

The young night assembled, the gold and mauve of the sunset only minutes vanished, the darkness still fused with their glow. Nebula of early stars. The child was purposively still in the wicker chair, in her dark corner of the verandah. Two large rectangles of light were printed on the blackened floor, flanking the central door, which were ajar and printed its own slender parallelogram of light. Below, a car ground on the shelled driveway, following its curvature, disappeared and stopped, she could tell, just beneath where she sat. A car of unfamiliar luxury: a limousine and European. It was Mr. Travilla, the maestro and guest of honor. She heard the laughter of a lady, floating up from the patio in the rear, where the early guests were already drinking and talking. She pictured them, having seen them only minutes before. Paper lanterns, pink and yellow-green, were strung out in the trees, a little enchantment from the Orient. The ladies, she thought, were styled each in their own way after Claudette Colbert, their hair parted on the side, short and fluffy with curls. Their hips flattened in their organdy gowns, mid-calf length, V-cut necklines. The slim ones. The stout ones wore finely woven straw hats, ribboned, wide of brim and dipping down in front. They looked like aunts she wished she had. They all smiled down at her, as she walked through them, with perfect mouths of lipstick and white teeth. The men took no notice, standing in closed circles, joking and laughing heartily. Their suits were double-breasted, either dark or white linen, no bright colors in the masculine styles of the thirties.

Two long tables were ladened with little things to eat. Press-glass dishes of chocolates, stuffed dates, divinity fudge; a huge oval platter of deviled eggs; pickles and olives (pimentoed) in smaller trays; a crystal bowl of pink punch for the ladies.

*The men were served bourbon mixes from a makeshift bar under
the back verandah.*

*She awaited the fuss that her father would make over Mr.
Travilla's arrival. Not unbecoming deference, though, to her.
Two important men meeting and sharing a common eminence.
The one, a young lawyer, gaining daily in renown, the other the
conductor of the New Orleans Symphony Orchestra, honored
and known by all.*

*Mr. Travilla's white mane of hair shone. His
double-breasted suit was deep blue, with a yellow pin stripe,
unfamiliar luxury from far off Italy. Mrs. Travilla's profile was
like a Greek statue, her lustrous black hair pressed into Marcel
waves. Tulle and lace throughout her cream gown, which was
cut in a low circle, the very beginning of the crevice of her full
bosom in sight, unfamiliar luxury. She seemed museum quality.*

"Ah, Maestro, we're so happy you could come."

*The Maestro lifted his arms (conductor-like), smiled
broadly, his eyes luminous with affection, "Maurice, my boy, to
come to your beautiful house is always my pleasure." He
embraced the younger man, rocking him and patting his back; so
much the earthy peasant to be so brilliantly sensitive to
his music.*

*Mrs. Travilla extended her hand which Maurice bent to
kiss. Not satisfied, she leaned in to kiss his mouth. She took
both of his hands, her face beaming with admiration, "So
handsome, Maurice. I am in love with you, my dear."*

*Maurice was all boyish smiles, a little blush, but
composed in his youthful charm. They locked arms and entered
the house.*

*"Mildred, the Maestro is here." Maurice's voice echoed
down the long breezeway.*

*The darkened verandah was left to the child, who gripped
the arms of the wicker chair, and inhaled an enraptured breath.
The moon, three-quarters and waxing had appeared over
the levee.*

Who was this pretty, placid girl? Her hand groped again, and
he fed it another cigarette, sparking the Zippo's flame as she turned.

A cardinal darted from an oak and alit upon the brambled broken fence; he danced and whistled for his mate, who darted from the oak to join him on the fence. They both danced and sang and flew off into the underbrush. A twisting little breeze blew a strand of chestnut hair against her placid cheek; she coiled it around her finger and let it drop to unwind on her shoulder.

"When did he die?"

"November twelfth, 1936, of a weak heart, he had rheumatic fever when he was a boy."

"What did you and your mother do then?"

She pulled at the grass like a bird does, tossing the blades as she yanked them off.

"Oh, we lived on here for several months until everything legal was settled, and she moved us to Dallas, to live with my grandparents."

"But now you live in New York."

"I moved there two years ago, to make money," she pushed out her lips to show displeasure of New York or money. Or both.

"How do you make money?" He followed in her displeasure, giving the "m" in "money" a little pop with his lips.

"I am a legal secretary, it pays the best for girls without a college degree." So, he mused, no college degree. Fortune awaited him yet; by astute judgments and not by credentials.

"I have saved every penny, for the house. You think I am silly?"

"No, no indeed. Very smart."

"In another year I will have enough."

"Is it for sale?"

"Yes, of course. Nobody wants it but me. Look at the way it's tumbling down."

He looked at the house, thinking how he never thought of houses himself: to own one, to be a part of one, as she was to this one. Or to live in one in some special way. To him, houses were the "Inside" to the world's ranging "Outside": to sleep in, to eat in, and to leave when you wanted to live your life.

"You really love that old house?" He hung his head, looking straight down at the grass because he was embarrassed at what he had just said. He had never before thought of feeling that way, loving something wooden and old. How old was his shotgun?

"You might say that."

"Your father loved it like you do?" He did not know why he was asking such questions. He knew it was the truth and that's why he said it, because she was thinking it. He fed the groping hand another cigarette, reaching across to light it, so that she did not have to turn. "I don't think that he would have sold it, like *she* did."

Mildred Duplantier in green was stunning and the envy of women of pale coloring. Her auburn hair suggested unpolished rubies, and was thickly bodied with a natural wave. The small, flat mole high on her cheek was as black as her long lashes. Her skin ruddy and olive, neither, something finer and rarer. Lustrous, ebony pupils surrounded by pure liquid white, alabaster. The only make-up, lip rouge to shape a cupid-bow to give the thin top lip the same rich curve as the bottom one. She was giving a touch to this cupid-bow with her pinkie when Maurice and the Travillas called her down the long breezeway. Had they caught her in the secret of her narcissism? The oval mirror, a pool, deep and private. She waited a telling second before she turned to Maurice's call. The moment was safely hers, she noticed. None of them were looking her way. The Travillas flanked Maurice and seemed to be nibbling his cheeks. She moved towards them, lifting her arms like a sleep walker, an invitation to the Maestro to embrace her. The old lecher, holding her closer and longer than she felt necessary. She slipped an arm around Sylvia Travilla's waist and pecked her on the cheek, "Everyone is waiting for you two on the patio." Sylvia's eyes, hinting of the envy of an older beauty, scanned her up and down, "You are beautiful as always, my dear."

"Maurice, have you seen Claire, I can't find her", Mildred asked.

"She was on the patio. I gave her a glass of punch."

"I told her that she could stay up to hear Henry play."

The child, hearing them, appeared in the doorway. The Maestro half swatted and patted his thighs, "Come here, Clara, and give me a kiss." She shook her curls and romped into his arms. Pressed to his chest, she hugged him, receiving his kisses with little squeals and giggles.

*Mildred's hands poked at her Shirley Temple curls,
turning and arranging them, "Where were you?"*

"I was sitting on my chair, looking at the moon."

*"The moon was looking at you, you pretty little girl," said
Mrs. Travilla, with the usual charming mystery she had in her
eyes whenever she spoke to Claire.*

"The moon can't look."

*"It looks when it wants to, at pretty little girls." More
eyes of charming mystery from faraway Italy.*

A vehicle was approaching from the far bend in the road; they
looked its way, waiting for it to appear. It was an old pickup truck, a
fat man in a khaki shirt behind the wheel. *Cy Petrie, Produce, Poultry,
Yard Eggs* was printed unevenly on the door with white paint. The
motor roared, the muffler was rusted out like the fenders.

They watched it disappear around the curve, and continued to
watch as if the roar had become visible and was diminishing in space.
Clara exhaled a fleecy cloud, it pursued the forgotten roar.

"In Dallas everyone calls me Claire, but in New York I am
Clara." A faint coyness sparked in her eyes as she turned and smiled
briefly at him. Ronnie smiled back, catching that she meant that she
was sentimental and not eccentric. The mockingbird sang on from
the cottonwood.

"Do you want to see inside?" she asked.

"Sure." He picked up the cigarettes and the Zippo as they rose.
She started down, leading.

At the near side of the road they stopped, noting how tall the
house appeared from their new worm's eye view. The central stairway
mounted to the verandah from where, presumably, the rigging and
smoke stacks of the freighters could be seen. Across the road they
stopped again, noticing that there was less of the fence left than they
realized. The brambles and honeysuckle were thickly intertwined,
only two or three fence posts were still vertical. How to pass through?
Ronnie led her along the old fence line to go around, trying to press
down new little shoots of bramble as he went.

"Dewberries." She stooped where a purple vine was sprouting
dark green leaves and tiny white blossoms. "They're first cousins to
blackberries." A New Yorker returning to the South land, speaking of

88

berry vines as cousins, *en famille.* She held one of the tiny blossoms between two of her fingers, stroking it with a gentle thumb.

There was no sign of the garden, no azaleas, no camellias; everything was of the wilderness, thorny or toxic, a luxuriant poison ivy bushing up a hack berry tree. Ronnie beat a path with a hefty limb he had picked up. The weeds and brambles had grown up the first four or five steps of the stairway. He stepped them down as he ascended, pressuring each board with his foot and the spring of his knee, a test less for his own safety than for the placid girl who followed him. Should he extend a hand? The absorption of her eyes told him no. He continued to mount and test, leaving her to her private memories.

"Look." He followed down her pointing finger, where a small green lizard was spreading out his pink throat. (Lizard, lizard, show me your blanket.)

Whole sections of the verandah floor had rotted and fallen through. Ronnie stood and tested a section which was still intact and seemed remarkably solid. It would give passage to the central door which seemed unlocked, being slightly ajar. He awaited her; extended his hand and led her onto this safe section of the verandah floor.

"I think this can hold us," he said, springing his knees and squeaking the boards. She went on past him to the door. She pushed against it with her shoulder and it opened, dragging heavily on the floor. He waited at the door sill as she struggled on with the heavy door. It came stuck at right angles to the wall, and she slapped at her shoulder, dusting it.

"Come in," she said. Her eyes calm yet hallowed in the semidarkness of the wide breezeway which ran the entire length of the house. She stepped into the doorway to her left and he followed. Bright dappled patterns quivered on the floor, emblazoned by sunlight striking foliage outside of the broken out windows.

"This is the living room." She smiled quickly with her eyes, which grew distant as quickly again.

"Over there," she began again, "is where the piano was." It was against the wall opposite the doorway, in the left hand corner. Radiant, reflective edges of light darted all about her shadowed pointing arm and hand.

"And here, an Oriental rug," slowly sweeping her arm to encompass the floor; "and there . . ."

Henry Madere's hands curled around his knees, his face a study of quiet respect as he listened to the Maestro. He was being talked to, he knew, so that he would not be nervous when he started to play. The talking was low and intimate in the manner of conductor to soloist. The Maestro's voice was pitched to be clearly heard in the hum and murmur of conversation about the room. Henry had apologized for having selected the Moonlight Sonata *to play. "Don't be silly," Mr. Travilla had said. "It is not any less a Beethoven sonata because of its popularity. Everyone tells me you play very well, I always enjoy Beethoven played by young talented men like yourself. The young play Beethoven with energy and innocence, that is the way it should be played. Make mistakes, my boy, but play it the way you feel it." As the Maestro himself conducted, with unmasked earthiness.*

Mildred came over to tell them that everyone was ready. The Maestro clutched his shoulder and said something that Henry did not hear. He straightened himself on the stool, he was ready. Mildred led Mr. Travilla to his chair and seated herself. The room became silent.

The child floated off with the first touch of his fingers to the keys. The moon was looking at you . . . . she pulled the curtain back an inch and gazed out past the verandah at the black and silver night. The night spilled in through the slit she peeked through. Muffled metal clanging, water chugging, hoarse hooting of horns, the nighttime river mingled with Beethoven. She heard all of these together and separately as only a child could, among adults who paired Henry's fingers, moving and striking, with the notes heard, his stretching neck and closing eyes striking their inner feelings as his fingers did the keys. Clara lived inside the music, inside the night--the night music. The moon chugging up the liquid sky; the clanging clouds pushed and hooted along. Moon night, moonlight, chugging, chugging . . . .

It was thus. A meeting between a dreamer and one who dreamed not. Who was Clara Duplantier, a girl so peaceful with such a greedless claim on what she wanted, born out of a seeing from within, unpossessing and serene? And he, broken hearted and on the run, mended somehow by the sparking of a Zippo, the clearing of paths, providing safe passages. Happy service for the Knight of the Torch.

They stood, in the way of a finale, on the shambled verandah, sharing the narrow island of solid boards, looking across at the rigging and smoke stacks, listening to the grinding and chugging of tug-boat motors; and the mockingbird in full, soaring song, whistling over the occasional purling of the cottonwood. Rippling breezes wisped strands of chestnut hair against her placid cheeks. Curving,tranquil lips expelled fleecy clouds. Neither of them moved or talked in an expanding relaxation that made a mockery of time.

A sudden quavering of her breath resolved itself into a sound that was part grunt, part sigh. She looked at her watch and held it to her ear.

"Say, it's four o'clock, and I'm stranded."

"Stranded?"

"I'm afraid that I took a taxi out here."

"I'll give you a ride, I have my car." Poor Plymouth, juiceless and--empty? The realization socked him, making him twist and scratch his head. "If it starts."

"Motor trouble?"

"My battery is dead, and I'm probably out of gas."

"Is that why you stopped?"

"No."

"Quite a man of mystery, aren't you?"

"What?"

"You spend an afternoon with me without introducing yourself, and now you offer me a ride in a car that is out of gas and has a dead battery. You could be a bank robber for all I know."

"I'm sorry, my name is Ronnie Hingle. About my car--it's a long story."

"It must be quite a problem to send you out to Algiers without gas." They were walking over to the Plymouth as they talked.

"Well," he hung his head and kicked at a phantom stone.

"Too personal, huh? Sorry for intruding."

For an answer he flashed a smile, opened the Plymouth's door and slipped in behind the wheel.

"Let's give it a try." At the turn of the key, the motor turned over and ran as smoothly as if it had been tuned the day before. Well, how could you figure it? The royal carriage running with the needle jiggling at empty, its driver and battery recharged. Wondrous.

They crossed their fingers and made it to a service station on Highway 90.

Who was this quiet girl, born to privilege and money, working so diligently in New York? Anyone with an ounce of brains would have advised her to forget this promise--a child's promise, after all--because in 1950 to buy back and restore her father's old house was not a sound investment, a terrible one, in fact. Old houses of this vintage, located in the wilds of the lower coast, had lost both their charm and value in the prosperity following the war, given way to a new, eager market for suburban houses. In consequence, Maurice's house had long since been abandoned by the new owners and was already in a serious state of dilapidation. Mildred had been wise to sell it in 1936.

But Clara could not forget her father or his house. Through the years, she had kept a photograph of him in her wallet, sporting a youthful mustache, with his foot upon the bumper of his Model-T Ford and his shirtsleeves rolled up to the elbow. He is laughing with open mouth while his bulldog sits on the Ford's hood, looking away and uneasy about his perch. Maurice holds the brutish dog with a slender muscular forearm. The photograph appears faded, as though the existence of the person whose image it preserved were tethering dangerously on the edge of extinction. He seems the very essence of innocent youth, so poignantly and vulnerably callow--young in a way that his daughter was never young, The date on the back of the photograph was 1926, a year before he married her mother--two years before Clara was born in 1928.

She had been kept away and told nothing during his sickness. But, of course, she didn't have to be told. She was eight and knew he must be dying. Why else would Mildred, her mother, be crying so hard, drying her tears and embracing her. Clara accepted his death in her child's mind, withstanding the empty feeling of his absence to begin the process of recovering what she knew could be salvaged of him.

On the day he died, her mother went away with Grandmother Rawling, leaving her with her nanny, Marie. Marie cried, too, as she busied herself, cleaning and cooking, checking on Clara who sat quietly on the verandah watching people walking on the levee. Everyone told Clara that Maurice had gone to be with God. It was better than saying he had died. The pitiable November sky hanging over the levee was as heavy and gray as granite. Small groups of ducks flew by every once and a while, struggling in the heavy air, and frigate birds spreading their great wide wings hovered high above in the thickening mist. The fading green levee grass seemed to lose its color, sucking the wet vapors of the clouds.

She didn't care that the weather was sadness itself, it did not add to her sadness. When her mother moved to Texas to live on Grandma Rawling's ranch, she didn't care either. She had already decided leaving the lower coast and Algiers was only temporary.

There were only women in her new home on Grandmother Rawlings' ranch, outside of Dallas. Grandfather Rawling had collapsed and died on his horse more than ten years before. The only other men on the ranch were the Indians who lived in the stables and took care of the horses. The big house stood starkly on the great dry plain, smelling strongly of oil-rubbed leather and peppery Cumin, odors she associated with Texas men, as though her grandfather, whom she didn't know, was still present. Texas, she quickly learned, was a land of men, horses, pick-up trucks and luxury cars.

Grandma and mother drove often to Dallas to shop, sometimes taking her. She actually preferred to stay with Anita, her new nanny and Dolores, Anita's daughter. Anita and the other servants were treated like family. A Miss Graeber, who talked with a German accent, came during the week to teach Clara and Dolores. In the evening after their lessons, the two girls rode their horses across the mesa, stopping in the dark blue-violet gloaming to watch the sun slip down off of the land's edge. Dolores had the broad face and somber eyes of her Apache ancestors. A closeness developed between the two girls without words. Words, however, were Dolores' gift. She read and mastered all of the literature offered by Miss Graeber, and began to write her own stories. Clara felt such pride for her friend. Years later when Clara would leave Dallas for New York, Dolores would continue writing stories about the great open country of her forebears.

It had not been easy for Clara to leave against her mother's strong protestations. Mildred had no way of understanding why her daughter would do such a thing, and would have prohibited her if she could. Clara held firm, though, and bore no resentment, explaining her reasons as best she could.

Grandpa Hypolite, Maurice's father, whose legendary reputation as a magistrate extended beyond Louisiana, helped her find a position as a secretary in a large law firm in New York. She had inherited this grandfather's stoic spirit of independence. The Algiers house had been his home. When his wife Stella died, Grandpa Hypolite had presented the family home to his son Maurice as a wedding present--reasoning 'better it be a house for a family than the haunt of an old mawkish widower.' His daughter-in-law, Mildred, had thought this gift a wonderful gesture, a house she could live in with great pride.

But in her distress over Maurice's sudden, youthful death, Mildred sold the house and moved to Texas. Grandpa Hypolite felt no bitterness towards her about this. He had little attachment to the house since the death of his beloved Stella, who had reigned over it with such grace. It was a house extended beyond its time, built by the rugged old ante-bellum plantation gentry. But now in the heedless, new, post-war optimism the veterans with their unexpected social mobility created by the generous bounty of the GI Bill had developed a passion for pristine, new suburban brick cottages, complete with garages, lawn ornaments and kitchen gadgets--the perfect fulfillment of the promise of America's new wealth and prestige. By 1950 Maurice's old house had progressed steadily into a ruinous state and Clara was advised by her real estate agent, to buy, if she must, as soon as possible. "Before it fell down,"agent Cora Lang thought.

One might have supposed that Clara was seeking adventure in New York, and should have been furthering her education instead. But she had no time for either adventure or higher education. It was adventure aplenty to return to Algiers and live in her father's house--more even than mere adventure, especially for a girl possessed of such serenity.

In New York, Clara practiced her regimen of saving money, talked to Grandma and mother on the telephone (her mother no longer attempted to dissuade her) and wrote regularly to Dolores in these early years while Dolores was still at the ranch. Dolores had not yet gone to study at the University of New Mexico. What she and Dolores lacked in blood kinship they provided spiritually--like compensatory sisters effecting a distant equilibrium--Dolores in New Mexico in the arid desert West, where she finally settled, and Clara under the lachrymose skies of Louisiana.

As time went on they would stop writing letters. Dolores would mail Clara copies of her books. Without having to explain her reasons, Clara knew that Dolores understood why she needed her father's house, and why she had forgiven Mildred for selling it.

How could Mildred understand her daughter or her eccentric plan, conceived in some recessed, hidden part of her childhood memory, where, like an angel, she hovered above time and the simple logical consequences of practical existence, and yet, so ironically, could discipline herself to focus on the most concrete of human endeavors, namely, saving money in New York city. Why did she not simply get on with her life?

Chapter 11

*W*hile Ronnie was meeting Clara and destiny, I rode the streetcar up to Sheila's house on South Johnson Street. We were to study for our Moral Guidance exam, scheduled on Monday.

As usual, I approached the Rosenberg's house with some expectancy. Perhaps my nervousness was of my own making, although I think that Bernie Rosenberg's callousness was at least partly responsible. Bernie was Sheila's father, who taught sociology at Xavier College, a Negro, Catholic school.

I arrived at ten o'clock and was startled to find their front door wide open. But I shouldn't have been; it was always opened, especially on bright spring mornings.

Bernie was sprawled out in a big easy chair in tennis shorts and shirt, pressing the strings of his racket, being his usual phony casual self, throwing his hairy legs on and off of the wide arms of the easy chair, as he spoke and smiled in that off-handed, out-of-class professorial way he had of holding forth. Emerson Lynn, Xavier's great composer, I noticed, was perched on the edge of his easy chair, and had his well-shod feet close together. His rich brown face was a complexity of eagerness and natural ease, but his dark eyes were snapping with a certain edginess. He knew as I did, that when black and white were conversing on a bright Saturday morning in an all-white neighborhood, that the front door should be closed. Bernie's voice rose and fell as it wished and at times must have carried out into the street beyond the opened door. Emerson's rich baritone was pitched low and soft.

This was by no means my first meeting with Emerson. But, as usual, Bernie had introduced us as if we were strangers. And any minute Sheila would burst into the room and introduce us again. Emerson and I endured. We had already shaken hands in that careful, tactful way that Negroes and ninth-warders warily met in the fifties. And yet, each time Emerson and I came together in the Rosenberg house, we were introduced separately by each member of the family.

"Ha ha," laughed Emerson each time, "Bobby and I are old friends, fellow saxophonists."

This was true, but a bit distorted. I played the saxophone in the St. Aloysius marching band very briefly; while Emerson was one of the best reed men in a city renown for its jazz musicians. But there I went at each introduction, rising to offer him my white hand. Emerson only smiled good naturedly.

"We've done that once already, Bobby."

This particular morning was very special, a little celebration. Last night the Rosenbergs and I had attended the premiere performance of Emerson's "Song Cycle", performed by the New Orleans Symphony Orchestra and the famous Xavier Choir.

It has never been explained to Bernie's neighbors that he taught at Xavier. They thought, I was almost sure, that he was with the Tulane faculty. Perhaps they preferred to believe this.

The conversation lulled and Bernie began to fidget, suddenly rising to his feet. He hit a phantom ball with his backhand, complaining as he did how his game is falling apart. He stroked viciously with clenched teeth, leaving Emerson and I gaping at the splendidly toned, wiry muscles of a man who was at least in his middle forties.

"If we all played tennis well," Bernie said, "it would be a happy world." At this Emerson and I exchanged silly, brow-jiggling smiles. If Bernie would close the front door, he would have a happy neighborhood, that would be a good start.

He came to rest from his stroking, legs astride, racket across his chest like a man in a cigarette ad, beaming down at Emerson who beamed back. Between Bernie's stroking and the performance last night their eyes were aglow.

"Emerson, let's face it, you are a genius." Bernie said, smiling triumphantly.

"Oh, no," said Emerson, "I'm just a cat who was born to the right lady and prays to the right Lord."

"No, it's discipline, Emerson, and talent. A cat without your genius can pray all he wants."

Emerson smiled broadly and shook his head, pitying his irreligious friend.

I looked up to see Bessie Rosenberg, Sheila's mother, standing in the doorway with a tray of martinis in stem glasses. What a handsome Creole lady she was, waiting there with endearing anticipation for Emerson to look her way. A clearing of her throat and the tinkling of the glasses did the trick; she held the tray aloft, in tribute to him.

Bessie smiled as only Creole ladies can. "Congratulations, Emerson. It was beautiful. I cried."

Emerson rose to meet her, taking the tray from her and setting it down on the coffee table. They embraced and kissed, in full view of the open door. It was very beautiful and spontaneous, the kind of sharing that is the privilege of good friends in the privacy of their homes. I restrained myself from getting up to close the door, knowing how it would be misinterpreted in this house.

Sheila appeared and congratulated Emerson with a kiss. The three of them circled like Greek dancers, ready to lock arms and explode into a joyful dance. Only my seated presence prevented this. Bessie and Sheila looked my way and back to Emerson with sweet, questioning smiles.

"Ha ha," laughed Emerson, "Bobby and I have met. We're old saxophone comrades. Remember?" They giggled and followed his lead to find a seat and drink the martinis.

Here's to Emerson Lynn, musical genius. Martinis are such wonderful drinks. I forgot that the front door was open and was stirred by my memory of last night's performance. Emerson's songs were moving and powerful: *Song of the River Willows, Song of the Pelicans in Flight, Song of the Golden Cypress at Dusk, Song of My People.*

Sheila read us the review in the *Times-Picayune*. Three columns, all laudatory. Emerson began to tell us about the symphony he was writing. But then I lost the thread of conversation, strange names and terms: Copeland, Schoenberg, harmonics, tone-row. But in the thrill of my private buzz, I had my own thoughts. We had more martinis, and I was tempted to tell Emerson about Harold Boudreaux, the great black first baseman from the ninth ward. After all, if Harold had gone to high school, I'm certain he would have been spotted by a major league scout. I was so warmed by the intimate talk and the martinis that I was even tempted to tell them about Cats and his tragic fall. It's very fortunate that they were talking over my head, or for sure I would have spilled my guts about Mama Gomez and Marais Street.

All in time, I reminded myself; there is plenty of time to tell all the stories that need to be told and so many stories I want to tell. Besides, how could I explain Marais Street and the ninth ward to this little group--what would they think? Off I went, nevertheless, dreaming and telling stories to myself. It was the martinis that had stirred me, and Emerson Lynn and the memory of his songs. How long had I wandered--and so far, so quickly? I woke up suddenly with Sheila pulling on my arm, drawing me back to whereever I had gone? I didn't know--exactly--or even approximately. I had totally forgotten about the Moral Guidance exam, but Sheila, always the good student, made eyes at me, reminding me that we must be off to the library to study.

I rose, slightly tottering and reached out to shake hands enthusiastically with Emerson, nodding and smiling, bringing my two hands together around his "It was so good to meet you Emerson--I mean to see you again,ha ha. I really want to hear that symphony you're writing, and your songs--they were beautiful. Really."

"Don't worry, Bobby, you will. You will." Emerson held me steady. (Is not music the food of love? And martinis?)

At the door, Bessie squeezed mine and Sheila's hands, delivering a warm and intimate message with her eyes. Even Bernie bobbed his head with a happy smile.

Outside we fell into an easy stride. The March wind blew hard, cascading through the leaves. Sheila nestled close to me, squeezing my arm and kissing me tenderly on the cheek. This was also my mood, but I was suddenly reminded of what Philip told me this morning about Ronnie. This was a day of kisses, cascading leaves, songs, of hands reaching across racial barriers, and in my joy I felt a pang of regret for my friend Ronnie Hingle, for I knew from what Philip told me that Ronnie must be miserable at that very moment.

"Sheila," I said, "did Philip tell you what happened to Ronnie?"

"About him and the nympho?"

"She's not a nympho, she's a bitch."

"She needs therapy. I feel sorry for girls like that."

"Sheila, listen. She is *not* a nympho, will you please listen for a change?"

"Bobby, do you know what a nymphomaniac is? It's a disease, it's tragic. . ."

"Yes, Sheila, yes, you explained it. But Cher is *not* a nympho or anything else Freudian. She doesn't even drink. That's all over with anyway. Ronnie got kicked out of Tulane."

"It's no wonder. Girls like that are very destructive, to themselves and others."

"It had nothing to do with her. He flunked out. Philip said he had a big problem with one of his teachers. A guy named John Stuart Mill, or something like that."

"*John Stuart Mill!* John Stuart Mill is dead."

"He is? Well, that shouldn't have influenced Ronnie's grade."

"John Stuart Mill died in the nineteenth century. He was an English philosopher."

"Oh yeah, well maybe this guy is his great grandson."

"He was a Utilitarian."

"Does Tulane have something against Utilitarians?"

"Forget it, Bobby."

"I'll bet that Cats knows who John Stuart Mill is."

"Who's Cats?"

"A Jewish philosopher."

"Nineteenth century? I never heard of him."

"You don't know everything, Sheila."

"You made him up. You're always making things up. Push your glasses up."

"Do you want to hear what happened to Ronnie?"

"I guess so. You'll probably make that up, too."

"This is the truth and it was terrible. Cher left him stranded out on the lakefront in the Cadillac at one o'clock in the morning, and his Plymouth on Freret Street wouldn't start. He had to walk all the way home, on Poland Avenue."

"What are you talking about--where did you hear this? Where's Poland Avenue--?"

"Philip told me--it's the truth. Poland avenue is way down in the ninth ward, know where that is?"

"Sure I do," she said, smirching. "It's downtown, where you get roast-beef poor-boy sandwiches."

"Everything you know is in books, Sheila."

"I guess that's where Cats, your Jewish philosopher, lives."

"That's right, and have some respect--he came within a hair of being your Attorney General, sweetheart."

"*Sweetheart*!--you're had too many martinis. Are you trying to talk like Humphrey Bogart? Push your glasses up."

She was right but I was coming out of it--the wind was beginning to clear my head. Anyway, what did Sheila know about roast-beef poor-boys, or Jewish philosophers? But wasn't that the problem between us? My sweetheart didn't know anything of ninth-ward culture. What happened to Ronnie could very well happen to me. At least Sheila and I were Catholics, thank God for that. Sheila wanted to meet Mama Gomez, but I wasn't so sure.

I was seriously considering asking her to come down to the ninth ward with me, to the American Legion dance on Spain Street to hear Russ D'Antoni and his Macaronis.

"Say, Sheila, why don't we go down there tonight?"

"Go where?"

"To the ninth ward. I'll take you to the American Legion dance."

"All the way down there, we don't have a car. I don't like to dance anyway. I thought we were going to the Civic Theatre to see the Alex Guiness movie?"

"Philip will be there. Come on. You can meet some of my friends."

She frowned. "I don't know, Bobby. Way down there?"

"We could get a roast-beef poor-boy at Martin Brothers. Whatsay?" I must have been drunk inviting trouble this way. Either that or I had the devil in me. Sheila might change her tune about English Utilitarian philosophers if she ever met Cats. But what if Cats lets me down? He was brilliant, but he was no match for all of Western Culture. None of Freud's theories apply to the ninth ward. Polly Sansone put out all right, but it was not because of primitive lust. What Polly had was a hot box. What would she tell her analyst?

101

"I'm so depressed, doctor. All the boys want to do is grab my ass. I'm miserable. What's wrong with me, doctor? Is it unreigned infant sexuality, is that it?" What is wrong with ninth-ward girls? Are they immune to nymphomania? Polly was going to marry young and have kids. She'd get fat, lose her teeth, drink RC, and never give a second thought to her primitive lust. If Mr. Charlie had a daughter, could he have an Oedipal conflict with her? Or for that matter, Augie? Augie was too busy making a profit at the expense of boogalees to accomodate his daughter's Oedipal conflict.

Why did I love Mama Gomez, who was not the color of my fair skin, or of my lineage, whatever it was? Shouldn't I have been turning this city upside down looking for my real Mama and Daddy? Did I want Sheila to meet and love Mama Gomez as I did? Was that possible? What was I asking?

Sheila finally agreed to go to the dance.

The sun was setting on the Rosenberg's modest Georgian cottage. Its little columned portico grew darker by the minute. The terraced lawn darkened to green velvet and the yew trees flanking the entrance turned as black as India ink.

We were sitting in Bernie's tiny Fiat. I had made a terrible mistake, but it was made in all innocence. We planned the evening perfectly. I went home on the streetcars, got dressed and came back here to pick her up, or was she now picking me up? The fifties mores demanded that I pick her up, but there was to be this slight deviation. We were all dressed up. Well, I was all dressed up. That's why Sheila was sitting behind the wheel, glaring out of the windshield in silent rage. I was wearing my powdered-blue sports jacket, and my striped knitted tie, knotted in the Windsor manner, made popular by Frank Sinatra. My pink shirt was wide-collared. We called this style the *bold look*. My scholarly sweetheart was wearing a simple cotton print, trimmed very minimally with a lace collar. Very nice for library attire, but all wrong for a dance at the American Legion Hall. Her hair, though full and curly, was also very simple: parted down the middle and left to fall naturally onto the shoulders. What did I suggest? A black taffeta skirt and ballerina slippers. She wore saddle oxfords instead. But couldn't she, I pleaded, at least have tied her hair up into a ponytail. You would have thought that I had asked her to shave it off.

"I'm not in high school anymore," she said. "What kind of dance are we going to?"

A very ironic response for a woman who would wear pre-faded jeans in her forties. She said my own attire was tacky. Had I blown it? Would I have to sit through another stupid English movie, wondering what in hell everybody was laughing about?

"Philip is expecting us." I said meekly. I had made every concession, and now I was pleading. I said nothing at all about the midget Italian car. We might be laughed clean out of the ninth ward. Uptown did not meet downtown in New Orleans without tough diplomatic bargaining. It occurred to me while Sheila was ignoring me that Bessie Rosenberg (nee Livaudais) was probably related to the Marignys. How ironic, indeed. The ninth ward was where these great Creole families had their fabled plantations. The streets still bear their noble names: Marigny, Villere, Urhquart. Could Sheila not consider this a kind of eternal return? There were portraits, dating from the Eighteenth Century in the Cabildo, our Museum of History, of Creole ladies who bear a striking resemblance to Bessie. The bloodlines were very strong.

"I'll go," she finally said, "But only because Philip is expecting us." I would have told her that Ronnie might be there, too, if he had recovered from his tragedy with Cher.

As the Fiat rolled down St. Charles Avenue, the sun's lingering rays deepened the colors of the azaleas all along the Avenue--magenta, rose and mauve. The oaks cast long, violet shadows on the the streets and parkways. Night jasmine wafted the air. I turned to Sheila's darkened silhouette and touched her hair. It felt like shadows. Did she feel, as I did, the steeped intimacy of a night coming swiftly down, veil upon veil? I gushed so because I was in love and the jasmine perfume was moist in my eyes.

At Lee Circle, the general folded his noble arms atop his great fluted column, framed darkly against the deep blue transparent sky, where the first icy stars began to appear.

The street lights popped on as we circled around the monument entering the run-down commercial section of the Avenue--dingy store-fronts, cheap rooming-houses, an occasional lonely figure standing in a dark doorway. At Poydras Street, a tranceful wino whirled unsteadily beneath the street light. The ruptured neon bar sign above him blinked asthmatically. We looked ahead, awaiting Canal Street with its bright lights and eager throng.

On Canal Street, the Fiat inched forward into the intersection against the flow of pedestrians who refused to give ground, or heed the signals commanding them to walk or not walk. When they gave her an opening, Sheila gunned the Fiat, and we went sailing across the broad thoroughfare. (One should notice when one crosses Canal Street that the streets change their names. Canal Street divides the city into uptown and downtown, or, in the old days, into French and American sections. Small wonder that tourists in this city get so confused.)

The trip from Sheila's neighborhood to mine was such a great distance, traversing centuries--what trauma we experienced, busting through the cultural barrier, which separated uptown from downtown--Sheila from myself.

We turned down a little side street, and Sheila was spitting out profanities. "What the hell kind of street is this?" The Fiat hit a pot hole and went sailing in the air. Here in the ninth ward there was one street light at each corner, and it was not nearly enough. The gutters were wide and deep. Look out! Sheila hit the brakes just in time. "My God, I can't see a damn thing. What's that? A canal?"

"A drainage gutter, my dear."

"A gutter, it must be three feet wide. Do we have far to go? I'm a nervous wreck."

"Just two more blocks, sweetheart."

"Listen, Bobby, you better cut the sweethearts, or else. I should have never consented to come down here in the first place. Tell me where to turn."

"Right--here!" I yelled, and she whipped the Fiat around the corner missing the gutter by inches. She stopped, lowered her head and muttered angry profanities. "Shit, damn." she craned her neck out of the window and whistled. "If I go in one of those gutters--goodbye, Fiat."

She was too preoccupied to notice that the American Legion Hall was just up the street. The kids were gathered on the banquette yelling and hooting as Sheila parked the Fiat very carefully. What had I done? Wasn't this a mistake? Had I suggested it, or had she suggested it, we would have gone immediately to the Civic to see Alex

Guiness. Instead, we trudged across the street, crunching oyster shells along the way. I unbuttoned my jacket to appear casual. Sheila led the way. No one made way for us. The entrance was blocked. Sheila nudged past a dark boy, whom I did not recognize.

"Say," he yelled after her, "Who's you, lady." I hustled up to catch stride with Sheila, and he yelled at me. "That your broad, skinny?" He made the whole crowd laugh and was satisfied, I hoped. There was no point in answering him. Philip was waiting for us. Where was Philip? As a precaution I pushed Sheila up the steps, which caused her to fling her elbows wildly, catching me soundly in the temple. I pushed her through the doorway where I knew Red Sterno would be standing, slamming his nightstick into his open, meaty hand. And there he was: all six-foot-two of him. Red had been, not too many years ago, a fair club fighter before he joined the force. This was his regular Saturday night station The sight of his red hair bristling on his thick, freckled neck calmed me down considerably.

"Will you stop pushing, Gomez?"

"We've got to find Philip, he's waiting for us."

"What's the policeman doing here?"

"That's Red Sterno; he's here to stop trouble."

"Trouble?"

"Don't worry, we're going to have a wonderful time." Where was Philip?

As we entered the main hall, Sheila's jaw dropped three inches. The floor was covered with sawdust and the whole place reeked of stale draught beer. The kids were gathered in groups of three or four, and they were yelling at each other, screaming and laughing. Nobody would lower his voice, the noise was positively assaulting. I spotted eight or ten powder blue jackets, exactly like my own, and knitted ties of every color. Sheila was the only girl without a taffeta skirt and ballerina slippers. The boys knocked back cans of beer while the girls sucked on the straws of their bottled Cokes.

The Hall was illuminated with rows of naked, incandescent bulbs, which glared down violently. When the band began to play these would be turned off, and the hall would become as dark as a cave. I had to find Philip before this happened. Sheila was yelling something at me, which I could not hear. I yelled back that I could not hear her, and continued my search for Philip. As I panned through the crowd my eyes were halted by a singular pair of hips, swaying beneath a flared, taffeta skirt. It had to be Polly Sansone, and it was. Polly had draped herself onto a tall, heavy-lidded boy with glistening black hair. Her head rested against his knitted tie, and her eyes were closed. His arms were locked around her waist as he casually guided her hips. He seemed marvelously unconcerned, oblivious to both Polly and his friends who were all yelling at him.

In the meantime, Sheila was yanking on my tie and pointing at the doorway to the bar. She had spotted Philip, and we started over to where he was leaning on the doorjamb, drinking a beer.

When we reached him, we began to make goofy, silent-screen faces at each other. It was a joyous reunion. Philip placed his hands on Sheila's shoulders, and rolled his eyes with delight at the idea of her being here. She smiled weakly and shrugged with mock resignation. As they communicated wordlessly and expertly about this irony, my own eyes are circling, searching for Polly's taffeta skirt; but the lights went out, the band struck up, and the yelling suddenly ceased. A trumpet and a trombone led out smoothly with *Slow Boat to China* over a sax which did rhythm, picking its spots with throaty six-note patterns.

My arm snaked around Sheila's waist and she looked at me with cool impertinence. "What do you want, Gomez?"

"This is a dance, sweetheart. I want to dance with you."

"All right. But no more sweethearts, or else."

Sheila's box step was confined to back and forth, turns were nearly impossible. Moreover, she put her left hand on my shoulder, instead of putting her arm around my neck. Her waist was rigid with her hips, precluding dips, ear nibbles, and other more stimulating contacts.

"Is this piece slow all the way through?" she asked.

"If it gets fast, we can stop. Kiss me."

"I'm warning you, Gomez."

It was enough that she was there at all, I guess. Polly, though, must have been giving that unconcerned boy all he could handle right now. This thought caused my right arm to tighten around Sheila's waist, which caused the fingernails of her left hand to dig into my right shoulder. The night was going to follow a ritual form, crossing barriers to meet somewhere between. We had Audubon Park which was neutral. In the meantime the darkness of the hall enveloped us, the saxophone took the melody and picked up the tempo; Polly swung out from her unconcerned boyfriend, and Sheila and I retired from the dance floor to speak with Philip who, like Audubon Park, was neutral.

At the break, with the bulbs glaring down again, I tried to weave through the crush with two draughts and a Coke. I arrived before Philip and Sheila with my left sleeve soaked, minus a straw for the Coke. Philip led us outside where we could hear each other. Red Sterno was gripping his night-stick on both ends, flexing the muscles in his forearms.

"Hiya, Red."

"Whatsay, Philip."

"Everything quiet tonight?"

Red smiled sardonically, showing yellow, separated teeth. "You never know, the night is still young." He turned to cast a wary eye toward the doorway, and I noticed an old brushburn on his jawline.

On the banquette, eight or ten dark boys were milling in a ragged circle. As we came down the steps, one of them bolted the circle, bent over, clutching his crotch, howling with both pleasure and pain. His assailant was Sheila's old friend, and he interrupted his triumphant laugh to measure the three of us.

"Say, Philip, who's four eyes?"

"This is my friend, Bobby Gomez." Philip answered, but this was not an introduction, and Baba Alvarez, whom I now recognized, did not offer his hand for me to shake. I put my hand on Sheila's elbow to lead her away; she went but pumped her elbow in my ribs twice as she did.

"The old broad's his girlfriend? She looks like my grandma," Baba said. Sheila's elbow reflexed on this remark, catching me neatly in the solar-plexus. My pain was tempered only by the assurance that Philip knew how to conclude his conversation with Baba. Baba was cocky, but not foolhardy.

Philip was chuckling good naturedly as he joined us, and poked me a little blow in my chest. Baba was glaring over at me, but he knew better than to do more than that. Sheila was glaring at Baba; what the hell did she think she was doing? "Baba is all right," said

Philip and poked me again. Baba led his troops inside; he was Red Sterno's problem now. There could be trouble. Sheila was smirking. "That one of the friends you wanted me to meet, Gomez?"

But now my thoughts were elsewhere. Where's Ronnie? "Say, Philip, did you ever get a hold of Ronnie?"

"Yeah, that's what I wanted to tell you. He called me right before I came over here, and you'll never guess, poor Ronnie."

"Poor Ronnie, what?"

"He met this girl in Algiers, on the levee."

"Algiers?"

"I hope she's normal." Sheila couldn't wait to hear of mental infirmity.

"What about the girl? Algiers, what was he doing in Algiers?"

"Search me, champ; but the girl is a secretary from New York."

"New York?"

"Jesus, Bobby, stop repeating and let him tell us."

"She used to live in this big house in Algiers when she was little. Her daddy was some kind of big shot lawyer, but he died when she was young. Her mother sold the house and moved to Texas, and now she's in New York and wants to buy the house and move back to Algiers."

"She must be a nomad," Sheila said smugly.

"A nomad. I guess that's something abnormal and Freudian. I swear, Sheila."

"A compulsive wanderer, Gomez."

"O.K., Sheila. I'm sure it's horrible and depressive. I don't understand, Philip. Does Ronnie like this girl? Did he pick her up?"

"That's right, Philip, give him a context his little high school mind can understand."

"At least I don't think that everybody is Freudian, even before I meet them."

Angry shouts and loud noises came from the Hall. Here we go. Philip paid it little mind. "I don't know if he likes her, Bobby, I guess he does. He seemed very happy. He's going to help her transact for the sale of the house. What's a nomad, Sheila?"

But at that moment Baba Alvarez came flying out of the front door, and his troops tumbling after him. We were spared Sheila's explanation, courtesy of Red Sterno.

Red stuck his head out of the door and waved his night-stick. "You're out ya lil mothafucka."

On the banquette, Baba's friends were struggling to restrain him. "I'll shove that stick up your ass, ya red-headed cock-sucker."

Red banged the nightstick on the doorjamb and went back inside.

"What is he going to do? asked Sheila, folding her arms, as calm as you please. Philip shook his head and smiled.

"I'm laying odds he's closing the joint." Philip was probably right; the older Red got the less patience he had. And sure enough, out came the kids, cursing and complaining.

Philip put his arms around Sheila and me and pulled us close. He was chuckling again. "Well, that's it. Red is closing the joint."

"Good," said Sheila. "I'm hungry, let's get a roast-beef poor-boy."

"Where's your car, Sheila?"

"Over there, in the gutter."

"The Pontiac is on the corner, let's get out of here before the crowd gets too thick. You follow me."

Philip was here tonight for our benefit. Ordinarily, he would be visiting Mary Ann Schelleci on a Saturday night. Mary Ann was his fiancee, but he would not think of taking her to a dance at the American Legion Hall. Mary Ann was very shy.

A roast-beef poor-boy is as thin as your wrist and as long as your forearm, made with crispy French bread, piled high with gravy-soaked roast beef, shredded lettuce, tomatoes sliced translucently thin, and extra gravy if you dared, all of it ladled over with mayonnaise. It is unwieldy unless sliced in half on an angle. A dozen napkins and two yards of butcher paper are required to eat it without mishap.

Sheila wolfed hers down, and half of mine, coming up with gravy on her chin and lace collar, and with little globules of shimmering mayonnaise at the corners of her mouth, which I wiped away lovingly. She had gotten what she wanted from the ninth ward. And I, if I played it right, would get what I wanted on the ride back up.

The ninth ward had more to offer than roast-beef poor-boys and American Legion dances. In the seventies they would call the ninth ward the inner-city, and kids like Baba under-privileged, but perhaps Sheila was right when she said Baba was downtown trash.

It seemed a bewitching night as we turned into the entrance of Audubon Park. Its great garlanded piers welcomed us. The circular garden smoldered, appearing haunted, awaiting, I imagined, the caped and white-faced Bela Lugosi. Two bats darted about the naked maiden who centered the garden, an omen which Sheila ignored, but which I trembled at the sight of. She was right, though, this was a night to be ruled by gluttony and passion, not by evils of the spirit.

I fingered the lace of her collar, and touched her neck so lightly that she shook with a little chill. "What are you up to now, Gomez?"

"It's only twelve-thirty, let's take a turn through the park."

"The park is dangerous at night. We may be mugged." But as she said this, she was turning the wheel.

"A lovely night, isn't it?" Testing, I was.

She parked under a spreading live oak, and I grabbed her; but it was a mistake. "Not here," she said, elbowing again. She was right. Outside was the cool lap of the nighttime grass and the wide, black umbrella of the oak.

We sat for a minute or two; Sheila holding her knees together; me, half reclining, propped up with a right-angled arm, happy that the moon had set, leaving the stars so bejeweled and numerous. I pulled her down, and she yielded, as she always did in Audubon Park, to a long almost endless kiss.

Here we were--two Catholics, one orphaned, the other hybrid, huddled warm and cozy in the darkness of the night, beneath the shelter of a great patriarchal oak. How very safe I thought to be so protected. Sheila was so soft and smelled so good. I wanted more of her, more than her mouth, more than her cheeks and tender neck. I began to unbutton her dress.

"What are you trying to do?"

"Unbutton your dress."

"Those are snaps, not buttons."

And so they were. Three little effortless yanks and she was open to my hand.

"Bobby, do you love me?"

"Of course."

"Then shouldn't you remove your hand."

"My hand?"

"The hand that's holding my breast."

"This one?"

"Yes, don't you care that I'm supposed to be going to Communion tomorrow?"

"Of course, I care, but you ate that roast-beef after twelve, remember?"

"Communion is spiritual."

And so I began to slowly to remove my hand.

"I'm sorry Bobby, " she said, falling on me and kissing me so passionately that I had to break away or come in my pants.

How many times were we to get this far and stop, daring to lubricate but never daring to consummate. Later, in the seventies, we called such restrictions hang-ups, but in the fifties they were the law, a time when sex and guilt were both congruent and conflicting, and marriage was the great divide.

Sheila dropped me off, and I rode the streetcar home, tired and hot-nutted, a common Catholic ailment in the fifties.

I thought of Ronnie and the girl he met in Algiers--who was she? What would happen to Ronnie?

What would happen to Bobby?

Chapter 12

*C*ora Lang decided in that first minute that she would offer Ronnie a job. A young man with a golden smile and natural grace could sell houses. She was usually right about selling. Cora knew that to sell one needed to trust one's quick impressions, especially first impressions. And this is what she immediately noticed about Ronnie--keen instincts like her own--the way his eyes darted around and the way what he saw lit them up. It was the keeness of her own instincts that was responsible for her success. She launched her real estate business eight short years ago, at age of sixty-four, two years after her husband died. Now she was making more money than he, Herbert, dreamed of making as a CPA. And though she was happy about the money, it was her success that she really loved, more specifically the thrill and challenge of selling houses. Each house, she discovered, embodied a telling issue for her clients. No one gave up or took possession of a dwelling without some ritual rearrangement of their lives. She loved sharing their hopes, fears and disappointments, which she did with such sincere enthusiasm. How they came to depend on her? She possessed the gift of optimism, an unquestioning regard for all vehicles of permanence--land, house, those concrete essences of continuity and immortality. Buying a house was like putting roots down in the living soil, she would have said had words been her talent, it was the scintillation of her clear blue eyes which said so instead, a sweet vividness of voice inflection, and the careful grooming of her fine gray hair. She saw this same gift in Ronnie, in his smile and his unbiddened grace of limbs.

"Mr. Hingle, have you ever thought of real estate as a career for yourself?"

He blushed slightly at the offer and at her calling him Mister, looking toward Clara, who was showing pleasure and agreement with her wonderful quiet eyes.

"No, I never did, do you think . . . . "

"I most assuredly do, I need someone in my office now, you could start this week."

"Well . . . . ?"

"As long as you are going to be Miss Duplantier's representative here in New Orleans, I think it is only fair that you earn some commission. You'll need a license, which we can get busy on today. It's only a formality."

How could he refuse? Who would ever believe what had happened to him in these past three days? Clara and Mrs. Lang were smiling at him in this handsome office. Where had that strange brassy taste in his mouth gone? Or the ache in his knees, and the dark thing that followed him from Tulane, racing behind him on his getaway?

He remembered his idleness on the campus--the punishing lethargy, the heaviness of his arm, his dilatory eye, the burden of slow minutes. There was not a second to waste here in this office. Mrs. Lang checked her watch. The interview was over. "Yes, ten o'clock on Monday morning. We'll get started early, Mr. Hingle, I'm sure you will learn very quickly."

"Thank you, yes, mam."

Time cantered to a new usefulness, a rhythm of purpose, placid Clara combining calmness and efficiency. A schedule. To the hotel at three o'clock to pick up her luggage and check out, out to the airport by four, an hour for a sandwich and a drink, departure at five thirty.

The star of fire which leapt from each spark plug in turn was the picture before his inner eye, to his ear, measured stroking. There had been time in the crowd of events to tune the Plymouth. It cut through the wind. The passing trees danced across the mirroring windshield, the highway ahead narrowed and converged. As he turned he caught the stillness of Clara's usual contentment, her head level, her eyes forward, seeing and thinking congruent. Who was she, planning grandly to repossess an old, forsaken house, ignoring the years passing in between, holding to a single, unalterable blueprint for her life? What would she make of this old, ruined house that would glitter and fulfill? How did she dream boldly without noise, flourish or defiance? Dream. Clara dreaming beside him, and him learning to dream himself, with his eyes open, in the full light of day.

113

Ronnie was still in awe of airports. He was conscious of hiding a big-eyed curiosity. The polished contemporary character of the place was in such sharp contrast to the droll character of Poland Avenue and the ninth ward. He was enamored again of this strange glamour which hinted of a chic modern reality. He had had three or four flights in the service, and he felt now as then that he was walking among strangers, denizens of this modern world which had grown up so secretly.

In the airport restaurant, he and Clara discussed business as a smooth public address voice announced arrival and departure times of flights. Ronnie recorded dates and figures in a pocket notebook as the great engines roared outside on the runway. As they lingered over coffee Clara began to express gratitude to him. Her brown eyes met his directly. He felt together with her in her dream, in the calm step-by-step plan to accomplish it. Her smile, brief and full, enkindled affection.

It was very late in the day when Ronnie left the airport. The setting sun angled its rays over the flat land, struck high trees, hanging aureoles on the far reaching limbs. The Plymouth sped into the cool evening. When he reached the city it was lit up and buzzing with traffic sounds. He looked closely at the faces of pedestrians when he stopped at signal lights, at the faces of young girls especially. A joyous, private game: waiting for Clara to appear as some stranger on a street corner. What the hell, was he crazy? But he was smiling, he *was* crazy and happy. What else would happiness do to a practical man? He had thoughts and dreams he dared not tell even Philip. But there was something he had to tell Philip that could not wait until tomorrow. Philip would understand. The last sight of Clara held him, her brown eyes looking into his, her hand pressing his, he was drumming on the steering wheel and humming a tune. Philip, where was Philip?

Chapter 13

The summer was upon us. It had rained daily for more than a week. The silky flag lily's yellow and red blossoms appeared, limp and graceful. We were soaked and mosquito bitten already and only, as yet, a week into June, hardly enough time to savor the successful completion of our first year in college. Draining summer and the first summer crisis. Both Sheila and I were glum and hostile, battling the frustrations of a sensual courtship, embittered by a scorching uptown-downtown rivalry. More specifically bringing Mama Gomez together with Bernie and Bessie. It was all set for this afternoon, but with what haggling, a whole catalogue of resentments and fears, all operating secretly beneath the surface. We didn't want this problem of joining families and cultures. Who cared what the educated and cultured folk of uptown thought of my dark lumbering mother, who was really no natural kin to me? Why did I have to take seriously the ugly accusations of a snide uptown girl and her phony bookish insights? Who was ashamed of his family and background? I didn't say I was ashamed, sister (sister, indeed). If you don't think I'm good enough for you, Miss Uptown, say so. Love me. Yes, you love me, but you don't respect me. Cats and dogs love each other--animals love each other, is that what you call love? And she who went to Mass every Sunday and received Communion told me not to be so Catholic.

We did love each other, and wanted to have this whole gorgeous summer day to ourselves, to be alone and in each others' arms. As we were, indeed, only last night beneath our sinful oak in Audubon Park. As sinful as beleaguered Catholics could be with her arbitrary stricture against disrobing, pressing our hot bodies together until . . . . and not a single unfastened button or unsnapped snap. "Bobby, we can't, you know we can't." "I know, Sheila, take off your blouse, I won't touch you, I swear." "No." "Please." "No." "Please." Wasn't it enough to remain pure, without having to reconcile uptown with downtown, legitimate with illegitimate, educated with uneducated? Especially in this seductive tropical city, with its hot moist breath of southerly winds; its sweet, fermenting growth, begging to be touched and veiling the rational eye. The air clung and the blood bound.

What did I fear about this meeting of families? That Mama Gomez did not have a decent dress to wear? Would she take the trouble to comb her hair? Shoes. She didn't even own a pair. Let's forget all those little details and speculate on what engrossing topic of conversation the cozy group could hit on. How much feet shuffling, head ducking, eye averting, chain smoking, nervous sipping of coffee would be required to fill those long awkward minutes once we discover that we had nothing in common? Would Bernie let off his thinly disguised lectures to say a few simple words about simple matters? And I could well imagine Bessie, gracious lady that she was, forcing some empty flattery about Mama Gomez' taste in clothes. We could get drunk and forget all the phony politeness and have it out, why not? Let's call it off."

"Look, Gomez," she lectured, "nobody including Mama Gomez is worried about this meeting but you. We're all looking forward to it. It is all in your head." "That's right, throw it all to me, everybody relax and leave all the problems to old Bobby Gomez who happens to be the only one with the sensitivity to know when things can go wrong. I can handle it, the rest of you can be your best innocent selves, I swear."

"You just worry about yourself and everything will be fine. Taking care of yourself does seem to be a major problem now that you have managed to work yourself into an hysterical state. Calm down."

"O.K. O.K. I'll calm down. Just you answer one question for me. How is Mama Gomez going to get herself in that goddam midget car? Y'see, I'm not being hysterical, I'm just being practical!"

She laughed. She laughed, in fact, right out of control, until tears rolled down her cheeks. Like it or not, we were on our way.

Who could have known what awaited us on Marais Street that day? Certainly not me, her only family. She had sent me off early that morning to pick up Sheila, so we could come back down to pick her up. I was nervous, wondering, amid all of these complicated arrangements, why, in the first place, I was sent to get Sheila, and finally how in heaven's name was she going to stuff herself into that tiny Fiat. When I asked Sheila again, this time calmly, but with barely suppressed cynicism, she told me not to worry.

"O.K. O.K. I won't mention it anymore, but don't expect me to perform a miracle."

Sheila and I arrived at the appointed ten o'clock. I had every reason to believe that we would find her in her market get-up, as I had left her, strands of her black hair hanging loose from a hasty roll, stomping around in the kitchen, gruff and sullen, the-devil-beware glowing from her South Sea Island eyes. Who knew her better than I? But, as it turned out, I did not. There was something different, I noticed, the moment the Fiat stopped. The front door was partially opened, and said unmistakably: welcome. As we mounted the steps, a subtle fragrance, something herbal and fresh, came to us. I tapped lightly on the door. Why? This was my home, and the door was open. What did I mean by tapping--a warning that the enemy approached? Straighten up, clean up, my God! This is my uptown girlfriend I have with me. Can't you manage to look respectable?

"Let's go in, silly, she's expecting us. Calm down."

"What's that smell?"

"I think your mother has made some tea for us."

"Tea?"

"Yes, tea. Yoohoo, Mama Gomez, we're here."

From within a voice of sweet tones sung out, "Come in, honey." We did and there she sat, her dark face aglow with her all-conquering Polynesian smile, sparkling white teeth, and full cheeks studded with youthful dimples. It took me several stunned seconds to recover from the sight of her. Her hair was coifed with smooth braids, not a single errant hair; the bright yellow dress she was wearing was one I had never seen before. Its folds fell softly from her lap onto the couch, which had large white doilies on its scrolled arms, these too, I had never seen. What I could see of her thick legs beneath the long dress had the sheen of nylon, and shoes, white shoes!

Sheila sat beside her on the couch and they began to hug and kiss, tender little smacks on each others' cheeks. This was only their second meeting, and there they were in each others' arms, locked in sisterly embrace. On the tiny coffee table sat a large pitcher of iced tea and three tall glasses each containing a bouquet of mint and sweet basil. Their fragrance blended with some more delicious scent that seemed to come from Mama Gomez' person. When I looked more carefully I saw the three little jasmine blossoms pinned in her braid, over her left ear. She poured the tea into the glasses like a Grand Dame as she and Sheila continued to gush with affectionate smiles, I was mystified and still standing.

"Sit down, Bobby," my Mama said to me. I knew from the mischief in her eyes that she had planned this surprise, this unveiling of her dark beauty and youthfulness. Was there also a teasing coquetry in her eyes with this invitation? I was blushing, perhaps, twitching with an unfamiliar quickening of the blood. I suddenly had a crush on this tropical beauty. Oedipal? What? Oh, how Sheila would have sprung at me if she knew. Did she know? They were too busy holding each others' hands. I drank down half of my tea, and my nostrils and tongue savored the sweetness that seemed now to envelope me. Munificent womankind, these two beside me and this felicitous lady of a city. We invest our love, we miserly men, pinching every penny feeling, while they spend lavishly.

"Bobby, doesn't she look beautiful?" Tender Sheila spoke to me as she embraced and kissed my Mama.

"Yes, Mama, you look beautiful," I kissed her, too. How could I resist?

There were more people sitting on their front steps on this hot summer morning than I thought was normal. Heat waves rose from the brick banquette, the temperature would reach ninety degrees before noon. Across the way, on the sunny side, Mrs. Montegut was shading her eyes with the morning Picayune, with her other hand she fanned herself with a palmetto fan. Mrs. Liuzza and Mrs. Maeglich were conversing, they are on our side of the street. Beyond them, at the corner, Mrs. Giglio was making a show at sweeping the banquette in front of her grocery. These and other were looking our way. Mama Gomez was center stage, waving and smiling broadly, like Mamie Eisenhower. What the hell? Was I to expect Jack Bailey to come along and declare Mama Gomez Queen for a Day? It was Philip Rotolo who came along instead, in the Pontiac, smiling up at me conspiratorially.

"What are you doing here" I asked.

"Well," said Philip grasping his breast with mock hurt and indignation, "I am Mama Gomez' chauffeur."

"Chauffeur?"

Sheila led me to the Fiat as Philip escorted Mama Gomez to the Pontiac, and we were off.

"What is this chauffeur business?"

"Your idea, Gomez. You did want Mama to be comfortable."

"My idea, right, but nobody told me. Nobody tells me anything."

"I called Philip this morning. I guess I forgot to tell you."

I said no more. Who was I that I should know what mysterious forces were at work when uptown and downtown were coming together?

Bernie and Bessie were at their front door, which was opened as usual, They exclaimed their greetings and helped Mama Gomez up the stairs, gathering her into their arms. What headlong joy! The three of them, talking over each other, laughing with sheer delight. Bessie and Mama Gomez embraced and gushed. Sheila was tugging at my sleeve, making big eyes of tender reproach. I told you, her eyes said. I barely managed a loose smile of idiot's delight, but it was enough to acknowledge my miscalculation.

It soon became a noisy family affair with everyone gorging themselves with mixed cakes and drinking Bessie's delicious wine punch. Bernie was very attentive to Mama Gomez, filling her glass whenever it was empty. My Mama was flushed and giggling at almost everything he said. I had never seen her having fun, a magical transformation, but she was drunk.

"Mama, Mama," I started vainly, "that punch has wine in it."

"She knows," said Bernie, rising to fill her glass, and slopping it over the top.

My warning was, of course, futile. Bernie was, as I had expected, intrigued with my Mama's Polynesian lineage, and she, so usually mute and inscrutable on the subject, was willing to tell all, as much that is, as she could articulate in her drunken giggling state.

"No, no, no, no, I was not born in the Philipine Islands." She swallowed more punch and laughed as if she thought it was hilarious that he thought so.

"I was born here, in New Orleans," more gales of laughter as Bernie poured up more punch. "My father was a merchant seaman, twenty-five years. He was pure-blooded Filipino, and my mama, too. But me, I was born here, I never seen the islands."

Bernie sat on the end of his chair, eagerly devouring everything she said, and laughed as loudly as she did. The others laughed, too. Philip, in fact, was bent over in near convulsions. When I thought about it, I was also laughing. But what was so funny? We were all drunk, and Mama Gomez had the kind of infectious, high pitched laughter that demanded company.

And yet I was not surprised that we were one big happy family. In spite of all our differences, we were congregated to bring a Catholic marriage one step closer to consummation. Who were we with our mere differences of blood lines, education, etc., to head off such momentum? Bernie, if I haven't said so, was only half Jewish. His mother was a Hotard, good Cajun stock, and Catholic, of course. His liberalism, though indeed bold in the fifties, was not as radical as it first appeared. He was dedicated to an enlightened Christian morality, an avowed modernist who fired flaming language at any who condemned Picasso and abstract art; and yet, would defend monogamy and marital fidelity as part and parcel of what liberal Catholics in the fifties called the Natural Law. Sheila, for all that she claimed, knew nothing of Freud's hellish pessimism. Her analyses were no more than flashy collegiate pedantry. What Sheila feared was the disapprobation of Holy Mother Church, Oedipal conflicts notwithstanding. The Church, Sheila, Bernie and the rest of us knew, possessed druidic power, mastery of the underworld and overworld. In short, we were scared stiff of the sacred.

This brilliant summer day, burning so incessantly, licked us like some great mother animal, wine punch filled us with pagan dizziness, cake sweetness ached in our teeth, and an old seed seemed to burst in our ancient souls.

Bessie brought in a pot of hot coffee and we sat drinking it, lapsing into silence, smiling cozily and conversing quietly with the new affection we felt for one another. A family indeed.

Suddenly we heard the wind rifling through the trees outside and saw through the window black clouds cover the sun. It started to rain, and the shower, light at first, gradually gained force and volume, until finally it roared and pounded in our ears. The world seemed dreaming, sighing in an ecstasy of replenishment. Then, however, just as suddenly as it started, the rain stopped and the sun shone through the clouds, illuminating the room. Sheila and I, as the poet said, were entwining our eye beams, feeling already the intimacies that were in store for us later in the night. We wanted to be alone, but it was not to be, for the sunshine infused new life in the gathering, Bernie especially, who rose, rubbed his hands and stretched luxuriously. He turned, smiling to us, arms outstretched, "What a beautiful day, why don't we all go to the lake for beer and boiled crabs?"

"I'm stuffed," said Bessie, appealing for moderation. But it was not up to the clear-minded Bessie or to me. The coffee had only partially killed my buzz; I still felt very affectionate and wanted Sheila, but she no longer wanted me. She had joined Bernie who was tugging on my Mama's arm.

"Doesn't that sound good, Mama," said Sheila, tempting my Mama, "boiled crabs and cold draught beer--let's go."

And Mama Gomez, beaming anew and ready for anything, yipped with delight as they pulled her lovingly to her feet.

"Let's go," urged Philip, dangling his car keys, "we can all pile in the Pontiac."

We drove to the lakefront, marveling at the lovely unstable day, bringing sunshine one minute, brief little sprinklings of rain the next. As we sat eating crabs and drinking beer, looking out over the choppy lake, I could not help feeling good about my Mama having such a wonderful time. How many such days did she have in her hard life? It was indeed a big day for the mysterious widow, whose life was so little known, even to her son. I knew even less about her husband, Riccardo, only the scant information she had trickled out over the years. How many times had I looked intently at his photograph, (there seemed, amazingly, to have been only one!) trying somehow to know what kind of person he was. But it told me nothing: a pleasant Filipino man in Merchant Marine khakis beside a taller Caucasian companion.

"Mama, " I had asked her a hundred times," tell me what happened to him?"

"What happened? The boat blew up. Why you asked me so many times--the boat blew up."

His death and her grief were none of my business.

As we sat, savoring the spicy morsels of crabs, swift intermittent little gusts churned the lake, and long rays of sunshine pierced the dark clouds. Presently, though, the clouds were gone, drifted south; the showers ceased, and the sun took command.

Although I had not presented Sheila with the ring yet, this was our engagement day. I was saving this for the night hours, when Philip and Mary Ann would help us celebrate. How happy I was to have a new family and such a friend as Philip. I told him so, on the way home.

"Gee, champ," he said, smiling and poking me an affectionate blow, "I'm really moved, I feel the same way about you." He had been helpful for more than chauffeuring and such, being someone who could prop up my life or zing it along, no mere device, but a true bedrock. His own life was unfolding according to a well laid plan, an old New Orleans blueprint for sons and daughters of Sicilian immigrants, not simply typical but prototypical. Mary Ann Schelleci, his fiancee, with her tender brown eyes was perfectly suited to his purposes. Petite and oval faced with a sweet, endearing voice, a girl-virgin fused to matron-woman, having eschewed puberty and rebellion for family tradition. Were they matched as in days of yore? Perhaps, but very agreeably, if so. They joined dynasties: the dry-cleaning Rotolos and the wholesale-grocery Schellicis. The Schelleci store on Decatur Street was huge and abundant. In this impressive place odors crowded, widening one's nostrils: the mustiness of pasta (of every variety), the acridity of brine olives and baccala. To look at Mary Ann, you could not guess she belonged to such enterprise. ("Dagoes," said Mama Gomez, but she was like so many who were envious of those who built tradition and prospered.)

Mary Ann's own engagement ring was a posthumous gift from her great grandmother, a magnificent antique, two karats of flawless diamond, encircled with sapphires and mounted upon a Baroque platinum setting. To Mary Ann, who most frequently covered this ring with her right hand in public, not to tempt the lurking jewel thief, there passed a grave responsibility, one in fact, which though it belittled her, was a diminution wonderfully appropriate to her natural modesty.

It was good, explained Sheila, that it was Mary Ann and not herself who stood in this line of succession, not that she would wear her own ring lightly (one-quarter karat set in a simple white gold Tiffany setting would wear lightly at any case).

That night I couldn't sleep--the idea of getting married floored me; or was it the idea of leaving Marais Street and making a life somewhere else? The old neighborhood surely was existing on borrowed time, having no more culture than the movies and the simple lore of the street. None of us had wandered very far out of the confines of our downtown habitat. Sister Catherine and the nuns at the Annunciation Convent had been our salvation. Philip and I were nutured along under their tender and not so tender care, and passed on securely to the brothers of the Sacred Heart at St. Aloysius for high school, never leaving the solicitude and sanctuary of the Church. Not the case for most of the other kids in the neighborhood, who were herded into Colton Elementary, a big Depression-spawn public school on St. Claude avenue, where the complexions of the kids ranged from light pink to medium coffee, not including, of course, any of known African origins like Harold Boudreaux, Marais Street's *passé-blanc* first baseman, who was spirited in at Annunciation by the nuns, against only mild protestations--as long as it was not said out loud, was the rule. A few of the bright and ambitious kids moved on to S. P. Peters, where they could prepare to be a draughtsman or a bookkeeper, careers considered very good by ninth-ward standards.

And so it went: not poverty, ignorance, prejudice, ruined marriages or any of those other nameless kinds of wretched conditions in the ninth ward decided our fate, it was something else which I can't explain because I don't really know what I would have settled for if Sister Catherine did not have better in mind for me. I remember the day so long ago when she came over with Philip shortly before we graduated from grammer school at Annunciation. We were assembled in our sparsely furnished, poorly lit little parlor, with Philip and I seated primly on the sofa facing Sister on the hard-back chair I had dragged in from the kitchen. Sister leaned forward as she spoke, her sturdy, round face aglow in her flowing black habit. Mama Gomez sat in the shadows, on an old threadbare armchair smiling and nodding even before Sister began to speak.

"I've made arrangements for Bobby and Philip to attend St. Aloysius where they can get the kind of background that will qualify them for college." Sister had a dry businesslike sweetness, punctuating her good counsel with winsome smiles. Philip interrupted her several times with questions and comments. I was silent, college and acceptable standards of education were as yet beyond my range of understanding, but I caught the flavor of Sister's explanation and it brightened my spirits. I looked over at Mama Gomez and noticed that her expression had gone vacant; she was rubbing her leg to ease the almost constant pain she suffered from poor circulation. Actually, Philip was as ignorant of all of this as I was, but he never let what he didn't know slow him down.

At St. Aloysius, Philip and I became inseparable and gradually lost contact with the other kids in the neighborhood, most of whom dropped out of Peters to get on at the Jax Brewery where they cleaned up during the war years on overtime. It took some perspective for Philip and me to keep up with our Latin translations when the other kids were skipping classes to take in matinee double features at the Joy Strand, where the movies were decrepit and the house lights never turned on; but never mind the movies, nobody watched them. On a good day at the Strand a youngster could be propositioned by members of both sexes. All ages and all types showed up at the Strand for whatever was your pleasure. I remember on nights when we gathered on the street corner, how I would listen to Joy Strand stories with my mouth hung open and my eyes bulging. I was sure that life was passing me by. But all Philip and I ever did was listen, even if it seemed sometimes that Philip had such adventures. He had the knack of seeming more worldly than he really was, or in this case, it seemed doubly so because he would give the guys a lift in the Pontiac to the public health clinic for quick treatments. The Rotolos, in any case, had not worked hard for all those years in the cleaning business to have Philip catch clap at the Joy Strand.

There were other things, too, that Philip and I might have fallen into--dark things like heroin and reefers. These, however, remained a matter of curiosity and mystery to us kids in these early innocent days, when drugs were almost solely the province of jazz musicians and alcoholics.

But by the time Philip and I graduated from St. Aloysius and were drafted, the war was over, and we left the ninth ward for the army, feeling both disappointment and relief.

Last night I went on and on to Sheila about how great it was to grow up on Marais Street. Was it really so, or had I eschewed the harsh realities for a fabled remembrance? How glowingly did I recount those hot summer nights to her, when the whole neighborhood sat out trying to cool off. The banquette bricks were still warm from the torrid sun. We kids, even little ones like me, ran in the street playing ancient nighttime games while the grown-ups sat silently, lulled into fantasies by the wing-flutter of window fans whirring in the alley ways. Sounds came clearly through the auditory night; you could hear a cough far down the street. Men drank beer in their undershirts; on certain nights they took their radios out and listened to Joe Louis demolish another white man and break their hearts. Mama Gomez was a dark, indistinguishable mass sitting in our doorway exactly like I saw a black prostitute do over on Touro Street, working her frayed edged palmetto fan, its reedy swoosh merging with the gruff, companionable complaints she barked out to Mrs. Maegwich across the street. After the games, I sat below her on the bottom step, perspiring and panting from all of my running. The night seemed as though it would go on magically forever when suddenly she would utter a great agonizing sigh and lift her great bulk to fill the entire doorway, and we would go into the hot house to sleep.

On Saturday mornings Mama Gomez and I would strike out for St. Roch market to get any giveaways being offered: lagniappe liver and bruised fruit. On the way back we stopped at the Annunciation rectory to pick up our St. Peter and Paul food coupons from Father Perrier, the pastor. Mama Gomez would receive these charities without embarrassment and barely adequate politeness I thought. I would try to hurry her away fearing to be seen, not wanting to gush out thank you's to Father who was condescending and very stern, reminding me to attend catechism class on Thursday afternoons after school.

Mama Gomez dressed me on Sunday and sent me off to nine-thirty Mass. I never asked her why she didn't attend, nor, by the way, was there ever any discussion of adoption. Wasn't I a smart little fellow and knew the difference between brown and white? Philip Rotolo would accompany me to church--I only saw him on Sundays then, for some reason. He was very strong and full of confidence even as a child; he impressed me very much, especially when he would nudge me and give me a nickle to put in the collection basket, saving me the embarrassment of letting it pass.

The Willards from Mississipi moved next door around this time, and I met Dorothy, their little girl who was my age. She introduced herself through a crack in the fence. She was a sweet little orange-haired red neck wise beyond her years, who taught me one day in our alley how to kiss. I was very impressed but very frightened. We repeated these little affectionate probings a few more times, but nothing came of it, for the Willards suddenly packed up and left New Orleans. I didn't tell Sheila about Dorothy for obvious reasons. I never remember seeing Dorothy's father, but I remember her mother very well. She would look sternly at me from her kitchen window whenever she saw me looking over for Dorothy. She had her suspicions about me and Mama Gomez, as I learned from Dorothy, who tried to convince me that my Mama was a Negro. What a bold, forward little wonder she was.

The neighborhood was mostly settled except for families like the Willards and the Hellermans who were not red necks. Mike Hellerman was my first playmate, his father had a real estate agency and they lived in the only two-story house on the block. Mike's mother brought him over one Saturday when I was barely five and took us to the double feature at the Famous Theater. Although I didn't know it then, I had been wearing Mike's hand-me-downs. He was much broader, and Mama Gomez had to stitch rough pleats in the waist of his pants to make them fit. Later when I started school, nicer clothes mysteriously appeared, pants and shirts that fit. I suspect that we orphans were better treated than other poor kids. Mike, besides being fat, was as clumsy and unathletic as I was. We would wrestle for hours in his large, uncluttered basement. His nose produced a perfect pattern of beaded sweat drops; he sweated, in fact, from every pore in his body, constantly blinking his wet lashes. We were perfectly matched, he charging bullishly, and me, dodging and grabbing from the rear. But it was hard to get grips on a fat, sweaty kid, and we usually ended in a giggling draw, both drenched with his perspiration.

Mike and I, when the time came, had our troubles on the street getting left out of touch football games or being chosen last. We had to be satisfied with playing marbles and spinning tops or flying kites on the railroad neutral grounds on Elysian Fields Avenue.

Too soon, Mike's family moved away to a new suburb in Gentilly, and I never saw him again. I kept to myself for a while, squatting on the brick banquette after a hard rain when our streets flooded, gazing into the gutter water, surely the most disease-ridden slosh one can imagine, or sitting alone, counting box cars on Elysian Fields. I wore glasses even then and worried Mama Gomez when I went off on one of my strange trances. Sometimes I worried myself, like the time I was sitting on the front steps and followed a strange man, a tall lean man in a dark suit with deep furrows in his cheeks. I followed him to St. Claude where he boarded a streetcar, and remarkably so did I, without a cent for car fare. The conductor let me pass, thinking I was with the tall man. I sat down behind the man and watched him read a newspaper which he had folded inside of his coat. Eventually the man got off, but I stayed on to the end of the line, way down in St. Bernard Parish, where there is nothing really but swamps.

The conductor finding me his last remaining passenger came over.

"Where is your father, boy?" he asked, assuming the tall man was my father.

"I don't have a father," I answered factually.

"No father, huh," he said, smiling and patting my head. He seemed satisfied that I was simply another lost child and put me off at my stop on the way back.

I don't know why I followed the man or why at another time I walked out in my over-sized pajamas up to Rapp's open-stall market on St. Claude passing neighbors on their way to the grocery, unaware but awake. I sat down on an orange crate next to a stack of wire cages full of clucking chickens and watched Big Nick in his long bloody apron grab one chicken after another to slit their throats. He plunged them into a drum of boiling water, throwing them onto a counter to be plucked. I was soon splattered with blood, but could not tear my eyes away from Nick cutting throat after throat. Presently he saw me and stopped his work.

"What d'ya want, kid?" he snapped at me.

I didn't answer--I heard him but for some reason didn't think I needed to answer.

"Hey, Malcolm," he called out to Malcolm Rapp who owned the market, "look here."

Mr. Rapp came over and asked me what I wanted. I still didn't answer.

"I think he's sleepwalking, Nick," I heard him say.

"No, I'm not, Mr. Rapp," I informed him.

"You're still wearing your pajamas, son," he said, plucking one of my sleeves. I looked down and realizing for the first time that I was wearing my pajamas ran home as fast as I could.

"What could have caused these fugue states?" I had asked Sheila after bending her ear.

"You were just a dreamy kid, you still are."

"Dreamy--do you think something is wrong with me?"

"No, of course not; you're my little boy," she cooed, taking me in her arms. I nestled against her bosom, like a child.

"Am I your little boy?"

"You sure are," she said and kissed me. It was not the way a mother kissed.

The mere memory of it filled me with desire, and I stretched out luxuriously until, with my head against the headboard, my feet edged off the end of the bed. I was too big for the bed--I had grown up after all!

And so betrothed, we endured three more years of college to graduate, and on a rainy June morning in nineteen fifty-six were married right there on the Loyola campus in Holy Name Church: a somewhat small but lively reception following at the Rosenbergs' home.

Marais Street was represented by Philip and Mary Ann and Mama Gomez, of course. Before it was over, my Mama drank enough champagne to render her so jolly and beaming that her face shone with a dazzling pinkish glow. Her condition progressed thereafter, unfortunately, to one of sheer drunken exhaustion. She sat, near the end of the festivities, on the sofa, yawning and blinking, but beaming yet whenever anyone spoke to her. When she began swaying and dropping off, Bessie took her in hand and put her to bed.

Bessie was, of course, wonderful and the salvation of all of us, the entire affair bearing the imprint of her tastefulness; she was constantly helpful and seemed to be everywhere, for whatever was needed and of assistance to whomever seemed momentarily lost and uncared for.

Bernie, who drank as much as Mama Gomez, became more expansive than I had ever seen him, telling everyone how proud he was of his daughter and new son-in-law; I half expected that he would say that he was not losing a daughter, etc., but he never did, he seemed several times right on the brink of it.

The Jesuit fathers were there in force, lending their clerical worldliness. There was also a steady coming and going of Bernie's black colleagues from Xavier, who came with their wives, looking primly pleased and ever so slightly ill-at-ease, to present themselves to the host and hostess and then to Sheila and me, accepting a glass of champagne, but begging off when Bernie insisted they have another drink and stay longer. No one, save Bernie, thought any of this improper in nineteen fifty-six, it was what our socially conditioned sense of decorum allowed.

I was not quite myself through it all, standing around gawking at everyone and everything as though I was one of the caterers and not one of the guests of honor. I seemed to have developed temporary catatonia, and was continuously being pulled around by Sheila, who was as expansive as Bernie, introducing me to one beloved friend of the family after another.

Bernie's mother, a Hotard from Avoyelles Parish, certainly did not look like a home-spun Cajun woman: in fact, had she been introduced to me as Clare Booth Luce, I would not have blinked an eye. Her husband, who was Jewish and from St. Louis, was, on the other hand, pleasant and shy, looking a little uncomfortable in his suit. He might have been mistaken for a truck farmer. Actually, he was an attorney. God only knows how he ended up practicing law in Bunkie, Louisiana.

One look at Bessie's mother and father and one knew who and what they were immediately. I wondered if everyone in Bessie's family was so sweetly dignified and calm, and commanded such instant respect. It was their warmth, more than anything else, that made me feel so unreservedly accepted among all my new relatives, in spite of my always edging downtown reticence.

It was nice to have Bernie throw his arm around me and treat me as an equal. He usually gave me only cursory attention, mistaking my dreaminess for subservience. At Christmas, he had given me copies of Stendahl's *Charterhouse at Parma* and David Riesman's *The Lonely Crowd*. I held them in my hands in sullen ignorance.

"Sorry, if you've already read them," he said, "I figured everybody can use clean copies of standards for their library." Typical of Bernie's subtle intimidation. It pleased his liberal soul that I was poor and illegitimate, and more so that Mama was Philippine. But it was my decision to be a writer, if only a journalist, that was crucial to his approval of me. I speak, of course, of the demands of his ego. I was a practicing Catholic, and that finally was the reason he felt so good about the marriage.

That evening Sheila and I departed in the Fiat, our bags piled high on a luggage rack, and drove out of town, leading a merry and determined little caravan of cars, blaring their horns all the way out to Chef Menteur highway; and from thence on to Panama City, where I got, in one glorious day, a painful sunburn. But I suffered no further disappointments, in spite of the most smoldering adolescent anticipation I harbored of hedonistic delights. What happened, instead, was funny, real and wonderfully stupid. Sheila and I, as Catholics, no matter what else we fancied ourselves to be, were inexperienced and the discovery that we be could be comfortable amid so many forbidden intimacies was alone a great relief. Nakedness is surely not a natural state, not for Catholics, anyway.

We closed the curtains and blinds, turned off the lights in our cozy little motel room and grunted through our official marriage-manual act of consummation; that done with, we got down to fondling and simple affectionate explorations, we even dared to exchange street obscenities, laughing uproariously as we did. We took long moonlight walks on the beach and planned grand careers for ourselves.

In these years Clara began rebuilding her father's house, Philip finished law school and started his practice, Sheila got her master's degree in Special Education and was eventually appointed to the school board as curriculum coordinator, and I began my labor as a journalist at the Picayune. But it was Ronnie, in spite of his late start and failure at Tulane, who made the greatest progress as a realtor.

That we would go far we never doubted--or only privately. Success in our little Caribbean oasis, we are told, is an uncertain thing, where there is less future and more past--more past than any place has a right to--so much that we must remember, and even more that we can't forget. And yet we feel content to say that the Big Easy is authentically *easy*--its pleasures real and for the most part honestly come by, in spite of what they think about the quality of our cultural life, and our putative aristocratic origins, or how ruinously comfortable everything is, how we pay for security with freedom and repay talent with arrogance, driving the best away to more virulent, hellbound places. And so our culture, we are told, ambles along amid our easy pleasures, dragging with it a tattered collection of old ornaments--everything mixing and intermixing according to the shadowy legacy of old class distinctions and even older caste divisions--nothing we care to talk about: colors of skins, unpronounceable West Indian names, patois tongues, amalgamated emigrant enclaves scattered about among stately graveyards, beautiful churches, turgid canals, placid bayous and forbidden swamps. all contained in the curving embrace of the river and a buttressing necklace of lakes. There is just enough money to go round--besides the old money and the Texas money. What's left is for those who hustle for it. In a community where royal appointments in Mardi Gras krewes are the pinnacle of social prominence, even downtowners who are good at making money are at a disadvantage, unless, like Ronnie, they make a lot of money. Politics, however, is open to all. Not that I agree with any of this.

For Clara, it was a matter of doing everything in order, she was in no hurry. But what was she going to do about Ronnie? He called almost every day in New York and finally suggested that she return to New Orleans immediately instead of later. She agreed only after he secured employment for her with one of the Lang realtor attorneys. In the city, she found that Ronnie had become very busy. Cora Lang reported glowingly to Clara about Ronnie's success.

"He is so full of optimism--so good at finding just the right house for everyone."

Clara was proud to have introduced them. Having her back seemed to satisfy Ronnie, he stopped the daily phone calls. She was thankful for this, since she got busy too, making arrangements for the renovation of her father's house. She had things done as money became available. When she and Ronnie met they reported on what they were getting accomplished, the relationship became almost like a business. The affection between them was measured, he kissed her when he left her apartment. They seemed to agree, without saying so, that they should control their passion. Although it may not have been necessary. They seemed to have purposes beyond what a man and a woman in love expected of each other.

Clara had rare moments to walk along the levee during these years. From her side of the river, she could see the white obelisk monument at the site of the Battle of New Orleans on the Chalmette battlegrounds. On bright days, the sun shone brilliantly on its clean vertical planes, as though it were closer than she thought it to be, so very far across the wide water. Nearby, beside the rows of tiny anonymous grave stones in the memorial graveyard, flashed the white columns of an ante-bellum house, a distant twin of her father's house. The brown river flowed with hardly a ripple, it seemed old and silent, its fathoms of deep water, dumb to the fluttering music of the cottonwood. Black men, sitting quietly on the river slope, fished for catfish with slaughter poles. A more fanciful girl might have imagined Huck Finn and Jim floating down in their raft. Clara always saw things for what they were, she had no talent for embellishing reality, but also no shallow inclination to reduce them to their stark contours. Without effort or grandiosity, she allowed everything its largeness, transpiring in the magnitude of her memories, but of what was and not what might have been.

On a few occasions Ronnie dropped by, to catch her on one of these strolls. He always accused her of day dreaming and she accepted his friendly jibes with quiet amusement. What did either of these enterprising people know about day dreaming, he, planning hotels and plush shopping centers, she, resurrecting the very world of her childhood? But if it had been suggested to them that they were reaching for the stars, they were have denied it, these things, after all, were within the normal scope of what can be had by ordinary effort. That what they did seemed grand to others, never occurred to them. Nor had they thought it a breach of their romantic commitment to postpone the wedding because it interfered with the progress of their projects. Ronnie would laugh quietly but joyfully at Philip's teasing.

Sure he was ambitious, and why shouldn't he be? As if he could imagine that ruthlessness went into the bargain of being ambition. His dogged sense of purpose was merely to get what he wanted, which was what everyone wanted, but so few actually got, that he could actually get those things never amazed him. The great freighters anchored all along the river was a sight that pleased both of them, like the natural immensity of the sky and the river itself winding far away in the distance. Even the wind that would sweep with thrilling freshness in their faces did not suggest more than what ordinary life promised, indeed, nothing was promised except what they were willing to work for.

And so they progressed, and we admired them for their progress.

Ronnie had gotten Clara an apartment in Pirate's Alley near the St. Louis Cathedral. One dreary overcast autumn afternoon, as she drank coffee at the nearby Cafe du Monde, she was accosted by a strange woman dressed completely in layers of soiled black garments, her face hidden beneath a raggedy knitted shawl. She was tall and walked slowly with bent neck; as she came beside Clara on the banquette, the woman stopped, lifted her shawl to reveal a weather-worn face and fierce, accusing eyes, which she turned on Clara, raising her arm to point her finger. But neither the threatening finger nor the baleful gaze disturbed Clara, who felt immediate sympathy for this poor woman; surely, she thought, here is someone who lives in the hell of some old, painful guilt like a child scolded and sent away by her parents. Actually the woman was a well-known character in the quarter and her theatrical finger pointing was a source of great amusement to quarter denizens. Clara, however, did not know this lady or any of the other famous demented clowns that roamed the quarter. The city was proud of all these ridiculous people, a quaintness and cynicism lost on Clara, who took everyone seriously. For this very reason, perhaps, Clara, a true eccentric, felt kinship with this bizarre city, even if she could not account for what was bizarre either about herself or others.

On another occasion she had actually lost her way, astounding for Clara, who never before, did not know exactly where she was. It was a clear April morning and she found herself beyond the quarter on Elysian Fields Avenue, a wide street with an old railroad on a broad parkway that in past years carried people out to Lake

Ponchartrain, to the beach and the amusement park. Many of the houses appeared to be as old as those in the quarter. She could only think that she had allowed this unusual diversion on the strength of the day's brightness and freshness. Without intending it, she had fallen into a sentimental mood of years long ago. a sort of wakeful dreaming to mist her vision, even on such a clear day.

Clara's gift was to resist the pressures of time, much like the city itself, to allow the future only as the backwash of the past. It was as if she belonged to two different worlds or were two people, one practical, the other mirroring the deepest longing of the city to return to certain golden times in its history. This was the quality that Ronnie had responded to, and so ironically, because neither Clara nor Ronnie were naturally inclined to sentimentality.

Ronnie was soon Cora's full partner, Cora, at last could sit back and relax and watch Ronnie build the business; he began preparations for really large developments by purchasing key properties, like the decaying buildings at the foot of Canal Street that harbored the seamy bars that catered to the riffraff that regularly poured out of sea-faring freighters docked in the port.

It took Ronnie six years before he could put all the pieces of his project together, and nearly as long for Clara to complete the restoration of her father's house. The near completion of the two projects, finally gave them enough time to get married. Ronnie, though raised a Lutheran, at least in name, raised no objections to Clara's desire to be married in the Catholic church. In fact, the idea appealed to him very much, and he arranged to have the ceremony in the Saint Louis Cathedral in the high style of the city's most prominent citizens. A long parade of sleek, gray limosines picked up and delivered the bridal party, important friends and business associates. Philip was the best man and Clara's beautiful mother was the maid of honor; her grandfather, Judge Hypolite Duplantier gave the bride away. Sheila and I attended with Sheila's parents in a private car, following the procession of limousines up to one of the large stone mansions on St. Charles Avenue, where the guests were met by a doorman in livery, and danced to a Big Band orchestra, Ted Weems, I believe, and feasted on gourmet delights from Commander's Palace. Irma Doucet, the Picayune's society editor attended and reported on the wedding: a two-page spread, with photographs of the bridal party and their families, along with attending dignitaries. Who could have guessed that Ronnie Hingle had emerged but a brief six years before from the squalor of the lower ninth ward? Clara, however, gave no evidence of the radiant excitement of brides. I would not say that she simply endured all of the fanfare, it was more like her natural serenity added an air of elevated dignity to the proceedings. When I mentioned this to Sheila she ignored me, so flushed she was with champagne and grandeur.

Was this when I began my obsession with this woman, seeing her receive each guest with grace and simple charm? Did it start here, the slow build-up of symbolic resonance I began to attach to her person? Bride she was, as I had never seen before--to an entity greater than a mere husband, as though she were bride to the high maintenance of canons or standards. Or was I beginning to surrender to some secret deficiency within myself, a need to rise up from a dreaded lowliness, to claim reparation for a scurrilous, debased lineage? Sheila slept that night in the luminescence of Clara's beautiful wedding, and I in the aura of Clara's royalty.

After we were married, Sheila and I moved into a little shot-gun house just off Magazine Street and launched our respective careers. It was an old styled New Orleans neighborhood, with the usual mix: a few scattered black families, some new couples just starting out like ourselves, and transients--red necks, Latinos and such, but mostly older, long-standing residents who had inherited their houses from their parents. The only sign of things to come were a few medical students who lived more luxuriously in these modest houses than anybody else. They told us when we asked that they liked the quaint charm and the friendly people; I told Sheila they were slumming, and she told me I was xenophobic. She might have been right. I grew up in the ninth ward, but didn't live in our new neighborhood in the old style, but as a wary interloper from New York. The students were the only neighbors I talked to, and only because they were friendly and introduced themselves.

I was comfortable nonetheless, even if I didn't use the old corner grocery more than a few times. It was famiiar terrain, and I had it both ways: moving around with the freedom of a stranger, but knowing how to read those around me with the instinct of a native.

My deepest satisfaction, however, came from the familiarly dark kid who lived directly across the street from us with his widowed mother. He was the perfect amalgam of all such kids who resided in all the old neighborhoods of New Orleans. I never talked to him, of course, since we were shy, and because I was really hesitant to tell him of my downtown pedigree. There he was, nevertheless, whenever I needed him, like a road sign to the weary, lost traveler. I would peer through the window at him as he worked on his vintage Chevrolet, which he did faithfully every Saturday morning, moving and functioning with the unresisting calm of his uncomplicated kind, his innocent face braised by a galvanizing toughness which allowed him access to whatever he desired but relieved him of the burden of the unreachable. As I watched him, I gained the most secure feelings from his diligence.

I could have lived there indefinitely, since it provided me with both what I had escaped from but which nevertheless still resided rather invincibly in my bosom, plus just enough of the new to stop me from sinking into maudlin nostalgia and thusly in the heart of despair.

We lived there for ten years, making steady professional progress, years of great satisfaction. Our lives were filled with our careers. We saw only our associates and almost none of our close friends. Bernie and Bessie came over on Sundays for dinner; Sheila would pick up Mama Gomez sometimes to join us. Mama was less and less able to move around easily, but she never complained.

Then one day I came home and found Sheila sitting on the bed with swollen eyes.

"Why were you crying?" I asked. She shook her head and started to cry again.

"Is it Mama Gomez?" She nodded. I sat down next to her and tried to decide how I was going to react, but before I could make up my mind, something inside of me broke down, and I cried out in a voice I didn't recognize. Sheila pulled me down to her breast, and held me tight.

Mrs. Radosti had missed her sitting out and went to check on her. For days after we buried her, I cried in Sheila's arms. When my tears dried and numbness set in, I began to realize how our relationship as mother and son had been compromised, not simply because we were not tied by blood, but because in her dark exoticness, I had considered her subservient to the other saintly mother whom I didn't know, or knew only by impaired memory. The conflict knotted me inside, compounding my guilt. Had I been faithless to her, regarding her my inferior, my brown nursemaid, my mammy? I paced up and down, confessing all of this to Sheila, who, at first listened patiently, but I wouldn't let it go, and Sheila warned me about grieving so indulgently. Finally, when I was exhausted and my grief spent, Sheila suggested that we move. It was a perfect suggestion, made at a perfect time. We had gained financial security, and the neighborhood was now unbearable to me, reminding me of what I had lost and could never go back to, but also of what I feared sliding back into, filling me with the most desperate feelings. We were ready for different and more prestigious lodgings, and what more prestigious lodgings than the French Quarter.

Sheila acted promptly, hardly waiting for my approval. I resisted a little, more out of form than for any practical reason. I knew nothing of this old historic district--nothing, that is, about living there. I imagined living among people who were vaguely sophisticated and decadent. In the end I suppose we downtowners are puritanical. The prospects of a chic quarter society challenged me, since I didn't know either from my background or from actual experience who these people were: deviants of every exotic persuasion, no doubt. What it really came down to, however--and I am embarrassed to say it, was the dangers the Quarter posed to our secure Catholic marriage.

Sheila, of course, had no such fears. She told me that life among prostitutes, transvestites, homosexuals, lesbians, leather cultists and whatever else that I could not even imagine was exactly and only what one chose to make it. She said that the Quarter was at least not full of ignorant, superstitious people and that I should look forward to the civility and elegance of a more cosmopolitan life style.

It turned out that I had nothing to fear, there being no such thing as Quarter society, cosmopolitan or otherwise. It was so overrun with tourists that any possibility for community spirit was thereby canceled. The streets buzzed with lively, agreeable commercial enterprise, and one learned to fear, not the leather cultist, but the midwestern tourist. Once inside your apartment, moreover, you enjoyed a more comfortable kind of privacy than in regular neighborhoods where there was always the possibility of coming to cross-purposes with a neighbor you had befriended, friendship always being risky. In the Quarter your neighbor didn't really exist, and inasmuch as they did, they were seldom available as friends.

Sheila, of course, went right to work decorating, steeped as she was in preservationist aesthetics. For over a year, she roamed Magazine Street, rounding up antiques.

There is more to decorating a Quarter apartment than one would suppose, I discovered. One should, for example, be eclectic rather than consistent in choosing antiques, selecting individual pieces or sets for quality; it is not necessary that things go together; in fact, it is very bad if they do. When Sheila was done, the variety in our apartment included Hepplewhite dining chairs, Sheraton end tables, a chrome and plate glass Art-Deco coffee table, a Victorian settee and an oaken provincial bookcase.

This bookcase, which was quite large and handsome, was hidden by potted palms, to the frustration of those visitors who were curious about my reading habits. As the feature editor of *Dixie-Roto*, the local Sunday supplement, I was expected to be a reader, but of what, I wasn't sure.

Along with the antiques, Sheila purchased a long contemporary couch for our living room and two canvas butterfly chairs for effect. The object, I learned, was to strike just the right balance between casual order and understated sophistication by embracing both the venerably old and the radically new. To wit: in our bathroom were hung prints by Andy Warhol and Roy Lichenstein, whereas in our living room we had genre paintings by plantation primitives.

It was a set up that would have confounded my friends in the old neighborhood, who preferred chartreuse dinette sets and Naugahyde recliners as I once did.

My only contribution to all of this was two of my own carefully rendered still-lifes which were hung in the short hallway between the living room and bedroom where it is too dark to see most of the time. I was a Sunday painter for a short time. I gave it up on Sheila's advice. Actually, she consoled me when my genius did not burst forth--this is the way I believed it to be with painters, raw flaming talent spilling out onto the canvas. When this didn't happen I went back to thinking myself a writer, which I knew required discipline more than anything else.

I hope that I have not created the impression that I didn't appreciate Sheila's efforts. She was, after all, more than I deserved, and was, for a woman her age, attractive, healthy--I would even say Raphaelesque--and, of course, very well educated. Who else would have known the designer of those butterfly chairs (was it Thonet? Or did he design the bent-wood rocker?). You see how much out of my cultural depth I was with her.

Lillian, the maid, came twice a week, on Mondays and Wednesdays. For a brief time in the sixties she threatened to resign. Lillian is seventy -five or more and stand-offish and taciturn to the point of being rude because I suspect she thinks we are not the sort of people who should have a maid. She is as tan as a super-market bag. Sheila approves of her reserve and never complains. In between Wednesdays and Mondays the apartment is left to gradually collect dust, rug stains and mold, dirty dishes piling up in our narrow galley of a kitchen. Although I should have known better, in my old fashioned way, I expected Sheila to be a housewife. She was, in a way, since she did clean when we had important guests.

By then Sheila had already risen to the top of her profession as an educator, with her appointment as director of the Department of Curriculum Development. She was perfect for the job, being a high-powered grantsperson, an absolute whiz at inventing creative programs for elementary schools, her main target being downtown underprivileged kids. I didn't always entirely approve of her programs since they carried the implication that downtown kids needed more help than other kids. I was proud of her, nonetheless. Her success continued, even after the demise of the Great Society, when she undauntingly milked whatever trickling appropriations the Republicans allowed.

We lived more or less comfortably and at peace with one another, I with her creative programs, even though I thought she knew next to nothing about downtown kids, and also with her decor, once I learned to distinguish among Hepplewhite, Sheraton, etc., and in time I no longer noticed the filth. I even accepted, at least intellectually, an equal partnership in bearing the responsibility for cleanliness and daily food. Actually, we ate out a lot, together sometimes, but often separately since our comings and goings with our busy schedules made it difficult to share meals.

The new decade turned, and things began to happen for Philip. He was a natural with his great, unshakable confidence. You never knew when you would see him on the evening news being interviewed about one of his cases or airing an opinion on a hot issue. His firm, Gagliano and Mouledoux, made him a full partner. By 1960 his name was becoming a local household word, and he was poised to enter the political arena. How proud I was to be his friend, to see him speaking with his deep voice and his rugged, unrelenting masculinity. Not to say that the Rotolo money didn't help. I saw him less and less though, only when he was part of one of my assignments. or when he would call me to cover one of his increasing public appearances.

"Bobby, can you get over to the Roovevelt tomorrow? How's Sheila? Can I count on you. When are you and Sheila going to start a family?" He would joke and hang up, I could hear other voices in the background. I could never decide whether I was being brushed off by my old friend. Philip seem to always move in a crowd. I would run after him with the other reporters after a speech and squeeze in for a question or two. I understood that he had to give the media most of his time. Politics and the electronic media were beginning a promising partnership, and young guys like Philip had a real edge on the old-guard ward politicians like L.C. Perrileaux, whose lack of polish permitted only the briefest exposure. Even Earl Long, great campaigner that he was, avoided TV.

I always held out the chance that Philip would ask me to handle his publicity, but he never did. He and Ronnie saw a lot of each other, regarding big projects concerning the city's growing tourist trade, and other more volatile matters, issues that were beginning to shake the very foundations of daily life. Fear and hatred smoldered in everyone's breast. Our lives, we realized, were changing radically. We longed for the simple, innocent patriotism of the great wars. It was hard to deal with the desparate feeling that we were moving inexorably to a point when there would be no turning back, when nothing short of the spilling of innocent blood would be needed to right things again. As I watched my friends grow bigger and bigger, facing the challenge of what lay ahead, I began to savor my own role as observer and commentator, though as a reporter, my commentary was very limited, I didn't do much of that. I was, however, soon to get my chance. As momentous events came with speed and fury, tumbling over each other, whistling and swirling, it was my responsibility to note them in the peculiarity of their details, and thusly to give substance to them, fixing them at least for a day in print. It was a way to console myself as I watched my friends, disappear in the distance. But there was always Clara, now that I think about it. I remember seeing her, in my mind, as Ronnie had found her, on the levee, returning over and over to her father's house, listening to the constant rhythm of the river. Her house had been restored by 1960, brought back to its magnificence, she would never leave it again.

And events rolled forward with results that none of us, not even Philip could have anticipated. Plans were worked out to launch Philip into politics; I was asked to report on the results of a meeting Philip and his father had with Kelly O'Doul and his precinct captains--Kelly was ward boss in our neighborhood, a stocky little Irishman with heavy dark eyebrows; his black hair was always carefully plastered down with Beryl Cream and some kind of make-up spread over his face to cover the bumpy scars from his teenage acne. Kelly was feuding with L.C Perilleaux, the encumbent city councilman of our third district, he had been bumped out in L.C.'s election campaign and he was very angry. Philip was quick to take advantage of the situation, meeting with Kelly and old Father La Garde, the retired pastor from Our Lady Star of the Sea. Differences between Kelly and Father La Garde were worked out, disagreements about very weighty matters about which there could be no final compromise, but Philip always knew how to handle such situations. Kelly and Father La Place occupied opposite poles in the political spectrum. Somehow Philip was able to give both of them what they wanted, although Father La Garde had his own way of getting what he wanted, and what he wanted most of all was to defeat L.C.Perilleaux, no small task because L.C. was allied to the city's strongest political organization, The Old Regulars as they were known. No one really gave Philip much of a chance to beat L.C. in 1960. But events would follow a direction of their own. What seemed impossible--that is, that Philip could actually defeat L.C. at a certain point began to seem possible. Forces in the traditional make-up of America's population were shifting like the inner core of the earth shifts to precipitate great cracking tremors, renting its surface. Not many saw it coming. I don't think Philip or Kelly did--I certainly did not.

Let me simply say here that this very first campaign of Philip's began to pivot on strategies that emerged from machinations of very complex minds and unexpected developments. Not the least of which would involve Clara, but so ironically, because Clara had no interest in politics.

Chapter 14

After the momentous events of 1960, everything settled down, and for Sheila and me, one year became very much like the one before as we rested comfortably on our respective plateaus of success, giving no thought to the passage of time, years of inertia which brought us to our twentieth anniversary, a landmark that nearly went unnoticed. Bernie and Bessie came over to help us celebrate, but it was a lackluster affair. I suppose we thought our marriage had solidified and needed no ritual renewal. The elements of my life were flowing together: twenty years of marriage and I waited for something to happen. But nothing did, only a brief little stirring on Mardi Gras of all days, which set off a faint alarm, but a warning of what I couldn't imagine; a Mardi Gras it was among forgotten ones, during these years when Sheila and I were privileged to sit in the make-shift stands on Canal Street in front of the Boston Club to witness Rex, King of Carnival and Lord of Misrule, halt his parade in order to toast his queen. I say privileged, which it was for Sheila, who was thrilled to be a guest of the queen's and included among all the local celebrities in attendance; but for me, it was strictly professional: I was on assignment to take pictures and report the nature of the festivities.

Nothing seemed different that day as we took our places. Sheila was excited, as usual, talking to everybody around her, while I sat there with my camera, keeping my distance from the high-powered folk seated near me and from the immense madness of Mardi Gras. From our perch in the stands we overlooked the frightening spectacle of more than a million revelers crowding the great expanses of Canal Street for as far as the eye could see. The parade had stopped, and those gathered immediately around the king's float were momentarily quieted in hushed excitement, ready to erupt the instant Rex would hoist his goblet of champagne. I had him framed perfectly in my viewer, bracing myself for the explosion, ready to record the magical moment, the very zenith of the entire carnival season. But, alas, before I could snap the picture, the whole world went suddenly and violently askew; I found myself tumbling over, clutching my camera and flailing the empty air. My neighbors in their eagerness to applaud the royal couple had bumped me, and I might have fallen through the open benchwork of the stands if Sheila hadn't given me a good hard shove with her shoulder, knocking me back in the other direction. I wobbled finally into an upright stance, shaken up, checking for bruises and broken bones, and receiving some delayed verbal abuse from Sheila for my clumsiness when I realized I was missing the royal toast, that is, missing taking pictures of it. I began to frantically line up my camera, but I was stopped cold again--not by a blow this time--but by the sight of a beautiful young girl dressed as a clown. She was crowded in among the maskers who were thronged behind the low guard-railings along the curb, and seemed stunned by the drama of the moment, her eyes glazed and her mouth parted. I stared at her dumbstruck for what seemed endless seconds until a thunderous roar from the crowd brought me back. When I looked up, Rex was lifting his arms, saluting the cheering masses.

"You missed the toast," scolded Sheila, gesturing towards the king who was throwing his goblet down, stumbling as he did: drunk, I realized, from much more than champagne. His thin, knotty legs which were mercilessly sheathed in white silk caused him to totter unsteadily around his float with his chalky make-up and woolly beard, leering and nodding towards his youthful queen. He looked fearfully vulnerable and extraordinarily depraved. (By tradition, Rex is a successful business man, usually in his sixties, and his queen, or consort as she is so suggestively termed, is a debutante, a mere teenager.) I wondered, contrary to the claim that all of this is only supposed to be symbolic, if it was possible that this painted, lewd old man would tonight in some hidden, profane bed-chamber, actually lay hands on his young queen. My speculation, though absurd, filled me with strange exhilaration.

I began quickly snapping pictures as the king's float suddenly went rumbling off, leading the parade through the screaming masses. Rex waved his wand awkwardly from one side to the other, shimmering in his satin and rhinestones, taunting his subjects who cried out for him to throw doubloons, and although the krewmen on the other floats filled the air with beads and doubloons, Rex merely smiled his lascivious smile and threw nothing, for he was riches itself, the very baseness and allurement of the filthy lucre, a thrilling display of money and greed, I thought, almost uttering a cry of triumph; and I would have, if a hail of gold doubloons had not suddenly exploded against my face, a moment of supreme irony and also my great misfortune, because everyone, Sheila included, rushed at me to grasp the bogus coins, knocking me back on the seat of my pants, doubloons being fair game among friends, even relatives.

This second shock had the effect of calming me down, and as I carefully picked myself up, I spotted the girl-clown of my vision, screaming and waving her arms.

The last float was now passing, and I noticed the queen making her way down the stands to re-enter the Boston Club, attended by her maids, who gathered up the flowing edges of her gown, like wood nymphs attending Diana. Everyone applauded her; Sheila, in fact, shouted congratulations, calling her by her first name, which embarrassed me since Sheila before today had never laid eyes on this girl.

The crowd began milling. The sky above was as peaceful and clear as I had ever seen it, and as I gazed dreamily up into its perfect blueness, there appeared, quite unaccountably--because the parade was now well past--a single doubloon, turning and glistening in the bright sunshine, gracefully arching towards me. No one else saw it, evidently, for I was able to catch it by simply cupping my hand. It had come so gratuitously that I coveted it greedily, worthless piece of tin that it was, rubbing it affectionately with my thumb. I thought of the morrow, Ash Wednesday, when we Catholics would be reminded of our dry and inevitable mortality. I was also reminded, for no reason at all, of Clara whom we had not seen in years.

But I knew very well why my doubloon reminded me of Clara: her own image had been printed on such a coin in 1960. It had been years since I thought about this strange girl. She was, of course, no longer a girl as I was no longer a boy. So much had transpired since we knew Clara. For Sheila and me, Clara was neither here nor there, Sheila being from uptown, myself from downtown. Clara was from Algiers, that forgotten part of the city situated across the river from us. She had always seemed so removed from what affected the rest of us, living beyond ambition or ordinary desires, whether because she came from old money or old blood, or had simply lost touch with reality because she clung to an incomprehensible ideal, I didn't know. It was Mardi Gras, a day of celebration, but I--perhaps because of my little mishaps--had grown wistful. It seemed an infinite number of years since I had seen Clara.

The stands were emptying out. While I packed up my equipment, Sheila was pushing her way over to the mayor and his wife. He was surrounded; she would be a while. Watching her, I suddenly realized how fortunate I was to be married to such a splendid woman. What did I have to offer this brilliant girl--but reliability? It was surely this, my inherent dullness, that won her over. I am steady and dependable, a plodder, her perfect opposite, someone to hold the course in our marriage. With me she needn't sacrifice anything of her pride; I was her fool, willing to descend to any purgatorial depth. I would never give her away, never threaten her, be her side-kick, or even her dupe.

And yet, Sheila for all her vaunted confidence, was a fraud who had never faced down her demons, her panache but a smoke screen. She imagined herself invincible, in no need of my manliness. In all these years, only on two isolated occasions did she let down: once when a fearful nightmare overtook her and again when an insensitive co-worker, a Neanderthal of a man, yelled her down at a meeting. Both times she wept in my arms.

But, of course, this does not give her credit for what she, in her turn, did for me. She accepted me before I accepted myself, saving me at Loyola from defaulting to the most obvious campus phony, forgiving me my downtown crudity when I became as obtuse and hysterical as Oogie Pringle. She helped me also, I am embarrassed to admit, to overcome my skittiness about sex when I was so maddeningly and frustratingly shy, all the while thinking I was practicing control.

Beyond all of this, of course, was the redoubtable tradition of Catholic marriage in New Orleans, a powerhouse institution. Not that Sheila and I did not love each other--we did, and with passion, at least at first, even if it was never quite torrid. As Catholics, we were the beneficiaries of this ponderous endorsement, but to be sure, its victims as well. Catholic marriages in New Orleans have been known to survive in the face of the most debilitating mutual misery and still be productive in a hundred practical ways.

The street noise grew more excited; I could see the Canal Street crush achieve direction, pushing and shoving toward Bourbon Street, a great crawling animal, forming and reforming its shape, filing and squeezing into the narrow street. Sheila had finally made her way to the mayor's side, grasping his arm and speaking so enthusiastically that he smiled and nodded his head, acknowledging their old friendship I cynically inferred from my distance. It is hard for anyone to deny Sheila. She held on to his arm, speaking rapidly until he finally turned away to leave. But still flushed, she began to make her rounds among the remaining local celebrities; she had already introduced me to many of them, and although most of them were meeting me for the third or fourth time, they smiled as if I were a stranger. Before I could leave, she shouted an invitation to the whole group to join us at our apartment for drinks. They nodded politely and insincerely. It didn't hurt my feelings that they were so condescending; as a man who in a few years would be at the half-century mark, I was perfectly secure, both as to my age and my professional pride, I considered myself neither young nor old, disdaining milestones as extravagant nor did I seek respectibility as a reward for my professional efforts, whatever prominence my name would acquire would not become a distraction and hinderance. My byline was not a play for pride, certainly not for fame, but the public's assurance of my professional honesty. What I write is the truth. Journalists, I remembered thinking, are made up of very humble emotions, making up an ego modestly trimmed and suited to selfhood.

I smiled though, at that moment, in spite of myself--a tight, unwelcomed grin that registered in some closeted, dark corner of my mind and for the most fleeting of seconds, as a nasty swag of moral pomposity. This was something, I decided, slinging my equipment bag over my back that I would have to deal with later. No more Mardi Gras' for me at the Boston Club. Next year I would turn this assignment over to Tom Mahoney, my assistant. He and his wife will enjoy it I think. I hadn't told Sheila this yet. She impatiently urged me to hustle up after her, now that she had exchanged a few festive words with our mayor, and congregated among her peers. We were due back to our apartment to entertain the many guests that would be arriving all day.

Chapter 15

 t was, however, the Mardi Gras of the following year that etched itself deepest in my memory. But I could not have known what this pivotal year held in store for me.

That summer, at the end of the school year, Sheila was voted Educator of the Year, and I received an award for my feature on famous New Orleans' oaks. The future seemed bright as an early winter met us head-on, arriving with a vengeance, bringing freezing rains and arctic blasts through both December and January. We were hunkered down, ready to endure its last chilling unpleasantness, when one Saturday morning in February, Spring made a miraculous entry. It came streaming past our eastward window, across our balcony, filling me with nearly rapturous gratification. And although it was not to last very long, the azaleas and camellias, easiest of our flowery maidens, popped forth with their coloration; everything else would wait for a more authentic season.

In the meantime, I couldn't resist putting off going to my office, which I did mostly out of routine, and usually for no other reason than to get out of the apartment. How could I not be enchanted, even if I knew there were yet days, perhaps weeks, of cold, wet weather in store for us. I stepped out onto our balcony and stood beneath an absolutely cloudless sky surveying the comfortable geometry of balconies and patios, smugly trying to imagine being cold or sweltering in the heat and humidity of June when the monsoons would send the banana trees in our patios spiralling into outrageous growth.

When I stepped back into the apartment I set up my typewriter on a Sheraton end table near the window and pulled up one of the Hepplewhite chairs. For a number of years, with the coming of spring, even a false spring, I felt the urge to write, and this time the urge was particularly strong, but whatever it was in me that required words was buried too deep. I sat there for nearly an hour, mistily waiting for something to surface. I was incubating, I listlessly reminded myself. Indeed, I had been incubating for years.

The morning passed and I napped until early afternoon. When I awoke at nearly three o'clock, I went over to the typewriter and stared blankly with a gnawing sense of self-disgust at the empty sheet of paper I had rolled into the carriage. The light outside was fading, and I could do no better than grow bitter and petty, reminding myself of those times when I gave up my faithful old portable Royal to Sheila to type one of her urgent proposals, as if there wasn't enough creativity junking up those poor downtown elementary school buildings, most of which were constructed during the Gilded Age. (When Sheila took me to see what had been done to old McDonough 15 on Burgundy Street, I was shocked. The walls were plastered with smeary tempera paintings, and the classrooms and halls littered with swampy driftwood, crude palmetto weavings and Spanish moss. Bookshelves had been emptied of books and lined up with mayonnaise jar terrariums chock full of blue clay and gutter weeds. All of which Sheila said was very therapeutic and liberating. Hadn't I explained to her that creativity is not for everyone, especially not for downtown kids? Who should know better than I? Did I not climb out of the cultural morass of the ninth ward to be what I am today?)

By evening, I was watching TV, which depressed me to no end. I grimly endured, however, not giving an inch to what I was stubbornly maintaining was nothing more than the ordinary malaise of a hazy spring evening. Right through the local and national news, the early prime time sitcoms I sat, refusing to even check the schedule to at least give myself the privilege of personal choice.

By the time Sheila came in at about eleven o'clock I was watching David Susskind, whom I abhorred. Mercifully her presence allowed me to finally turn the damn thing off. She went into the bedroom to change into her pajamas. When she came back, she found me pacing up and down. I was really worked up. For what, I didn't know.

Sheila took one look at me and at the typewriter still set up at the window and arched her eyebrows.

"What's wrong?" she asked as she sank into the snowy cushions of our long contemporary couch.

"Nothing." I replied bluntly and continued pacing in front of her.

"Are you getting ready to start another novel?" she asked and yawned hugely, not to be impolite but because it came suddenly upon her; she looked very tired.

"And what if I am?" I fired back with an edge of hostility that I wanted to take back.

"Well," she answered, returning me kind for kind, "you're forty-six, you know."

"I don't see the connection."

"I mean if you were going to write a novel, you would have done it long before now. If you really want to write a book, you could rework and compile some of your best features, but you don't have to do that either; you don't have to prove anything to anybody. Most people would already consider you a success."

"Are you saying I can't write a novel?"

"No, but I don't see you as a frustrated creative writer. Whatever has put this idea in your head has to do with something else."

"With what?"

"I don't know, that's for you to figure out."

"I'm a good writer--why couldn't I write a novel?"

"Haven't you tried?"

"Yes."

"And?"

"Those were false starts," I replied helplessly.

She yawned again, it was really very late.

"Don't let me keep you up," I said glumly.

I was more irritated than was normal for me. I almost never became this annoyed about the apartment being messy, or about Sheila's absenteeism. That night, however, I felt like yelling at her back when she finally did go off to bed. How dare she go to sleep so smugly. Her success, if one could consider it such, was hardly the kind one might settle for in middle life. In fact, her entire professional effort suddenly seemed sham and spurious. What did those downtown kids need from her (uptown bitch): certainly not her sporting assistance to be aware of their crummy enviroment? If I knew downtown punks, they were aware of things that would make Sheila blush.

Oh well, I thought as I began pacing again, I'll write a novel if I want to. If it's in me, it'll come out, and if it's not--I was really worked up and couldn't understand why.

It is true that this urge to break upon the literary horizon came upon me every spring. In the past, however, it had only succeeded in rendering me starry-eyed for a day or two, just abstracted enough to send me to open windows to look out into the vacant distance. It was usually pleasantly sad, not at all upsetting. I am not by temperament given to driving ambition or grandiosity, and Sheila was perfectly right when she said I should consider myself successful.

Nevertheless, something had stirred within me; it had come without warning and with more than the usual dissatisfaction I had felt at those times when I realized how parochial I, *Dixie-Roto* and New Orleans were. How could I deny that *Dixie* was the very breath and voice of the Philistines, or that this city was not simply complacent, but militantly complacent. I usually said to myself at such times, and only with a little rancor, that I knew my place, that I was not superficial like certain hotshot liberals I knew. Perhaps I had felt a little too honorably dutiful as an editor of a publication that brought so much wholesome pleasure to so many. I was not one of those purple stylists who routinely and ruthlessly exploited the causes of minorities and crime victims. What I did for these causes was done quietly and without fanfare.

Oh, how damnably sincere and honorable I had been! It had always been so for me, that this very caution and self-righteousness has corroded whatever verve I've possessed.

I closed my eyes, and as I sat there stewing, the visual field beneath my lids was muddy and reddish; I squeezed my eyes tighter and the field turned a bilious green. I opened my eyes and looked around the apartment with disgust, reveling with willful spite at the signs of Sheila's neglect. How could she, I thought, with anger rising in my breast, so confidently think that her sham career was important enough to warrant such irresponsibility? I was driving spikes of hatred and self-hatred into my heart. I had to stop giving into this feeling of dread and misery, the source of which was neither Sheila nor the messy apartment. It was too late in the night and too early in my life for me to be thinking so blackly of my future.

So I did the best I could, which was what I'd been doing for some time. I curled up on the Victorian settee and watched TV. In fact, I watched all of the late night movies. It was a better selection than usual: an inchoate western classic with Randolph Scott, followed by a Japanese monster, and at about four-thirty I was awakened by the insistent tooting of trombone staccatoes during a scene that was both sinister and fast paced. I believe it was an old Claudette Colbert melodrama, but I couldn't be sure, for I was done for and finally fell into a deep sleep.

In the morning I awoke with a headful of old memories and an eyelid toasted by a sunbeam which found just the right angle through my eastward French window. The old plastered ceiling above me appeared in the soft morning light as serene as a Monet painting with its overlapping circular water stains of mellowing sepia. I had dreamed of my childhood, and as I lay, not fully awake, my life in the old neighborhood began to play back to me; all it needed was a Max Steiner score. Why doesn't this happen when I'm sitting behind the typewriter I thought, I could spin so rich a tale of old New Orleans. If only I pondered--but the water stains on the ceiling began to drift, and I dozed off again.

The dream that I awoke from this time seemed to have risen from the fathomless depths of my consciousness, my mind glowed in the wake of its magic. I blinked my eyes against the blinding light flaming through the French windows. What was I to do on such a splendid opalescent morning in the afterglow of this vivid dream?

Inevitably I grew more clear headed, and lay there waiting to hear Sheila stomping around in the kitchen, clattering dishes and banging pots. But there was nary a sound; she was up and gone as she usually was on Sunday morning. Even the observance of the Sabbath did not deter her from her duties, though until a few years ago we attended Mass together. She was at the Napoleon House, no doubt, having a Pim's cup with some jerky federal examiner, one of those eastern liberals. I had seen enough of them with their pre-faded jeans and beards. I could see him sitting across from Sheila with his shit-eating grin, waiting for her to stop for breath so he could kick in one of his dreary one-liners.

But I really didn't care where she was. This unnatural spring which seemed almost spiritual with its light rippling across the ceiling had induced my dream and put me in touch with something I had not been in touch with since I didn't know when, maybe never, but maybe at a time too early for me to remember, or a time that had been crossed out of my memory. I was still held, at any rate, in the glow of the dream. I had dreamed of old friends, not only as old friends but old friends revisited and remembered in some magical way. The dream was disjointed: a mosaic of vivid scenes. I saw Philip, back in the old neighborhood, as we had been, young, perhaps more glowingly young than we had ever been. And Ronnie, too, working on his old Plymouth. But the most radiant image was of Clara. I came upon her, as Ronnie had, on the levee, the wind blowing her hair and combing the grass, against an unbelievable blue sky.

I hadn't seen Clara in years--or Philip and Ronnie, either. It was so odd for me to have dreamed of Clara. She was such a strange, lonely girl, and I never knew her very well. I don't think anyone knew her well, not even Ronnie who was married to her.

But hadn't she touched each one of us in some very special way? Or did it just seem so because of my dream? I was willing to believe almost anything, for the dream seemed to have reached into the mystical regions of my past. It seemed, in fact, to have exceeded my own past and connected with an archaic, universal past, as if Clara was not simply someone I knew, but rather a distilled feminine essence, a finely wrought prototype that might have inspired Phidias in his rendering of Athena.

I lay there lolling in the reminiscences of this dream, surely in some way I was still dreaming the dream. I don't know how long it was before the real world finally began to reassert itself.

Gradually, however, little by little, it did: a creak of floor boards I never noticed before, the warm sun on my cheek and forearm, the gritty sound of my hair scraping gently on the settee's velvet. It was as though I was re-entering my body. But even then, what remained of the dream held me in its aura.

Eventually I arose and walked slowly into the kitchen and made myself a cup of instant coffee. I carried it over to the typewriter, sat down on the Hepplewhite chair and stared out of the window.

Irresistibly, I began drifting back again--I could not stop myself. Old memories came unbidden. It was so quiet I thought I heard the new season ticking somewhere off in the distance. When I next tasted the coffee, it was cold, and I was back on Marais Street watching Mama Gomez moving ponderously through the back door, the light from the backyard flickering all around her huge frame. I shook my head and turned to the typewriter and began to type, hardly aware of what I typed. Ironically, I wrote, not of Mama Gomez, but of Clara, my fingers and mind having a rare lyrical connection. It went on page after page. When I stopped, there were ten pages stacked next to the typewriter. As a writer, I had never had such a rush of fluid thought. It was surely more than mere thought.

I leaned back very pleased and was about to read what I had written when I heard Sheila unlocking the door below. Bad timing, I grumbled to myself, noticing only then that the morning had slipped away, the sun already high, leaving my balcony cool and shadowy.

Here came Sheila all right, and with a guest. Yes, I was sure of it, there were heavier steps--a man.

As they entered I straightened my pages and placed them face down under a paper weight. Sheila introduced me to this prissy, bespectacled guy, who looked at first glance, like John Dean. When I shook his hand, I asked him if he was from Massachusetts. He said he was from Kansas. He was dressed very neatly in a three piece tan suit. His name was Ed Lehmann. He really didn't seem like such a bad guy. Sheila had carried in a box of Popeye's fried chicken, her idea of introducing midwesterners to local cuisine. I don't think that she expected to find me at such loose ends, or at home at all maybe. But as it was, there I was, still in my pajamas and robe. She had no choice but to invite me to eat with them.

When we were seated at the table, I noticed Ed staring forlornly at his fried chicken. He asked for a knife and fork. I was already licking my greasy fingers, which made Ed smile. I think he thought I had done so for his amusement.

"Make yourself at home, Ed." I announced, tearing a wing apart with gusto. Ed turned away from me then, realizing that I was not trying to amuse him or offer him the benefits of southern hospitality. Sheila gave me a funny look. She was surprised, as I was myself, at my rudeness.

Ed took no offense, however, and picked up what I assumed had been an earlier line of thought, explaining to Sheila between bites how neighborhood schools relate geographically to everything in their immediate area.

"It's exactly the same patterns Claude Lévi-Strauss found in primitive villages," he said, fixing Sheila with his owly stare. Sheila stopped chewing in order to listen more intently.

"Lévi-Strauss," said Ed, turning to me, "is a structural anthropologist." But before I could respond, he turned back to Sheila and went on elaborating, speaking of "lifestyles" and "environments", drawing diagrams on the table with his finger. I got a picture as he continued of old Lévi-Strauss living it up in Geneva, autographing boxes of his books for shipment to America, throwing down truffles and champagne and sending off big deposits to his Swiss bank. What the hell is this country coming to, I thought, Ed Lehmanns all over the land, diagramming neighborhood lifestyles, sending downtown kids out in search of their environment, encouraging them to collect empty-lot flora and insect life, and any other kind of stuff they can find, most of which they probably steal from somebody's back yard.

In my day, the idea was to get rid of the old environment before you went to school: scrub it off your skin, dig it out of your ears. Manny Tardo, I remember, always brought a lot of environment with him, it jumped out of his well-oiled hair and set off coughing spells all around him; Miss Ziegler would send him home.

When lunch was over, Sheila and Ed were off to an afternoon meeting. As Ed shook my hand, he thanked me for the delicious lunch, which I thought was a Kansas brand of sarcasm until I saw him sincerely rubbing his stomach. Fast food and home cooking are the same to Ed.

"Say, Ed," I yelled as he reached for the door, "if you liked that chicken wait till Sheila cooks red beans for you."

Of course, there was no chance that Sheila was going to cook red beans for Ed or anyone else, especially me. Before Ed could respond, Sheila grabbed his arm and pulled him out of the door. Well, I thought, who has time for home cooking when there are so many lifestyles and environments to round up.

When they were gone I walked over to the window, picked up my pages and began to read. They were not so bad, a bit too earnestly introspective, somewhat static and surprisingly philosophical for me. It could have been a sketch for a short film, in which the camera would move along slowly, showing the terrain, then halting to find this lone figure of Clara, sitting on the levee, panning slowly then in a wide arc, letting the audience imbibe the full significance of her isolation.

It was Clara's lot to be lonely, but I wondered if anyone remembered that she was a celebrity in 1960, when her picture appeared on the cover of *Time* magazine. It was very brief fame that came and went in a flash. And it was freakish, too, for it came about by virtue of the very oddest happenstance. Those who are too young to remember, I think, would find it incredulous, but it is true.

The incident was local and of only local interest, so why *Time* came to feature it is, in the end, unaccountable, a one in a million oddity. The incident itself was odd, even in New Orleans where oddity is often the rule. It was an unprecedented mock coronation in which Clara was crowned queen of the third district, staged solely for the benefit of Philip Rotolo's fledgling candidacy for a seat on the city council. Astounding that so nutty an idea was ever conceived in the first place, and even more astounding that it actually came off. And unbelievable that it was brought to the attention of *Time* magazine. Still, such a thing really happened. I think that even if *Time* had discovered it merely as an amusing little vignette and stuck it down in some little corner, it would have been surprising. But the fact that it was their cover story strains credulity.

Stranger yet is the fact that almost no one in this city remembers. Perhaps, though, not so strange, for in 1960 *Time* magazine was not regular reading for most New Orleanians, who even today customarily ignore national publications, unless they have to do with sports. Beyond baseball scores, weather reports and parade schedules, our citizens, for the most part, are not much interested in news. So it really isn't surprising that not more than a mere handful of our people remember this story. This is certainly true of downtown, and only a few university-based liberals are likely to recall it; and even if they do it is because they find the ninth ward where the election took place so amusing.

It is always the same with *Time* and other outsiders: the same, superior, elbow-nudging, winky, what-next treatment. I remember, for example, how *Time* dealt with one of our governors who went temporarily beserk. When his wife had him committed, *Time* was amused. When he escaped and took to the open road with an exotic dancer, they almost fell over laughing. And more recently, when a certain oversized local district attorney picked up a few suspicious characters in connection with a certain assassination, we were referred to as a raffish, rococo city, and the district attorney himself was dubbed the Jolly Green Giant. Is that really funnier than Massachusetts electing a black senator just because he happened to look like Claude Rains and talked like Adlai Stevenson?

I remember Clara's freakish fame very well, even though I've tried very hard to rub it out of my memory, and if I could from the collective memory. But it would be impossible for me to forget, for it was because of one of my stories that this unlikely coronation took place, and because of my subsequent actions that it was passed on to *Time*. I was a young reporter and very flattered--but I lived to regret it, because I was made a prized dupe and the joke they made for the whole country to laugh at was on me. Chalk it up to youthful ambition and stupidity; I should have seen through their fawning interest. I took no end of kidding from my colleagues at the paper and was treated by my good friend Philip Rotolo with rather stiff, condescending patience when I tried to apologize for embarrassing him in a national publication at the very outset of his political career. I could hardly blame him, and it became a taboo subject between us.

As for Clara, it must have been even more humiliating, she was so shy and reserved. The cover of that issue was designed to be the very broadest kind of joke. One wonders how she was talked into it, I don't know by whom--it wasn't me. It was embarrassing for Ronnie, too, I'm sure, to whom she was already married. I suppose she agreed because she was told that it would help Philip.

Ronnie and Philip have moved on in their careers and might be willing to laugh about the whole thing now, and I can, too, finally see the humor.

Perversely perhaps, as I sat there, just left off reading my little meditation on Clara, I was not thinking of her queenship as funny or odd but as oddly significant. I was still in the spell of my dream. Wasn't there something really queenly about Clara irrespective of that silly incident? Or did the dream make it seem so? Dreams do strike very deep sometimes. I remember Sheila telling me this years ago when she was switching her allegiance from Freud to Jung. Of course, I heard much more about Jung and the collective unconscious than I cared to know, though I found Jung less scandalous and more interesting than Freud. Sheila is nowadays much less the fierce theorist even if she now espouses the views of Lévi-Strauss who is after all fairly harmless when compared to Freud.

But finally I had enough of my dream and my old memories. I closed the typewriter and put it back in the closet. I left the pages neatly stacked on the coffee table under a brass paperweight that was stylized to resemble a Brancusi bird.

The day was drawing down; the light had such a dolorous cast that I suddenly felt unlocated and empty. Why was I so terribly sad when I should have been fervid and passionate, wasn't it spring, if only a brief, preliminary spring? It had come time for me to put myself on the line, or at the very least to find someone to love me.

What a primary creature I had become!

Chapter 16

I was frankly happy that this weekend of strange revisitations was finally over, and welcomed going back to work on Monday. But I had not reckoned with the persistent magic of this vagrant, unscheduled spring, and instead of toiling away in my office, and thereby regaining my sense of practical living, I went drifting off, permitting my staff to take up the slack.

I stood, nearly the whole day, behind my desk, hands dug deep into my pockets, staring out of the window. My young secretary, Bernice Waguespack, came in carrying letters for me to sign and found me thus. She called me several times, I think, before I responded, but I merely turned around and nodded and turned back to the window.

"You're really out of it, aren't you? she asked. As I turned to her, she smiled rather too sweetly with a hint of motherliness.

"Yes--spring fever I guess." I replied and turned again to stare out of the window.

"Is this weather going to last?" she queried, walking over to join me at the window. We both looked out, she with her hands folded behind her back.

"I don't think so," I finally answered, my voice a low drone rising dreamily from my trance. "Winter will come again," I added gloomily.

"I hope not," she said, still sticking by me, knowing how lost I was.

I hoped not, too, but didn't say so because I was drawn again back to my week-end dream which nagged me still with flashes of memories.

"Mrs. Waguespack," I started, unlodging an undue heaviness from my throat, and wondering as I did, why I was calling my secretary Mrs. Waguespack, when I usually called her Bernice. She turned to face me, bringing her feet together in a subtle mockery of a military gesture and also of my uncalled for formality.

"Bernice," I began again, but too stridently this time. My neck stiffened and I broke off.

"Ahem, Bernice, my dear, I wonder if you would be good enough to place a call for me to a Mr. Ronald Hingle."

"Place a call?" She replied with just enough good natured ridicule, still trying to lead me back to the real world.

"Yes, you know--I want to talk to him."

"Oh, I see. Why sure. Should I *place the call* now?"

"Yes, of course, now; why am I talking like this--place a call--I never say place a call, do I?"

"No, you don't; it must be spring fever as you say."

"But you shouldn't be making fun of me."

"I wasn't," she said impishly.

"You weren't?"

"Well, just a little." Bernice is about 25 and kind of cute.

"I see, well, go place the call." I ordered faking gruffness.

Why was I calling Ronnie? I didn't know, certainly not to ask him about Clara, I wouldn't dare. Shouldn't I have been calling Philip instead, who was my best friend. Or had he been my best friend? Of course he was.

Actually I had decided that morning to call Ronnie while I was shaving. I think that I had again dreamed about Clara last night, although if I had, the contents of this dream had already gone back into oblivion. Perhaps the dream was also about Ronnie.

At any rate, I had decided to call Ronnie even though I didn't know why. It was no doubt because of the weather and all of these dreams and because all of this had made me so goofy. I wasn't, of course, going to ask Ronnie about Clara, and I certainly didn't consider for a moment that we would renew our friendship, if we ever had a friendship. What I wanted, I think, was to hear his voice again. It had been over ten years since I had either heard or seen any of my old friends. Just why this had suddenly made me so keenly bereft, I didn't know.

Anyway, I thought that if I could speak to one of them I would no longer feel so lost, and Ronnie seemed the logical and least risky one to call. Moreover, I had invented a legitimate reason for contacting him. I would do a feature on him and all of his developments.

160

I was anxious, nevertheless, and when the phone buzzed, I picked it up with thumping heart.

"I have your call to Mr. Hingle."

I recognized his voice immediately.

"Hello, Ronnie, this is an old friend of yours--Bobby Gomez." There were an interminable few seconds of silence, and I almost faltered. "Philip Rotolo's friend from the ninth ward."

"Why, yes, Bobby, Bobby Gomez, of course, It's been a long time, Bobby."

Suddenly, however, as his voice came rolling back to me over the many years of our separation, I froze with the realization of how totally strange we had grown to each other--I nearly hung up. For a flashing second I could hear myself say, "Jeewhiz, Ronnie, don't you remember me? I know we weren't really close, but we came from the same place, the ninth ward. Let's get together and talk about Philip and old times . . ." But I came to my senses, not before, though, my eyes had moistened with a few gratuitous tears. What a ridiculous, maudlin fool I had almost revealed myself to be. I told him straightway that I wanted to do a story on him as a developer, telling him I was the editor at *Dixie-Roto*. He expressed surprise, I guess I thought there would be a chance he already knew. But now I was on firm ground, my proposal was valid; Ronnie was, after all, the city's most important developer who had already built three or four hotels at the foot of Canal Street.

Of course, Sheila with her Junior League background, had informed me what a travesty Ronnie's hotels were, how they destroyed the *toute ensemble* of the Quarter. Sheila and the *Courier*, a fly-by-night French Quarter rag, had this shitty attitude about progress, and went off half-cocked whenever anybody so much as cut down a thin sapling. The buildings Ronnie had torn down on the fringe of the Quarter were shabby and roach infested anyway.

He accepted immediately as I knew he would, and I set up an appointment for an interview on Friday morning, asking him if my apartment would be convenient. He hesitated but then agreed, asking for my address. It bothered me a little that he hesitated. But why not my apartment, wasn't he my friend? Nevertheless, the prospects of having him over to our apartment caused me some regrets.

After I hung up, I felt very confused about what my motives were. I seemed to remember that Ronnie was a little suspicious of me, and perhaps only accepted me because I was Philip's friend.

At five o'clock as I was finishing up, Sheila called and told me that she and Ed Lehmann were having dinner out; I had expected this.

I got back to the apartment just in time to see the light fade and went directly to the kitchen to heat myself a can of soup. I guess that I could have called one of my friends for dinner, but I couldn't think of anyone. I could have gone to a bar and had a drink, but I don't drink, not alone anyway.

The next morning, when I told Sheila what I had done, she hit the ceiling.

"Why did you have to invite him up here, you haven't seen Ronnie Hingle in ten years?" She was right, of course. I wanted to say it was different because Ronnie was my friend, but I wasn't convinced of that myself. I told her that I would call him and change the place to my office but I didn't. On Tuesday I told her that it was all right, that I didn't expect her to be here when Ronnie came, that I wasn't going to entertain him, just interview him.

She gave a sigh and frowned; she looked frustrated and I could see her point.

"Look at this apartment," she complained. "It's filthy."

"It was clean enough for Ed Lehmann, why not Ronnie Hingle?" I tried my hand at a sardonic smile, but it was wasted on Sheila who was busy reviewing the filth.

She stayed home on Thursday and cleaned the apartment. When I got home she was vacuuming. I went into the kitchen and poured myself some orange juice and waited. When she was finished she looked at me with an expression of triumph and resignation.

"There," she said as she put the vacuum cleaner in the closet. "You're on your own now," and went off to shower. The place looked beautiful.

I could not understand why it was so important to her that the apartment look good for Ronnie. I really did understand, though; Ronnie was one of our old friends who had become very wealthy and that was something in addition to mere success.

When she emerged from her bath I poured us a glass of sherry, and we sat together and talked. It was like old times.

I was standing on my balcony Friday morning when Ronnie arrived; he was in a taxi, I had expected him to drive up in a Jaguar, or a chauffeured Rolls. He was wearing a light pin-stripe suit that smelled of money. He hadn't changed much; he seemed a little thicker in the face but more handsome for it. His slightly lantern jaw fit him better. He appeared not to have gained a pound and was as lithe and graceful as ever. When I opened the door I noticed deep crows feet at the corner of his little round eyes and a little gray at the temples, but otherwise the years had treated him well. As I let him in I must have been gawking, for he was looking at me expectantly. I think I was checking his hands to see if they were pink and rough as they always were in the old days when he worked constantly on his old Plymouth and had to scrub them with mineral spirits, or did I expect to see a lump deforming the shape of his svelte thigh--a grease-encrusted spark plug in his pants pocket? I recovered and offered him a seat, and he sat in one of the butterfly chairs but rather testily, looking around for places to put his hands.

"Interesting chair." His tone possessed the subtlest kind of ridicule, which I tried to ignore.

"Yes, it was designed by Bonet." This caused him to raise his eyebrows, and I knew that the visit had every possibility of being disastrous.

I got my note pad and sat down on the settee opposite him and started the interview. He began to relax. I asked him all the right questions, about his meteoric rise and plans for the future. But all the while, I thought of other questions: what about your old Plymouth, Ronnie, the one you had at Tulane? I didn't, of course, nor did I ask him about Cher, his old girl friend from Tulane who broke his heart, or about how he flunked out of Tulane in a year in Business Administration. (How about this for a headline, Ronnie? TULANE DROP-OUT GIVES CHALLENGE TO HOUSTON BIG MONEY.) Most of all, I wanted to ask him about Clara.

I told Sheila about the interview, but she didn't seem interested. I started to ask her if she remembered Clara, but I didn't; all of this was ancient history anyway.

When my story on Ronnie appeared in *Dixie*, we made it a cover story. I used a fish-eye lens to get a shot of him looking up at the hotels. He called me and thanked me. I didn't, of course, mention his ordeal at Tulane or anything about his relationship with Clara.

Chapter 17

The day that Sheila and I met Clara was indeed a long time ago. What I remember may be pure invention, but I do seem to recall it so clearly. A torrid August afternoon, out on the wild fringes of our familiar city: where must we be, I thought? It had taken Philip at least an hour to drive out here. I was struck by the seeming quietude of the place, and yet there was activity and sound all about us, the wind which whipped our hair into disarray, the shrill whistle of innumerable birds darting about, bustling sounds which came to us from over the levee. There we were, a handful of people, suddenly aware of a vastness and multiplicity our city life had not prepared us for, swarming over the land, flailing away at the underbrush, not knowing what kind of wild creature or lost treasure we would stumble upon.

There was the moment when Sheila and I first laid eyes on Clara, that serene and simple girl who among all of us knew where she was going. And as I reflect upon it, it was all the more amazing that she did since the whole world was steaming in the other direction. There she stood, though, pursuing a childish dream with astounding level-headedness. But if her plan was so blatantly unrealistic, why were we gathered in this pilgrimage, searching for God knows what in this wilderness? Mere feminine curiosity for Sheila, one could suppose, to know what quality of womanhood had spurred Ronnie to such industry and clearmindedness. But she knew immediately that Clara was devoid of devious intent, that Ronnie had not been snared or duped, but blessed, as we were all to be, by a stubborn naiveté that allowed a pure vision. Sheila had decided on the drive over that Clara was ruthlessly decadent, and expected to find a fatuous snob, alternately giving orders and ignoring we who had come to serve her. What prey for Sheila's venom. Instead, we found this placid, if unlettered, Madame De Stael, who was so shyly and calmly grateful for our interest, so disarmingly reticent to speak of what she so fervently felt. We were touched by the way she hesitated to burden us with what she considered a private responsibility, and yet wanted, and in a strange unruffled way, to share it with us.

And what did Ronnie's father, Mr. Charlie, think of Clara? He was there to give advice about the cost and feasibility of restoration, being one who was experienced in all areas of construction. You would think that he, wise, practical boogalee that he was, would have straightway told her what a stupid idea it was to spend money on an old broken house out in the boondocks. And yet, there he was, fairly bowing and scraping, stepping out ahead of Clara in a lively, courtly manner. He climbed all over the old house with his clipboard and pencil. We were amazed by his agility. We heard him from above in the attic knocking on the roof beams. "Solid cypress," he kept yelling and laughed triumphantly whenever he did. "It's all here," he said in the end, handing Clara the clipboard, "I tried to estimate it close, it's going to take a lotta work, Miss." Philip pounded him on his back and congratulated him.

We had all gathered in what was once the living room to drink the cold beer that Philip had brought in an ice chest. I remember hearing gnats, mosquitoes and bees buzzing outside among the leaves. The hot August sun and the beer were buzzing inside of our heads. How strangely silent we were, sitting on the dusty floor, leaning against the walls. Sweat was trickling down from Mr. Charlie's sideburns and streaking along his bony cheeks, he was overheated from all of his climbing and was gulping his beer with great relish. Clara had folded her legs under and sipped quietly, it was her cool presence and the great volume of the room that had this strange effect on us: dreamy speechlessness, summertime stillness. We, Clara excepted, were wondering why we were here, why we felt enchanted, why we were so solemnly quiet when suddenly Mr. Charlie belched loudly, letting out a long, satisfying, "A-A-A-A-A-h!" It was just as well for it was a peacefulness we did not understand.

"Excuse me, Miss," he said to Clara, "if I sit here too long, I'll fall asleep." With that he bolted up and started walking, "Let me see what's left of that front porch." Philip chuckled and started after him. Clara and Ronnie remained sitting, smiling like angels. (It seemed to me that they should be left to their privacy so I got up and gave a lift to Sheila, giving her a quick wink as I pulled.)

"Sheila and I are going to check out the back yard," I said, causing Sheila to give me a fierce look, both the wink and 'checking out' annoyed her. But we were soon out behind the house among weeds that ranged over our heads. "Now, what is this all about, Gomez?" Sheila demanded when I pulled her towards me, as I pecked her cheek and nestled in the crook of her neck. "My goodness!" she hissed and pushed me away, exasperated. "My little bride, " I offered. "Your little bride, you're ridiculous." But she was yielding to my embrace when footsteps from the house above brought us to attention, and Clara's voice drifted down to us. It was an awkward moment, both of us wanting to eavesdrop but neither of us willing to admit it to the other. Clara was wondering why all of the fruit trees had died and why the hack berries thrived. Ronnie didn't know. I looked around at all of the weeds, trying to imagine what Clara started to map out for Ronnie: fig trees over there, peach trees here, etc. We listened as she went on outlining her plans in that wonderfully calm way she had of holding forth. She had enough money, or nearly enough, to purchase the house and restore it. It is such a big house for just one person. But it was not a house to live in economically, it was, in fact, not economical; she would have to furnish it very gradually with antiques and she would have to do all of her own cleaning.

I knew, and I think that Sheila did, too, why she wanted to do all of this. Clara was not at all like a Southern aristocrat or even a Creole aristocrat. She was not planning a life in the grand manner, how could anyone ever imagine her to be. She was just resourceful and patient, and so untemperamental, no Bette Davis twitches, remarkably unglamorous for someone so pretty. No one would imagine her doing anything dramatic and extravagant, and yet this whole plan of hers was extravagant in the extreme. Her reasons were personal. The young are expected to have personal reasons for what they do, but they rarely plan so patiently to get what they want. Being young means to have new fantasies weekly and daily and to suffer with innocent self pity, the morning would bring a fresh cause for a broken heart.

She was only eight; so the funeral, the arrangements for moving and the trip to Dallas seemed to her very well managed events. Her grandma, the Texas one, guided her through all of this, taking her away from both families when the emotions of grief threatened to overcome. They went on long rides in Grandma's Chrysler with the radio turned to a station that played symphonic arrangements of popular songs, and ate in charming, quiet restaurants, attended by waiters wearing black vests and black pants. Delicious seafood, fried shrimp, fried oysters, trout amadine with side orders of French fries, ordered especially for Clara, and ice cream served in tall stem glasses for dessert. They went shopping on Royal Street, stopping in four or five antique shops until they finally bought a small garnet necklace for Clara. "Isn't this lovely, just perfect for you, Claire." Then on to Canal Street, where they bought a blue party dress to go with the necklace. Maison Blanche, the biggest department store in New Orleans, sold a line of high quality milk chocolate, all of it full of chopped pecans. Clara ate enough of it to make her feel overfull and nauseous. She became sluggish and started to trip over her own feet. But Grandma Rawlings knew exactly what to do about that. They went to Walgreen's Drug Store and sat in a booth, ordering a cup of tea for Grandma and an Alka-Seltzer for Clara. The drug store was new, clean and air-conditioned, in minutes Clara felt fine.

The only noticeable change in her since her father's death was a certain moodiness, or was it a new calmness, but one inappropriate for a small child. Or was she depressed and unwilling to talk about it? Her grandma thought it was a good sign, Clara cried only once, and very quietly that one time. No one knew if she was adjusting or not. She seemed more grown up, somehow, quieter and more composed. She did what they suggested, but she had always been a cooperative child. The change was very subtle, a child less prone to whine or fidget, the new Clara was the same manageable child but more like a young lady. She did not laugh or giggle nearly as much. This prompted Grandma to prod her ribs. The tickling got a short little spasmodic giggle from Clara. Grandma smiled and Clara smiled, she seemed to understand why they wanted her to show signs of happiness. Acting like a young lady was fine, but a child should not become morbid.

All of her toys and dolls were forgotten when they moved.
Actually they were packed up and sent to the Salvation Army.
Her mother made a little scene over the forgotten toys, and took
Clara out to buy new ones. She seemed just as pleased with her
new things. She had not shown any disappointment about
losing her old things. She had, in fact, forgotten those things.
What she had not forgotten, though, was the big house that she
had left behind and the youthful father who brought such gaiety
to living in it. This she remembered from year to year, filling her
memory of it with vivid details.

It was not like Sheila to condone this plan of Clara's. Sheila put
great store in saying good-bye to the old world and hello to the new
one. A tradition has to stand on its own bottom, prove itself valid.
What of this old, neglected house, down here in what Algerines call
the Lower Coast? In the fifties everyone considered these old houses
impractical, too big to keep clean without servants, and who could
afford to have servants. They fell down by the dozens up and down
both sides of the river. Only a few were saved by retired doctors,
usually Italian doctors. The *Nouveau Riche*, Sheila called them, and
what was worst, dago nouveau riche. She meant that money was no
good, was dangerous without culture and good breeding. It is hard to
tell what Sheila considered good breeding; her own half-Creole,
half-Jewish mixture meant nothing to her, she said. Lineage was bull
shit, so was race. That one has an enlightened mind, a willingness to
understand and learn, that's important. I knew that line all right.
Liberal snottiness, and assholeness, came of hanging around too
many universities. It was the trick of being facile and contradictory,
for Sheila enjoyed both the privilege of having good breeding and the
privilege of condemning it. Sheila was afraid, she told us, that Dr.
Tamourello if he was not advised correctly would enclose the rear
verandah of an ante-bellum house with jalousie windows, call it a
solarium and load it down with kitchy bric-a-brac, or what was worst,
uproot a one hundred year old oak tree to make room for a kidney
shaped swimming pool, complete with a Florida style cabana, and
paint it, here she made a hideous face and shivered, AQUAMARINE. I
was embarrassed that she spoke this way in front of Philip, but he
laughed heartily, and seemed otherwise pleased to know what to do

and what not to do with an ante-bellum house. It was strange, and the more so, since I knew that Philip thought highly of odd shaped swimming pools and aquamarine cabanas. He was destined to build a big red brick villa in an exclusive lake subdivision.

With Clara that day, Sheila was sisterly, they went walking on the levee, leaving the men to consult with Mr. Charlie about the restoration. Give an old construction man an old house and he becomes ecstatic about its sturdy cypress members. He took us into what we supposed was the dining room and showed us in the corner where the plaster had fallen away what this house was made of. He poked through the lathing with his screw driver, stabbing vigorously at the solid timber beneath. "Do you know what that is?" He looked at Philip, ignored his son Ronnie, and finally at me.

"Do you know what this is?" Nobody answered as he glared and wagged the screw driver at all of us. Still nobody answered, and I became uncomfortable. "That, my boys, is a twelve by twelve, solid cypress. They ain't used twelve by twelves in houses for fifty years, too expensive, it'd cost a fortune today." I had the feeling that he had built houses like that many times, and maybe he had. Through the window I could see Sheila and Clara sitting on the levee, smoking and talking away. As always I wondered what could two people have found to say so much about.

Was it their common Creole heritage, a searching exchange about the Livaudais' and the Duplantiers: so that in just a few minutes, following the families back two or three generations they would find that they were related, or that a famous member of one family had a famous meeting with the famous member of the other? But no. When I asked Sheila later, she told me that they were talking about Clara's job in New York.

Mr. Charlie would have us understand that this old house will be standing long after all of those brick subdivision houses had fallen down. He grew ever more bitter about the carelessness of the Modern Age, the cheap materials and the poor workmanship. He lifted his denim peaked cap to mop his brow, where the ruddy sun worn area of his forehead made a line and began the white skin of that protected by the cap. His brown hair had gone mousy and was plastered down on his bullet head. He was a swamp man turned proletariat and yet was more faithful to the tradition in the Old South than its aristocratic scions. His pride in that old house worked him into a rage, for its promise of permanence could only be appreciated by a workman like himself. Beneath its flutings, its ceiling medallions, its dentured molding, was its twelve by twelve backbone, as tough and enduring as Mr. Charlie's hatred of all surface trim. Strip away the Classicism, the elegant Old South skins, and there would remain the monolithic twelve by twelves, right-angled to each other, post to lentil, vertical to horizontal, the simple grandeur of forces working for strength and support. How was it, I thought, that this most unlettered man, a boogalee, had put his faith in Platonic form, that he preached against the deception of mere appearances with the vehemence of St. Thomas himself. But at this moment, as I was making of Mr. Charlie a Pythagorean metaphysician, and of his screwdriver the cubit of the Golden Mean, Philip sneaked up behind and goosed him. He sprang up with a great HO-HO, did a Bojangles number, and turned on Philip with an expression of raucous good humor. Philip stood his ground, smiling sardonically.

"I've had enough of your bullshit, old man," Philip announced, handing Mr. Charlie an ice cold Dixie beer. And that's exactly what Mr. Charlie wanted. Philip may have believed in the permanence of structures, but he knew that such ideas were beyond the ken of mere men, who must not take themselves or their ideas so seriously.

Mr. Charlie muttered, emitting a ragged guttural laugh, "Dago cocksucker." I was relieved. Ideas, especially great ideas, make fanatics of men. It was a good thing boogalees could be goosed into this realization. Philip was a good politician, he knew how to remind men of ideals of their earthly bodies. A few beers, said Philip, and a few laughs.

I looked up just as Sheila and Clara came walking down the levee. Sheila was swinging her arms gaily, bounding along as her momentum carried her down; she laughed with an open mouth and talked with her head lifted upward as one talked under great skies of snowy cumulous clouds along the banks of wide majestic rivers. Clara's arms were at her side, as she measured her descent, her head turned down, but even from this distance I could tell that she was smiling. They seemed fast friends, and their friendship filled me with a big summertime joy.

Is my memory of this day distorted? Had we indeed locked ourselves in such heart-warming, rousing companionship, feeling the adventure and thrill of this project, of bringing this ruin of a house back to its former brilliant life? Perhaps not, but it seemed so. Who can tell how glorious was youth when viewed from the battered vision of middle age. In New Orleans we drink cold beer on hot August days until our minds become squeaky and our spirits dream-sodden; we glaze out through bleary eyes finding the world soft and comfortable, and we will agree to any proposed plan, seeing in the future, endless hot summer days of sweet companionship with ice cold beer to make us perspire freely. To sweat and dream, no wonder that most of these old houses have fallen down. But this was not so of Clara, who was half-Texan, and part-Yankee. She had been lured back to this easy, graceful city, but she knew that there was work to be done, business to be transacted. What of gracious culture her Creole father had given her softened her brown eyes and chestnut hair, but she avoided excesses of relaxation. Behind her sweet sobriety sparked the Texas talent for building empires and drilling wild-cat wells, even if she and other Texans know less of what should be done with their fortunes than we drunken New Orleanians; she knew the importance of getting the job done.

We were like ten year olds building a club house, for whatever secretive reasons ten year olds build club houses. What more did we need than ourselves? A construction man, Mr. Charlie, a legal advisor, Philip, who planned to go to Law School at Loyola, a historian, Sheila of noble Creole blood, Clara and Ronnie, project director and assistant project director, and me, chronicler so that those of succeeding generations would not forget what we did.

The other day, when I asked her, Sheila claimed that she did not remember any of this. It was all very well for her to pretend this, since she has had such success as a special educator, writing proposals, running from this school to that one, checking to see if there is enough of the environment stuff strewn about the buildings to impress the feds, who come inspecting, (they want to make absolutely sure that the level of creative enterprise is high enough to warrant the spending of so much of the taxpayers' money.) She had taken possession of her importance, her fortyish authority, and was simply too busy to remember whatever foolishness she might have been up to in her adolescence. Clara was a sweet girl, she said. She hoped that Clara and Ronnie were doing well. She either did not know or chose to ignore the fact that Ronnie and Clara have been divorced for almost three years, and that Ronnie was married again to Cynthia Lyles, a Junior Leaguer presently serving as Director of the Vieux Carre Commission, and interestingly enough, a Newcomb graduate in Fine Arts. I had seen her on TV, introduced as Cynthia Lyles Hingle; she was not more than twenty-five and looked like Jinx Faulkenberg, with the athletic glamour of a chorus girl. She was too young to have known Cher at Newcomb, and yet I could not help wondering if Ronnie and Cher did not now move in the same social circles. But even if they did, I don't suppose that either one of them would likely make anything of it. It is only sentimentalists like myself who constantly brace themselves against the emotional excitement of meeting old friends, especially old girl friends. It's hard for me, even now, not to be titillated when I have a passing thought of Gloria Schwartz, who was my first real date and who gave me my first kiss. I don't count the alley experimentation with Dorothy Willard, we were both children and knew hardly anything of real love.

"Why are you asking all of these questions?" Sheila asked, "you're trying to make something out of Clara and her old house, aren't you?"

"I sketched a few things for a feature."

"Yes, I know, you left them out, and I glanced through them. It looked like something a little more ambitious than a feature."

"Not really, but Clara did make the cover of *Time*, remember?"

"Jesus Christ, Bobby, you can't be serious. That was a joke. But I guess it would make a good feature. Or maybe you could just dig up that issue and use a shot of the cover for the 'Pictures Out of the Past' section."

She was sitting on our long contemporary couch with her feet up on the coffee table as we talked. Her arms were folded, and she was screwing her head around, arching her brows and narrowing her eyes. All of which made me self-conscious.

"Why are you looking at me like that?" I finally asked.

"How am I looking at you?"

"Like I'm a psychiatric patient."

"I'm sorry, I was just curious about what's going on in your mind lately. You seem restless."

"Restless?"

"Yes, restless and preoccupied, I think you're going through middle life crises."

"Sheila, don't analyze me, please."

"I'm not analyzing you, but you are middle age you know, and you're very worked up which isn't very normal for you."

"I'm not worked up; I don't know what you're talking about."

"I'm talking about how you stalk around here lately. Like right now. Stop pacing and sit down."

I stopped pacing but didn't sit down. She smiled at me. "That's better. Now tell me, don't you have some crazy idea about writing a book about Clara?"

"Maybe I do, and if I do, what would be crazy about it? After all, I'm a journalist, I write for a living. It's not like I'm Sam the Plumber."

"Who's Sam the Plumber?"

"Nobody, I made him up, but you get my point."

I didn't want to explain it to her. But it's just as well, because she had to go. Another meeting.

Chapter 18

*S*houldn't I have complained about Sheila reading my sketch? I didn't, of course, since I had left it out knowing or hoping that she would read it. And how would it have been, also, if it were known how ridiculously flattered I felt that she even read it, or how absolutely exhilarated I became when she said it was more ambitious than a feature. Me, ambitious in Sheila's eyes? Did I think--grasping at straws--that the word "ambitious" referred perhaps to a perceived high level of literary quality. Surely, though, she referred instead to the inflated importance that I, the writer, intended in the very manner in which I wrote the piece--in short to my grandiosity.

Why didn't I ask her outright and directly what she thought of it as literature, instead of trying to justify my assumed intention to write a novel about Clara, which I had no intention at all of writing. It was surely the height of something--my defensiveness, my immaturity, my passive aggressiveness. How easily indeed did I slip into glum recalcitrance with my wife, who had demonstrated many times and in so many ways, a willingness to discuss openly and honestly even the most stupid ideas.

But it was true, I could not tell even Sheila, good ole pal that she no doubt would have proven herself to be, just how proud I was of this little sketch. Nor could I have revealed that I had considered using Clara's story for a novel, however fleetingly. In fact, if she were not a real person, and had I invented her out of whole cloth, who could tell?

I had my wits, though, and my very formidable insecurity, and did not even for a moment seriously consider writing such a novel. This sketch was only eleven pages and had exhausted my meager literary inventiveness; the vast journey through a hundred and sixty thousand words and three hundred pages was out of the question.

But if these pages were so meager why was I clinging to them as though they were the lost fragment of a wreaked hull. I began to read them with fervor, pronouncing each word to myself.

Was I lost, as Ronnie was when he came upon Clara sitting upon the levee, reaching out to her, claiming her as my private vision? Had not Sheila detected in these pages the ruminations of a man drifting without direction, yearning for literary glory? I was digging deeper and deeper, trying to find solid ground. I wanted to think that Sheila meant to encourage me, but it seems obvious that she was warning me not to tear my life apart to examine it.

The edges of these few pages were already fuzzy from handling and would no doubt be frayed before this long morning was over. Something had happened with the arrival of that brief little spring--something more than my usual enchantment. I had seen Clara seated on the sloping earth of the levee like some eternally peaceful goddess, and wondered what could anyone ask of such a girl? She seemed eternal, forging harmony and forgiveness between earth and sky; here, at least, I knew there would be no violence unleased upon earth from an angry, passionate heaven. I saw her clearly with the wind blowing against her cheek, the gulls circling above her, draughting sea designs. It was a vision in which I could find solace, knowing that there was, after all, a source of inner peace in the world. And it came to me that Clara's promise to herself and its fulfillment was the gratuity from which Ronnie, Philip and I had drawn favor: Ronnie, who was leading us into the future, Philip, lately mentioned for a cabinet post in Washington, and me, Robert Gomez, feature editor of *Dixie-Roto*, I, too, owe something to Clara.

And yet I don't think Philip, or even Ronnie, who had been her husband, thinks very much about Clara anymore. My own memory of her, in fact, had been thrown into oblivion before it had been resurrected---dare I say miraculously--by of a vivid dream.

I began to read the pages again--one last time:

> Whenever I think of Clara, it is as she must have looked that mild April morning in 1951 when Ronnie came upon her sitting on the levee before her father's old house............

On Sunday, winter returned, just as I had predicted it would. It would be three weeks before the true spring would begin, and with it the unexpected breaking up of my life.

Part Two

Chapter 1

"There's no art to find the mind's construction in the face."
W. Shakespeare

February 1975 - Three weeks before Mardi Gras.

*W*hen something finally does break in our lives, we suddenly realize how impossible it was for us to have read what must have been a clear and peculiar pattern. In hindsight, however, we may fool ourselves in thinking that we saw the certain signs of an unexpected shift in events announcing itself.

In any case, all seemed normal for Sheila and me that February. The brief spring passed and we returned to the usual kind of bleak weather, pale streaking currents of wind blighting our greenery, chilling our tropical souls one last time; and rain, not the fresh clear downpourings of June, but the cold, lethargic, inevitable drippings, the day and night long, from a dreary winter sky. And if we had not been numbed sufficiently by what seemed endless gray days, we surely must have been, even more so as I look back, by the tedium of an unfulfilling marriage.

Not that I thought so at the time. Indeed, everything in our lives was on a steady course, and there seemed nothing at all to fear. We had both achieved what could be called local success, and did not need to add anything to a life that brought in a regular bounty of ordinary and reliable satisfaction. I should say *I* did not think such additions were necessary. As it turned out, Sheila was not nearly so content as I thought I was, and, in fact, I wasn't either.

Nevertheless, except for a few rankles here and there, and my new restlessness which Sheila deemed significant, I detected nothing that would have tempted me to predict anything but steady progress and inevitable longevity for our marriage.

179

But things did change for us, and they started to change, in my way of calculating, that drunken night at Brennan's. We had gotten drunk in public places before, but not nearly so drunk and out of hand as on this particular night, although I can't say that any of us there took special notice of this unprecedented degree of drunkenness. Now, however, I see very clearly how it was, the sudden but imperceptible letting go of old restraints, my theory being very precise. Just one more martini than we could really handle, and presto--the worm turned. It is perfectly true, though, that this one-martini-too-many theory of mine could be thought highly imaginative and even exotic considered in the light of what really took place that night. I'll admit, it wasn't all that obvious. I myself did not come to this conclusion until the following weekend when we attended the Beaux Art Ball at the Royal Sonesta Hotel. It was only then that I realized how sadly lacking our marriage was.

If it is true that portentous events imprint themselves on our memory, I think my theory is right, for I have a vivid memory of that night.

Dining at Brennan's was nothing unusual for us. It is customary to do so during the dreary days of February. We make do as we look forward to brighter days, with the greenery of Brennan's patio, which is roofed over with glass during the winter months.

On the night in question, we were guests of Margaret Joubert, one of Sheila's colleagues, and her husband Louis. Their invitation was especially welcome, for it had been raining softly and quietly for three days and we were depressed because of our confinement. It was more than we could bear, waiting for the dim light to grow even dimmer at the close of each day, when the slow, trickling rain would resolve into a mist and lure us to our French window to watch the great northern wind rolling the gray clouds southward. For these three days the sun had not so much as glimmered through with even a partial light. It was just three weeks before Mardi Gras, and all of this rain made me think that the make-shift stands that the residents of St. Charles Avenue usually erected along the parade route would warp and need rebuilding before the parades would begin.

For me at least, the prospects of dining with Margaret and Louis were only mildly pleasant. They sat on the New Orleans Council for Children's Art, Margaret being its director.

I liked Louis well enough, he was a good natured Cajun who always had a good east Texas dirty joke for me, and was otherwise warm and friendly, like all Cajuns. Margaret, I found dull; she was from Iowa and spoke brassily and endlessly of the politics of writing proposals for creative programs for our underprivileged downtown kids. She had more dedication than Sheila.

Don't ask me why she and Louis were married to each other: He was from Lafayette, Louisiana, heart of Cajun country; she was from Iowa, heart of God knows what. Happily, however, they were rooted to the earth, devoid of neurosis and able to laugh at everything, including themselves.

Margaret told us of still another proposal, the new program would have the uniqueness of educating the imagination and sensibilities. She spoke of the worn out, hung up, stodgy training of the mind. What are the minds of our children--waste paper baskets to be filled up with disconnected scraps of information? Was it my own littered mind she spoke of? Heaven knows, I have junked up my brain with countless items of sheer uselessness. Her blood fairly boiled over the intransigent clunkiness of traditional education. It is hard to imagine, listening to her, that she was a very normal, practical woman. She seemed to have a religious fanaticism about the creativity of children. If only they could be allowed to be free, the teachers should let them experiment. When she spoke this way she flipped out her hands as if she was shooing chickens. Of shooing chickens, I think she knew quite a lot, being the kind of squarish, raw boned farm girl from Iowa who could be trusted with any kind of practical task. Of art, I was certain that she had not a clue.

Louis cared nothing for art or creation and would modestly admit it if you asked. He was a geologist and served on the council as chairman of the entertainment committee. Cajuns throw the best parties; they know enough of despair and will drink heavily and cook up a good gumbo if they feel the least little sadness. They know that you can only hope to stay a step or two ahead of your old enemy.

Louis made our dinner very pleasant, he ordered up one martini after another; he knew that with enough of the juice we would begin to relax and have a good time, even in a place as stiff and phony as Brennan's beautiful green patio. It has every appearance of tropical enchantment, tier upon tier of hanging fern, a jungle of potted palms set all about between the tables which are levitated on slender wrought iron supports, the chairs are articulated with the same calligraphic metal. It is only after you enter that you become aware of how flat and exactly like an architectural rendering the space really is, you and others trying to strike elegant poses, to appear as much like the fashion plates who habitat such renderings.

But after two martinis the picture changed. I demanded that the waiter move the palm that nettled my hair and tickled my ear. He dropped the obsequious smile and gave me a sincere one, he knew. He snapped his finger to beckon a bus boy, "Get this thing out of here." Our neighbors exchanged silly, knowing smiles. They knew, too.

Louis was more tickled than anyone else, "Don't like the trees, heh, boy?" But Margaret was glum, this was her favorite restaurant, not because of the food, being midwestern she couldn't tell good food from bad. Sheila laughed with Louis and at the same time flashed disapproving eyes in my direction. The waiter offered the menus, but Louis sent him back for a third round of martinis. This third one did it for Margaret. She started talking fast and loud, going on about how crazy and fun loving people from New 'Arleens' were, how it is a wonder anything gets done, etc. When Margaret laughed, she was some teeth and more gums, a wet, healthy, pink mouth. Not even Louis' tan firmness could match the pinkish glow of Margaret's health. She would never understand either New 'Arleens' or art, and yet she had taken both of them unto her heart.

And then to my great misfortune Sheila got drunk, and very surprisingly decided to give me away to our friends. Usually when drink works adversely on Sheila she becomes morose and not hostile, but this night was to be different in every way, and my dear wife proceeded to blind side me. I had never known her to do this, her prey when she was bad tempered was more typically someone remote and worthier than myself.

How could I have known also that it was my secret literary ambitions that she would light upon.

"Listen," she announced, casting her eyes about with a sniggering little smile. "Shall I tell you what Gomez here has been up to?" Of course I couldn't imagine what she was referring to, and neither could Louis who was looking around for our waiter.

"For one thing, hon," said Louis, "he's getting drunk. and for another, he's getting ready to take an ax to these trees." Cajuns just love it when their friends get reckless and threaten to bust up the place.

"No, no," Sheila replied, batting her glowing eyes, "I mean what he's doing at home." She reached over and seized Louis' hand to insure that he get her meaning.

Louis' eyes widened with intrigue, "What's he doing, cher?"

"Yeah," I put in impatiently, "what am I doing?"

She ignored me, speaking directly to Louis, "He's writing a book!"

"Uh-ooooh," Louis hooped, rolling his eyes; but you could tell he was disappointed--what did an old Cajun know about writing books.

"He's writing a book about a queen," Sheila continued, her eyes and smile full of irreverent glee, but Louis was stopped cold. He really didn't know what Sheila was up to. Margaret, however, was not markedly interested.

I, of course, was struck dumb and generally flabbergasted, but also inwardly braced that this little group would think that I was writing a book.

"Oh, Bobby," entreated Margaret, "Really? A book about a queen? Don't tell me--Marie Antoinette, right?" A fair enough guess for a midwesterner, given their romantic notions about this old French city.

"Ho-ho-ho-ho," yodeled Sheila. Margaret jumped up and down on her chair.

"A Mardi Gras queen!" More ho-ho's from Sheila, and I tried to kick her under the table. Margaret gave up.

"Tell me, Bobby, this sounds so interesting."

"Don't ask him, Margaret, he's keeping it a secret, ask me."

"I don't care who tells me, tell me, Sheila," she patted my hand. "You shouldn't keep this a secret, Bobby, If I were writing a book . . ."

"Shall I tell her, Bobby?"

"I don't care what you do, Sheila, this is your game."

"Gomez is writing a book about a ninth-ward queen!"

I didn't know what Sheila was up to either. I had never seen her so obviously and publicly out-of-order. Ordinarily when Sheila treated me with disrespect, it was clear that she was only kidding. I was being kidded, all right, but it looked for all the world as if she was doing so seriously and with relish. She was swaying a bit, shaking her head as she talked and had brushed away a few strands of her hair which had fallen over her face.

But, when I looked closely, I could tell that Sheila wasn't really looking at me, and that I shouldn't take this banter about my writing a book personally. My literary efforts held no fascination for Sheila, and were to me merely my springtime arousal, not that a novel about Clara's story was such a bad idea.

"Clara, my dear," I declared, pointing my finger at Sheila authoritatively, "was only a ninth-ward queen, but a queen nonetheless, and I wager her story could ring a bell in this city's old collective unconscious. As an old Jungian you surely would agree."

"I don't know what the hell you're talking about," she replied disinterestedly, looking down into her empty martini glass.

"Who is this Clara?" Margaret chimed.

"Gomez' queen, Margaret." Sheila grunted, turning her Martini glass upside down.

"Well?" Margaret asked, making eyes and squeezing my hand.

"Well, what? I replied innocently.

"Are you going to tell us her story?"

"Sure he is." Sheila volunteered, "He's got her made out to be a regular DuMaurier Rebecca."

"Oh, stop ridiculing, Sheila," Margaret scolded.

Actually my drunkenness had reached a blissful stage--I felt triumphant and ready for anything.

The waiter returned with the menus, and this time I sent him back for more martinis. If Gomez was going to tell his friends a story, they would have to wait for their food, and risk serious drunkenness. The waiter didn't look pleased, the place was packed, and people were waiting for tables.

When the martinis arrived, I pulled my chair up closer to the table and spread my napkin out smooth and flat, a formality which got the attention of the other three, even Sheila perked up. Gomez was going to tell all. Louis and Sheila lit up cigarettes, Margaret started to wiggle her ass on her seat like a school girl getting ready for her teacher to begin the lesson.

"Back in the fifties," I began in my best barroom style of narration.

There was a break in the story when the waiter came up again and made us understand that we had to order.

"O.K.," I said, and told him to bring crawfish etouffee all around and a bottle of good Sauterne.

"No etouffee," he said, casting a suspicious look at Louis. We all realized that the waiter was also Cajun, how else would he have known to connect Louis with etouffee. But you would have never known, because he was effecting a Parisian prissiness. A Cajun homosexual is a rare creature, but there he was, sniffing and checking his manicure. Louis curled his lip in disgust, and I changed the order to Coquille St. Jacques. He nodded, wrote it down and pranced off, rocking his narrow hips.

It was interesting that my listeners were engrossed in my story. They seemed sober somehow, and were taking small meditative bites of their Coquille St. Jacques. On I rolled, telling the tale, it seemed to me, better than it could be told in a book. The fag Cajun waiter cleared the table and asked if we wanted a check. "Not yet," I said, checking around and getting nods from the others. I ordered a glacé something or other for dessert and coffee. Louis called him back and added four brandies to the order. "Oui, Monsieur," he was really pissed, the fruit. Louis yelled something to him in patois, Cajun French which caused him to scamper along too fast; he confounded an oncoming waiter and hipped the corner of another table, bouncing dishes and glasses. Louis yelped and banged the table. There is no ire like that of one Cajun for another.

But the story continued, Sheila and Louis were chain smoking, Margaret urged me on with humming, cooing expletives: M-m-m-m, wow, etc. They were in the palm of my hand, and nobody was more surprised than I.

I had withheld the names of the characters, since this was a real story about real people. I called Ronnie the hero or the protagonist, Clara the queen or the girl from New York, Philip an Italian boy from downtown, Cher the Newcomb deb, Sheila and I, of course, by our real names; and I left out the parts about Sheila's family and mine, this is to say, Bernie and Bessie, Mama Gomez, and my unknown real parents, and so forth, Mr. Charlie being the hero's father, and Miss Thelma, his mother.

But there was no lack of color in my spinning of the tale. Ninth-ward life in the early fifties I painted vividly, the wonderful mix of the place, rich with poor, black, tan, yellow and white habitating in close proximity.

Today the ninth ward is called Bywater, and it has gone completely black. The whites have all moved out to Metairie, a lily white suburb in Jefferson Parish. No one goes down there anymore. If they did, they would see that it is not any longer of a piece: some of the shot-guns are painted unusual colors, salmon pink, bright yellow, magenta; in the old days it was always white with dark green trim. Some have been bricked up in front with blond or gray decorator bricks and fitted with aluminum windows, the old blind shutters and low cypress steps having been removed. Corner groceries and bars have been remodeled into residences; these have the strangest appearance, the work of jack-leg carpenters using any assortment of materials: cinder blocks, jalousie windows, exterior paneling, aluminum awning, all made to fit together in the best cubist tradition of juxtaposition. On the streets big luxury cars are crammed in bumper to grill; there are no driveways or garages in the ninth ward. All manners of fast food packaging litter the streets and bricked banquettes, fried chicken buckets, burger wrappers, French fry bags, plastic six pack rings. HUD, the federal agency has had its day down here, one is reminded of the barbarians in Ancient Rome, quarrying stones from the Coliseum to build primitive hovels.

We could stall no longer, the restaurant was empty, but our waiter kept a respectful distance. When we beckoned him over, he came swiftly, bowing and smiling, asking if Messieurs and Mesdames enjoyed their dinner. Louis paid him with his credit card, but tipped him with two crisp twenty dollar bills. He was so pleased and surprised that he forgot himself and winked at Louis. Oops! It could have been trouble, but Louis was looking the other way.

The temperature was in the low thirties, and the wind howled down the narrow streets. We huddled together and averted our faces, trying to yell to each other through shivering lips. Where to go now was the question, it was only eleven o'clock. Louis leaped out ahead, turned and started to walk backwards, barking orders like a drum major. To the Napoleon House! This was an old fashioned crowd, we four; youngsters did not go to French Quarter bars like the

Napoleon House, such places are relics of the more pleasant bohemian days of the fifties when college kids roamed the Quarter in search of what they quaintly called coffee shops, but were actually old neighborhood bars. As the college kids came in greater numbers the regulars removed to bars on the fringes of the Quarter. The owners put in a hi-fi phonograph, bought a stack of classical and semi-classical records, added a table with a built-in chessboard, and began to thrive again.

The paintings on the old plaster walls looked dreary and tired, they were all crooked, tilted this way and that, a thick film of grease and dirt blurred their surface, they were unattended and looked at--all these years. I judged them now in my cranky middle age as bad to terrible. I used to think that they were hot stuff, especially the pink abstraction; now I knew: pink is a terrible color for abstract paintings.

Old faithful Tiger waddled up to take our order. Tiger had gotten rounder with the years. Sheila and I greeted him warmly, that Tiger recognize us as two of the old guard was important, like Picasso and Gertie Stein come back to Cabaret Voltaire. Tiger acknowledged us, and we exchanged pleasantries about old times. I didn't think that Tiger knew us from Adam, he was like the old Chimpanzee in Audubon Zoo, many pass his way, but it was always very brief, too brief for real friendship. Do you remember Sal, Tiger? Oh, yeah, he was in here last week. He was? Sure was, ha, ha, he looks good, too, ha ha. And he took our order and waddled off. Sal Messina has been living in San Francisco for ten years; but I would not doubt that Tiger saw him last week, he sees many of us old friends, years are like weeks to old friends. Good old Chimp, always there, in the same old cage.

Margaret asked me to finish the story, but I declined. Sheila and Louis were talking about the Beaux Art Ball, laughing their heads off about the kind of costumes they would wear. Louis wanted to go as Bonnie if Sheila would go as Clyde. He put on lipstick, fluffed his imaginary curls, mowed down the sheriff and his deputies. They laughed and laughed. My feelings were hurt, I really did want to finish the story, but Gomez wanted rapt attention and nothing less. If they begged me, maybe.

Margaret joined in the fun, thinking up crazy costumes. "What if I go as the Statue of Liberty, smoking a cigar." Midwesterners cannot tell jokes, they know nothing of irony, much less madness;

they think up something illogical and try to palm it off as a joke, not realizing that a joke must have a twist that curves down and then up, it risks madness in order to achieve joy.

I was really glum now, alone and disappointed, a story must have an ending once it has begun. But what was I going to do with this group? I had not been consulted about attending the ball, but I knew why they had decided to go. It was the spirit of Carnival, the old collective unconscious, this miserable weather and the liquor. The Viennese with their bizarre, labyrinthine minds were not nearly so unconscious as we New Orleanians. Had Carl Jung been a resident of this city, he would have seen nothing startling or unique about the collective unconscious, up goes under here and under goes top, and nothing is amiss.

And around and around went my head. Louis kept ordering up the drinks, and my imagination began to soar. It came to me that Clara's queenship was more than mere political shenanigans, even in New Orleans, a city which after all only pretends to be democratic. Clara's image loomed before me like Banquo's sons before Mac Beth, and I saw her privileged succession, the deeper layers of her royalty, of Louis XIV, her patriarchal lineage, and the matriarchs from which she derived: Athena Parthenos the Protectress, the White Goddess of Chartres and the Venus of Willendorf. That's why I should write about her, I suddenly wished to declare. But as I came to myself I saw that my companions were huddled in drunken laughter, and I was very much alone with my thoughts. Nevertheless, Clara was, as I now vividly saw it, the very manifestation of Our Lady of Prompt Succor, the city's patron saint to whom all of us go for comfort and help with our miseries and tragedies and are soothed, in spite of our wanton indulgences. Were not Clara and Our Lady, I recklessly concluded, the Big Tit?

A new drink was set down before me, and I drained it off. Sure, I thought, Clara and Our Lady, it's so obvious. Like I said, an ordinary cab driver knew this. What the hell did Carl Jung know about contradictions compared to New Orleans cab drivers? But should I say all of this if I write this book? Would not my theme be gutted and all of its hidden secrets revealed? The reader would know as much as me, the writer!

The pink abstract painting swam before my eyes, floating softly, as in the old days. We had many drinks here, and I was really bombed as they said in the--when? The seventies, the sixties, the fifties? As I pondered I thought maybe a bad painting held a greater secret than a good one. Maybe--my eyes floated, my mind drifted; Tiger was looking over at me smiling--he did know me! Did he also know Mama Gomez and my real unknown parents? Was he really my uncle and was too embarrassed to tell me?

The next week the parades began, and we all hoped for good weather when the first fleecy clouds of spring would come drifting across an immaculate cerulean sky. Margaret had made up her mind, she was going to the Beaux Arts Ball as Cleopatra, Queen of the Nile.

Chapter 2

*J*ust why we attended the Beaux Arts Ball was a mystery. It's nothing more than a collegiate dance, there is nothing to gain for mature and successful citizens by attending. Tulane's students of architecture sponsor this affair and have patented it after the Beaux Arts Ball in Paris of scandalous fame. This ball, however, has never been scandalous but rather tame and pleasantly fashionable. The costumes are usually rented and nothing like the wild funky inventions of street maskers on Mardi Gras. It is the only Mardi Gras ball at which all of the maskers may dance. At important balls, such as Rex and Comus, only members are so privileged, the rest watch.

So, you see, it is poorly considered and never attended by anyone of social prominence--a lot of snotty uptown kids, upstart professional types, lawyers, college teachers, architects of course, no one really important. There is no prestige in getting invitations, ours were provided by Murray Waguespack, my secretary's husband and a young architect. If you are interested you can crash without an invitation.

Ronnie was, of course, too wealthy and too well-married to be seen at this ball, likewise Cher, if she still resides in New Orleans. Of Clara, I could not say, as Ronnie's ex, she was certainly entitled to much better, but I don't remember that she was much of a socialite. It has been many years since anyone has seen her. Had not Bessie married a common Jewish- Cajun like Bernie, and had Sheila married better than she did, they, too, would be entitled to better, the best in fact. As it is, Bessie's marriage was tantamount to a defection to a lower station. You see how it is, a matter of money and old family tradition, but mostly a matter of money.

Come to think of it, how could I have written a book about Clara, not knowing her whereabouts, or about Ronnie who would have been my hero.

It comes from not doing enough research, of not having a proper outline.

Our decision to attend could be regarded as the function of the season, that is, Carnival, since it was made in such a drunken manner, stunned as we probably were by the cold winds of winter and detecting in some mindless, primordial way the first distant stirring of the coming spring.

Ordinarily, in my sobriety, I try to avoid Mardi Gras. It is not within my usual purview to accommodate the kind of outrageousness that attends Carnival. Perfectly normal people go nuts and behave without modesty or dignity in public streets. Amazing transformations are witnessed, feet grow cloven, eyes slant and gleam, lips swell to fullness, glistening with lewd saliva. Men dress up like women, law abiding citizens like thieves, hard working businessmen take off their clothes and beat tom-toms like savages. The rich show open contempt for the poor and sling bogus coins and cheap trinkets to the greedy masses, who shamelessly fight and claw each other for this worthless loot. I have seen children and old women, struggling against one another, snarling like weasels, ready to maim. Doesn't everyone, in fact, in their savage heart covet shining useless things and stand ready to kill for them?

And yet, I suppose, we decided to go to the Beaux Arts Ball for the most innocent of reasons, to have fun perhaps, and not at all as I was prompted to speculate to be led down a strange new path in some arcanely designing way. I say this in spite of the fact that my attendance at this ball changed my life drastically. I would like to believe that I was aware that our decision to attend was still another indicator, more evidence that the pattern had been ruptured, and that our marriage was unraveling. But in all honesty I didn't have an inkling.

In fact, not even when it happened did I realize that my life would never be the same. It wasn't until the next morning when I began to tremble with--what? Was it fear or joy?

I remember very well, it was eight-fifteen in the morning. I was sitting at my eastward French window, looking out at the gray February sky. From this vantage point the roof tops of the French Quarter could be mistaken for the Latin Quarter in Paris, if one were not too familiar with Paris, as I wasn't, and if one were dreamy, which I was. A V-formation of dos-gris ducks made their way across the barren sky, seemingly pumping their wings in slow motion. I sat there, of course, not with the dewy drowsiness of an early riser, but achey-headed and numb-tired. We had returned from the ball but an hour hence. My eyes stung and blinked from want of sleep; I knew without aid of a mirror that they were red-rimmed, hollow and glassy. I was waiting for the aspirins I had just swallowed to take effect.

A stranger walking into this room would have had some need of an explanation at the sight of me. I wore skin tight white leotards, black military boots, a royal blue velvet vest over a silken, blousey sleeved shirt; a waxen lock of my hair was curved into a big "C" and laid on my forehead. I was rocking the Hepplewhite chair that I sat on, back on its hind legs, pushing off the wall for balance, now and again, with one booted leg. And I was frankly admiring this svelte leg, knowing full well that this member whenever it would be unsleeved of said Empire attire was spindly and had the slightest tendency toward bowness. But I had other reasons for believing that I possessed a well-shaped Napoleonic leg, and although the costume itself did the trick, the illusion was sharpened immeasurably by the image I entertained of Bernice Waguespack's face. I perused that face with eidetic clarity; the slender up-turned nose which pulled the upper lip to a shallow soft apex, revealing a row of white teeth where the lip had been lifted by the tilt of the nose; this and her wide-open blue eyes gave her face a delicate expectancy, a virginal vulnerability. The nostrils quivered, the eyes darted, an expression at once helpless and passionate. I remember those eyes going cross and closing tight right before I kissed her. I was leaning against the bricked patio wall in the Royal Sonesta Hotel. An empty, wintry patio it was, the wind whistling over the roof tops above us. We had danced out there, sidling and walk-dance stepping the way drunken passionate couples did when they wanted to be far from the maddening crowd so that they could embrace and kiss.

I had asked Bernice to dance out of duty, since she was my secretary and colleague. We danced very close, so close we thought because the other dancers were pushing us together. We barely moved in the tiny space allowed us. But when the dance was over we did not pull apart, again because we were being pushed together. We talked as two strangers, as shyly as two teenagers newly met, our faces inches apart, eyes welded. How have you been? Fine. You? O.K. Silence. Nice dance. Yeah. Silence, Well? We who saw each other five days a week and had never hesitated a moment in any other conversation before this. The music started again. Dance? O.K. And we started to weave through the throng towards the patio, stopping along the way to press closer, a few inadvertent murmurs, full of meaning, but not a word.

She fell against me with her slender body, pressing and directing her pelvis. It was a kiss without reserve. Mouth open, tongue deep.

Bernice, though not a raving beauty, has her pretty days. Last night she was costumed as duBarry or dePompadour in a full Rococo blond wig with a coiled lock falling along her narrow cheek, a black beauty mark, a hoop skirt which ballooned out behind her as we embraced; a tricky matter to find her buttocks among all these satin billows, but I did, with her help. How resourceful was passion that when hands searched for ass and lost their way, ass found hands. There were more kisses and more hunting around among folds, pleats, tucks, to find other sensitive parts. In street clothes there is no telling what could have been done, as it was, the intricate paraphernalia of both costumes defeated us, pants without fly, etc. Before we went back in to the dance I looked into her eyes and said quite sincerely, "Can I see you again?" Her eyes twinkled with amusement. "Yes, as a matter of fact, on Monday morning." These were our parting words.

We would indeed see each other come Monday morning, the question was: what would we do? My headache was gone. The day was grayer yet, the wind whipped in across my balcony, rattling the windows. Two pigeons struggling to keep a steady course went careening and disappeared over the roof tops. Footfalls and muffled voices ascended from the street below, a pack of tourists braving the weather, searching for whatever action there was in the Quarter at eight-thirty in the morning.

Should I not have felt guilty about Bernice? I didn't, I felt wonderfully light hearted and exhilarated. Bernice was 25, I, 48; why should not a man who was 48 feel wonderful for having kissed a girl of 25. I did, but I also wondered if the girl was not at that moment full of regret. A party caper--well, old girl, you really did it, got drunk and let the boss kiss you and feel you up. Better put him straight on Monday; apologize, tell him how drunk you were, please don't get the wrong idea. We'll just forget what happened and get back to work, like always. Or did she pine deliciously and wistfully as I did with the memory of it? I was relaxed and wide awake, something new within me hummed. From what reservoir came this energy which at once becalmed and tingled? What did it mean at my age to tell myself that I was in love? A mere matter of hormones, the age old story of a middle-aged man gone crazy with longing for young girls? Or, as they said in the sixties, an ego trip? Whichever way you say it did not match the way it felt. A time when reason and science failed, and only poetry would do, if one was a poet.

My one conscious regret concerned Murray, Bernice's husband, who after all had provided us with tickets to the ball and for whom I had real affection. Murray was an architect, an earnest young man who wanted to put his talent in the service of beauty and humanity. I had been charmed many times by his pudgy boyishness, seeing him sweeping his thick dark hair off of his forehead and telling me of Frank Lloyd Wright's Broad-acre City, or Lewis Mumford's concerns over the disappearing sense of community in big cities. I listened and understood why he did not want to work for a large firm, doing hack work, and so struggled on his own, but was his own man and retained his ideals. There had grown between us a kinship, a rapport of souls, whenever we met we fell easily into searching discussions of deep matters, of good books, good music and of the problems which beset mankind the world over, he responding to my maturity, I to his youthful idealism. And Bernice, sweeping into my office to mock us men for our seriousness.

"O.K., you two, break it up." Her favorite men, the boss whom she respected and the husband whom she loved. How wholesome it was before this betrayal. You see how it is Murray, old man, I loved you dearly, as a son, but Pan piped, and I lusted for your wife, grew weak at the sight of the elfin turn of her nose. There was nothing I could do about it, it is the way men are.

Sheila was sleeping and unaware, what did I mean unaware? Was this how it was going to be? Think about it, Gomez, I told myself, you sit here with a heart bumping away, planning a double life of contradictions and endless intrigue. Be practical. It was nothing, the kind of fling that one has at a Mardi Gras ball. You know how it is at Mardi Gras, the old rite of spring, lambs bounding, goats prancing, the bewitching fragrance of new growth filling the air. Did I imagine that Bernice and I were the only ones? When Bacchus ruled by night, love was everywhere. There are no strangers among strangers with passion. No need of names or of common recognition (the reason for the masks, you see). Did it occur to me that my wife, Sheila, found some friend-stranger, stranger-friend, and was lying in bed at this moment as wide awake as I, with her own memory of passion?

What will happen on Monday at the office? What would happen . . . ? I was very sleepy and would have to remove to the little Victorian settee. There was no life in that gray sky, one could not imagine that in a week we would have Mardi Gras and this city would go mad again.

I had a little dream, snoozing on my Hepplewhite chair; a crow lit upon the grillwork railing of my balcony. He fretted and hopped in his arrogant crow way, jumped down onto the balcony and up to my eastward French window, and tapped against the glass with his bill. I awoke with a start, half fallen from the chair. He flew off, did I see him? I shivered, how cold, how very cold I was. "Bernice, my love, lie with me on my settee. Warm my old bones with your pliant young body."

Chapter 3

I arrived at the office, woolly headed and with the shakes, which I haven't had since my youth in the ninth ward. Since the thing with Bernice at the Beaux Art Ball, I had been revisited by a veritable avalanche of old memories. A regular Marcel Proust I was all weekend. Like the time when Raymond Lowery fixed me up with Shirley Hymel from down below in St. Bernard, fixed both of us up, I should say. The old trick of fifteen year olds double dating with the same girl. Shirley was easy, said Raymond, she would kiss us he knew, and who knows, let us play with her tits; two tits, two boys, barbaric are fifteen year old boys, we should all blush at what we did at that age. The plan was to meet her in the last row at the Arabi Theatre, which we did. The tiniest formality with introductions: Hi, Shirley, this is Bobby. Hello. She kept her head down, but I could tell that she was no peach. When the movie started, Raymond went right to work. He had her head angled over and down, nearly pinning it to the wooden arm between their seats. It seemed like fifteen minutes before they came up for breath, and me, bug-eyed without a glance or thought for the movie--what movie? Down went her head again, low sounds of murmuring and slobbering; Raymond was inept but effective. But what about me, I was thinking. I needn't have worried, Raymond did not forget. When he came up for air, he gave me the go ahead. But you know what happened, I put my hand on her shoulder and got the shakes so bad that my seat began to rattle, my knees were beating a ratti-tat-tat on the seat in front of me. I did the only thing I could have done; I took a seat way up front and watched the movie. On the way home on the streetcar, I asked Raymond if he played with her tits. He said he did, but I think he lied, if he had he would have told me without my asking. Raymond kept no secrets from his friends.

Bernice was not at her desk in the outer office. The Mr. Coffee was clean and unplugged. She could have been home with the flu, it was flu weather in New Orleans; it was raining softly outside, the sky gloomier and grayer than ever. She didn't have the flu; it was nine-thirty, a mere sickness would not have precluded a phone call. She was home for the other reason, whatever that reason was. There were at least two possibilities: she hankered for me as I did for her, but didn't know if she could handle it. Or she didn't hanker and was mortified about what happened and needed a little time to think up a tactful way to tell me.

Call her? No good, I was shaking all over with the thought of it. Such a dumb thing, an unused phone, sitting there without a hand to grip it, or a mouth to speak through it.

There was nothing to do but get to work. This was a very slack week at *Dixie-Roto*. The Mardi Gras issue, due this Sunday, had been prepared with the usual standards well in advance. There had to be something to do. A busy man is not a perplexed man. A perplexed man preaches to himself mouthing platitudes, and so remains idle and more perplexed. I tried my hand on the phone, testing, but it shook badly.

O.K., Gomez, get up and get going. I went to the file cabinet and pulled the folder on the New Iberia Crafts Festival, scheduled for March 20th, something we were preparing for the Sunday after Mardi Gras. I went through the 8 by 10 glossies which I had taken myself. They were good, very good. Ordinarily I could have gotten very excited about good Cajun ladies weaving on sturdy cypress looms and crusty old Cajun men carving duck decoys with such wonderful detail that the ancient Egyptian sculptors for all of their four thousand years of unbroken tradition were put to shame.

The phone rang. Need I say that I jumped. "Well, brother," I to the phone, "you speak at last; is it she for whom you whistle so merrily?" No time to prepare, pick up the receiver, say hello and act normal. "Hello." It was Ralph, our managing editor. "Yeah, sure." A last minute change in a layout. I was hardly listening. "Do what you want, Ralph. I can live with that." With what?

I shook and had wild palpitations. I was slowly deciding that I couldn't live like that, a nervous wreck, talking to my phone instead of into it to the human person on the other end. Something had to be settled, I had to know, so that I could get back to living my life, whatever kind of dull middle-aged life it was. So I picked up the phone, a mere instrument of communication, and dialed the dumb thing. On the third ring I wanted to hang up to stop the shakes, but on the fourth she picked it up.

"Hello," but it sounded, I thought, like "hollow": hello-hollow-hollow-hello. It was the voice of a woman who had been sitting alone with her thoughts, and waiting.

"Bernice?"

"Yes."

"Are you sick?"

"No."

"You didn't come in today."

"I know."

"You are not sick?"

"I said I wasn't"

"Why didn't you come in?"

There was such a long silence that I thought the phone was dead or that she had quietly hung up by easing down the button. "Hello, hello, Bernice."

"Yes."

"Are you going to tell me why?"

"You know why."

"Bernice, don't you think we should talk about this?"

"I don't think that would be wise."

My own silence now. I heard her quietly clearing her throat. She would not resume, so I had to.

"What are we going to do?" I asked.

"You tell me."

"Let's talk."

"It wouldn't help, it would only make it complicated."

"We have to work together, you know."

The sound of her even breathing was now very distinct, she was not going to respond. I couldn't tell whether I was thrilled or heart sick or both. My ear burned.

"You are not going to resign, I hope."

"I don't know yet."

"But that wouldn't be fair."

"Fair, what's fair. We have a mess; it's got to be cleaned up."

My silence again, I heard her breathing quicken. Was she about to cry?

"Bobby, I'll call you back." Click.

So strange to be turned upside down when you are almost fifty. To realize that you have been nearly dead for so long and didn't know it, never even suspected. I was crying and knew not for what. Warm, ample tears, a new clear saliva collected in my mouth.

At ten o'clock I decided to risk a quick trip to the men's room. If she should call while I'm gone . . . . you see in what a storm of flying moments I moved. I was too fast and more than the usual few drops streamed down my leg; I would soon reek of urine. No time even for the quick glance in the mirror, checking for any new signs of aging. Back to the office, and to him who waited with me, brother phone.

My desk was pure havoc; neat stacks had been picked up and dropped, contents of folders emptied, desk calendar knocked askew. And then my memory played a nasty trick. I couldn't remember what Bernice looked like. A confusion of near resemblances, one or two came close, but the sheer effort of concentration turned my mind's eye blank. From here it was a matter of groping around, trying to find the way back by the use of rough approximations: Evelyn Keyes, Bernice looks like Evelyn Keyes. Bernice did not look like Evelyn Keyes, but they were the same type. Deborah Kerr, the same type.

It was ten-thirty-five. If she hung up because she was near tears, she has had enough time to recover; if she meant it that she would call me back, that is, wanted to talk to me. It occurred to me now that she may have been interrupted; heard Murray at the front door. If Murray was home and I called, it would not seem strange, I was her boss. I couldn't sit here much longer wrecking my office and pressuring my bladder, I had to go again. I would go to the men's room, come back and call her.

This time I gave the member a proper shaking, let the water trickle over the finger tips, tucked the shirt, smoothed the hair.

After the phone rang for a long time, I wearily counted the next ten rings and carefully set the receiver back on its stand.

I knew a lot of men who drank because their nerves were gone, or because their life was sour and flat or just commonly when they were beset by trouble, and presently they said to themselves and then to their friends that they had a problem.

It was not easy for someone like myself to stir with rage and so be tempted to commit violence. I was instead, in my confusion, merely sick at heart, and I would go on, I knew, sinking deeper and deeper into this misery. How very odd that other men would turn to drink or worse and I had no desire to. Was it that I accepted misery like I accepted everything else, that to resist it would be tampering with my naturalness--my wholeness? I was logical, I will go the wrong way if it is the right way. Other men are led into vice against their will.

Ordinarily this is how I would have acted, but this time I decided to get a drink, many drinks.

Damn New Orleans and its Mardi Gras. The sky was thick and sullen, it hung low, nearly to the chimneys and roof ridges of these old houses. The tourists walked along trancefully, their eyes full of wonder as they gazed at these narrow grave streets. They seem expectant, waiting for a secret to be told or a clue given. They were strange to those beside them and to themselves, eager to drink deeply of the strangeness of this strange place. It was the weather, half-toned, and the place, an old place. I walked along, edging along the sides of the buildings. The tourists, three or four abreast, gave no effort to their stride since they were not going anywhere, but I moved like a thief, slipping through the slightest opening. When I brushed their shoulders, they looked at me, not annoyed, and went back to their wonder. I, the natural wonderer, had purpose and a place to go.

I was making my way out of the Quarter to what was presently called Faubourg Marigny, a section just beyond the French Quarter. I was going to Johnny Matranga's Bar, which I'd only been to once with Philip, and that many years ago; but I knew that it was still open for business.

When I walked into a bar named Johnny Matranga's and looked behind the bar for Johnny and saw a short Italian man with silver hair I said to myself: that's Johnny. But I was wrong as always. A regular, two stools down called, "Sal, two more here." Sal Matranga? I would never know. Sal walked over to me, leaned on the bar with his hands before him and looked me in the eyes, a level look, not friendly, not hostile. "I'll have a double bourbon with a little water, on the rocks."

Sal didn't ask me with his eyes if I was troubled, wanting a double bourbon. It was no trouble for him to mind his own business. Sal would serve me double bourbons all day and all night and never blink an eye. This was the right place.

I slipped the bourbon. This was the right drink. Do you know that Bernice's face popped right up; not any of the same type, Evelyn Keyes, but the very Bernice whom I love. Did Sal know that he had canceled a gray day, along with the strange wonderment of New Orleans tourists come to Mardi Gras, and painted the face of the beloved? It was the bourbon Sal would say and your own loving heart, not me.

The walls of this bar were textured to look like stucco, painted yellow, gone to ochre with the years; near the ceiling they were enunciated with a stenciled frieze, swaying California palms alternating with stylized Pacific waves; at mid-wall were a continuous row of framed photos. From where I sat I could make out that they were snapshots which had been enlarged, of events happily enjoyed right here at Matranga's Bar: flag raisings, Mardi Gras', Johnny's birthday. I was interpolating for no details were clear to me from that distance. I knew, though, even from there, that these pictures were vintage 1945 to 1955 or thereabouts, and that probably none had been added since. The juke box was a 1950's streamline model, with peeling nickel plated trim and an old turn table with a selection arm. With the dropping of a nickel, (a quarter?) the selection arm pulled a platter from the row, flipped it level and set it down on the turn table: a machine imitating a sequence of human executions. In the fifties technology was wondrous, it was something to fear (beware: soulless machines will replace real men); in the seventies, technology was truly wondrous but known now to be dumb, microscopic circuits powering and connecting invisibly and silently, but doing nothing more amazing than what we poor humans have been doing for centuries. Today, ordinary file clerks and secretaries show open contempt for computers. "What went wrong? You know, it's that dumb computer, I have better brains up here in my own head. Don't talk to me about computers."

Dean Martin sang *That's Amore*. My companions here were all veterans of World War II. It was clear that they were old friends yet they did not talk to each other as if they were; but rather as people who had been waiting for hours at a bus station and had started up a conversation with their neighbor, to have someone to complain to and kill time with. Thank God for beer and bourbon, or we would see ourselves as a wise observer does. I was the only one who was technically alone and in love. But I wouldn't have bet on that, I had caught these men at their morning leisure, any number of afternoon rendezvous may have been in the offing. This is the way with people in love, to feel very special among all the rest.

Sal came over to me, right on time; like all good bartenders, he kept his eyes on the drinks and not the customers; mine was down to the last sip. He casually laid his arm on the bar and leaned forward, the hand poised to pick up my glass; his eyes asked if I cared for another, and that it was of no consequence to him or to Johnny if I didn't. I pushed the glass to his hand and nodded. Sal was wise: make no foolish, unnecessary conversation and everyone could relax and be free to dream, think or speak as he pleased.

Sinatra sang *I've Got You Under My Skin*, the juke box was, no doubt, being fed with house quarters. Frankie's perfect Bronx diction held each vowel to its shape, his voice lingered without slurring and bit off phrases and modulated endings: Cole Porter from Paris speaking through the mouth of an Italian-American urban-tough kid-man, who preferred Las Vegas to Paris, a New Yorker exiled in the desert West as Porter was in Europe. My mouth was delicious with bourbon and Bernice's kiss, remembered. I licked and pursed, refusing to swallow the bourbon until it burned my gums. Pain and pleasure, pleasure and pain.

I was trying to remember exactly what prompted me to go over to the table where Bernice and Murray sat the other night with other young people. They were quite riotous I recalled. I was strolling around the dance floor aimlessly, getting in the dancers' way, being bumped and spilling my drink. I had stopped to watch a gigantic Daniel Boone, with a real red beard, and what looked to be authentic buckskins. He was big enough to be an offensive tackle and probably was. He was performing beautifully, a big graceful clown, hooping and laughing, dancing with great skill, artful sashays, bumps and grinds to give envy to Kalatan. His mirth had drawn a circular audience around him; his partner could have been Rita Hayworth, costumed and made up to perfection as Dracula's daughter. She did no more than a casual rumba, tossing her hair with nearly stationary feet; but her ass was a wonder, and she moved it as if she was quite literally getting it on. I was sucking the rim of my glass, which was by then empty. And then . . . . that's right. Someone behind me put a hand on my elbow and called my name. "Bobby?" Female. I turned, I remember, and put one boot forward, letting the weight settle on the other, and I must have tucked in my chin and brought my glass up in front of me. The lady before me reared back a bit, smiled and said: "Or is it really Napoleon."

"No, it's really Bobby." I said, coming out of my contrapposto, embarrassed that I had done something so theatrical. She wore a long formal dress, a little old fashioned because of the puffed sleeves and V-neckline, but of a rich, expensive fabric of some kind, brown going toward gold. Her brown hair was combed back off of her forehead and pinned on the sides with simple gold barettes. She smoked, turning her head politely to blow the smoke out to the left of me. I judged her to be my age, but well kept. She wore almost no make-up, light pink lipstick, maybe a little mascara. A single crease was beneath each eye with delicately etched laugh lines at the corners; she had been pretty and still was. She turned her head and looked at me quizzically, "You don't recognize me, do you?"

"Of course I do," I lied. "How have you been?"

"Oh, very well."

It was then that I saw Bernice, waving to me from her table. There was something about her eagerness that made me want to go over immediately. I was also talking to an attractive lady whose name I did not know, and I did not want to talk to her any longer, under the pretense of being her old friend. "Excuse me," I said, I"ll be right back." I went over to see Bernice. I had intended to point this lady out to Sheila on the chance that she knew her. But then I asked Bernice to dance and forgot.

It was Clara, of course. But it couldn't have been, I was mistaken. How could I have not recognized Clara, even after all these years? It was her, though, I was sure. Wow! I pounded the bar.

Sal looked up and nodded to me, "Be right there." Oops. I hoped Sal didn't think that I was being disorderly, he ran a good bar. But I just couldn't get over that. Clara. Wow! I was going to write a book about her and didn't even know her when I saw her.

Sal came over with another double bourbon, and I quickly swallowed what was left of the one I had. But none of my confusion perplexed Sal, he had seen lonely men pound the bar before.

I took the long way around back to the office: up Esplanade Avenue over to Rampart, etc., not only to avoid bumping into the tranceful wandering Mardi Gras tourists, but to sober up; that last double bourbon hit me like a mallet. I knew that I was weaving but I couldn't help it. When I looked up I had to exert great effort to bring the double image of the world back in line. Meeting Clara and not recognizing her made me look through the wrong end of the telescope, looking back over the long years. How far from my youth, our youth, mine, Clara's, Sheilas, Ronnie's, Philip's? I knew suddenly how old I was; and how young was the girl I kissed and thought I loved. I could be her father, she my daughter, in ten years she will be 35, me 58, in twenty . . . . adding, subtracting. . . .

I was less drunk suddenly, but I was getting depressed, the cold damp air blew into my face and cleared my head. A gust kicked up and I looked up to see that the clouds were finally moving. Maybe the tourists would stop dragging their feet, but as I neared the corner of Conti and Exchange Alley they were still in their wonderment. The wind hit them hard, their coattails and skirts waved like bunting, but they were zombies yet, strangers in a strange land. In the forties where this slow procession of midwesterners, Floridians, what have you now moved pranced the gay young heroes of World War II, calling all civilians, friends, and stranger, Mac. "Nice going, Mac," to the street cleaners, throwing the words back as they walked swiftly on in little coveys; sailors with their hats, jack-deuce, their flared pants flapping, wearing their smiles and battle ribbons casually, at their ease, for they had known war and now peace, and America was great. They were everywhere, Leathernecks and Infantry men, we had our best Mardi Gras' in those years following the war. Being young heroes they knew that their casual gaiety was a gift, and they must have known that it was a brief gift, because they spent it like easy money.

I met Ralph, our managing editor, at the lobby concession, on his coffee break. For as long as Ralph had known me he had treated me with perfect respect. He was a certain kind of bald headed, unself-conscious man you are apt to encounter anywhere in this city. They handle authority with ease, do their jobs efficiently, are relaxed, have the knack of giving orders without being either high handed or condescending. So when he saw me tousle-haired and wobbly he merely smiled, "Where the hell have you been, Gomez?"

"Having a few drinks, Ralph. Don't I look it? Are you going to fire me?"

"Maybe. Are you really drunk, Bobby?"

"'Fraid so. Do I look that bad?"

"Bad enough. Get yourself a cup of coffee and comb your hair."

"Don't you want to know why I've been drinking?" I was offering an explanation because I had no intentions of explaining anything to him. It was also a New Orleans style of banter.

Drunkenness is common here and does not need explanations. Ralph knew this style and smiled, "A little early Mardi Gras party, huh? Why don't you go home and sleep it off," and he patted my shoulder and walked off.

A slow, strange day. I drank coffee and used the glass shelf that held Twinkies, Hubig pies and other sweets for a mirror to comb my hair.

I thought of Clara at the Beaux Arts Ball. What was she doing there? Did she still live in her big house on the River Road in Algiers?

When I went up to the office Bernice was there.

Chapter 4

*K*enny McDermott and Kathy Watson were at the water fountain. They shot nervous glances my way as I approached. As well they should--be nervous. They were seeing each other. A big clown laughed in my head; I felt kicked in the ass: meaning I was going Ha, Ha, Ha to myself. Bobby laughing at Bobby--Kenny and Kathy, Bobby and Bernice, and who knows who else? A regular one reeler we had going, Leon Errol rubber-legging it around, trying to stash three blondes in three different closets because his wife was at the front door arriving unexpectedly from visiting her mother.

That's right: it was funny. How you say, hankie-pankie in the office, ha, ha. Old Bobby and skinny Bernice. Well, well.

Well, well, I said as I heard the electric typewriter clicking away in my outer office. Shush! said Leon Errol, finger to mouth, legs becoming soft noodles.

Well, well, is what I said, but she kept banging away, all business. "Hold on," she shot at me without lifting her head. The carriage slid along; she was as furious at her typing as a man tying up a boat in rough waters. There was nothing for me to do but sit in the visitor's chair and wait.

If someone should walk in . . . if someone should walk in they would find a man in his own office, albeit, in the visitor's chair, looking over at his headlong typing secretary, his mouth ringed with a simp's smile. Only the smile could have been considered fishy. Why did I want to close the door? That would have been fishy.

Her spare cheeks quivered with the fury of her typing. Her skin looked transparent and silky, blue veins showed through; she was paler than I remembered. Remembered? The world is new and old to those in love; the beloved is from the distant, fabled past, has returned to be remembered, glowing in the keenness of the present moment. She was wearing jeans, unsuited to her slimness and inappropriate for office attire, there was no time for protocol on a day so unusual and tentative. She simply came as she was, for her coming was not the usual everyday coming. Neither was her fierce typing usual. I was made to wait, allowed enough time to look things over, sniff the air, and would thereby understand that I was not to come at her too fast. There was to be a business-personal manner of dealing with personal business. Be off-handed as if nothing was amiss. Please, no Tristan drinking of poison. Be cool, like Cary Grant perched on the edge of a chair, head cocked, brow arched, hand twisted backwards grasping knee: "Very well, my dear. We are to have business as usual," strokes chin, smiles to self, "I like that, really; never did approve of improper displays of emotion, not the thing."

She came to rest. At last. Her hands still on the keyboard, head down, she heaved a welcomed breath. "Finished." But she spoke only to herself. I wore the simp's smile yet; it was my awkward way of appearing boyish at 48. She looked at me with a calculating, uncertain gaiety that sputtered all about her expression. I was to speak first.

"What are you typing?" I meant *why* are you typing, but that was too fast. Business-personal.

"Your letters, Bossman." She was throwing out half smiles, pivoting in her chair, looking for places to put her hands, a marionette whose manipulator absently diddled with the cross-wood control. What could I do to make her relax? Or bring myself out of my stupor: I sat in my chair leadened and hunched over, with my hands intwined and thrust between my legs, unable to unfreeze the simp's smile from my face.

I got up finally and walked to the edge of the desk, "I'm glad you came."

"Why?"

"Because I wanted to see you."

"You saw me the other night."

"That's right, I did."

"And you see me every day of the week."

"That's right, I do."

"So?"

"So, I wanted to see you today, and every day."

"This is a mess, you know."

"What's a mess?"

"Everything."

"I don't think it's a mess."

"Murray and I are getting a divorce."

"Bernice, I hope . . ."

"Oh, no--I'm sorry. It's got nothing to do with you."

Someone walked by in the corridor then, and we both looked out with startlement.

"Let's go in my office," I said, motioning with my head.

I closed the door halfway.

"Is it true, you and Murray . . ."

"Oh, everything's all right now. We've been talking about it, and we both think it's the best thing to do."

"I'm sorry"

"Don't be. Murray isn't, and neither am I. At this point, we're very calm about it, and relieved.

"Then why were you crying?"

"Well, if you don't know."

"I'm sorry, I didn't mean to fish around . . . you said everything was a mess."

"Everything is a mess. I decide to get a divorce, and right away I start chasing after a married man, another woman's husband."

"You weren't chasing . . ."

"You know what I mean."

"You're married, and I was chasing as much as you were."

"With a man it's different."

"I don't believe that." I was trying to console her, but she was claiming superior knowledge. Older men can console younger women, but women are wiser about love and heartbreak at any age. Was that my role, counselor, mentor? I wanted more.

We fell silent, she looked down in her lap at her folded hands. I looked at my own hands on my desk, also folded. We looked up and our eyes met. We were silent.

I came from behind the desk over to her, she stood up to meet me, but when I tried to kiss her, she turned away, "No, Bobby, I don't think so."

"Why?"

"You're married, you and Sheila . . ."

"I don't understand."

"I messed up my marriage, I don't want to mess up yours."

I didn't believe her. Women talk a lot about guilt, but when it comes to their passion they know guilt only by its spelling, if they can spell. Either she simply didn't want to kiss me, how you say, I didn't turn her on; or this was a spurious bargain whereby I had to complain about Sheila and tell her how lousy my marriage was before I got my kiss. Furthermore, she, like all women, loved to bust up marriages.

I turned her head around and kissed her, and she kissed me back, and that was that.

*B*ernice's Toyota was egg-shell white, but the bucket seats were unexplainably maroon. She was rubbing the steering wheel, which was black, shining it with her palm grease; I, more idly watched the gas pump register, spinning away, ding, ding, gallons of gas, dollars and cents. Between us on the battery cover, which was white, set a boutique style box of Kleenex. I felt like a burglar in a stranger's house who suddenly stopped stuffing jewelry in his sack, having noticed a worthless, personal item on a dresser top, a box of tissues. A thief is homeless, and steals in vain. We drove on Magazine Street. The street was still damp from the morning rain, but the sky was cloudless, not quite as blue as it would be very soon. The sun burnished the windshield, showing it to be a surface of many marks, scratches, and etchings. It was a day of fine details shown, of calm, vacant minds. The warm sun laid in our laps; outside the air was dry and chilled. We were speechless, a silence for our eyes which saw everything: the fine dust particles on the dash and the sun-cleaned sides of houses and shops in the far distance.

Magazine Street looked like the Quarter did twenty years ago: a jumble of antique shops, second-hand bookstores, corner groceries, po-boy restaurants, Latin American dives. We could have parked, Bernice and I, if we had been simply a couple out for a morning drive, and strolled about, nosing around in any random shop, looking but with nothing in mind to buy, holding hands and bumping each other in the way that carefree couples do. As it was, we drove with more purpose to a friend's apartment, Bernice's friend, not to visit the friend, name of Sharon, but to feed Sharon's cat, his name: Tolstoy.

The ridicule that Sharon deserved for naming a cat Tolstoy would go by the way, Bernice might have thought that Tolstoy was a cute name for a cat, and anything your best friend did, naturally, would reflect on you. We were gradually getting to know each other, in this different way.

Sharon, like so many New Orleanians of this day, had gone off to the Mississippi Gulf Coast to get out of town for Mardi Gras. Many other natives, I happened to know, stayed home on Mardi Gras day and watched the parades on TV. No one knew what these danger signs meant, or just how far things had really gone. Who were all of those people thronging the streets?

Sharon was divorced, Bernice told me, after six brief months of marriage and lived alone with Tolstoy. She was into ceramics and organic gardening. "Really," I said no more than I had to. Who was I to judge? "Sharon has it together," said Bernice. Had what together? I told myself a joke. Her shit, same joke: should shit be together, I mean is it better for it to be together? Did Tolstoy have his shit together? I saw rows of Sharon's pots lined up against the walls of her apartment, some contained her shit, others, Tolstoy's shit, out of them grew great healthy tomato plants, ladened with red ripe tomatoes.

Officially, we were going to interview Miss Julia Reilly, a fabulous miniaturist, who did portraits of entire families on pieces of smooth mahogany the size of silver dimes, with the aid of a specially rigged microscope. Miss Reilly, of course, was also out of town for Mardi Gras visiting friends in Lafayette, or so she told me last week. You see how carefully we covered our tracks. This was my plan which I carried out by the simple means of telling Tom Mahoney, my assistant, that Bernice and I were going out for this interview with Miss Reilly. Tom looked at me somewhat stupidly, wondering why his boss seemed to be checking with him, the assistant, for permission to leave the office. Bernice, the secretary, did not know why she was to go along. Imagine. She didn't approve, but she came, after all I was the boss. "Where are we really going?" she asked in a manner impatient and disrespectful. "City Park." Not Audubon Park, you know why. "Oh, no! Not the park, that's tacky." She presumed much and was right. "Very well, where would you like to go?" "I don't know, you're the boss." I was baffled, yesterday in my office in the heat of our passion, the burning issue was, where could we go. There was not enough time to go, even if we had hit upon the right place. That was yesterday. Today I had freed our day and thought of the perfect spot. How lovely on such a sunny, crisp day to have been parked beneath Suicide Oak, its great limbs stretching out forty feet and touching the ground. Beneath this ancient tree fourteen desperate men ended their lives, by various means, bullet, poison, slashed wrist, hanged with loop of rope from the great black limbs. True fact. Was this not just the spot? Instead we were on our way to perform a duty, this was a work day, and it salved her conscience to perform a duty, even if it was only feeding a friend's cat; this was her reasoning I assumed. I thought it was a great idea when she suggested it. Empty apartment, small duty to take no more than a minute (didn't Tolstoy need to be let out to put his shit together somewhere?). Perfect, and yet Bernice drove routinely as if we were simply going to feed Tolstoy, let him out or clean his litter box as the case may be and then leave. Did she really intend it to be this way? I could not believe it, although it was true that nothing had been discussed. It would, of course, be my idea if we did take advantage, she had promised Sharon that she would feed Tolstoy. When I thought about it, I did not ask Bernice to dance at the Beaux Art Ball. She didn't ask me. It was decided in some other oblique manner. "Hi, boss. Boy is that the right costume for you. The Emperor Napoleon, the tyrant of *Dixie-Roto*," she kidded. I was the farthest thing from a tyrant. She had taken both of my hands as she continued to needle me with high spirits. "Well," she said still holding my hands and looking at me sweetly, "you better get back to your table." But I asked her to dance, and she accepted, "Sure, why not." My idea, the dance.

Sharon's apartment was nothing but one big room on the ground floor of a large Victorian house. This room was appended by a bath and a small alcove which served as a kitchen. Everything was in the room: bed, bookcases, record player, sofa and coffee table. I saw no evidence that Sharon was into ceramics, and there were no tomato plants. Many house plants, however, ferns, philodendrons, purple Wandering Jew in hanging pots. Sharon had done well, two Maxfield Parish posters and a Guatemalan rug. The bed, ahem, was a big double one piled high with throw pillows.

But where was Tolstoy? Betwixt stove and wall, I found him. Bernice was in the big room, calling him; you don't call cats, you call dogs, who know their names, happy-sad creatures ready to make fools of themselves for any stranger who would pat their heads and scratch their furry hide. For cats, you must search in darkened, secret places. Two great golden eyes peered out at me. I was impressed, Tolstoy was the biggest black cat I had ever seen, he was the size of a hefty fox. He came out only when I backed away, and went swiftly to his feeding place to settle into a fluffy ball, his tail rising like a serpent. Such a magnificent cat perhaps deserved a name like Tolstoy. "There you are," scolded Bernice, still treating him like a dog. "Ma-a-a-a-a," said Tolstoy, the serpent tail snaking about with impatience. As she bent to fill his bowl I could not help noticing that she did wrong to wear pants. For pants one needed an ass with shelf and deep under curve, some thickness in the thighs. This very meagerness, though, was her charm. It was all I could do to stop myself from placing hands there. Did I say that Bernice looked like Evelyn Keyes? This is somewhat misleading, it was much more accurate to say that she had a body like Audrey Hepburn, whom I had never seen wearing pants; you know, frail, callow, wanting of tender touch and gentle handling.

Bernice tended to the litter box as I went round Sharon's room in search of I knew not what. Her book case, a simple affair of stacked bricks and shelving board, held two or three dozen books, mostly paperbacks. The collection was overbalanced with science fiction, which was in turn overbalanced with Robert Heinlein. Sharon was into Heinlein. A hardbound jacketed copy of *The Greening of America* (rare) which looked too new to have been read. But that was not what I was looking for . . . no, it wasn't there: *War and Peace*. All the same, Tolstoy was a noble cat, worthy of his name.

Bernice entered from the kitchen, dusting cat litter from her hands. She completed the job, wiping them on her pants. Her expression was that's that, next business, stubbornly refusing to acknowledge the fact that we were alone in an empty apartment. A tryst unacknowledged is not a tryst yet. What if I had said, "O.K., let's get back to work." Boy would she have been surprised. I hoped.

What this situation needed was a catalyst. Sharon was not the type . . . but just maybe? I walked myself into the kitchen, opened the cabinet and started to move things around, (Bernice looked on with interest, didn't she?). "Ha, here it is." Dry Sack Sherry two-thirds filled. Better to be bourbon or gin, but this would do.

"What are you up to?" Sheila, now Bernice. What is it about you, Gomez?

"This."

"What's that for?"

"To drink, naturally."

"Shouldn't we be going?" There was, though, a certain testing of the wind running beneath the question.

"O.K., we'll go, but first let's have a drink."

I took her arm and led her over to the sofa. "Just one."

"All right, just one."

The moment was right; not much sherry was required. I kissed her first and then she was kissng me back, and we were in a hurry to get to the bed, throwing pillows off onto the floor. She asked me to close the blinds and turn off the light. Good idea I thought.

"Bernice," I called searching the bed. I found her slender arm.

"What are we going to do?" She asked.

"What--what are we going to do? You know."

"Shouldn't we take off our clothes? Or is this going to be a quickie?"

"A what?"

"Take off your clothes."

"Oh, yeah--right"

I stood up and shed my clothes, kicking off my pants that wouldn't let go.

"Bernice," I whispered, returning to bed. "Where are you?"

"Here," she giggled. "I'm right here, calm down."

And she was; I touched her belly and her ribs. She took my hand and lifted it to her breast.

"Kiss me," she said. I pulled myself up to her mouth.

'No, not here--down there."

"What?"

"My breast."

I kissed her breast, so meager and so soft. She murmured softly. It was different--different than Sheila.

"Lie down," she said. "On your back."

She came over, straddllng me, sitting up. "Are you all right? Can I touch you?"

She managed everything. I closed my eyes.

"Yes, yes," I heard myself say. She rocked slowly. It all seemed miraculous.

"Did you?" I asked her afterwards...........

"Yes," she said, curling up beside me, kissing my shoulder. We lay there nearly sleeping, floating.

"I want a cigarette," she said, stirring.

"I didn't know you smoked."

"I don't, except now after sex--after making love." She left the bed, turned on the lights, and returned with a lit cigarette and covered us.

"Why didn't you and Sheila have children?" She said, blowing out smoke with a mouth made for whistling, like a junior-high schooler smoking on the sly.

"I don't really know, she just never did get pregnant. Then, about ten years ago she got a hysterectomy."

"Did you practice birth control? You're Catholic, aren't you?" Bernice was Catholic, too, I thought.

"I'm a Catholic, all right, and so is Sheila. Believe it or not, we didn't practice birth control, or even rhythm."

"Did you want children, both of you?"

"Yes, I guess we did, everybody expects to have children when they marry."

"Are you sorry that you didn't have any?"

"Yes, I think so." Then I said for some reason, "I am adopted."

"Are you? Really?" She squeezed my hand.

"Yes."

"How do you feel about that."

"I don't know, I don't know what it's like not to be adopted."

"Who raised you?"

"Mama Gomez."

"No father?"

"No."

"Why do you call her that?"

"I don't know, I always called her that. She was a Filipino."

"She was?" She squeezed my hand again. "She died?"

"Yes."

"I don't understand--how could she adopt you?"

"She knew my parents and had just lost her husband and we became very attached to each other at the orphanage. Sister Catherine worked it out, I think, because she couldn't bare to separate us."

"Do you know your real parents?"

"No."

"Why not?"

"Nobody ever told me. I don't know their names, but I know them in a way. I lived with them until I was five."

"Bobby?"

"Yes."

"Hold me." I held her.

"What's wrong?" Me.

"I'm crying."

"I know, your tears are wetting my shoulder."

"Sorry."

"That's all right."

When I woke up it was dark. I didn't know where I was. Then I remembered. Is dying like this? Waking up in the dark, not knowing where you were and remembering. What time was it?

The floor was cold, a good hard pine floor, but cold. A married man must know the time. Marriage is always knowing what time it is. My hands groped around the kitchen wall. I was looking for the light switch and found it. There on the wall was a cozy little clock: Round, with an apple and leaf appliqué circled around. It was seven-eighteen. What would Sheila think? If she was home.

Phone, where was the phone?

Wait. Was it seven-eighteen in the morning? No, of course not; it was too dark.

I put on my clothes and made coffee in Sharon's kitchen. Bernice hadn't stirred. I was colder somehow with my clothes on than when I was naked. Tolstoy came rubbing against my leg, serpent tail rising like a Hindu's cobra. What heft; he nearly pushed me off balance.

I sat, freezing, sipping hot coffee, looking at a mosaic of my life. It was a feeling of something wanting to begin, despair moved off of dead center and nervousness. Sheila and I: an old tree, thick with mistletoe, sparse of its own leaf.

215

Something within me wanted to be home, where I usually was at seven-thirty. And yet, I had dreamed many times of being here, where I was. I was thrilled and anxious at the smell of Sharon's kitchen and of Bernice's skin. A nose on the scent. At home I smelled nothing, where everything was of a piece.

Philandering is a funny, old fashioned word. It is what an old uncle does. The old fool, chasing after young girls. Why does a man do that, he's got a fine home, a fine family, a good wife. Whatever possesses . . .

This is an old fashioned city. Sheila and I were an old fashioned married couple. Bernice was old fashioned, needing sherry, fancying herself chasing after someone's husband. Was she my mistress? It takes more than one lay. Mistress is an old fashioned word. Not even in New Orleans would you say that you had a mistress.

Bernice got up, huddled in the blanket, squinting, half-stumbling as she came.

"Why didn't you wake me up?"

"You slept so peacefully."

"What time is it?"

"About eight, seven . . . fifty-two to be exact."

"That coffee?"

"Want some?"

"Is there another cup?"

I got a cup and poured her some coffee. She tried to hold the blanket and the cup, and the blanket slipped, exposing her shoulder and breast. "Here," she handed me the cup. She pulled the blanket back over her, and I pulled out the other chair for her.

"Do you think that this is an old fashioned city?"

"What?"

"New Orleans, do you think it's old fashioned?"

"I don't know, I'm cold."

"Drink your coffee." Steam rose up from the coffee, warming her face as she sipped.

She'd got a firm grip on the blanket and began to drink in big swallows, draining the cup.

"More?"

"Please."

I heated up the coffee and poured her another cup. Billows of steam enveloped her. She drank and shivered. Her hair was messed, pushed up on the back of her head, her skin seemed wilted. I must have looked as bad. How old did I look? Another cup, down the hatch.

"That better?"

"Much. What are we going to do?"

"Spend the night."

"Be serious."

"I am."

"What am I going to tell Murray?"

"I thought you were getting a divorce."

"I am, but I don't have one yet."

"You're old fashioned."

"Wha-a-t? You got something about old fashioned?"

"It's the whole city, you and Murray, Sheila and me."

"Bobby, what's wrong with you?"

"Don't worry, I got my shit together."

"I better get dressed."

"Wait."

"Wait?"

"Why can't we spend the night?"

"You're crazy, I'm getting dressed." She went stumbling off.

We said good-bye to Tolstoy and went into the cold night. The sky was . . . what? Clear and brilliant. The darkest blue; stars, whitest. Specks so far, so clear. Mars glowed.

It was freezing, we shook and shivered. The motor warmed.

I felt alive and cold, as clear within as was this night outside. Every light was brilliant. On houses fell sharp, clean edged shadows. Even the wind, when it blew, seemed to make straight lines. A cold crystal night.

Sherry was what Sheila and I drank, when we drank alone. It's a good drink for a husband and wife in the comfort of their home. Did I say what Sheila told me last night? She was leaning far into the mirror, putting on her make-up. I had just arrived home and found her thus.

"Going out?" I asked.

"The gang from D.C. is down and we are taking them out to dinner."

"We?"

"Margaret and I."

"Oh."

"Why don't you warm up that pizza in the ice box, I had it for lunch."

"No, thanks."

"O.K., you're on your own, though."

This did not mean that she came home every night and cooked for her loving husband, even if it sounded that way. "Hey, Sheila, guess who I saw at the Beaux Art Ball?"

"Who?"

"You'll never guess."

"Who?"

"Clara."

"Yes, I know, I saw her, too."

"You did?" She did!

"We had a long talk, doesn't she look terrific."

"I almost didn't recognize her."

"She and Ronnie are divorced."

"You didn't happen to mention anything about my sketch."

"Your what?"

"You know--my sketch about Clara."

"Of course not."

She was putting on her coat and checking around for what she might be forgetting. "I'm leaving, you can find something to eat, can't you?"

"I'll manage, don't worry, have fun."

If I did write Clara's story it would be allegorical, and set in the future. 1999. That's right--it would go like this: The signs of America's fall are everywhere present. There is great confusion in Washington, states have seceded from the Union: California (naturally), Nevada, Massachusetts, and Ohio (the last straw). Louisiana has done nothing decisive, the governor, a mulatto of noble Creole heritage and originally from Haiti consorts with the restored Shah of Iran--has been, in fact, living in the Shah's palace for quite some time with his harem (ex-show girls from Las Vegas). In his absence, Abraham Long, a direct descendant of Huey's, has taken over, with the support of Northern Louisiana Protestants and the Standard Oil Company. They persecute Catholics and Jews, driving them south to New Orleans where they find sanctuary. NASA has been converted into a munitions factory and an army raised so the city is well able to defend itself against the onslaughts of the Neo-Long faction. The city government has dispersed, and the Tourist and Vieux Carré Commissions have merged and taken over. They have been up all night in hot debate. And finally they reach a decision; they abolish the democratic form of government and restore a monarchy. Clara (or whatever I shall call her) is declared Queen of New Orleans. The decision to have a queen instead of a king is what kept them arguing all night. The new coalition government, you see, is composed mostly of women. The novel begins with the subsequent headlines in the *Times-Picayune*: RESTORATION. Type-face as tall and bold as that used for PEACE at the end of World War I and II. March 15, 1999. This morning, at five-thirty, the New Orleans Parish Coalition government voted 15 to 7 to abolish the present city government and to establish a monarchy, etc., etc. Oh yeah, Philip is made head of the Catholic Church in New Orleans, since Rome is also in disarray. I will have to call him other than Philip, of course. The blacks (I almost forgot) leave *en masse*, stealing every yacht at the Lake Pontchartrain Marina and sail (?) to Cuba where they overthrow whoever has by that time succeeded Castro and revert to Voodooism.

I fell asleep on the Victorian settee and dreamed of Bernice.

Chapter 5

$\mathcal{I}$ was looking at my assistant, Tom Mahoney, who was talking to me, telling me something. I was looking at his mouth and not his eyes, a sure sign that I was not listening to what he was saying. I think Tom knew, he had stopped talking and brushed at his lips with his fingers. My eyes might have been a little crossed. Tom had two overlapping lips. Tom was the most patient of men, he went on talking. He was probably repeating something. Then he smiled.

"Where are you, Bobby?"

"What?"

"I said, where are you?"

"I'm sorry, I was somewhere." But I was right here looking at his mouth. Where was I?

Tom smiled his big tooth smile. He was a big black Irishman, blue-bearded with thinning dark hair. I have seen Tom on picnics in swim trunks: a hairy beast. He shaved all the way down his neck to his collar. A bear for work. A Leo with a smile that filled the room.

"Bobby, is it all right with you if I do it this way?"

"Of course."

"You didn't hear a word I said."

"I trust you, Tom."

He smiled, "O.K.," and he was off.

"Tom."

Stopping and turning, "Yeah."

"I *did* hear what you said."

"All right, Bobby." Smiling.

It was a replay, but I heard him. Where was I?

New Orleans is old fashioned. I opened the bottom drawer and looked down into it. A glass bottom boat. There it is.

A thin folder: two items. A half-column article, headlined, "Queen Needed." Yellow and brittle. Dated October 25, 1960.

Second item: three and a half column article with pictures, headlined, "Here is Your Queen." Brittle, dated November 2, 1960. The item I added was a slip of paper, a sheet from my scratch pad: Clara, beneath, 368-4995.

I first looked under Hingle. I found Hingle, Ronald, office address and residence; also Hingle, Cynthia Lyles, office address and residence, and Hingle, Charles (Mr. Charlie). Two columns of Hingles, I thought there were more. I then looked under Duplantier. I found: Duplantier, Clara, residence on Pattison Drive (the River Road). Paper in folder, folder in drawer. One-third column of Duplantiers: rarer.

Bernice moved through interstices. When we greeted we were jolly. "Good morning, Mrs. Waguespack, sweetie." "Good morning, Mr. Gomez, dearie." Last night when she dropped me off, I leaned over to kiss her, and she pecked as I did. Like husband and wife, but we knew that that was wrong. We parted not knowing, and we don't know now.

We had to stop at every corner to let the people pass, on their way to St. Charles Avenue to see the parade. They half ran, the sirens wailing, motorcycle police ahead of the parade pushing the crowd back onto the curbs. Those passing before us had two blocks to go before they reached the Avenue. Suddenly packs of black teenagers broke into the streets, running full speed, and men and their wives hustled their children along, more excited than the kids, who looked up at them and said, "Is it coming?" and were yanked along. It was impossible for us to pass. We were excited, too, hearing the sirens. We could hear the clamor of the crowd on the Avenue. We stopped in one intersection after the people passed and looked to the Avenue at the parade rolling by. The big floats rumbled by, green, pink, yellow, the masked krewemen throwing beads and doubloons. The crowd reached up; I was leaning over, my head on Bernice's shoulder, looking and smelling her hair, which was stale-sweet. I kissed her hair, she smelled like Sharon's bed, I did, too, probably. Sinful bed; it was thrilling. "We have to go," she finally said after we had watched three floats pass. Mardi Gras through the crystal lens of a brilliant, clear night. The metal of the Toyota's hood shone.

Something had backed up from the Gulf over us, a cloud pattern. It was once more gray and muggy, raining softly. Everyone asked if the parade would be canceled. Krewe of Proteus tonight. It takes the whole year to plan a parade, so they are almost never canceled, save hurricane or flood. Bernice had already mentioned to Tom and me that she and Murray were eating out with friends and going afterwards to the parade. This was according to her plan "to be good at least until the legal separation is final."

"How long will that take," I asked.

"A few weeks, maybe a month." No good, I thought to myself.

"Don't you want to see me?"

"Of course."

"But you are willing not to for three weeks or a month."

"I think that's best, don't you?"

"Do you know who Andrew Marvell was?" Bernice was unlettered a year of college at LSU in Baton Rouge where she met Murray.

"No."

"He wrote a poem about his mistress, who was a master at procrastination. He told her that love can't wait on this or that thing, it is urgent, it must seize the moment. We have to love when we can, while there is still time." I felt lousy saying this, showing off, letting her know how miserable I was. But it was the right foot note. Nobody listens to poets. My God, why don't we have time for love.

"You're old fashioned."

"There you go again, ha, ha."

I should have charged her for the lay. Ten bucks, please. You need tiding over again before the separation, I'm available. Ten bucks, cheap. I was going to Matranga's after work to have a bourbon or two, and listen to Sinatra, the kid-man from the desert. Go to the desert, said the prophet. Nobody said that, it came winging from my bitter heart.

The day would not end. I was at Tom's elbow, meaning to look busy, but getting in his way. He had taken over with me day-dreaming, floating off during conversations. Tom knew that I would be back, but not today.

At eleven-thirty I suggested to Bernice that we take an early lunch. But she hauled out a brown paper bag; she had brought a sandwich and was eating in the office. "O.K. Mrs. Waguespack, sweetie." I headed for the door to have lunch alone, but I had to come back to get my raincoat and umbrella. She looked up at me from her typing a bit frightened, I thought. This was not my day for reading signs, maybe it was a look of triumph.

Down in the lobby concession I leaned against the wall with a Coke in a paper cup and Mrs. Drake corned beef sandwich, which I didn't feel like eating. Mae Morgan who I was staring at was in her forties and had a good figure, her hair was thick and wavy, jet black, strong featured like an Indian, a full mouth surrounded by strong muscles. A sexy lady. Why had I not noticed before? She was talking to . . . I didn't know her name. Once or twice Mae shot a quick glance over to me, wondering why I was staring. My rain coat was buttoned and my umbrella was hooked onto my arm, a man prepared for the rain who was eating in the building. Mae shot another glance. I sipped my Coke and stared on. Was Mae married? Yes. She wore a diamond engagement ring and a wedding band. New Orleans is an old fashioned city. Mae looked like Anna Magnanni, the same type, calves like a half-back. When she glanced again, I thought I would wink, I bet she would jump out of her skin. Old fashioned, this city.

Last night I found a note on the ice box from Sheila: "gone to the parade." I went to the bathroom to take a leak and look at myself in the mirror.

I am the kind of man who is better looking at 48 than I was at 25. A little thicker, a mustache for ruggedness (I should have mentioned this before, a man with a mustache forgets that he has one after a while); most of my hair was left, no gray, wearing it longer covered part of my ears. I wore stylish glasses, air force style, slightly tinted. How did Clara recognize me: Napoleon with a mustache? Going to sleep was out of the question. I took the Hepplewhite chair to the eastward window to look at the stars. I heard the sirens. The parade was on Canal Street. Things were busting loose. The krewemen save most of their doubloons for Canal Street. As the floats turn onto the big thoroughfare they fling them high into the air by the handfuls. The coins glitter in the air, turning round and round. Tinkles are heard all around on the pavement where the people are down scrambling, killing each other. If you come up with one you are the happiest man in the world. It's true. A worthless, golden thing clutched in your hand and you are as happy as a man can be.

I got to thinking about Clara. About what really happened. Wes Collins, a local stringer for *Time-Life*, told me that they were interested in my story. I couldn't imagine why. "Well," said Wes, "it is a novel way to campaign, staging a mock coronation, a queen in New Orleans, Mardi Gras, you know. And L. C. Perrilleau is Rigaud Perilleau's brother." Rigaud Perilleau was a segregationist who made national news by pulling a black priest off the altar in a white Catholic church down-below in St. Bernard. Wes had passed the story on and *Time* did a column and a half on it, with a marvelous photo of Rigaud, a bloated, corrupt, defiant man with glinting eyes and twisted mouth.

Wes thought that there was a possibility. "If Rotolo," he said, "beats Perilleau they might go with it. L.C. is as big a bigot as Rigaud, just not as well known. Philip is young, hence a liberal; you know how *Time* hates southern bigots. And the Queen, New Orleans, the queen city, Catholic and all, the kind of local color that makes those guys lick their chops."

I was excited, fool that I was. But sure enough those jerks came down: guy named Weinberg or Sternheim, another named Hilton, they called him Hilt, you know, New York guys, and a Japanese photographer. I had called Philip when Wes told me that it was a possibility. "Is that right? *Time Magazine?* You think there's something to it, Bobby?" "Think so, Philip. Wes is very hopeful." "All right, then, let's not disappoint them."

To tell you the truth, Philip thought that the whole idea was crazy, the idea of staging a coronation. Said that he only went along at first because he was pressed by Father La Garde. Father La Garde you must understand was an 86 year old retired priest with a mind as crafty as what's-his-name . . . Machiavelli. He lived in the rectory at Our Lady Star of the Sea Church, where he had been pastor for many years before his retirement, forced retirement, when he was 82. And the bishop worried about him, not his age, or even his politics which were liberal, but his drinking. He stayed crocked most of the time. In his favor, he drank very expensive wine, so it would be hard to call him a wino.

Philip told me about that night in the rectory parlor. Father La Garde opened a bottle (Chateau-Lafitte, Rothschild, 1947). "A glass or two in the evening helps one to relax, don't you think, Philip?"

"I wouldn't argue with that, Father. How old are you now?"

Father La Garde was really smiling broadly. He knew what Philip meant. He looked like Jacques Cousteau, same type; but was much warier than Cousteau. Knew himself better than others knew him.

"Been talking to the bishop, Philip?"

"Not lately, Father, ha, ha."

Father poured up two glasses of wine.

"I liked your speech the other night, Philip."

"Thank you, Father."

"Nice touch about the queen. Good people down here, they do deserve better; perhaps a queen as you said."

"Came right off the top of my head."

"Yes, I know, Most people would have said a king."

"That might have been better."

"On the contrary. More wine?"

"What do you mean, Father?" You drank wine with Father and asked him what he meant at your own risk.

"A queen is much more appropriate. She's soft like a mother, a mother to all of us."

"Like the Blessed Mother."

"Yes, that's the general idea. But I mean that the idea of a queen fits this place, the ninth ward and Algiers, too. Good people, fun loving and innocent, like children. Whereas other cities, northern cities would do much better with say a Viking king, a warrior. We're tropical, warm like the bosom of a woman. You see? More wine?"

"You're over my head, Father."

"Well, Philip, you might seriously consider this idea of a queen."

"Back up, Father."

"I mean it's a creditable idea. That's all."

"A queen instead of a councilman? This is America, Father."

"A councilman and a queen. How would that be? Nothing unconstitutional about symbols. The American eagle, for example."

"Not a real queen, then."

"Well, real in a way. Even real queens are symbolic. More wine?"

"Father, excuse me, but I don't know what we are talking about." Philip was dizzy; less from the wine than from the talk about symbol and reality.

"With the help of a queen I think you may be able to win this election. That's very important to me; Mr. Perilleau and I don't get along, as you know."

"Father, if I tell the voters that the Blessed Mother has appeared to me and asked me to be their councilman, I think that I might be considered nuts. The bishop for one . . ."

"If Our Lady appeared to you, Philip, it would not be a mere political matter. I am talking, my son, about a publicity stunt. More wine?"

Our Lady Star of the Sea church stood on the perimeter of St. Roch Playground, which comprised about four city blocks, marked off into playing fields, baseball diamonds in the summer, gridirons during the fall. The church was known the city wide because of Fisherman's Mass. Special permission had been given the pastor to celebrate a Mass every Sunday at three o'clock for early rising fishermen. A good idea, these men must get an early start. They hitch their boats and drive down St. Bernard, to Delacroix Island and points beyond: Venice and the Chandeleur Islands, going for specs and red snappers. If there is anything that the men of this city enjoy more than drinking beer it's catching speckle trout. But even good ideas don't always work out as planned.

Father Prescott, Star of the Sea's dour pastor, celebrated this special Mass himself. Pacing forth from the sacristy, chalice in hand, his eyes would sweep across the congregation, at what he saw, and not to his surprise, for it was thus every Sunday, he would scowl, eyes clouding with an anger he must suppress for sacramental purposes. There would be but two rows of starchy fishermen, with a cowlick or two dangling from the caps which they had removed, their eyes still puffy from sleep, and a small boy innocence in their slightly parted lips. Beyond these, however, and the object of Prescott's ire, were all manner of all-nighters. Good Catholics, they come to Mass for it is a sin, a mortal sin, if they didn't, but there was little left for the Lord. Bedraggled and bleary-eyed though they were, they had to stay awake, for Prescott's orders to the ushers were to throw out the drunks.

In 1960 it was thus, an adolescent put on a rented tux, took his best girl to his senior prom, swigged four or five shots of whiskey in the men's room, danced and sweated all night to a local swing band, got a kiss in the cab, and ended up here at Star of the Sea. But he had a great time. He really did. It was great to be a Catholic in 1960.

What Prescott wanted he said in his sermon, was folding money in the collection basket. Electricity is very expensive, at three o'clock in the morning there is little more that even a good priest can tell his flock.

The park which Star of the Sea looked out over, St. Roch Playground, was the very site of my athletic youth. Here the Annunciation Bombers gave battle to the St. Roch Bullets and all comers. Doing double duty I played the game and reported the news. A paragraph or two in the parish bulletin: Annunciation Bombers edge past St. Roch Bullets, 56-52; or if it was baseball, 36-35. The Bullets always played us close.

What clinched it was something that Wes Collins stumbled upon. Actually at this point, the whole idea was slowly spinning down the drain. Sternheim, Hilt and the Japanese photographer were not down yet; it was this stumbled upon piece of information that cranked things up and sent them flying to the Crescent City. The problem had been who would be the queen, how would she be chosen. Besides, Philip had gotten very busy and had no time for such foolishness, said I was a prize asshole for writing such an article, and he was a prize asshole for drinking with a wino priest. I forgot about it, and Wes had, too, until this little fact came drifting down like a fallen leaf and stuck in his ear. Clara Duplantier's grandfather was none other than old Judge Hypolite Duplantier, who, aside from being a distinguished Creole magistrate and legal scholar, was the judge whose restraining order had stopped Rigaud Perilleau cold. Rigaud had to stand by spitting and fuming while the Negro priest returned to the Church to celebrate Mass on a regular basis. A major victory for the liberal cause in 1960. Rigaud was the undisputed lord and master in St. Bernard Parish. Not a hair moved or a finger crooked unless Rigaud gave the nod. It seems a simple thing to us today for a federal judge to stop a bigoted political boss in such a manner as this, but in 1960, things were different. To shackle Rigaud Perilleau in St. Bernard required legal astuteness, determination, and moral conviction; and Hypolite Duplantier was 76 years old in 1960.

"Look here, Bobby," said Wes, "if this Duplantier girl would agree to be the queen, I think I could put this thing back together again, that is if, and only if, Philip would be willing to make civil rights an issue in the election." He was right, but I knew that Philip dared not say a single word in favor of integration; the ninth ward and Algiers were very conservative. And this was such a harebrained idea, anyway, I didn't know why Wes persisted. But Philip, and I really don't know how or exactly by whom, was talked into it. Wes for sure and maybe old Father La Garde. It was actually a very logical thing for him to do. He had no chance to beat L.C. Perrileau anyway. Nothing to lose. And yet in 1960 what Philip did take courage, if courage it was, perhaps it was daring, or some vague stirring within him to be heroic; heroes, I think, are frequently the result of peculiar circumstances striking a chord in the hearts of bold men, calling them forth. I think my friend Philip was a bold man. What ultimately happened was astounding. The blacks came out to vote, and Philip won. It was the first time that blacks had voted in such numbers since the days of Reconstruction.

But this was not why *Time* decided to make this a cover story. Oh, they liked the idea of old Hypolite's granddaughter reigning as queen over territory wrenched from an old bigot like L.C. Perrilleau. They even included a sidebar on the old judge and his family, including his son, Maurice, Clara's father. What did it for the cover story was this shot of Clara, taken by the Japanese photographer. In it, she bore a striking resemblance to Elizabeth II. And there were those beautiful shots of the parade. That's right, there was a parade; this is New Orleans. Three marching jazz bands and doubloons struck with the image of Queen Clara. Most of the whites voted for L.C. Perilleau, but they came to the parade, and made it a gala affair. This is an old fashioned city, and who is to say that its people would not give serious consideration to having a queen to rule them. The Queen of New Orleans.

Father La Garde in full vestments placed the crown on Clara's head. It was a very dignified, solemn ceremony, the same, I was told later, as that used by the Bourbon kings of France, abbreviated I am sure, staged on the front steps of Star of the Sea. This was as far as the bishop and Father Prescott would go. The parade followed, winding all through the diamonds and gridirons of St. Roch Park.

There was some talk of the blacks taking over, but that didn't happen until the seventies. Mr. Charlie held forth about this at Steckmann's for some time afterwards, I heard. I happen to know, though, that Mr. Charlie got drunk on his ass at the coronation and had to be dumped on the back seat of Ronnie's Cadillac and be driven home. It was three years before this in the spring of 1957 that Ronnie and Clara were married. And some years after that their best man, Philip, ascended to old Hypolite Duplantier's judgeship. Philip is today, of course, our junior Senator in Washington, having unseated, in another upset, F. Martin Bougeoise, whom everybody had thought was elected for life.

But this was ancient history as Sheila said.

Later, as I snoozed on my Hepplewhite chair, I dreamed.

The Lady on my balcony turned to face me, extending her arms out from her elbows, hands turned upwards; round about her golden crown was a circular pattern of silver stars. Doubloons rained forth from her finger-tips onto the balcony. They tinkled away, piling up, overflowing, and fell from the balcony to the streets below. The people were down scrambling and grabbing; I couldn't see them, but I could hear them screaming with wild excitement. Snare drums went rapatatap--rapatatap, bass drums: BOOM-rapatatap--rapatatap--BOOM. A band struck up. I fell--half fell, pushing myself back up with my left hand. The parade was passing two blocks over on Royal Street, in full swing now from the sound of the band and screams. In my right hand was a doubloon, but it was an old one, dated 1960; on one side was Clara's embossed profile: QUEEN OF THE THIRD DISTRICT circled around. On the other side: VOTE ROTOLO FOR YOUR COUNCILMAN.

Chapter 6

I did wink at Mae, and she smiled back, blushing a bit I thought. She was distracted in her conversation with--was it Ethel? She glanced over more often now, not listening anymore to Ethel, she had shifted around to face me more squarely. She could look right past Ethel, and Ethel was none the wiser. Well, well. I relaxed my stare and smiled. The question now was who could stare the other down. I won easily. She became fidgety, checking her wrist watch, looking up at the wall clock, and threw a little smile to Ethel. Ethel turned around and looked directly at me. She wanted to know what the hell was going on. Nothing much, just a little eye game. As the lunch crowd began to drift toward the elevators, Mae cast one more glance my way, and she and Ethel turned to leave. Some day, Mae, my dear, some day.

At two o'clock I asked Bernice the wrong question and started trouble. She was standing at the corner of my desk, looking over two letters which she had just taken in.

"What say we have a little drink at five o'clock?"

"I told you that I was going to be busy."

"Just a short one, half an hour."

She looked at me with eyes which pleaded for mercy, "Please, Bobby, don't make it difficult. Don't make me say something ugly."

"O.K., sweetie, I get the message."

"See, you're mad."

"I just got turned down, of course I'm mad."

"But it is your fault." She was right.

I went down to the lobby concession again, to have more coffee. Maybe Mae Morgan would show up. The place was deserted, just me and Sylvestor the attendant. Sylvestor didn't talk unless he had to; he had his nose buried in a paperback, Harold Robbins I guessed. We all do the best we can. Real life just doesn't do it sometimes--most of the time. If I was not careful I was going to get very depressed.

An old speculation came to me. Something I had been working on, and half avoiding. There was probably nothing to it. I saw Sheila and Jules Bergeron in the Old Absinthe House Bar one day last August. I was just walking past, and there they were sitting at a table across from each other. I stopped to go in to join them, but suddenly changed my mind. Did I detect some intimacy between them? I stood there looking in at them. They were laughing quietly about something, Sheila tracing the rim of her glass with her finger, Jules talking with little gestures of his hand. Jules was an old friend from our Loyola days. Actually he was more Sheila's friend, I never liked him. Jules was a Cajun gone bad to my way of thinking. He taught French at Loyola and had never gotten over his Ph.D. Most Cajuns had too much culture to seek higher degrees in French literature. There was no end to what Jules would tell you about the French Symbolist poets, especially Paul Valéry. Beware of a Cajun who could recite whole poems by Paul Valéry. In the old days at the Napoleon House Bar, he would hold forth for hours on end. He was a fresh Ph.D. then just out of school on his first teaching assignment, but only two or three years older than Sheila and me, having been a prodigy. His students, Sheila among them, who flocked around him, would actually ask him to *do* Valéry. "For Valéry," he would say, almost smacking his lips, "I need a stimulant." The stimulant required was a glass of Chartreuse. You should have seen him: tiny glass aloft, twisting it delicately to let the light shine through the green liquid, eyes sensuously half-lidded, one sip, and he was off. And no none, Sheila included, understanding a single word. Was he *doing* Valéry that day. I don't think so, I think he was doing something else, and that's what concerned me. Nothing happened really, I dared not stand there too long. I walked on, brushing it off. They probably ran into each other and were having a drink for old times sake.

Would it bother me that much if Sheila were having an affair with Jules? I was having an affair with Bernice, that is, I hoped I was, only time would tell. I didn't know. Sheila and I knew each other like an old glacier knows a mountain slope, ancient carcasses lie beneath the snow.

Sylvestor read on. Thank God for best-sellers, Sylvestor was sixty or more, and had never known the passion of a beautiful woman, from the look of him. Does this fire ever burn down? Drinking that bitter coffee and watching Sylvestor read a Harold Robbins novel was very depressing.

It was four o'clock, and I had to decide whether to go back to work or to go to Matranga's for a double bourbon. I decided to wait until five o'clock and catch Bernice when she came down. What to do in the meantime? An hour was a long time for a man in my condition.

I had to go back up. Sylvestor was looking over at me. He might want to tell me the story of his life.

My chair was turned to face the window behind my desk. Nothing moved. In a few days Mardi Gras would hit that dull, gray sky. The roof tops were wet and forlorn; it rained a mist. It needed a Breughal bird, soaring into the cold blankness. Winter wrenched the heart of this tropical city. It would end in the forty days of Lent, following on Fat Tuesday.

Today I was a poet for myself; I sang old songs and listened. I needed a drink and an intimate talk with a woman. I had something to tell, something I had never told before.

Behind me the typewriter clicked away. A maniac was banging on it. What was she thinking that her flying fingers did not know? All day long I had been composing words to tell her. My heart was full of poetry, it came unbidden to my ear. If we could have been alone to speak to each other . . .

The typing stopped, and she was stepping into my office, "Bobby," softly like a mother who called her child to see if he was sleeping. A man looking at a winter sky should be gently wakened from his thoughts, "Yes."

"Are you all right?"

"Now that you are here talking to me, there is nothing wrong."

"What?"

"I said that it is good to hear your voice."

"Why are you so quiet?"

"I was thinking of you."

"Someone might hear you."

"You're right, I should be more careful, but it is true: I was thinking of you."

"I believe you, but you shouldn't say it here."

"What did you come in here for?"

"It's four-thirty."

"Is it?"

"I was thinking of leaving early, I have finished everything."

"May I leave with you?"

"No."

"I'll just walk you to the garage to get your car."

"What good will that do?"

"We could talk along the way."

"Someone might see us."

"Everyone will see us; what of it?"

"You know what I mean."

"What about it?"

"All right, but I'm going home."

"Let's go."

Outside it was freezing. We walked separately, hands thrust in our pockets. It was even too cold to speak, and I had so much to say; but it was not practical. We walked briskly, our one object was to get to the garage so we would be warm.

There was a little waiting room with a glass front where the customers could get out of the cold to wait for their cars. There were ten or so people there, and it looked packed.

"Look, Bernice, can't we go for just one drink?" I suggested.

"You promised."

"I know, but we haven't talked, it was too cold."

"What are we going to talk about?"

"I have something to tell you."

"Can't it wait?"

"It can, but I can't."

"I'll get caught in the parade traffic." She was right. In an hour or so the police would block off the main arteries from here in the Quarter to Uptown where she lived. You had to go miles out of your way through narrow, seldom traveled streets which would be congested with other confused drivers trying to find their way.

"We'll get your car now, and find a place in your neighborhood."

"Why can't you wait until tomorrow, I'll have lunch with you, I promise."

"By tomorrow I'll be a wreck, have mercy, please."

We were still standing outside of the waiting room in the open garage. She was shivering, "I don't care what we do; I just want to get out of this cold."

"Give me your ticket and go into the waiting room."

The weather in the Toyota was colder than it was outside. There was an early gathering of people on St. Charles Avenue along the parade route. They stood around, without mirth; they had the look of people who had witnessed an accident and were still stunned by what they saw.

Bernice and I were trapped in the misery which I had created. I could not help myself. She drove without aim, like a cab driver on his last hour of duty. I could think of nothing to say. One of us had to speak soon, out of sheer practicality.

"Where are you going?" I finally asked.

"Nowhere."

"We have to go somewhere."

"You know a place?"

What about Tall T?"

"That's on Carrollton?"

"Yes."

"You been there?"

"No, I've seen their sign. It looks like a college hang out."

"Murray's going to be waiting."

"It's not five yet. What time does he get home?"

"Five-thirty."

It was hopeless, I couldn't talk to her then. What did Marvell do about husbands? In a poem you can do anything--say anything. I should have been at my eastward French window writing a poem. Is it the same: being in love and having a poem to write? One is a function of the other. But which of which? "Bernice."

"Yes."

"Drop me off at Tall T. I'll have a drink and catch the streetcar home."

"I can't do that."

"Yes, you can, I'm at fault for this situation. I'm sorry I caused so much trouble."

"I told Murray that I would go to the--"

"I know. Drop me off. I'll be fine."

"Are you mad?"

"Of course not. It's my own damn fault. Besides, I like to drink alone, ha, ha."

She leaned over and kissed me with expression, "I'll see you tomorrow."

Tall T was slick-rustic: rough milled planking, carved fraternity escutcheon, a parchment bill of fare: something between pirate den and Texas ranch. It reeked of text books and blue jeans. My waiter was a yellow-haired, smiling youth. Tulane would never change.

"A double bourbon with a little water, on the rocks."

"A double, sir?"

"Right"

"Call brand or bar brand?"

"Old Taylor," anything, just get it here fast.

Every effort had been made to make this place warm, comfortable and adventuresome. It had recently been done over. The old map sepia wallpaper was very handsome; for tables, old cable spools had been sanded and finished with fiberglass, one could not help passing a hand over them. Each chair was a heavy, generous captain's seat, with curving arms for the elbows, contoured bottom for the ass, the sitting was pure luxury. Why, I was asking, did I get the distinct feeling that I was in some college boys' dorm? There was a phantom whiff of locker room, caked shaving cream and soiled athletic socks. I could have been some freshman at Kansas State, lost in an alien world, ready to shake hands with my roommate, "Hi, Bobby, Bruce Deerfield, welcome aboard." For all I know there were parents of my generation from the ninth ward who had sons named Bruce. There was no one responsible for this place, no enlarged snapshot of its opening, happily enjoyed and drunk to, no jolly collage of licenses, permits tacked randomly about with carpet tacks, or first dollars earned, proudly framed in dimestore golden frames. Thank God for bourbon, if, and heaven forbid, the bourbon here did not bear the acrid flavor of stale nineteen year old sweat.

It didn't, bourbon is bourbon the world over. So, I mused, this was why Ronnie was lost at Tulane. The whole place stank of freshman underwear. It wasn't John Stuart Mill, at all. Mill was a very sensible man, a Utilitarian, who wanted the best for his fellow man, even Catholics are willing to admit that now. Ronnie had a fatal case of the dormitory stinks, coming as he did from Poland Avenue where shot-gun and corner grocery were redolent of oyster juice, oily luncheon meat, and nutria musk from down-below in St. Bernard. Did not Cher in her own foolish, farcical way know how to drink bourbon, true alcoholic or not?

What do you think my waiter's name was? No, not Bruce but Rick, would I lie, I heard the bartender call him so. There was near the entrance a pay-station telephone with chained directory, and I was tempted to flip through its pages, a little research. I would wager that I would find: Remison, C. Anderson (Cher's father). Did I not hear a few years back from an unknown source that C. Anderson Remison was king of Comus? One would never know for sure, the identity of the kings from this oldest of the Mardi Gras krewes were never revealed.

I sat there, sipping bourbon, feeling like the little ninth-ward rat that I was. A Proustian odor of fried liver came curling up my nostrils. I knocked back the bourbon, the ice rattled against my teeth. Where are you, Bobby Gomez? You don't even know who your mama and daddy are.

I had to go. There wasn't enough bourbon there at Tall T to exorcise whatever spirit pervaded the place. I had to go sit at my eastward French window and read the big gray sky for new signs.

The evening was dark and cold, casting no long summertime shadows, nor did it deepen the hue of flowers and grass. I could have frozen to death, standing there on Carrollton Avenue. And perhaps I would have; but as luck would have it, Bernice came pulling up to the curb in her Toyota. God bless midget foreign cars.

Chapter 7

The Toyota was jockeying along Carrollton Avenue headed for Tulane Avenue whose natural extension was the Airline Highway; we were going to turn left onto the highway and zip up to LaPlace, a small Cajun town but twenty miles upriver from New Orleans. There we planned to sup on chicken gumbo, made with the best Andouille sausage in all of southern Louisiana. My idea. The din of the parade crowd was but a reverberating memory in our ear; we were getting out of town for Mardi Gras if only temporarily.

"What are you doing here?" I had asked, opening the door, bent over low enough to look in at her, a big smile plastered across my face.

"I like that, aren't you glad to see me? Hop in."

We sat there smiling the same wide smile, holding hands over the white battery cover. Holding hands sometimes gets it all.

"What happened?"

"Murray called and said he would be working late, not to expect him home until very late."

"Oh."

"What oh?"

"Just oh."

"Oh is right, I think Mr. Murray has a girl friend." Mr. Murray, old fashioned but cute. What did she think I was?

"Are you hurt? That is if it's true that Murray has a girl friend?"

"Honestly? Yes, I am. It's true all right, this is the third time this week he's working late. I happen to know who it is, too. Stubby little Stella McNamara. He's finally got a girl short enough for him."

"How tall are you?"

"Five foot six."

"So am I." She kissed my hand. Such intrigue, delicious intrigue.

"Should you be so hard on him, considering?"

"We had a date, a date's a date."

"Technically true, I myself am happy that Stella is such a charming little midget."

"Selfish."

"Sheila's been home late all week, too."

"Don't joke."

"I joke not. Sheila has been coming home late for years."

"Oh, Bobby," squeezed my hand.

"I am not accusing her; she is very busy. She's got people down from D.C. to entertain, meetings, one thing or another. In a way I suppose I would like to believe that she has a boy friend."

"Feeling guilty?"

"Not that so much. Well . . . better not say anymore."

"Say it."

"It would be the height of self pity."

"You're silly, if she is running the streets at night, I bet she's fooling around."

"Maybe she is fooling around, and maybe I don't want to know she is. A man has more pride in these matters."

"Do you have any proof that she is?"

I told her about seeing Sheila and Jules in the Old Absinthe House Bar.

"That's no proof."

"They were leaning towards each other when I walked off."

"Are you sure?"

"I'm sure, I've tried hard enough to forget that they were."

"I'm sorry."

"Why? I feel great! Telling you was really like telling myself. I've lied to myself too long. Kiss me." We smacked hard and laughed out loud.

"Who is Jules?"

"A rotten Cajun Ph.D. and close associate of Paul Valéry."

"Who is Paul Valéry?"

"Never mind, kiss me."

*M*iss Jeansonne, our waitress, wanted to know if my daughter wanted a cocktail before dinner. I gave Bernice's hand a fatherly pat and ordered her a double dry martini. If Bernice drank martinis I doubted that she took them double. The double was to let Miss Jeansonne know that I knew that she knew that Bernice was not my daughter. Cajuns, especially Cajun women, are nobody's fool.

"Wall, suga, you lak that cocktail your Papa bought for you?"

Miss Jeansonne was from hereabouts, she told us; had been living on the River Road all her life in the same house her grandpere built with his own hands. You heard Cajuns tell you things like that so often that you were no longer impressed. But it was true, there were little Acadian cottages all up and down the River Road, built by grandperes with their own hands and still inhabited by their granddaughters. Who would believe that there were such people as Cajuns? Unspoiled, French-speaking peasants, earthy, smarter than ten Creoles and fifteen red-necks, true mechanical geniuses, they had converted from trappers to petroleum engineers in one generation, knew more about drilling oil than any Texan, you pick your Texan. Good at anything they took a mind to, even French Symbolist poetry; come to Louisiana and see for yourself.

I was really surprised to see Bernice poking around in her gumbo wanting to know what was in it. I explained and teased her. "I don't believe that you're a native and don't know." Her name was O'Neill, which meant that she might have been from the Irish Channel and therefore been deprived of more than chicken gumbo. Miss Jeansonne was at my elbow laughing her head off. We were her only customers on this slow day, and she was taking a special interest. Cajuns are very friendly and will include themselves in any fun available. When I invited her to join us, she rolled her eyes, "Mais no, you are customers, I got work to do." But she was not offended, or thought for a moment that we felt crowded. She explained to Bernice how Andouille sausage is made, step by step and offered to write it down. Her own uncle made the sausage we were eating; he was eighty-one years old that year. Bernice made a pig out of herself, accepting the seconds that Miss Jeansonne offered at no charge. Good food, a lot of laughs, a typical Cajun evening. Miss Jeansonne went all the way to the front door with us, hung herself out in the cold night and waved us off. She made us promise that we would come back soon.

I thought of Tall T, smelling of adolescent laundry. In four or five months the rough planking would fall down, the captain's chairs would grow wobbly and peel, the sepia map curl up at the corners, not by any rough house vandalism, but through sheer neglect. A Chicago chain would sell it to a St. Louis chain and it would be redecorated and called *The Screaming Jean* or some such.

Miss Jeansonne waited tables at Robichaux's which was owned by Ridley Robichaux, her cousin. He owned, besides this restaurant, two oil wells down in Golden Meadow. His mama and daddy, Miss Jeansonne's aunt and uncle, lived in an Acadian cottage on the River Road; he had built himself a big, rambling brick bungalow on the Airline Highway and landscaped it with evergreens. In a few years he would try to buy a house in the Garden District in New Orleans, failing that he would build a Greek-Revival villa in a lake subdivision and join a Mardi Gras krewe, Babylon if he could. He wanted nothing more than to have his daughter "come out" as a maid one happy Mardi Gras season at the Babylon Ball. But if you visited him at his villa, he would take you back to the kitchen and give you a good cup of French-drip coffee, drinks if you wanted, and a bowl of chicken gumbo made with Andouille sausage.

From Carrollton Avenue to LaPlace we traveled through stolen hours from the eternal reservoir. On the way back on the River Road, (we took the longer, scenic way back to the city) time overwhelmed us, a loud tick-tock in our ear. We checked our watches for the time, turned on the radio to double-check; we had to decide what we were going to do, if not for the rest of our lives, at least for the next several hours.

The night on the River Road was dark beyond all imagining, the levee a black, flanking wall. Bernice had clicked on her brights; they cut swatches of light out of the blackness ahead, like a miner's helmet-light that beamed its way in a shaft. Curves were hardly made out and had to be felt around. The Toyota leaned like a quarter horse working cattle.

This blackest night muffled us. Only the gumbo, solid and warm in our stomachs, prevented us from buoying up into its ether regions. I searched the side land for Acadian cottages, but there were only black trees on black sky, and the felt slumber of old Cajun men, deepest slumber. Words entered and went hallow in my mouth. Bernice was quietly pressing brakes and turning wheel, and these movements too were swallowed up. It seemed the longest moment before she spoke, "Bobby."

"Yes."

"We're not lost, are we?"

A chuckle went hollow in my throat, and I could only manage, "Of course not." But the sound of it was not reassuring to either of us.

"Are you sure?"

"I know that the River Road will take us to New Orleans, trust me."

"What are you thinking?"

"About how cute you are to think that we may be lost."

"I've never been this way before." The conversation had two levels, didn't it?

"The road or what we are doing?"

"Are you thinking about that?"

"Aren't you?"

"I wasn't until you mentioned it."

"What are we going to do when we get back to the city?"

"Go home, of course."

"What do either one of us have to go home to?"

"You're blowing this up, aren't you?"

"Not if you feel anything like I feel."

"How do you feel?"

"Very close to you and alive for the first time in a very long time."

She silently pressed the brake and turned the wheel, she had the hang of it now, the Toyota rolled like a ball bearing around the curve. She digested what I had just said.

"How do you feel?" I ventured.

"I am not sure."

"I don't mean to commit you."

"I'm sorry, Bobby, of course I feel close to you now. Isn't that obvious?"

"Then shouldn't we take advantage?"

"Advantage?"

". . . of this night."

"I thought we were."

"I mean: why don't we go to Sharon's apartment. Tolstoy is waiting dinner, isn't he?"

"I fed him earlier."

"Technical, my dear."

"If we do, we'll be missed."

"Don't make me laugh. By whom?"

Another curve, and another silent, deft execution.

"Don't you want to go?" There was a lowering, pitiful register to my voice.

"Of course."

"All right then."

"For a little while, anyway."

"For as long as you want." A light ahead; it hung over a solitary gas pump before a small grocery store. The Coca-Cola sign said: E. Boudreaux, Ice. Beer.

Tolstoy was waiting at the door for us. He threw his weight at us, arching his great back, serpent tail twisting like a tentacle; he wove around and between our legs.

"He's hungry, Bernice. Are you sure you fed him?"

"No. I lied."

"You're tricky but cute." I took her in my arms and kissed her. My friend Tolstoy was winding round our feet. Her eyes caught light from somewhere when we broke, "What was that for?"

"For lying, and because I love you."

"I better feed him before he knocks us over."

She moved through the dark to his feeding place in the kitchen and switched on the light. I found my way to the sofa and sat to wait. When she had given him his food she moved behind me and put her hands on my shoulders, "Did you mean that?"

"What?"

"That you love me."

I took her hand and pressed it to my mouth, "With all my heart."

We were entwined on the sofa, lost in a deep, unending kiss. It seemed long and yet too short before Tolstoy was back winding round our legs, "What's wrong with him?" He was too furious in his weaving. We were forced to break.

"I don't know, I gave him lots of food. He must miss Sharon." she petted him, called him softly, trying to calm him down; but he wove more furiously yet.

"He needs to go outside."

"He has his litter box, he never goes out."

We were thinking that Tolstoy, a great golden-eyed beast, brought us some message from beyond, that his weaving was our own furious weaving--no mere black cat but some spirit within. His restlessness increased, and he suddenly bounded up in our laps.

"My goodness." She stroked him heavily pushing down his fur, determined to calm him. His heaviness pulled us out of ourselves. From his warmth we felt how cold it was, how very cold the room was.

I pushed him onto her lap and rose, "It's cold in here, what does Sharon use for heat?"

"There is a floor furnace I think." She stroked him still, and he jumped up on her breast.

"Where is the thermostat?"

"I don't know, at the entrance, I guess."

I searched at the entrance and found it, bending to make out its calibrated face, "Here it is." Somewhere near the bathroom we heard the burner flare up.

The light switch was near the thermostat and for some reason I switched it on. It was a mistake. An undercurrent of despair pulled me down, now that I could see everything clearly. Bernice petted Tolstoy who was still and calm, she looked around distracted by the sudden illumination. Her eyes glinted with new alertness.

"What time is it?" I went obediently to the kitchen.

It was one-seventeen, "Nearly one-thirty."

"That late?"

"What difference does it make?" I actually snapped. Why was I annoyed? I went searching through the cabinet to find the sherry. It was right in front where we left it. But I knew that it wouldn't do: it was a drink to be comfortable with, a drink with warm, glowing coals, I needed one with fire.

"Is there a package liquor store near here?"

"A package liquor store?"

"Yes, do you know where one is?"

"There's an all night drive-in grocery on Prytania, it sells liquor I'm sure. What are you going to do?"

"I'm going out to get a bottle of bourbon."

"Bobby, wait."

"What?"

"It's getting very late."

"I don't care how late it is. I'll be right back. Where are your keys?"

"They're here. But, Bobby, I'm worried about the time."

"Let me worry about the time. Give me the keys." I struggled upwards, against the undertow.

The pint of Early Times fitted neatly in my hand. The pint, I was thinking, was a relic of the twenties, still contoured to fit back pockets. Did I remember empty pint bottles like this one, lying over on one another, scattered about on a worn-through kitchen linoleum, the way they smell when empty, fumy and gaseous? I had not drunk bourbon until recently. I come late to my passion. But I would no longer deny myself. I drove with one hand and slugged bourbon with the other, and felt the fingers clutching my gut loosen their grip.

I went straight to the kitchen and got two glasses and joined Bernice on the sofa. Tolstoy was curled up, sleeping at her side, "He's sleeping," I whispered.

"Yes, I think he was cold." The room was warm and comfortable.

She cast a wary eye at the pint, already opened, and the two glasses, "What are we going to do? You have already been drinking."

"That's right, and I feel much better. Here let me pour you one."

"Are we going to get drunk?"

"That's the general idea."

"Do we have to get drunk to do what we are afraid to do when we are sober?"

"I used to think that people who drink were weak. But I realize now that we are all weak. Maybe, in a way, it takes courage when you know that you need to. Here, drink up."

"With nothing in it just like this?"

"It's the best way, and the fastest. Don't you want to make love to me? Drink, I'm going to put the lights out." She took a little gulp and her eyes watered, but when she recovered she drained the glass.

We whispered to each other, words hardly spoken and barely heard, fallen across the bed, still dressed, petting each other and unfastening buttons, pulling zippers down with care, unhooking hooks, whatever had to be loosened, helping a twisted arm out of a sleeve, rolling gently like children in summer grass, patient with every little detail. Words, more soft words for every step of the way, sweet, warm kisses here, there, wherever we were at the time. We were drunk with bourbon and with a released love we had never known before. We told each other this, "Never have I loved this way, I feel like giving you everything," a foreplay long, sweet and loving: "Foreplay," did I hear that technical word? Did I speak it, or her? It mattered not who spoke, who heard, what was foreplay, what was gentle handling of member, what was gentle, sliding penetration, rhythmic rocking, pressing, holding, waiting, and asking: "Now?" "In a while, my love, hold me, hold me." Sleeping, in a drunken, loving sleep, but kissing and pressing yet.

The windows were so bright with sunshine when I came awake that I knew that it was their brightness which had awakened me. Bernice slept on her side, one leg pulled up, an arm under her head extended out, the hand over the edge of the bed. I kissed her, sunshine kiss. Was it spring, or was the sun already high, breaking through a still cloudy, wintry sky? I went to the kitchen to look at the clock, enchanted, but with a slowly dawning presence of mind. It was not yet seven. Spring? Mardi Gras is calculated by the cycle of the moon, it marks the ancient turning of seasons, a pagan remembrance.

I did my morning stretching, wondering: what was that last night--that fumbling of amateurs, drunken blind-man's buff exploring, and . . . what? Crawling across the floor to the bed, tickling and giggling along the way. Bourbon babies, not knowing anything of lovemaking or its seriousness. The pint laid on the sofa, half tucked between cushions, uncapped and exuding its gaseous fumes; lozenges gleamed along its contours: the work of the early sun filtering through Sharon's gauzy window drapes. Elfin Bernice, skin as callow as a six year old's, teeth smooth pearls bared by the usual lifting nose and rising lip. Her eyelids were blue-veined, violets floating in milk. Old Bobby was stretching like a puppy, feeling frisky enough to romp about the sunny room.

When would I realize the seriousness of this situation? Had we been reported missing? But there was time yet in Sharon's springtime kingdom. Tolstoy, who knew more than I did, slept near the point of Bernice's toe, and must have dreamed of eternity stretching out. There was no rush to make a crisis here.

Sharon's little kitchen was puffing steam and humming like a factory. Water boiling for coffee, toaster busy with its constant, one-note melody. I sat in my boxer shorts, neither smiling nor frowning, having no need for a special face to meet the world with.

Seven o'clock by the apple clock. I shook Bernice, calling her a drunk, an adulterer, and other profane names; whispered gutter language for love's sake. She opened her eyes and tried to burrow under the pillow. "You think it's funny," she told me when I lifted the pillow. "It's spring," I said, stroking her arm. "We're in trouble," mumbled she. "Let's have breakfast first," I said, "and then we will figure things out." "We're in real trouble," she spat out as best she could against the muffling sheet. "I know, I know."

I had even found a little orange juice and some margarine for the toast. A feast, no less.

The most serious problem was the rumpled clothes, having been rolled on, slept on, and . . . Bernice looked down at herself, now fully dressed, assessing the damage, then over at me, also fully dressed. "This will never do." Two winos trying to press out wrinkles by hand, picking off little worms of sheet lint. "Awful," she bemoaned. She went rummaging around in Sharon's closet and found an iron and an ironing board. Good old Sharon, on her own but well equipped. We stripped to our underwear and felt for a few minutes like husband and wife, she in her bikini briefs and bra pressing with vehement energy, me in my shorts making passes at her and getting poked for my trouble. Bernice in her briefs would wilt the strongest man: a tender Olive Oyl.

Eight-thirty by the apple clock, and we sat in the kitchen, showered, well-pressed and well-groomed, having the last of the coffee. What were Murray and Sheila thinking, we were thinking.

"We have to call them, you know," she said, sipping her coffee, riveting me with her blue eyes over the tilting cup.

"Of course we'll call them."

"Have you thought about what you are going to tell her?"

"The truth."

"Be my guest. It's your funeral; I'm getting a divorce, remember."

"You've committed adultery."

"That's not funny. Please be serious."

"You're right. All right. I'm going to call Sheila and tell her that I met an old friend and got drunk with him at Johnny Matranga's bar, and that I am now at the Morning Call having coffee and donuts. You can tell Murray that you were irked at him for working late again. Came over here to feed Tolstoy and decided to sleep over. See, simple."

"Do you think that they will buy that?"

"Maybe they will and maybe they won't; but they can't prove anything. Unless Miss Jeansonne tells. And Cajuns don't tell."

"O.K., you first."

"Why me?"

"It's your plan."

I reached for the phone which was on the wall above the table. I had to call before my confidence ebbed. I dialed and listened as it rang. Bernice and I were looking at each other like two convicted murderers who had just been told to rise to hear the sentence. Three rings and she answered, "Hello, Sheila?"

"Bobby?"

"Yes."

"Thank God. I've been worried sick. What's gotten into you? I was going to call the police. Don't ever do this again."

"Don't you want to know where I've been?"

"Well, I think that I have an idea, I called Murray earlier this morning." What!

"You called who? Murray? Why did you call him?" Bernice rolled her eyes with great histrionics, but was careful not to make a sound.

"I called Tom Mahoney, too, and he said that you and Bernice left early. I can just about guess what you two have been up to." Great going, Tom.

"What do you think Bernice and I have been up to?" Bernice slapped her head a great silent blow.

"I can just imagine. Good old Papa Gomez giving advice to the lovelorn. I think that you are very kind to do it, but you and Bernice should have at least called. That would have been considerate."

"She was really broken up, Sheila. I couldn't let her go home like that, you understand."

"Of course, I understand, but it's almost nine o'clock in the morning. Where in the world have you two been all night? How is she now, I know that the poor girl has been going through hell."

"She is fine. Now. Did you know that she and Murray are getting a divorce?"

"I've been knowing it for weeks, Murray is pretty broken up, too."

"Does Murray know that Bernice has been out with me all night?"

"He was the one who figured it out. He knows how much respect she has for you."

"Well, I'm sorry that I didn't call earlier. We're having coffee at the Morning Call. By the way, we drove out to LaPlace last night to have dinner. Gumbo. I'll be home shortly."

"All right. But I won't be home when you get here, I have an appointment. Better take advantage of your Saturday and get some rest, you're not as young as you used to be you know."

"O.K., Sheila, see you later."

"Oh, Bobby."

"Yes."

"I hope you and Bernice didn't do anything foolish, something you might regret."

"Don't be stupid, Sheila, I'm old enough to be her father."

"You never know with men your age. I'll see you later."

Bernice was sitting there, her mouth half open with the most amazed, amused expression she would muster, "You really are something."

"What do you mean?"

"I've never seen anyone lie with a straight face like that before. You ought to be a spy, you'll never get caught. Amazing."

"What was I supposed to say? Bernice and I have been shacking up, a lot you and Murray know. We'll be home as soon as we clean up. Anyway, it's your turn now, let's see how well you do."

She grabbed the phone, dialed and waited for him to answer. No answer. She hung up. She should have been relieved, but she looked forlorn. "He wasn't home?" I asked.

"No."

"Maybe he's working, you know architects, always making deadlines."

"I know what he's working at all right. He just couldn't wait to get his hands on that little bitch."

"Now, now. Under the circumstances I should think . . ."

"Oh, shut up!"

"What?"

"Shut up!" She was crying. What the hell?

"Bernice?"

"Leave me alone, please."

What was I supposed to think? Was she jealous? She loved Murray. He had broken her heart. Did I think for a moment that she loved me? Was glad to be rid of Murray? Whose heart was broken? I could have cried, too. There was a salty taste deep in my throat. Bernice was crying in her cupped hands. I got up and went into the big room. On the sofa the pint gleamed with bright starry fire. It contained but a few futile amber drops.

I was alone in this big room, filled up as it was with Spring's first sun. Spring is saddest of all for the lonely.

The sun burned my cheek. I must have dozed off. My head was lying back on the sofa, my feet propped up on a little brown ottoman. Tolstoy slept near me. It was quieter than it should have been. Bernice was gone or was sleeping. The bed was empty and made up. In the kitchen the table was cleared and things had been put away. She could not have left me. But she had. The pint was gone. I could have used those last few drops.

I thought that I was going to cry. A dry, tearless, choking cry by the way it was rising in my breast. But there was a click, a small click, at the front door, and Bernice opened it and entered. Her face was long, and she looked at me only briefly. "Where have you been?" I demanded.

"I was out walking."

"I thought you left me."

"No. I'll take you home now if you like."

"That's all right with me."

"All right, let's go."

"Bernice?"

"Yes."

"I'm sorry I made you mad, I didn't . . ."

"I'm not mad at you, Bobby, I was upset, I'm sorry I yelled at you."

"I appreciate that, but I don't mind telling you that it really pissed me off. I don't think I deserved that."

"Well, I apologized. What do you want me to do?"

"I want you to be honest with me. If someone as young as you can be honest."

"What is that supposed to mean?"

"I mean that I feel like I have been used."

"Used?"

"That's right. Something, someone to tide you over while you're getting over Murray."

"That's ridiculous, and you know it."

"I don't think it's ridiculous. You ought to know what you're getting into when you do something like this."

"This was all my idea I guess."

"No, but you're over 21 and ought to be responsible for your actions."

"Thank you, Mr. Gomez. Coming from you I certainly appreciate the advice. You're old and wise."

"That's enough, Bernice."

"You're damn right that's enough." She marched herself into the kitchen.

We could have sat there all day in separate rooms, but I didn't have time for that. She didn't owe me anything, she had her own problems. I went in to her.

"Bernice, this has gone too far. All those things I said were stupid." I bent over her and kissed her cheek. "You want to hear something interesting?"

"Yes, I do."

"I'm writing a book." so I lied; maybe it would be worth it.

"You're kidding."

"No. I really am. Would you like me to tell you about it?"

"That would be nice."

"You must swear yourself to secrecy, because it is a true story."

"It's not about us, is it?"

"No. It's about something that happened a long time ago. About the same time that you were born, I think. In what year were you born?"

"1950."

"The very year that this story had its beginning."

"What is it about?"

"It's about a queen, a real queen."

"A queen? Do you know a queen?"

"Yes, I do."

"Of what country?"

"Of right here in New Orleans, the ninth ward and Algiers."

"A Mardi Gras queen?"

"No. A real queen and her friends."

"This is a real story you said, about real people?" She patted her cheeks dry. They were blotched red, such delicate skin.

"Yes, it is."

"You know these people, or knew them?" she blew her nose, but kept her eyes on me. A little story is what we need sometimes.

"I know them yet, they live right here in New Orleans. Today."

"Is it all right to write a book about living people? Legally, I mean?"

"I don't know, I may have to change the names."

"Won't they recognize themselves anyway, if the story is true?"

"Yes, I suppose so."

"Was she really a queen, the girl?"

"Yes."

"How can that be? In New Orleans?"

"I'll have to tell you the whole story."

"I got nowhere to go. Tell me."

"Are you sure?" I asked. she smiled now, finally; and seemed relaxed. And so was I. Finally.

"Tell me about this Queen in New Orleans. You want to, don't you?"

"Yes. Very much. Let's make some more coffee, and I'll tell you the whole story."

Fresh coffee, two relaxed people in a little kitchen in old New Orleans, and a story to be told. Outside the new Spring wheeled its opalescent light.

"Back in the fifties . . ."

Tolstoy was running around the room in a wild frenzy. He scampered across the floor, onto the bed, onto the floor, across the back of the sofa. He was driving us crazy, the story was interrupted,

251

and there was nothing to do but to go in and see what he was up to. He was up to Krazy Kat business, and we watched him go round five or six times before he rolled over and had a little duel with the corner flap of the bedspread, "What's that all about?" I asked.

"Who knows?" said Bernice, rolling her eyes, her old jolly self again, "I like her. She's neat."

"Who?"

"Clara, she is the queen, I assume."

"Yes, you could tell?"

"It's quite obvious."

"Well, it could have been Cher. She is very rich."

"It couldn't have been Cher. She had no class. What is Ronnie's last name?"

"If I tell you, you will recognize him."

"Really, tell me; I don't like suspense."

"Hingle, Ronnie Hingle."

"Ronnie Hingle, the hotel man. Hingle-Lang Real Estate?"

"The same."

"Murray knows him. He has met him anyway. Is that all true about him, flunking at Tulane and everything?"

"Every word."

"You can't write that, he'll sue you."

"I wrote a nice story about him in *Dixie-Roto*, didn't I?"

"That's right, you did."

"Maybe he won't mind me telling his story in a book?"

"But I still don't understand how she became queen, especially of the ninth ward, why would the ninth ward have a queen?"

I smiled, "Yes, it was very unusual, and it was certainly not Clara's idea."

It was hard for her to believe what was being suggested--a queen? Bobby Gomez, one of Philip's friends, a reporter for the Picayune was there with another reporter whom she didn't know. Philip had driven her and Ronnie to the church--or the priest residence and ushered them into the parlor to meet an elderly priest who offered them seats and wine. He was very charming. They sipped wine and talked informally for a while. The old priest looked constantly over at Clara, and she could have sworn his eyes lit up.

"I am staring Clara, please excuse me, but I had no idea......You realize my dear that you have the most remarkable effect, I mean you are so composed. Here we are planning something very akin to Mardi Gras, and when I look over at you, I think you are....."

"I am what?" She asked.

"You are queenly, I hope that doesn't embarrass you."

"I have never thought of myself that way." She didn't think, as the grinning Philip was thinking, that it was the wine. But even if she thought the priest was exaggerating Clara sat there with her usual calm self and did, in fact, look queenly. That is the quality that she had always conveyed to Bobby Gomez, who kept his thoughts to himself. Ronnie was, of course, smiling, too, for Clara was his--that is, she was going to marry him.

There was still the question of why there was to be a queen in the first place, because it wasn't Mardi Gras, it was September. The priest asked the other reporter, whose name was Collins, to explain. He was very serious, this reporter, explaining that they were going to stage a mock coronation and have a parade afterwards to kick off Philip's campaign for city councilman. This was Philip's first time running and he needed something--well, sensational--to get people thinking about him, who he is and so forth.....Clara smiled, yes she understood but why her? The reporter explained further, reading from his notes. Her family had a proud tradition in the city. Her name was known, especially in connection with certain liberal causes. The public would make the association. Otherwise, Philip's opponent was almost certain to win, with his powerful political connections. She would be helping Philip. Didn't she want to stand behind the political heritage of her father and grandfather, who was still living and almost a legend in Louisiana? The priest told her how much he admired her family. Yes, of course, she was willing to help in any way she could. She was proud of her family--the Duplantiers'. But for her to be a queen, even for one day caused an elementary confusion. When she looked in the mirror she saw an ordinary girl with regular features, and brown hair--how can they make a queen of her? She would do the best that she could to make up for how ordinary she was, but....? Even if the old priest thought she *was queenly. He was only flattering her, she knew. Ronnie told her later that he was very proud of her and her family, and that what she going to do for Philip's campaign would also help him in his project to erect a new exclusive shopping pall at the foot of Canal street, a project that would bring some of the most famous department stores, to New Orleans and revitalize Canal Street, once one of the premier thoroughfares in the United States. She was distracted because of his use of the word 'revitalize'; it is a word that she couldn't imagine Ronnie using not too long ago when she met him. He was dressed in a beautiful blue suit, he had become very polished, his hair trimmed, he was clean shaven, his nails manicured and his teeth as white as could be, he smelled of very good cologne. She wondered why she was not more pleased with these improvements, since he was going to be her husband. Of course she was pleased, she concluded, who wouldn't be?*

Everyone was excited about the meeting, about Philip running for city councilman, about her becoming queen of the Third councilmatic district which included the ninth ward and Marais street where Philip grew up. Clara felt a little rush, herself.

"Did Clara ever get the house fixed up again?"
"Yes, that's the next part of the story, sit down."
"Was it like it was when her father lived there?"
"I think so."
"Did you see it?"
"Many times."
"Tell me."

Chapter 8

M r. Sol Ulysses' complexion reminded her of dried bay
leaves, tiny black moles were sprinkled over his cheeks
and forehead. One could not, if one was from New Orleans,
help thinking of file gumbo. She smiled, remembering his speech:
resonant, musical, rising from deep to higher registers. A calypso
lilt. One expected sultry, slurring speech from Negroes, words
formed more with the lips than with the hollow palate--the
blues; and a high-spirited, yukking laugh when they are joyful or
derisive. But Mr. Ulysses, she knew, was from Trinidad, and
hummed an island tune when he was pleased. "Life is sweet,"
she heard him say when particularly happy, which no local
Negro could ever be imagined saying. He was explaining to her
how this long row of avocado trees must be protected from the
frost. They were grafted and would bear fruit, no eunuch house
plants sprouted from supermarket seeds. She walked out from
the patio along one of the brick pathways that curved along
the rows of slender saplings; the left-most one swelled to a
circular base for a latticed orchard gazebo, its fresh painted
white members sheening in the warm sun of mid-May.

Mr. Ulysses was a member of the team. Team was not
quite the word for them, even though they worked together as
one. She could not believe that so many had come forward to
help her, after the solitary years in New York with barely an
acquaintance now and then, lunch companions from the office,
a young man to take her to a show (none were encouraged). She
was firm of purpose and resisted loneliness. Making deposits in
her savings account was what she looked forward to, and
finding new ways to save a few dollars; six extra dollars for the
weekly deposit, ten more one week when she ate nothing but
cottage cheese for lunch. But she knew she must be sensible and

carry none of these deprivations to extremes. She expected the same austere life in New Orleans. But then she met Ronnie by sheer accident on the levee. To this day she did not know why she invited him to sit down with her and then told him everything--practically the story of her whole life. Not like her at all. She felt very contented, even serene, sitting on that levee. She must have looked lonely sitting there; he certainly did. Who stopped their car in such a deserted spot to speak to a stranger, especially a girl? A lonely man with a problem, or a rapist. But Ronnie was not that, she could tell instantly by the slow, distracted way he got out of his car, and by the graceful way that he walked. Still, she knew, she took a chance. But there was no calculating weighing of the balance. It was something about the shy way he became confused when she questioned him. But why did she tell him the story of her life, that's what she did not understand.

Mr. Ulysses did not have a degree in landscape architecture (that's what it is so called), but Dr. Sherman Meyers who did have a degree, three in fact, recommended him. Dr. Meyers was a member of the team, one of those who had refused pay. Philip Rotolo, a brand new lawyer, with the firm, Gagliano, Moledoux, and now Rotolo, was the one who put her in touch with Dr. Meyers. "He is an old friend of your father," said the ever smiling Philip. Philip smiled because he was full of confidence, and Ronnie because it was so natural for him, and, one suspected, because he was hiding his shyness. Philip did the title work absolutely free. Another member of the team, he was Ronnie's best friend, and it was no wonder. Still, friend or not, she was overwhelmed. She sent him a check, and he sent it back. And he would only accept a nominal amount for the act of sale.

"Your father could have been mayor of this city if his time was right, my dear." Dr. Meyers smiled, too, because he was so comfortable with himself. He was retired from the Tulane School of Architecture, but was busier as a consultant these days than when he was teaching. Ph.D. in Federalist Architecture from Davenport, Iowa. In that year, 1957, he considered himself a preservationist, out of love for his adopted

city and its rich heritage, but had also encouraged an interest in good contemporary architecture, a fine line, he said, and a puzzling dilemma in this city where progress and tradition had shunned each other.

It had been six years since her meeting with Ronnie in the spring of 1951. She had not thought that it would be that long. Her other life had intruded for three of the six years. Grandmother Dolly Rawlins had died, and Clara returned to be with her mother in Dallas. It was slower going during those three years. But for Ronnie, it was a time of great strides. He had done all that Cora Lang had expected him to do. In three years they were full partners, and the Hingle-Lang sign with its fleur-de-lis appeared everywhere. It was no trouble for she and Ronnie to be engaged for those three years and for the two following. Ronnie was buying property in the Treme area and at the foot of Canal Street, the groundwork for developments he was planning in the sixties while she was biding her time, and had had some arguments with her mother about the wisdom of the plan. She explained to her mother over and over that it was best for her to return to New Orleans, and to wait five years to marry.

She had for over twenty years corresponded with and on occasion visited her Grandfather Hypolite Duplantier. If there was ever anybody just like her it was this independent old widower. They were always happy to tell each other of their plans, and were warm and affectionate when they met, but never complained to each other or gave each other advice. Had she asked him what he thought of her plan, he would have said that it is a good plan if she thought that it was a good plan. He would have been willing to help her with it, if she had asked him to, but she did not ask him.

She had not asked anyone. The members of the team had come forward to help her of their own volition and out of their generosity. Ronnie included. During this year while the house was being restored she had never known such generosity or been so warmed by companionship.

Mr. Hingle, Ronnie's father, called Mr. Ulysses Coca-Cola. He referred to the popular calypso tune of the late war years, Rum and Coca-Cola, sung by the Andrew Sisters.

Mr. Ulysses did not seemed to mind, and Mr. Hingle did not mean derision by it, it was just his rough way of being friendly. He was an independent contractor now, since his son's success in real estate. She thought sadly that he had had such a hard life. Clara had barely gotten to know Ronnie's poor mother who died two years ago of diabetes, and had enjoyed this new life of luxury for only a short time. She was the sweetest, simplest person she had ever known. Ronnie was more like her, Clara thought, than like his father. Mr. Hingle called Dr. Meyers 'Prof', and had thrown up his hands a number of times during the restoration over suggestions made by the professor. What the 'Prof' and little Clara wanted, he would declare, was all right with him, even if he knew better, and off he would go, mumbling that he only went up to the fifth grade, but knew a little something about the construction business. He drank cold beer all day long and perspired even on cool days. His body, she was sure, would never grow old, it seemed to be made of coiled wire . When his men did not understand his instructions, he would push them out of the way, pick up their tools and do the job himself. Such language! Clara was sure that he did not know that she was standing so close.

Now, in December of that year, she and Ronnie were going to be married. In May the house had been finished. They had not planned it that way, but she thought it was fortunate and convenient. The house would remain in her name. She decided to give it a name, which as far as she knew, it had never had. She named it Maison Maurice, after her father. She and Ronnie would live there after their marriage, of course.

What was left to do, Mr. Ulysses was telling her, was the planting of the St. Augustine lawn in the front yard. He would come out and check on things during the coming months, everything was going to be beautiful. This was the most beautiful job he had ever done. A beautiful garden, a beautiful orchard. He had two gold teeth, and when he smiled she was sure that he was conscious of showing real gold in his joy. "Don't forget the house-warming, Mr. Ulysses, you and your wife are invited, and I'll be very disappointed if you don't come." "Wouldn't miss the party, Miss Clara." He gave her more of his golden joy before he left.

She had an appointment that afternoon with Mr. Marcus Scipio, legendary interior designer of New Orleans; an old thirties Trotskyite, Dr. Meyers told her, who consorted with Diego Rivera in Mexico City and with certain local Cubist painters, hereabouts, in the Bohemian days of the twenties when William Faulkner and Sherwood Anderson lived in the French Quarter, then a Sicilian ghetto, famous for his modern furniture and interiors during the late thirties, the only tiny effect, Dr. Meyers complained, that the Bauhaus had in old New Orleans. For Clara's house, however, he had selected Victorian furniture and Oriental rugs. Mr. Marcus Scipio (a professional name) was a handsome, silver-haired octogenarian, an old friend of her father's, enlisted by Dr. Meyers, and had acceded to her demands to accept a nominal fee for his services, out of sheer courtesy.

The appointment was not for a few hours, so she had time to walk down her orchard path and sit for a while in the gazebo.

She flipped the Zippo and lit a cigarette. She inhaled deeply and blew out the smoke in one long smooth stream. A mockingbird squawked in one of the new peach saplings. The bird was deciding, thought Clara, if she would build her nest in a tree with so few leaves. She hopped up to the topmost limb and began to sing. Mockingbirds, when they have found the right perch, will sing for long minutes on end. This one did, until there were four snubbed cigarettes on the bricks beneath her feet.

There was something in Bernice's eyes which interested me. It was a feeling for Clara and for me, the story teller. There was also behind this feeling, I thought, a new sadness, one that had come to her this very day perhaps. It had to do with her broken marriage with Murray, and with the passage of time. She felt and could see, if she were a visionary, the ponderous earth turning on its axis, the tongues of fire leaping from the sun, and the great distance their rays must travel to reach us through Sharon's windows. It is the peculiar sadness of a new springtime noon, and of a story told. I had told her Clara's story with a quiver in my stomach, and a new intensity. It came to me from I knew not where.

Part Three

Chapter 1

*U*ntil Bernice was fourteen years old, her mother and father took her regularly to Sunday Mass at St. Peter and Paul Catholic Church in downtown New Orleans. St. Peter and Paul was a poor parish in a poor neighborhood. Its pastor, Father Conner, although well-off himself, was profligate. He spent money like water in barrooms and expensive restaurants and attended the horse races during the season at the Fairgrounds. As a consequence, the church was in poor repair. Its red bricks were blackened, paint peeled from its wooden doors and the interior was dark and smutty. The statues were covered with a film of cloudy grease. It smelled of melting holy candles, incense smoke and older odors.

Bernice and her parents sat in the first pew whenever they could. It was seldom that they did not since her father was a methodical man who arose early. They attended eight o'clock Mass.

The great crucifix above them was the centerpiece of the church. When such a huge expensive statue had been purchased was a lost fact of history. It was larger than life size, and was placed next to the pulpit. Its style was the very ordinary nineteenth century church style of Italian Renaissance statuary: painted plaster of Paris, picked from a catalogue of an Italian manufacturer of holy statues; though, to be sure, it was clearly one of their most expensive items. Bernice was enthralled with it. And with Him whom the statue represented. She supposed that this feeling was a religious one. Christ was rendered in the ideal of physical beauty retained through the centuries from the ancient Greeks. His marvelous head was turned upwards on a wonderfully muscled neck, his mouth parted in exquisite agony, eyes rolled up beneath a pained and furrowed brow; lovely, copious locks of auburn hair entangled in a handsome crown of thorns. The blood which rolled down his cheeks was not grotesque or offensive. The magnificent muscular body curved down into a contraposto, a wedged platform of wood supporting the pierced-through feet. If crucifixion was a form of execution reserved for the most despicable and contemptible criminals, it was a fact lost to Bernice. This man suffered with passionate magnificence. Such a small child as herself did not suppose that there was a penis beneath the draping loin cloth (more, certainly, than a mere loin cloth which by definition is meanly shameful in its inadequacy to cover a man in the indecency of his suffering.) Her eyes would linger on the canting pelvis and athletic thighs. Her gaze produced a feeling of innocent desire, a stirring of blood she was entitled to, being so young. Nonetheless, it was an arousal of physical longing for warmth and contact with human flesh. Bernice paid no attention to the ceremony of the Mass and felt the sermon was distracting, so strong was her infatuation with this crucified Christ. She was thin and pale, but her body was healthy in its inner workings in spite of her seeming frailty, but her passion did not torture her as passion would torture a saintly girl who would come even at age nine to a momentous conflict between sensual and spiritual longings. She was blessed with normality and health, but she had inherited her father's callow elegance.

As she grew older she became more and more confounded by the incongruity of the immature body and her generous passion. When she was twenty she could have given to any man all that he needed. Unfortunately her physical attributes were not the ones men were attracted to. Her nose turned up, showing her nostrils, and took her upper lip with it. Her lips, in consequence, were naturally parted in her usual demeanor. Her teeth were white and even. Her skin was transparent like her father's and let her veins show through. Their hue, though veiled, were sparked in their blueness by her clear blue eyes. Her eyes were wondrously tender and receptive when she was aroused to passion, and she was easily aroused if given the opportunity. But few men got past her thinness, she would never be voluptuous.

She would have made a wonderful model, for she was elfin and pubescent, but what fashion photographer could have discovered her? She was born to simple folk in downtown New Orleans. None of the clothes available to her suited her. She needed to be discovered; she needed to be created, as Twiggy was. The men she came to know were as puzzled as she was about herself. They knew that they held a beautiful, passionate woman in their arms, and yet--they knew also that her beauty was rare; and they did not have the sensitivity to respond to it. That she kissed them with the passion of a woman with more obvious attributes puzzled them even more. They clung to her and were puzzled all the more by their arousal. In their confusion they did not come back to her. She could only suppose that she was unattractive and would have to settle for what she could get. The physical beauty of the crucified Christ at St. Peter and Paul Church was her ideal. She thought, rather bitterly, that she was born without beauty, that beauty was a rare gift.

Her mother's name was Reba, Reba Marchand, before she married John O'Neill. Even in her pious attendance at Holy Mass, Reba could not conceal her fiery nature. How was it that Reba was so dark and full-bodied and Bernice was so pale and thin? Was not conception a blending, a striking of a balance between extremes? Reba's hands were smooth and strong, like those of the crucified Christ, long-fingered and marked on her nails with perfect half-moons. When she stood up during the reading of the Gospel, she gripped the back of the pew in front of her, so incessant was her need for action and adventure. This restlessness would be the undoing of her marriage to the mild, methodical John O'Neill. Reba was like her father, Alcide Marchand. He was a shrimper from down-below in St. Bernard Parish. A brown man with the marks of the wind in his face. Who could tell what went into the making of this man's body and countenance? In 1959, when Bernice was nine years old, Alcide was 74 and showed no signs of slowing up. He had held tight reigns on Reba. She married John O'Neill to escape this tyranny. John married her because she was as brown and passionate as her father. But Johnny O'Neill was not the man for her. He did all he knew to do to keep her. He was steady and gentle, quiet and patient during her rages. But when Bernice was fourteen, Reba broke every dish in the house and left John for another man. Bernice was glad to see her go. She was ashamed of her mother and her whole family. Their dark eyes and loud voices frightened her.

Bernice looked like her father in every way. She was proud of this, the close resemblance tempted her to believe that her mother's blood had no part in her making. On Reba's part, there was a confusion. Why had she been given such a thin and sickly child?

Through Reba's veins coursed the blood of many races. Those who lived in the marshlands below New Orleans were descended from the privateers of colonial days. They were richly cross-bred: Negro, Indian, French, Spanish and God knows what else. Bernice was happy to be done with the mystery and richness of this heritage. Many of Reba's people had come to the city and over several generations lost the distinctiveness of their blood lines.

Reba loved Bernice with all the dark wildness of her marshland culture. But from the very beginning Bernice rejected her. Reba had no way to understand this rejection. She would have done anything to win her daughter's love. John's reserve and her pale daughter's rejection of her love became more than she could bear. She had a simple, savage heart. John had stood back because he needed order and temperance in his life, this coldness was more devastating than Bernice's hatred. After all, she could understand the violence of blood against blood. If John had fought her, things would have been different; but he did not know how to fight. He was by nature aloof. Nothing could have saved the marriage.

Bernice was more like her mother than she realized. This was her contradiction. Her passion for the crucified Christ was the love that she denied her fiery mother, for Reba's savageness was a match for His magnificent agony. Her body had the grace and power so admired by the ancient Greeks, the same that had been retained over the centuries, and had stirred Bernice. The Christ was a poor manufactured version of powerful sensuous beauty. During her life, Bernice would come to understand that her own pale body was powerfully sensuous in spite of its appearance. But, in 1959 she was innocently stirred by the Christ, sham replica that it was, and knew nothing of the complexity of feelings she had for her mother.

In the morning she was awakened by her father. He shook her gently but did not kiss her. She wanted him to kiss her. Her mother smothered her with hot kisses and powerful embraces. She fought her mother with all the strength of her frail body.

The early morning sun was too weak to light the kitchen. Her father's face was engulfed in shadows as he drank his coffee. He had poured her a glass of milk. She preferred coffee, but drank the milk knowing that her father was concerned for her health. Her mother always gave her coffee. She thought her mother indulgent and irresponsible for doing this.

It was so dark in the kitchen at this hour that she could not tell if her father was looking at her or not. She knew somehow that he wasn't. He seldom spoke to her in the morning. She imagined that he was thinking when he was so quiet. She admired him for this. John O'Neill was quiet because he enjoyed the half-darkness of the early morning. At this hour the world was fragile and whole, when Reba would awaken the morning peace would be shattered by the onslaught of her great force. She heated up the stove, switched on the light; the sun seemed to rise by the command of her presence. The coffee turned acid in his stomach. She was always too much for him.

The family had a standing invitation to join Alcide, the grandfather, for Sunday dinner. Alcide was a widow these past twenty years and did his own cooking. He cooked a huge pot of pungent chicken gumbo, and boiled shrimp in'his backyard. He hugged and squeezed Bernice, kissing her with a slobbering mouth. His breath was dark with strong tobacco. It was more than she could bear. He and Reba talked noisily about all of their friends and relatives. After they had eaten she and her father would go for a walk, leaving her mother with all of the dark, loud people who came over to visit. Alcide told Reba many times that he could not understand why his granddaughter was so thin and pale. He thought that his blood was stronger than that.

She and her father would walk to the edge of the bayou. Water hyacinths and lily pads floated on the surface. Her father told her the names of the birds they saw: white egrets, pin-tail ducks and raucous kingfishers, which reminded her of her grandfather, Alcide. They saw nutria and armadillo and parts of the bayou's surface was churned by blue-gills and goggle-eyes swarming for floating particles of food. All of this teeming life should have brought joy to the heart of a child like herself; but she could not dissociate this fecund spectacle from the frightening energy of Alcide and Reba.

Sunday after Sunday they went down below to have dinner with Alcide, and their walks became longer and longer. Her father would sit beneath a huge oak tree, leaning against its great trunk, and rest his eyes. She imagined that he was meditating. He was actually resting and trying to forget what he knew to be the inevitable breaking up of his life. Reba was seeing her old beau from down-below, Raymond Treadaway. Raymond was brown and powerful like Alcide, and had a way with women. John felt helpless to stop what was happening. He felt guilty, thinking his own blandness was the fault of Reba's slutting ways. He did not realize that his daughter admired him for what she supposed was the elegant reserve of an educated man. He knew that he was not well-educated or well-cultured. He had gone to Warren Easton High School and to Soule's Business College. He was a bookkeeper. He lacked a verve for life and felt defeated by the challenge of life itself. Since he was a good Catholic he could not consider suicide, although at times his desperation brought him to a flashing realization that this would release him from the torture he endured.

Bernice was fourteen when Reba left them for Raymond. Alcide and Raymond had a violent argument, and only their difference in age prevented them from coming to blows. Raymond was as powerful as Alcide and stood him off. He took Reba over the river to Venice which was near the mouth of the river, even deeper into the marshes.

John moved out of downtown New Orleans and away from St. Peter and Paul Parish. He rented a little shotgun cottage in the University section of the city, near Carrollton Avenue. He set himself to the task of raising his daughter. He sent her to Dominican High School for girls and encouraged her to go to college.

When they moved it did not occur to Bernice that she would not see the crucified Christ any more on Sundays. She was to stop going to church after she graduated from high school and went off to Baton Rouge to college at L.S.U. Away from the reserve and refinement of her father she found herself seeking sexual adventure. All of her boyfriends were physical eccentrics. Short plump boys, thin boys with twitches. She lusted after the well-built, handsome athletes but knew they could not possibly be interested in her. She consoled herself with the fact that some of her boyfriends were intellectuals, or the creative types from the art department. Eventually she found Murray Waguespack, a student in the School of Architecture.

Murray was from uptown New Orleans. His father was an architect. Murray was very self-conscious about his height (he was only five-foot three) and about his pudginess. Bernice was three inches taller than he in her stocking feet. He had a brooding sensitivity which was actually a defense against his feelings of inferiority. Bernice took his brooding for profundity. He flaunted what little knowledge he had to impress Bernice. He told her that his father had given up his ideals as an architect. "My father is a hack," he said viciously. Bernice was impressed, but she was merely giving in to her own feelings of inferiority. She had never known of architects and the style they promised to living. She was ashamed of her poor background and succumbed to Murray's brooding arrogance. She was not attracted to him physically. He was pudgy, with heavy eyebrows and thick, coarse black hair. His lips were thick and always moist with childish saliva.

They fell in love one night in the darkness of a summer night in the Greek Amphitheater on the L.S.U. campus. They had drunk a six pack of beer, and in the summer darkness Bernice forgot Murray's deficiencies and made love to him. It was her passion that led the way. She practically undressed him and laid him down in the grass. Murray was overwhelmed. His self-consciousness fled, no woman had ever done as much for him as Bernice did on this lovely summer night. He had been a virgin. He asked her to marry him, and she accepted.

She dropped out of school to support Murray when they were married. He refused to ask his father and mother for money and she admired him for this. Murray struggled through his last two years of school. He made mostly C's. He did not have the intelligence and talent to be a good architect.

During these two years they had many friends on the campus. They lived in the Married Dormitory. Every week somebody threw a party. Bernice was accepted among all of these intelligent, creative students. It was fun while it lasted. At one of the parties a lanky art student with soulful eyes made a drunken pass at her. She put him off, but she had been tempted. Murray had not proven to be a good lover. His passion was compromised by his self-consciousness which came back soon after they were married. She knew that he was having second thoughts, her body was thin and inadequate; and she in truth had many second thoughts about Murray. At times he looked piggish to her. He complained to her about her lack of education. She saw him for the pompous, babyfied runt that he was. His coming graduation from the School of Architecture was the only thing that cheered her up. As the wife of an architect, she imagined that their life would become fashionable and comfortable. Wasn't that all a thin, pale girl could expect?

At another party, a quiet, softly handsome student talked to her half of the night. They left the party and walked around the campus. His name was Michael Prat. He was gentle and self-effacing. He reminded her of her father. He was studying to be a landscape architect, and spoke to her of his love of nature. His sensitivity stirred something in her. He was actually attracted to her, but she imagined that he liked her because she listened so well as he talked about himself. Michael thought that she was beautiful, he had admired her from a distance at some of the other parties, but he did not tell her so. She felt this admiration but could not believe it. Their hands brushed as they were walking, and he apologized. She smiled and told him that he was very shy. She took his hand, and they walked on hand in hand. They stopped in front of the Campanile, the most famous landmark on campus. They were silent. When he turned to her, she put her arms around him and kissed him. She pressed against him, and he responded. He finally broke, and became flustered and embarrassed. She had not been ready to stop kissing him, but she could tell that he was upset. He apologized. "You are married, and I should not have done that." They walked back to the party but the spell of their attraction for one another had been broken. They seemed to hurry along. Bernice had pangs of guilt. Her Catholic faith pinched her, even though she had only been married by the justice of the peace. She planned to be married later by a priest. Michael was from New Orleans and was also Catholic.

She looked for Michael at the next party, but he was not there. He had decided not to go to a party if she was going to be there. He was deeply in love with her. He saw her once at a drive-in grocery, and greeted her in a warm friendly manner; but she could tell that he was standing back from her. She had harbored the memory of their kiss in front of the Campanile, and could only suppose that he was not as attracted to her as she was to him. Nothing happened.

She forgot about Michael. As Murray's final year of studies put more and more pressure on him, he became irritable and high handed. He could not confess to her how his confidence had been drained by the challenge of his final assignments. Had he been sensible he would have forgotten about his ambitions to be an architect. Bernice felt the prospects of Murray's lack of talent, but she fought off the idea of his ultimate failure in his profession. But in spite of this dogged optimism she began to resent him very much. He was spoiled, ugly, and indulged himself with the most childish self-pity. She thought of leaving him. One day in her misery she actually picked up the phone to call Michael. But she didn't. She told herself that she was not a quitter, that her frustration was her own fault, that her passion for Michael was self-indulgent.

She worked as a secretary on the campus for the department of Modern Foreign Languages, and one afternoon while she was working late, her boss, Dr. Bellows, asked her out for a drink. He was middle-aged and dignified. She was shocked and confused. Was she now an easy target for any lustful middle-aged man, because she was so thin and unattractive? She politely turned him down. The next week she saw Dr. Bellows leaving with a young female student, a plain girl in every way. Bernice was appalled by the sordidness of this sight, and felt vaguely soiled by it. Had she not been tempted to go with Dr. Bellows herself? If he had been younger and more attractive, like Michael, wouldn't she have gone?

But she survived these two years, and Murray graduated. They moved to New Orleans. They rented an apartment near Tulane University.

Back in New Orleans Murray became more of a problem. His father offered him a job but he refused. He wanted to make it on his own, but became more frustrated by his lack of confidence, and wasted most of his time. Bernice had gotten a job for *Dixie-Roto*, the Sunday magazine section of the *Times-Picayune* as a secretary. She was again their sole support. Murray's mother gave him enough money to open his own office, and he went off every day to sit in his empty studio to stew in his frustration.

Her father came over to visit in his dutiful way. She noticed how stooped he had gotten, his black hair was graying at his temples, his fine transparent skin was withering and sagging. He looked more defeated than ever. He told her that he was sorry that she did not finish school, but that she had made a fine marriage with Murray, an architect. Murray was indifferent to her father. Sometimes she detected in Murray's expression when he looked at her father a profound sense of disgust. She began to see her father as the lonely, lost man that he was. Where had his elegance and culture gone? Were these only illusions of her youth?

She thought, at times, of Reba, her mother. She had a strange urge one day to call her. Reba and Raymond had gotten married. An old priest in St. Bernard secured by some means an annulment from her marriage to John O'Neill. Within the year they had a child: a dark little girl. The child was now ten years old and was the image of Alcide, her grandfather, who was very proud of her. Alcide had gotten over his objections to Reba's marriage to Raymond. He knew this marriage was right, and that Reba's marriage to John O'Neill was wrong.

Bernice wanted to see her half-sister. A memory of her mother's affection came back to her. She imagined Reba nursing a child. It became a vivid image which aroused a warm feeling she did not understand. Did she love her mother after all? The question came and went but she made no effort to answer it. She thought that she wanted a child of her own. But the thought of having Murray's child repulsed her. Thoughts of the old neighborhood and of St. Peter and Paul Church came to her. The crucified Christ loomed before her mind's eye. She was filled with faith for her religion. Motherhood seemed to her a delicious, powerful salve. She could save her soul, be released form the emptiness of her life. She came very near to proposing to Murray that they have a child, but one look at his pudgy immaturity caused her to change her mind. Her frail body became a burning altar of passion. It came to her suddenly that Reba would understand. She thought of calling her, but she faltered--how could she go to her mother with such feelings, had she not hurt Reba? Had she not denied her own mother her love? This realization shocked her, she tried to forget that it came to her.

Bernice's job at *Dixie-Roto* gave her the only relief she had from her life of frustration. The work was pleasant and interesting. Her boss, Mr. Robert Gomez, was easy going and personable. The magazine supplement specialized in local culture: colorful personalities with interesting hobbies, well decorated homes, etc. Mr. Gomez seemed to take a special interest in her and even became friendly with Murray. At their first meeting he and Murray talked for over an hour.

Murray secured tickets to the Beaux Arts Ball which was sponsored by the architecture students of Tulane University. He invited Mr. Gomez and his wife. At the ball Bernice drank too much and overstepped her bounds with her boss.

That night in their apartment (it was Saturday night) when she and Murray got home, she began to feel guilty and confused. She decided it was time to ask Murray for a divorce.

"Murray, I want to talk to you."

"I'm very tired, can't it wait until tomorrow?"

"I want a divorce, that's what I want to talk to you about, if you want to wait until tomorrow to talk about it, it's all right with me."

Murray looked at her very hard; she had shocked him. "What brought this on?"

"Our marriage is lousy, and you are just as unhappy as I am. Anyway, your mother told me that you have been seeing Stella McNamara. Don't you think it's about time we get rid of this useless marriage of ours?"

"My mother lied. She's always trying to make trouble for me. I've not seen Stella in years. Do you believe her?"

"Yes, I do."

"You're wrong. I'll call Mother in the morning and prove it to you."

"It doesn't really matter, Murray. Even if it isn't true, I still want a divorce."

She thought of her mother again, and felt a sudden need to call her. She began to cry and tried to muffle her sobs. She didn't want Murray to think she was crying over losing him. Murray turned over and grunted. They were both awake. It seemed like hours before she finally fell off to sleep.

Chapter 2

*T*he sun poured its light through Sharon's windows. Bernice was looking straight through me, her countenance rapt and glowing, washed in the tender light of the new spring. She was dangerously close to succumbing to its dread beauty. It was a visage which, as I looked upon it, hollowed my breast. I felt inert, my breathing barely audible. I knew that this was no simple paralysis of my body, but the fading of my very soul. I reached across the little table and roughly caressed her breast (so meager and yet so ample to my touch). She came to attention, blinking her eyes rapidly, and I could tell by her startled look that she knew how deeply she had sunk into emptiness. She looked down at my hand on her breast with the peculiar, curious wonder of a child, slightly jerking her head and knitting her brow.

Am I back? She seemed to say. Where was I? Am I safe now? Is that why your hand is on my breast?

I smiled. She smiled back and placed her hand over mine. We had saved each other, and in the nick of time.

"Would you like to call him again?"

"What?"

"Murray. Would you like to call him again."

"Why should I?"

"To tell him where you are; he may be worried."

"Why are you worried about him?"

"I'm worried about you and about me, about how you feel about me."

"May I be truthful with you?" She said, "I know now that I never loved Murray. I was angry because I didn't want her to have him. That makes me a terrible person, doesn't it?"

"That makes you a weak person, not terrible."

"I don't think Murray and I ever really loved each other. Neither of us is anything to look at and together we're a riot. Mutt and Jeff."

"You're feeling sorry for yourself."

"But it's true, I'm not attractive, if I were . . . "

"You wouldn't have to let an old married man have his way with you."

"I didn't mean that, and you know it."

"It's lucky for Murray and me that you're not beautiful."

"Stop trying to put words in my mouth."

"The kind of beauty you're so envious of, my dear, is not real, it's an illusion."

"Do you think I'm pretty?"

"Stop the shit, baby."

"Well, do you?"

"Why don't we start talking to each other, like one person to another."

She started to cry. But she was still looking at me, trying to be the person I had asked her to be. Tears were rolling down her cheeks, her nose was running, and she was trying to keep her mouth from breaking up. She choked with the words she was trying to say. I could have gone to her, but I was waiting for her to find composure on her own. She knew this and was fighting for control. She would not even use the napkin which she was crushing in her hand to wipe her face or blow her nose. Her head jerked violently with the sobs which erupted from her throat, and which she would not let through; the air came gusting through her nose. It was disastrous. Big bubbles of snot swelled from each of her nostrils. It was so embarrassing or funny that she suddenly began laughing and heaving great jetting exhalations.

"Would you please excuse me while I wash my face?"

"Yes, of course. I'll heat up the coffee. When you return I'll tell you the rest of the story."

"You look very nice," I said when she returned.

"Thank you. Have you written this book yet?"

"It's in process."

"I've never known anyone who wrote a book. Isn't it hard?"

"It's worse than that."

"I'm like Cher in the story, only not as pretty. Not feeling sorry for myself, mind you, just making an observation."

"There is a little bit of Cher in all of us."

"But I am not at all like Clara. She was so sure of herself. She's like a character in a book. Didn't you make her up; she isn't real, is she?"

"No, she's real, I saw her at the Beaux Art Ball. Maybe you remember her. When you called me over to your table I was talking to her."

"You were? I don't remember seeing anyone talking to you."

"I didn't know it was her. I didn't recognize her. I only realized it afterwards."

"Has she changed that much?"

"I don't think she has; but I think that I have. I was looking in the mirror the other night and I didn't recognize myself. I saw my mustache, which I had forgotten I had, my glasses, my hair style; it was like a Groucho mask. At the ball I thought that I was Napoleon, and Clara shook me out of it. 'Is it really Napoleon,' she said. I said stupidly, 'No, it's really Bobby,' as if to reassure myself. Just now, when you were crying I saw your mask melting and breaking away. When it had fallen away, you were there, and I realized that my own mask had fallen away, and I could see myself in you. Are you hungry?"

"Starving."

"Let's go get a po-boy and I'll tell you about Clara's house-warming."

Chapter 3

F *lood lights, hidden among the azaleas, lit up the columns and the verandah, creating a spectacular effect from the levee or from the far bend in the road. The fresh white paint glistened, and on that clear night, the highlights fairly flashed. In that year of 1957, Maison Maurice had no close neighbor, save the freighters anchored in the river whose mast lights offered the only relief from the darkness of night. From the drainage gutter, which ran beside the road, frogs croaked loudly; cricket cries became so loud and constant that one soon stopped listening to them. There was, besides the pristine glow of the freshly painted house, the savoring aroma of new soil piled up around each new shrub and tree. The wide gravel driveway was lit up by other floodlights attached to the side of the house. The cars arriving, turned into the drive and were directed to parking places by James Timothy, a Negro who cleaned the Hingle-Lang real estate offices and looked after Ronnie's cars. James was curt but not surly with his directions, but did not offer to open doors. He greeted those who greeted him with a sober "Howareya." There was no tendency toward a slouch or a shuffle in his gait. He walked with the dignity and spring of a high jumper.*

In the parlor, Mr. Hingle had finished his bourbon and Coke and was headed to the bar for another. He was less ill-at-ease now, but still very excited about being here. He liked the glitter of the crystal chandeliers, and the rich intricate design of the Oriental rug, but most especially the comfortable fit of his alligator shoes. They were matched by a perfectly fitting brown tropical-worsted suit. If one could have overlooked his thickly calloused hands and the tell-tale division on his forehead between weathered and unweathered skin, one could have mistaken him for a businessman. Philip Rotolo was looking him over, shaking his head with disbelief and admiration. Philip's shy little wife, Mary Ann, was smiling her approval as well. She followed Philip's every lead, nestling close to him. She nuzzled softly into his heavy shoulder to tell him something. "There's whiskey in this Coke." He smiled with mocking amusement, "Drink it, baby, you won't get drunk." She looked down into the drink with mild horror and crinkled her nose, "I can't. Can you get me another one with plain Coke?"

Mr. Robert Gomez of the Times-Picayune *stood in front of the Italian mantle-piece talking to Mr. Marcus Scipio. They were exactly the same size but of widely different ages. Their positions were calculated to take in the panorama of the whole room. They were a rare pair to be party companions, being both listeners and observers. As they talked to each other, their eyes were circling, taking in everything. Robert's wife, Sheila, was standing nearby, talking to Mr. Emerson Lynn, a Negro musician from Xavier University. She stood close to him, her drink nearly touching his necktie, going on about something, perhaps music, aiding her words with her wonderfully expressive eyes. Emerson's eyes and mouth seemed prepared to smile, but the smile ebbed and never came. The beautiful caramel girl whose hand he was holding was his wife, Priscilla. In the next linking island were Mr. and Mrs. Bernard Rosenberg, Sheila's parents, talking to Clara. He was leaning back against the concert grand piano and pushed himself off from it, gently rocking himself. The similarity between Clara and Bessie was too striking to miss, they could have been sisters, but because of their age difference, more probably aunt and niece, or even mother and daughter. Following on to the next group, Mr. Sol Ulysses was drinking something red which was mixed especially for him, scooped from the punch bowl and laced with imported 151 rum by the bartender. He wore a yellow suit, of unfamiliar fabric and cut, and black and white shoes. He flashed his golden joy at Judge Hypolite Duplantier, who was the only one at the party wearing a tuxedo. Judge Duplantier was broad of face and quite handsome at age 72, his white hair thin and wispy. Mrs. Ulysses was somewhat misshapened, having a pregnant-appearing belly, but was otherwise pleasantly pretty, her skin being* cafe au lait *with a fleshy mole low on her jawline. Mr. Clifford Duveneaux, a Negro jazz pianist, was the remaining member of this group. He stood beside the judge, as if he was his body guard or manservant, but, of course, was neither. Clifford seemed doubtful about his purpose for being at this party and paid little attention to what Mr. Ulysses was saying.*

Dr. Sherman Meyers was standing beneath the arching entrance talking to Ronnie and Mrs. Cora Lang, who followed his words with bright, animated eyes (he told some story which, though not a joke, was building towards a punch line). Ronnie stood by, with his easy smile and graceful stance, in the breezeway and peered now and again down at the front door, through the beveled glass panels which made a bediamonded kaleidoscope of the mast lights on the river beyond. It seemed (the kaleidoscope) the perfect image to express what Ronnie was feeling on this brilliant night. He could have sung with a voice that would reverberate down the long passage of this breezeway, if he were a singer, or fly among the bright stars beyond, if he were Peter Pan. Ronnie's happiness was not a conscious thing for him to marvel over, but rather a sharp, vibrating energy which traveled from his toes to the roots of his hair and down his arms to the tips of his fingers.

The only seated guest seemed also to be the happiest. She sat alone on the long Victorian sofa, it was a necessity because of her bulk and swollen legs. She was Mrs. Flora Gomez, Robert's mother. The reason for her wide, dazzling smile was her simple joy at being in this beautiful house. She was dark and wore a pink camellia in her black hair; one linked her with Mr. Ulysses in his yellow suit. But they had not been introduced, and in truth she did not care to meet him.

Upstairs in a bedroom Mrs. Mildred Duplantier, Clara's mother, was preparing to come down. She sat at the dressing table looking at herself in the mirror. The only changes in her face over the years since she lived in this house were a hardening of its contours and a slight darkening of the skin beneath her eyes. Her demeanor had stiffened, and it was more difficult than ever for her to register her feelings. At 41, she was still strikingly beautiful, but it was a beauty which had hardened into a mask. More than a dozen men had proposed to her during the intervening years, but she refused them all. She liked the simple, uncomplicated life of a widow. She was concerned now about walking down the stairs to meet the guests. She thought of it as an entrance when all eyes would turn her way. As usual, she wore green to complement her auburn hair.

Downstairs, Emerson and Sheila had prevailed upon Clifford Duveneaux to play the piano. He usually charged seventy-five dollars to play at parties like this, but tonight he was a guest and among friends. He was not so sure about this, but he trusted Emerson and Bernie Rosenberg, who insisted that he come. He also had to admit that he liked Clara, though he had not said more than a few words to her.

He ran down the scale with his left hand, picking out a little blues motif on a high octave with his right, stopped to move the bench an inch closer, and brought his hands together again.

Heads went bobbing and feet tapping.

Mildred made her entrance without notice. She stood beside Ronnie in the breezeway. Marcus Scipio at the mantelpiece looked over at her and was stirred by her beauty. She had the habit of meeting the eyes of such admiring men, but was hardly conscious of what this did to them. Even a heart as old as Marcus' beat a little faster under her gaze.

Clara, who was standing behind Clifford, looked up from his hands, flashing across the keyboard, to her mother standing beside her fiancee. Such unremitting beauty, she thought, was both fascinating and strange. Her own mother, because she was so beautiful, was a stranger to her. Her mother, she could have reasoned further, because she was so beautiful was a stranger to herself.

Mr. Hingle nudged Philip's ribs. He had noticed Mildred, too, and smiled and straightened himself up, but Philip bent him over with an open-handed, back-handed blow to his mid-section. "Not for you, old man, not for you," said Philip with his smiling eyes. Mary Ann nestled closer, wanting to know what was going on, "Nothing, baby, nothing."

Clara, who liked jazz well enough, was wondering if Clifford knew any Beethoven. Robert Gomez had wandered down the breezeway and out of the front door and stood on the verandah. He was trying to imprint this night indelibly on his memory.

Clifford was improvising Tea for Two, *with right hand lightening runs, melody inversions, in the style of Art Tatum. He went pianissimo: delicate, plaintive, "Tea for two, and two for tea." Up above the stars were making music, over the levee the river made music, Robert's heart made music, this last came from he knew not where. He felt the presence of someone else on the verandah. It was Clara. She was smoking and looking out over the levee. She thought that she was alone. A scene from* The Great Gatsby, *Robert thought, when Nick had wandered out of his house and found Jay Gatsby looking out over the bay, supplicating to the night and to Daisy. But, unlike Nick, Robert decided to speak, he was no Nick Carraway and she was no Jay Gatsby. Nevertheless, he wondered if it was true that all romantic tales are not essentially the same. "This is a lovely party, Clara." "Oh, I didn't see you standing there." "Sorry, I hope I didn't startle you." "Just a little." There was everything left to say, and then again there was nothing left to say. They were not characters in a novel, so they went back into the party. Clara needed to announce that buffet dinner would be served on the patio. Oyster patties (oysters stewed with white sauce in little flaky pastry shells), platters of boiled shrimp and boiled crawfish, chicken livers en Brouchette, a baked ham and a baked turkey, a mixed green salad. Makeshift tables had been set up on sawhorses and paper lanterns had been strung along the rear patio.*

It was out here in the patio where there could have been trouble. There was an acute awareness of the racial mix. This party was a freakish event in 1957. None of the guests doubted Clara's motives, there seemed to be no deviousness in her; and they felt also a special albeit unexplainable devotion to her and her house. Some would forget that they felt this devotion in 1957. Those who had never broken bread with members of another race had decided to make the best of a bad situation. There were two long tables and decisions must be made. The night was saved by Judge Duplantier who took Clifford Duveneaux along with him to sit together at the far table, Emerson and Priscilla Lynn followed, bringing with them, Sheila Gomez, Bernard and Bessie Rosenberg. Philip Rotolo, who had never known hesitation in his life took Mary Ann to the other table, bringing with him Mr. Hingle and Mrs. Flora Gomez whom he had assisted down the stairs. Clara and Robert Gomez sat at this table, too, because there was more room on the benches. Mr. and Mrs. Ulysses, who were both without guile, sat here, too. Sol did not notice the gruff demeanor of Mrs. Gomez whom he sat down next to. It was fortunate that Clara was sitting next to her on the other side, and her son Robert next to Clara. Ronnie sat on a separate folding chair at the head of the table.

Mrs. Cora Lang and Dr. Sherman Meyers had seated themselves separately, at the little wrought iron patio table, and its matching chairs. Mrs. Lang's eyes were darting as brightly as a wren's; her head was cocked and her mouth formed expressions of titillating interest. Dr. Meyers told her another story which, from the look of her, must have been building to a rousing climax. Upstairs in the dining room Mildred Duplantier and Marcus Scipio had set their plates down and were talking. Marcus was thinking thoughts which an eighty-two year old man should be very cautious about thinking. But Marcus had never in his life been cautious, not in his socialist youth or through his very active middle age; he had buried or divorced four wives, and discarded an unlisted number of mistresses. Mildred liked Marcus' natural sophistication, his unfaded handsomeness, and his old age. She had never been ruled by her passion, which even she had to admit was not a strong enough passion to rule anything or anybody. It would be very nice to be seen about town with this good looking, sophisticated old man, and otherwise, regarding less public matters, uncomplicated. She could have been wrong about that. Marcus had already squeezed her hand twice during this conversation.

Mr. Hingle was eating like a savage, with a viciousness born of honest hunger and unwanted hostility. He was trying by dint of gorging to ignore Mr. Ulysses who instead of eating heartily was smiling golden smiles and talking his head off. If he talked like a regular nigger it would not be so bad. Working with Coca-Cola was one thing, eating at the same table was something else. Mrs. Gomez had demanded in her sweet giggling way all of Clara's attention for the same reason. That left Robert on an island to think his own thoughts, which was very much to his liking. It was a beautiful mild mid-May night, and he felt the enchantment of the paper lanterns overhead, and of the river noises coming muffled from over the levee. If any ugliness should disturb the peace of this table, he knew that Philip would be able to handle it. Mary Ann was dumping half of what she had served herself onto Philip's plate.

Robert would report the bare facts of this party in the Times-Picayune: a listing of the guests, of what was served, of the entertainment provided by Clifford Duveneaux, no racial designation following names, as was done on the sports page with the reporting of boxing results. It was possible to think of this party as having a special symbolic significance happening as it did now in 1957. It would be remembered by the guests as a private celebration for Clara, an ordinary house warming. More might be made over it, Robert thought. In this year of 1957 it was only a passing thought, he made no notes that night.

Emerson Lynn, after dinner, told Clara that Clifford Duveneaux was a musical genius. He could play anything; Beethoven sonatas, jazz in the style of Art Tatum almost better than Tatum himself. Clifford told her that it was Emerson who was the genius, he was only a performer, Emerson created music, he was a composer. If she had the sheet music, which she did, he would be happy to play the Moonlight Sonata. She told him how silly she was for wanting him to play the sonata--a brief little story of little Clara who remembered hearing the Moonlight Sonata one night long ago in her house when her father was still living. He didn't think that she was silly at all, and only hoped that he could play it well, since he had to read *cold. Clifford was very sentimental but didn't often show it. He thought very well of Clara for making this request, he only hoped that the other guests would sit still long enough. For the unsophisticated a sonata could be an eternity.*

Chapter 4

*M*y story gave Bernice an appetite, she ate like a horse, polishing off an oyster loaf and a slice of apple pie a-la-mode and confessed that she was still hungry. She was telling me how she had not noticed what a sensitive and profound person I was until today. She told me this, I know, because of the story she has just heard.

The little greasy spoon we ate in, was a long established po-boy restaurant and bar on Magazine, rather mysteriously called The Boathouse. We were surrounded by old-timers, most of them were sitting at the bar watching the midday news on television. A group of them were sitting at a table having coffee with the guy who owned the place. Our waitress was a red-headed Thelma Ritter. She wiped the linoleum top table with vigor. She did everything fast, not to rush her customers, but because she was loaded with nervous energy. Places like this could be comforting if you were in the right nostalgic mood. On the back wall the lunch special was hand-printed on at little chalkboard: white beans and rice, mixed vegetables and cole slaw, $1.95. The kitchen stank of old meatless soup. Time had stopped here; it could have been 1932. The old timers wore faded flannel shirts and labored for their breath.

Today, however, I could not bear to look at the defeated countenances of these old men. Their missing teeth and pink porous noses filled me with despair. Bernice and I had to decide what we were going to do. The day was hazing into the afternoon. Tonight was the Bacchus parade. It was the newest and richest parade, born of new Texas oil money and a new tendency in New Orleans, to imitate Las Vegas, a celebrated clown as king each year, Bob Hope, Jackie Gleason, and this year, Red Buttons.

The story was not really finished. Bernice had just asked me if it was. Does a real story have an end? "How do you think it should end," I asked her. But she was lost, lost even to herself. She stared past me into an emptiness. An old timer spit a shred of tobacco from his lips and spoke inaudibly with a loose half-opened mouth, his eyes aimed at the wall and beyond. The man he spoke to had his own angle of vision, and knew only from memory what his companion had said.

I paid the check and helped Bernice out of her chair, she was exhausted and like a child was ready for sleep and sweet dreams.

"Hey, kiddo. You gotta snap out of it."

"All that food--made me so sleepy." She yawned and fell against me. She was but a trifle, a sweet little sack of bones.

"I'll drive myself home. Do you think you can make it home from there?"

"Sure." But she snoozed already, nestled in the crook of my neck. At times I wished I was a taller man.

I walked around the living room, stuck my head into the bedroom, knocked on the bathroom door and opened it. "She's not home," I said out loud to myself. There are times when a man can talk to himself without fear for his sanity.

The eastward balcony was shaded, the days were still short. Time for some shuteye on the Victorian settee. "Shuteye?" Had I ever used that word before? A movie word. Edward G. "Good night, Edward G."

Around ten o'clock I was awakened by the parade, Red Buttons heaving doubloons with both hands. I turned over. Good night, Red.

At nearly seven o'clock I got up and went into the kitchen and read Sheila's note, it said: Mother and Dad are coming to dinner today and I'm sleeping late. There is a roast in the oven, when you get up, turn the oven on. Sheila. She always signed her notes. I guess everyone does.

In the shower I had the comforting thought that I was washing away evidence: cologne, make-up, a subtle skin odor which I can smell at will (a mere figment of my memory?). I had the thought that I should creep into the bedroom and sniff around Sheila while she slept, and maybe go through her pocketbook. Bernice and I made no arrangements to meet or call. When I shook her last night, she roused herself immediately, slid over to the driver's side when I opened the door. No husband-wife good-bye peck. Was it good-bye forever? Everything back to normal, Sunday dinner with the family.

When I had dressed, I did something that I had never done before. I left the apartment to get coffee at the Morning Call. It was another perfect day, sunny and chilled, not a cloud in the sky. The streets were surprisingly empty, King Red Buttons kept everyone up late last night, his majesty and his followers were sleeping late. It was only seven-thirty or thereabouts. The streets had already been cleaned, I saw only a random peanut shell here and there.

At the Morning Call there was a table of old timers. They looked chipper, fresh coffee steam and bluish cigarette smoke wreathing about their heads. Were they going fishing on the Sunday before Mardi Gras? It was too late, they would have been long gone by now, already putting the ice chest and gas tank in the boat. It was just possible, however, that they would be going fishing on Mardi Gras day. It was more and more the custom for old timers, and for younger men. On Mardi Gras day Sheila and I would be deluged with family, friends, friends of friends, acquaintances, acquaintances of acquaintances. It was the fate of anyone who had a French Quarter apartment. A base of operations, all of these people called it; they would be coming and going all day. Strangers laid out on my sofa and on my Victorian settee. Sheila would have booze and a baked ham, long crispy loaves of po-boy bread, a quart jar of mayonnaise, a bowl of potato salad.

My waiter took my order: one coffee. I had to tell him if I wanted it black, *cafe au lait* is what is served here with beignets, deep fried donuts sprinkled with confectionery sugar.

An Ohio man stuck his head in the door. He was ruddy, with close-cropped wheat-colored hair, middle aged. He cased the joint like a bank robber. All clear. His wife and another couple followed him in. The men wore casual sweaters, the ladies pant-suits. They were not the usual Mardi Gras tourists, but more the off-season summer types. They might have been from Kansas for all I knew, or Iowa. They perched alertly on their seats, ready for whatever was unique and interesting. The waiter was explaining about *cafe au lait* and beignets to them, the ladies nodded their heads and smiled enthusiastically, the men ordered up. The waiter was cynical but did not mind explaining, it was his job. He even managed a sour little smile.

More of them might have been on their way. I finished my coffee and left. Outside I stopped before a pay station telephone, staring at it absently, while the sun warmed my neck and shoulder. The directory was fat and dog-eared with overuse, some of the yellow pages were ripped out. I was as careless as all the rest, flipping roughly through the pages, the shelf was too shallow. I pressed the directory to keep it from falling free onto its chain. What had gone wrong with my memory? It was impossible for me to commit to memory one lousy phone number. It was listed under Murray's name. I had no coins. I went back into the Morning Call and asked the waiter manning the cash register for change. He gave it with reluctance, if the place had been crowded I think that he would have refused.

From this end the ringing was a buzzing, low and resonant. It rang four times before it was answered.

"Hello." Masculine. Murray. I hung up. Damn. What if he suspected it was me. He knew I was out all night with Bernice. He thought that I was consoling her. Now he would think that there was something else to it. But how could he know? Just a wrong number. Bernice and I should have a code. Two rings and hang up, then call this special number at a pay station phone.

The receiver was still in my hand, I was looking at the dial as if it was someone I was trying to recognize. I had more quarters. What the hell.

I dialed information.

"Directory."

"Do you have a listing for Senator Philip Rotolo?"

"One moment, please, the number is in your directory. 288-1515."

"Thank you."

It rang only once, followed by a click. An answering service. "Senator Rotolo's office. Can I help you."

"Yes. I would like to speak to Senator Rotolo."

"The Senator is not in now. Would you like to leave a message, sir?"

"I wonder if I could speak to his secretary; this is his answering service, isn't it?"

"One moment, sir."

Click. Click. The Ohio foursome emerged from the coffee shop looking as if they had won the blue ribbon. They carried in their stomachs a trophy, exotic food, something to tell the folks back home about. Their ruddy faced leader struck out for the Farmers Coop Market, the others trotted along, they had only a few days and had to see everything. People from Ohio are not so bad. I could have been born in Ohio myself. But, I swear, I couldn't even imagine it. There are special destinies, suited with precision for each one of us. A place, a time, circumstances so unique that we know not any other shape of happening but those indelibly marked with the "me" we have eternally known, "Yes, hello."

"Yes, sir, can I help you?"

"Are you Senator Rotolo's secretary?"

"Can I help you?"

"I am an old friend of the Senator's. I would like very much to talk to him, if that is possible."

"I could take your name, sir, and your number, and have the Senator call you back."

"Would you be disobeying any orders if you told me just where the Senator is right now?"

"No, sir. He and Mrs. Rotolo are attending a banquet in honor of Mr. Red Buttons at the Royal Orleans Hotel. If you will give me your name, sir, the Senator is very good about calling his old friends."

"That's all right. Just tell him that Bobby called."

"Sir?"

"Tell him that Bobby called. Bobby. Goodbye."

I went back in the coffee shop. Where were the old timers? They were gone. There were just four or five tables of tourists, the poised, well dressed type, from Massachusetts, Montreal, Los Angeles. I left before any of them saw me. Where the hell were the rest of those quarters?

Wasn't there a bar on the other side of the street? Montalbano's? Had old man Montalbano gone to rest? What about his sons? I don't remember ever drinking at Montalbano's, but I remember the sign, it was there for years. An adult book store is there today.

It was only eight o'clock, maybe eight-thirty. How could Philip and Mary Ann be attending a banquet this early? I didn't believe it.

I looked down the street and saw the midwesterners poking around the produce. One of the wives was yanking gently on a long plait of garlic. I didn't suppose garlic was a favorite in Iowa. I put my wallet on the phone shelf and started to look through random slips of paper from various compartments. None of them, however, were what I was looking for, so it was back to the battered old directory. I remembered suddenly that I had done this yesterday in the office. Or was it the day before? I found the number, but for some reason lingered while resting on my elbow. I stared at the page until the print blurred into a cloud of gray. When I lifted my eyes I looked again for the midwesterners but they were nowhere in sight. Far down the corridor of produce stalls there appeared the figure of a female, strolling leisurely. I strained my eyes to make her out but the distance defeated me. She continued walking away from me, disappearing into the bright mosaic of fruit and vegetables. It could be Clara, I thought to myself. Clara was on my mind. I knew that I should call her. How rude of me not to recognize her at the ball. She was probably home as she always was. I hoped that she could forgive me. I must drive over the bridge and down the river road to the Lower Coast to visit her. It had been so long since I had been in her beautiful house. When was I there last? Was it at the house warming? Was that the first and last time I had been there? It couldn't have been. Everything about Clara's house was so fresh in my mind. In the living room on the mantle stood the little bisque cherubs beside the antique American clock. Above the mantle hung Rodrigo Cuello's large Cubist still-life. Rodrigo like so many other neglected artists of the thirties had been Maurice Duplantier's friend. There were many other paintings, his collection was extensive. It seemed to me that I could remember where each one hung. How could I see all of this so clearly now, after so many years? Out in the patio along the little brick pathways were beautiful pieces of Newcomb pottery, planters and bird baths. And how lovely must the orchard be now. As I stood there the sun began to grow uncomfortably warm on my back. When I looked up I noticed that the woman I had seen walking in the Farmer's Market was now coming toward me on Decatur Street, but she was still too far away. I watched her as she drew nearer. She wore a very simple white dress and carried a small white leather handbag. I could tell that she was too young to be Clara. She was hardly more than a girl no older than Clara was when I met her. Her hair was jet black, several shades darker than Clara's. As she passed directly across the street from me, she looked up and caught me staring at her. We both dropped our eyes; she looked nothing at all like Clara. I began searching through my pockets for the remaining quarters. I dropped one in the slot and ran down the page with my finger to the number and dialed it. The phone rang six or seven times; no one was home. As it continued to ring I felt a keen sense of disappointment, I wondered if it was Clara's number or if she lived there anymore. Perhaps she had moved back to Dallas, but then someone said, "Hello." It was Clara. It was so good to hear her voice again.

Chapter 5

*T*he streets were filling up with tourists. They seemed less lethargic, laughing and talking with more spirit. As I walked back to my apartment I remembered that I had not turned on the roast as Sheila requested. It was just sitting in the oven, red and juicy. Raw meat for the Rosenbergs.

It didn't really matter. I'd just walk back to the apartment and turn the damn thing on, it couldn't be more than nine o'clock. I could feel better about one thing--I was going to see Clara again, tomorrow at two o'clock. It had been so good to talk to her again. She was the same old impervious Clara, treating my phone call like it was routine, as if it had not been almost fifteen years since we talked to each other. Perhaps now in one way or another I could write her story.

Sheila was up, sitting at the little breakfast table in her quilted house coat. Her usual breakfast was on the table: two fried eggs over light, an oval slice of rye toast and a cup of hot chocolate. All of it getting cold as she pored over the *Times-Picayune*. What did I have in *Dixie*? Nothing, it was the Mardi Gras issue.

"Where have you been?" she spoke without looking up from the paper.

"Just taking a walk."

"Something on your mind?" She looked up at me. Some small nervousness in her eyes made them blink more than usual. A tremor of the lower lip, but almost imperceptible.

"No. Nothing on my mind. It is such a pretty day."

"What time did you get home?" The third degree. She spoke casually but measured her words as if her tongue had to be manually operated.

"About four. Where were you?" Tit for tat.

"I left you a note. I was with Margaret and Louis and the people from D.C. Didn't you see it?"

"Yes. How was the parade? It woke me up."

"Bacchus gets better every year. The floats were ingenious. And Red Buttons made an ass of himself, he was great."

"Did you catch any doubloons?"

"Louis gave me some."

"I forgot to turn the roast on."

"I turned it on. How is the patient?"

"The patient?"

"The one you spent the night treating."

"Oh, Bernice. She's fine. Cried so much she's pooped out. Drunk, too. So was I."

"Where did all this take place?"

"LaPlace and Johnny Matranga's Bar."

"Matranga's? Where's that?"

"On Kerlerec. One of my old hangouts."

"It was not."

"Well, I mean, I went there once or twice. How do you know it wasn't my old hangout?"

"I know more than you think."

"What about the roast? Shouldn't we get it on?"

"I told you that I turned it on."

"Oh, that's right. When are Bernie and Bessie coming?"

"Soon, they don't want to stay late and get caught in the parade traffic."

"I think I'll take a shower."

"You already have. The mirror was all fogged up. Is anything wrong with you?"

"Just absent-minded like any Sunday. Guess who I called?"

"Who?"

"Philip. Gave me the run around. That's an old friend for you."

"He's a busy man. Why did you call him?"

"Just to say hello."

"Just to say hello, that's kind of frivolous, isn't it?"

"I guess so. What's on TV?"

"The TV's been broken for two weeks."

*B*ernie was now the head of the sociology department at Loyola. At Xavier during the tumult of the sixties the blacks tried to clean house, ran off white liberals, black Creoles, any body who wasn't a direct descendant of a slave. Things had settled down again, but by then, Bernie was at Loyola. He must have been 65 or so and still played tennis on a regular basis. Had something going at Loyola called the Coalition for Prison Reform. Took busloads of students to the State Prison in Angola every week. He made fine enemies of the warden and the district attorney: Interviewing murderers and rapists for TV, asking them if they liked the food, if the library was good enough, were there enough educational opportunities, did they get enough sunshine and exercise, did they have many conjugal visits with their wives or girlfriends. "This place is a hell hole. There ain't an ounce of rehabilitation in the whole place. No wonder I'm a murderer, wouldn't you be one if you had to live like this." Bernie wanted me to give this kind of stuff coverage in *Dixie-Roto*. He was teasing. *Dixie* was apolitical.

Bessie was still beautiful. Her hair turned a fine steely gray, and she was trim as a girl. When there was a fight, it was Bernie and Sheila against Bessie and me. Thank God for well-bred Creole ladies.

While we were having martinis, Bernie hit on an uncomfortable topic of conversation. He started to tell us about Jules Bergeron's new book on Paul Valéry, a definitive interpretation of Valéry's work. Jules had been acclaimed by scholars around the world. He was working on a book on Lautréamont. "Who's Lautréamont?" I asked. There was a time when I would pretend that I knew who all these people were. "You really don't know," said Bernie, smiling as warmly as Leonard Bernstein whom he somewhat resembled. "No, Bernie, I don't, should I?" "Well, I suppose one could go through four years of college and not hear of Lautréamont." It turned out that Lautréamont was a Surrealist poet, not a doctrinaire Surrealist like Andre Breton (who?), but a proto-Surrealist who wrote *Les Chants de Maldoror* a long, bizarre prose poem greatly admired by Breton and the Surrealists. He became a legendary figure for them, since he died young and never got the recognition he deserved. That really cleared things up. I couldn't wait to hear Jules "do" Lautréamont. Neither could Sheila, I'll bet. She had been very quiet. "Did you know who

Lautréamont was, Sheila?" "I had a minor in French, Bobby, remember?" "You are not answering the question. Did you know who he was?" "Of course I did." "I didn't mean to start a fight," said Bernie. "Oh, no fight, Bernie, it's just a shame that your daughter married a dumb journalist." "Let's eat," said Bessie.

Roast beef, green peas, mashed potatoes and Claret wine, California's best.

Coffee and pecan pie, Bessie's specialty.

"You know, I haven't seen Jules Bergeron in a long time. Must be years." I was swirling brandy. The snifters were a Christmas present from Bernie and Bessie. "I am happy to know that he is doing so well. We should have him and his wife over for dinner some time. What's his wife's name, Sheila?"

"What's that?"

"Paula Guiterrez, wasn't it?"

"That's right"

"Beautiful little hot tamale from Mexico, wasn't she?"

"From the Yucatan, I believe, Merida."

"She was one of his students, wasn't she?"

"Yes, that's right."

Paula Guiterrez was a dark little watch-charm beauty, with unblinking sultry eyes; she knew not to speak too often and to smile radiantly at unexpected times at men, who were unprepared, certain that they were being showered by a Northern light: knees buckled, cheeks flushed. They made excuses and dashed off. Heedless daring was required to answer her smile for smile. Jules was the only match for her. They became inseparable, the handsome Cajun professor and his student-sweetheart: a gangster and his gun-moll, he waxing expressively, she mutely ignoring the quick glances from the boys around the table; it was really difficult not to feast your eyes.

Sheila, who usually referred to her as a vapid, little bitch, had explained why brilliant men were attracted to mindless beauties. Her usual Freudian fare. I have forgotten how it went, something about a Ledean emptiness prompting an act of cruel sexuality, the vibrant heavens raping the dumb earth. A little Freudian irony went a long way at Loyola in those days. All the girls had a crush on Jules, but I don't blame Sheila for that anymore. I 'm not sure why I blame her. Philip said that Paula stared that way because she was so shy about knowing only a few words of English; but what did Philip know? He made mental notes whenever Sheila went to analyzing. Maybe they were both right, Paula, I would be willing to wager, still says v's for b's, or b's for v's, shit for sheet, and I had reason to believe that Jules was bored with her beauty.

Bessie came swiftly out of the kitchen, removing her apron. "Are you two going to the Mid-City parade?"

"Not me." I replied from the couch.

"I have to deal with my people from D.C.?" Sheila called in from the bedroom.

"What people from D.C.?" I was glad Bessie asked that question.

"They're from the National Endowment for the Humanities. Actually they are on their own today."

"Then you are not going to the parade?"

"No, Mother. I'm going to a reception at Loyola."

"At Loyola?"

"Well, it's funny that you all were talking about Jules Bergeron's new book. The French Consulate is giving a reception in his honor. I didn't think that you would be interested in going, Bobby. It's scheduled for two o'clock this afternoon."

"No, that's right. I wouldn't be interested in going. I had a grueling day yesterday. I think I'll just stay here and catch a nap."

"Look, you two," Bessie said, handing Bernie his jacket. " Bernie and I better get going, the traffic is going to be very heavy."

Bobby Gomez would find something to do. It was one-fifteen; Sheila better get started.

Chapter 6

*W*hen they had gone, I went to the closet for my briefcase where I had put some notes I had made on Paul Valéry two weeks ago, when the release announcing the publication of Jules' book had come into my office. I had the idea then of reviewing the book. It was not the sort of book that the *Times-Picayune* would usually review, no local color, a symbolist poet, unknown to the home folk, esoteria from academia. Perhaps there could be a short little article on page two or three, acknowledging Jules' accomplishment: LOYOLA PROFESSOR WRITES BOOK ON FRENCH POET. Nevertheless, it came to me that I might find some angle for a viable review. I made up a little fact sheet on Valéry gleaned from the *Britannica*, lifting a few of the better phrases, no one was likely to check. But there was nothing about the guy that remotely connected, I was about to give it up. Near the end of the release, they mentioned that Jules was working on a critical study of Lautréamont (who?), another French poet, which was going to be very important when completed, new information on obscure poet, etc. Well, let's give him a try. Volume 13, Jirasek, Lighthouses, page--814, LAUTRÉAMONT, COMTE DE (1846-1870). This was more like it. Lautréamont was a pseudonym. Real name, Isadore Lucien Ducasse. Born in the Americas, Uruguay, son of a chancellor in the French consulate. Ducasse sounded like a Creole name to me. For all I knew, he might have been Jean Lafitte's long lost grandson. Jean Lafitte was Louisiana's legendary buccaneer, who saved the day for Andy Jackson at the Battle of New Orleans, played by both Frederick March and Yul Brenner in the movies. Lafitte had a dark, mysterious past; no one knew his origins, some said he was the lost Dauphin of France; Uruguay would have been a perfect sanctuary (Where was Uruguay?). Let's see, Lafitte, same volume, page 594, LAFITTE, JEAN (1780-1825?) Lautréamont was born in 1846, that made Lafitte too old to be his father, but not too young to be his grandfather, hm. That would work. The article said that nothing authentic was known about Lafitte's life. Why was I doing this? My secretary, Bernice Waguespack, wanted to know, too. I had a mind to tell her. She was leaning over my shoulder, pressing what little breast she had against me, her breath wafting my cheek. "Do you know Dr. Bergeron?" "Yes, I know the gentleman." "Who's Paul Valéry, and--who's that?" "Lautréamont." "Yes, him." "They're French poets, like it says." "Are you interested in French poetry?" (Did the wafted breath grow stronger? No, only a middle-aged fantasy.) "In a certain way, I am." "I wish I was better read, Murray thinks that I should read more." "Murray is a snob, I think that you are smart as a whip." "Ha, ha, thank you very much, but I know better." "Would you like me to teach you about French poetry?" "All right." "We'll start tomorrow." "Ha, ha, I can take a hint, I'll get back to work." "No, no, don't go." "Sorry, I'm insulted."

When was that, two weeks ago--two hundred years ago?

Of course, Sheila is right--one should not refuse invitations from the French Consulate. One knew immediately that one had been invited specially, that one was special for having been invited. I had discovered Sheila's invitation last week in our bedroom, sticking out of the corner of her bag, a square envelope of thick vellum with a wavy glaze flowing through, crested. It was early morning and Sheila was still sleeping; I had just emerged from the shower. The envelope prompted no suspicion. A bill, it could have been, or a letter from the school board, a bulletin or schedule announcing a calendar of events, a piece of junk mail. I was massaging my still wet hair, enjoying the aperient keenness of my body, noticing again in the dresser mirror that freshness carries with it a glow of youthfulness. I plucked the envelope as I would have plucked a strange brand of mustard from a supermarket shelf, entirely innocently, and might have replaced it without examination, if distracted by anything, an itching ankle, some toiletry I had forgotten to perform. My eyes passed swiftly over the embossed words, over Jules' name like all the rest. Everything registered, but nothing stuck. The computer clicked to repeat. Well, had I been sniffing, poking around? No. A man who was sleuthing did not stand before a dresser mirror draped only with a towel about his waist, turning this way and that for different angles of his torso, and shaking his dripping locks, not unless he was a master of deceit. I resheathed the invitation; it was somewhat difficult because it was such a perfect fit, the corners had to be lined up with the edges of the envelope and slid in evenly and smoothly; three tries before it went in without buckling, six tries before the replacement in the bag was right with just that much showing, the point of the corner at ten o'clock (an old World War II way of spotting zeroes). There were damp spots on the vellum, but nothing could have been done about that. I went noiselessly to the closet for clean clothes and into the living room to put them on.

I was thinking, as I walked so softly, of our engagement night, at the Napoleon House, where we had gone to celebrate with Philip and Mary Ann. The place was packed, the collective voices of so many intelligent table discussions humming with flow and ebb, like distant surf on a calm night; the *1812 Overture* was building towards its final cannon-firing crescendo, but softly enough not to disturb the discussions. Mary Ann, who was not familiar with such places, was huddled next to Philip, hugging his ample arm, a pinball machine or juke box might have allayed her suspicions. She was whispering into Philip's shoulder, wanting to know if they served Tom Collins. Philip ordered her one, telling Tiger to load it up with cherries, her favorite; Champagne cocktails for Sheila and me on this special occasion, a bourbon and coke for himself. Two Tulane types were smoking pipes and playing chess just behind Philip and Mary Ann, and just beyond them, Jules Bergeron, Ph.D., and his retinue. Sheila had waved and yoohooed to him as we were getting seated, and he acknowledged us with a wink and a curt little two-fingered salute. When the drinks came, we toasted. Sheila held her hand over mid-table, turning it to flash her diamond ring. Mary Ann's eyes shone with brimming pleasure, she would have applauded if her hands had been free. It was a simple ring, one-quarter karat, elegant in its Tiffany setting. Philip leaned over the table, shook my hand and kissed Sheila full on the mouth.

I had slipped the ring on in the back seat of the Pontiac. Not the place and time I would have chosen. Sheila's point was well taken, I was stalling. "I hope you haven't memorized a poem?" "No." "Then let's have my ring, I'm tired of waiting, you're not having second thoughts?" "Of course not." What could I do? I really loved the way she bullied me, calling me Gomez. Mary Ann had laid her cheek on the back of her hand, turned around in her seat, an ingenuous witness, big brown eyes luminous with a lubricating tear. I slipped the ring on, and threw my arms around her, but too soon, I pinned her arms to her side, and missed her mouth, smacking part of a nostril and upper lip. "Oh, look, Philip," cooed Mary Ann. "Yes, look," said Sheila, breaking away. "King Kong kissing his mate. That's enough, let me see my ring." She was right, a brutal performance, and I moved towards her again with silken smoothness, but was stopped just short by a traffic cop hand, she pecked my extended, puckered mouth. "Thank you, darling, it's lovely."

I grew drowsy sitting on my Hepplewhite chair by the eastward french window. The fact sheet nearly slipped out of my hand. I could hear milling and the flow of excited talk below. The tourists were warming up. The sky was a fine washed blue. The sun was creeping nearer and nearer. Two more days to Mardi Gras, and I wished that it was here and gone, nothing could be done about anything until it was over.

An elderly couple I had never seen before was sitting on the balcony across the way. He was mustachioed and petite, like William Faulkner, his companion wore a blue babushka and linen pants. Strangers, but they didn't look like tourists. They smoked leisurely and sipped drinks, sitting nearly motionless with their legs crossed. They were looking out over the houses at the sky and spoke only now and then. I imagined their conversation to be simple, speaking in sentences of three or four words. A sad Sunday afternoon it was.

I put the fact sheets back into my brief case, and lay down on the settee. "Good night, Lautréamont." Jean Lafitte had died, leaving no authentic facts about his life, there is no trace of him, save a brief heroic act in battle, a subject for a painting, if we knew what he looked like. But who he really was and who he loved we would never know.

"Who are you?"

"Clara. Don't you recognize me?"

"I thought you were Marie Antoinette, or duBarry."

"It's only a costume. This is Mardi Gras, isn't it?"

"Who am I?"

"I don't know, where is your costume?"

"I am Napoleon, the mustache is a disguise. I have enemies. I want no more island exiles."

"Come with me, I will hide you in my house. You will be safe there."

"Are you Marie Antoinette?"

"No, I am Clara, why have you forgotten me? I have not forgotten you."

"Are you disguised? You have enemies?"

"No, of course not. This is a costume, it's Mardi Gras. Come quickly, take my hand. "

"No. Wait. I must know who you are."

"I'm Clara. This is only a costume. See, your enemies are coming."

"That's only a pick-up truck, my enemies are noble men."

"Like all great men, you are a fool."

"Who are they?"

"Your enemies, see they carry shot-guns. It's too late."

They were racing up the levee smashing clover and buttercups. Clara stepped in front of me, shielding me. They fired. Her blood spurted in my face, she fell, a gaping, bloody hole in her abdomen. Blood and pink satin. Oh no, no! No, no, no, no! The report of their shots rang in my ear. No! No!

I had nearly fallen from the chair. The phone was ringing. How long?

"Hello. Hello."

"Bobby, is that you?"

"Clara?"

Silence.

"Bobby?"

"Yes?"

She was crying.

"Bernice? What's wrong?"

"I'm sorry, have I disturbed you? Is Sheila home?" Crying.

"No, I am alone."

"Can I pick you up?"

"What's wrong?"

"Murray's left. Can I pick you up? Where's Sheila?"

"She's gone. Calm down and tell me what happened."

There was a long silence, I heard her blowing her nose.

"Bernice?"

"I'm here, wait, please." The words were obscured by a gurgling sound. She blew her nose. A horn. Such a delicate nose.

"I'm waiting, take your time."

"I would like to talk to you. Is that possible?"

"I'll go downstairs and wait for you. Hurry, though, there's a parade coming."

"Are you sure it's all right?"

"Yes, but hurry."

"O.K., good-bye."

The elderly couple was gone. Their drinks and ash trays were gone, too.

A drunk from Alabama stopped me. He was with his wife and another couple. He wasn't sure what Mardi Gras was going to be for him and his friends, something ultimate. He gave a rebel yell and offered me his drink, a scotch and soda in a paper cup. I sipped, knowing what was at stake for him. "You're a good guy. My pal," he said, putting his arm around me. His friend, who was really very shy, wanted to take me along with them. "Come on, look at this." He showed me a big wad of money, twenties, tens. "I'm waiting for someone, but thanks for the drink." They laughed uproariously, the wives rolled their eyes and pointed their fingers. They knew. "He is *waiting* for someone, 'dya hear that?" He hugged me, pulling both of us off balance. "We don't want to interfere, when a man is waiting for someone, well! Bet she's sweet as pie, right, pal?" "Right." His shy friend offered me a twenty. "Buy her a drink." "No, thanks." "Take it, I'm rich, we're all rich, right, Jasper?" "My pal doesn't need money, he's in love." Good old Jasper. Here came the Toyota. It swerved a bit, to avoid a tourist who had started across the street. She pulled up too close to the curb, scraping the tires. Jasper bent down and looked in at Bernice, "Don't worry, honey, we've been taking good care of him." When I opened the door, Bernice was smiling but not meaning it, she was still upset, "Who's your friend?" "They offered me twenty bucks to buy you a drink." "And you didn't take it?" "No, let's go. They might want a ride."

She drove along at a rapid clip, shooing tourists back up on the curb.

"Jasper said that you were sweet as pie."

"You know them?"

"They're tourists, how do you feel?"

"Terrible."

"How about a bourbon?"

"Just tell me where to go, I'm lost."

"Turn up Esplanade to Carrollton, we'll go to Tall-T."

"I thought you didn't like that place."

"I don't."

She took a gulp, made a face and nearly choked. "Good?" I asked.

"You're going to make me an alcoholic, like the girl in your story. What was her name?"

"Cher. she's a real person, it's not just a story."

"I think that you make things up." The next gulp went down smoothly, and she smiled.

"I can prove that she's real." I was half serious.

"How?"

"We'll give her a call. Do you want to tell me what happened with Murray?"

"The sonavabitch walked out on me. He said that I wasn't his intellectual equal."

"I thought that you two had already talked things out."

"We had, but he started it up all over again. He said that he was leaving. I asked him where he was going. He said that it was none of my business. I told him that I knew damn well where he was going. And then he said something about you."

"He did." This was the last straw for me. I had not planned on losing Murray's respect. A protégé, if he was that, was an important thing for a man my age. I felt a deep, scorching shame.

"He accused us of doing something." Poor Murray. Poor Bobby.

"You didn't tell him anything, I hope." I could tell by the way she lowered her eyes and bit her lip that she had. She was fighting back the tears, "I'm sorry, Bobby, I didn't want to get you involved."

"Baby, I got myself involved. Let's have another bourbon. Exactly what did you tell him?" She was all cried out. She blew her nose.

"I told him that we spent two nights together."

"You didn't tell him where, did you? And technically, it was only one night."

"Yes, I did."

"Jesus Christ, Bernice, you didn't?"

"You want to order another drink." The little bitch was smiling.

"I'll need a double. What's done is done. Did you have to tell him where, though?"

"I didn't have to."

"I feel so shabby, an old man like me taking his secretary to her friend's apartment when she's out of town. I never thought of it that way. With somebody else knowing, Christ."

"I'm sorry I told you. Are you afraid that Sheila will find out?"

"Of course I am. Do you want her to know?"

"Of course not. I didn't want Murray to know, I was mad and frustrated."

"Well, that's that, I guess, hey, waiter." I ordered two doubles.

We sat there with our heads down, staring at the table in silence. It was my hurt. I was old and did not have her youth and fire to blurt out the truth and cry when I was hurt. The kid put the bourbons down in front of us. He looked concerned and respectful. Maybe one of our loved ones passed away, "Is that all, sir?"

"Yes, thank you."

"Bobby?"

"Yes?"

"This might be a perfect time to call Cher. She drank bourbon, didn't she?" It took a split second for this to register--I started to laugh. How could I not chuckle? It came from the pit of my stomach. I began to laugh with gusto. All of a sudden, it seemed a wind blew away the black clouds. When I brought the laughter under control, my head was clear.

"Why don't we do that, I have been wondering about her all of these years." My eyes were gleaming with pure devilment. Bernice was smiling like a fox would smile who had come upon a vixen in heat, her scent drawing him to her, even as the hounds are howling over the hill. This was a crazy thing we were planning, "You said that she is a real person, didn't you?"

"I never actually met her. What happened with her and Ronnie happened almost twenty-five years ago. What excuse could I make for calling her, even if I could reach her, she may not be living here anymore; or she might even be dead."

"There is only one way to find out, isn't there?"

"You really want me to do it, don't you? I don't even know how to spell her name."

"Yes, you do. I'll ask the boy to bring the telephone book. Waiter."

"Bernice, what in the hell do you think you're doing? I can't call somebody I've never met, and, if I had met her, someone whom I haven't seen in twenty-five years."

"I'll call her. As your secretary. I am your secretary, you know. I'll tell her that we have her name listed as an ex-Mardi Gras queen, and we are doing a story on ex-queens."

"You are forgetting one thing. Today is Sunday. She will think that it's a crank call."

"No she won't. I know how to be convincing, I'm experienced."

The waiter looked puzzled. He thought that we were grieving. Now he thought we were nuts.

"Could you bring us a telephone directory, please." Bernice asked, smiling brightly.

"There is one on the pay station phone, ma'm, but it's chained," he added, a little bewildered.

"Isn't there one behind the bar, we have to look up several numbers. And bring us another round of drinks."

"Yes, ma'am, I'll see what I can do."

He came back with the directory, smiling, happy to provide this unusual service, "I'll get your drinks. You did want the New Orleans directory, didn't you?"

"Yes, you did very well, thanks. O.K., Bobby, what's the name?"

"I am not sure that I should tell you."

"That will only prove that you made her up." I didn't make her up. I know I didn't.

"The name is Remison. You can look under C. Anderson Remison. Smarty."

The waiter returned with the drinks. He still looked very pleased with himself, "Two Old Taylor's, on the rocks."

Bernice gave him a big smile, "You're a marvelous waiter."

"Thank you."

She was looking up the number. I had to stop her, "Bernice, what's gotten in you? You're crazy. I don't want to be haunted by some old ghost of my past."

"I'm taking care of this, you just sit there and drink your bourbon." She was drunk, and had hit on a weird way out of her troubled mind. Maybe it would work.

"Here it is. Remison, C. Anderson. 2214 Newcomb Boulevard. 866-4492.

"What! Let's see that. I'll be damn, the old bastard is still living. He must be ninety."

She went digging in her leather sling bag for a quarter. Unbelievably, she was going to do it. I had nothing more to say, just sat there sipping my bourbon. It was the same feeling as watching a close friend acting in a school play.

She had her back to me, dialing the number. She got somebody and was talking rapidly. She turned her profile toward me, and I tried to read her lips. She drummed on the shallow shelf, not talking, not listening. Someone was being summoned.

She talked again, smiling, secretary expressions lighting up her features. I listened. I was dizzy. What the hell were they saying? Who was she talking to? I began to look for cuticle tags on my fingernails, something to chew on. The longer the conversation went on, the more restless I became. I had to go to the men's room, but did not dare move. On and on, she talked. I hoped she was not telling Cher about the book. What kind of phony life had I been leading? Making up stories about living people. I had to pee, my bourbon was gone, and my head was beginning to tingle, the excitement was bringing on a headache. After a long time she hung up, a big smile was spread across her face as she walked back to the table.

"What happened? Tell me. I'm a nervous wreck."

"A maid answered the phone."

"Of course . . ."

"I explained to her that I didn't know Cher's marriage name, and why I wanted to reach her."

"She didn't think that it was strange that you were calling on Sunday?"

"No, she went immediately to call her. She told me that Cher was divorced and was using her maiden name again. She was very cordial, she seemed excited about the article."

"But . . ."

"Listen, that's the best part. Cher *was* an ex-queen. She was queen of Proteus in 1951."

"I can't believe it. I would have guessed Comus."

"See, you haven't done your research. There's more . . ."

"You talked to Cher?"

"Yes, listen. I told her what kind of article we were planning, and she said that she would be happy to cooperate. I told her that we would like an appointment to interview her, that we wanted to put in a few personal touches about each queen, like if they liked bourbon or martinis." A little explosion of laughter came from her, and she reached over and pressed my hand. "Know what she told me?"

"No, what?"

"She loves bourbon, drinks it all the time. She said it like she meant it. She has a kind of gravelly voice. I think she might be a lush."

"Maybe she has a cold."

"Maybe. At any rate, we have an appointment with her for this Friday."

She looked at her empty glass, "I want another bourbon."

"No more for you. I don't know what you'll do next. We're going to LaPlace to get some chicken gumbo."

Chapter 7

*S*he was dressed in jeans, her hair was fly-away, and her face was blotched. She was a mess, but her driving was steady. I was watching her. She had three bourbons in her. So did I.

The Airline Highway was deserted at this stretch. We were past the outlying sub-divisions, clear of the city. The canal to our right was clustered with blooming hyacinths. The sun was low in the sky, and came flashing through the tall trees, nearly blinding us. The land on the other side of the highway spread out into a wide prairie, appearing mauve in this late light.

"They were kaintucks."

"They were what?"

"Poor ignorant Bernice . . ."

"All right, now. What are kaintucks?"

"That's what the Creoles called Americans.

"I don't understand."

"They were from Kentucky. Hillbillies."

"Who told you about them?"

"Sister Catherine at the orphanage, when I was nineteen. Until then, I only knew their names. Sister waited until I was old enough to understand. His name was Alvin Harris."

"Your father?"

"Yes, he came from a very poor family, farmers. When he was sixteen he robbed a hardware store. They caught him and put him in prison. He was paroled in a year. Shortly after that he married my mother. Her name was Julie, Julia, maybe. Julie Williams, I was born in Louisville a year later. When I was six months old, he robbed again. This time he killed a man. But they didn't catch him. He stole a car, packed up Julie and me and took us to New Orleans. One of the first people he met was Riccardo, Mama Gomez' husband, who was a merchant seaman. Riccardo got him in the seaman's union.

They shipped out together, and became friends. He didn't even change his name. He was a fugitive, and didn't even change his name, I guess they only do that in the movies. On one of the voyages Riccardo was killed by an explosion in the engine room. I must have been about three years old. I don't know what happened during the next two years. Alvin, my father, went back to his old habits, I think. By then, from what I can piece together, he must have been a wino. I don't think he was home much, he was drunk or on drugs all of the time. They caught him breaking into a drug store and sent him to the state prison in Angola."

"What happen to him?'

"He was killed in a fight with another prisoner, stabbed with a knife."

"What about your mother?'

"She went back to Louisville, and got married and raised a family. I spent a few months at the orphanage, and Riccardo's wife, Mama Gomez, legally adopted me. That's the whole story."

"How do you feel about all that?"

"I don't know. It's like a piece of fiction.

"Why didn't you tell me this before?"

"I don't know. I guess I was trying to forget it."

"Are you ashamed of them?"

"Yes, I guess so. I didn't really know them, they didn't seem to be any part of me."

"But that's not true, they were your parents, you are of their blood."

"I know, but I didn't want it that way. When I was small, six or seven, I used to draw pictures of him. I put big scars all over his face. You know the kind of scars kids draw. I would draw heavy dark lines around his eyes; I think I meant them to be mean eyes."

"Is your mother still alive?"

"A few years ago, one of her daughters wrote me to tell me that she had died. I wrote a long letter back, and haven't heard from them since."

When we got to LaPlace, there was a sign on Robichaux's. CLOSED TODAY AND TOMORROW FOR MARDI GRAS. It was a nice drive. I asked Bernice if she wanted to go to Sharon's apartment.

Chapter 8

*T*olstoy was nowhere to be found. We searched everywhere. I told Bernice that he would come back. Cats don't get lost like dogs. She wanted to go out looking for him. Where do you look for cats at night? I opened the fifth of Old Taylor and slugged a drink right out of the bottle, it scalded my stomach. "Stop worrying, he'll come back." "But how did he get out?" "Let's eat the pizza, I'm hungry."

Someone knocked on the door. We exchanged looks of panic. Murray? Murray called Sheila. Murray *and* Sheila? We had to answer it, the lights were on.

I went to the door with a mouthful of pizza. It was a gorgeous strawberry blond, young, straight hair, very long, blue eyes, oriental bone structure. She had Tolstoy in her arms, lucky Tolstoy. "Oh," she said, trying to look past me, needing some explanation for the middle-aged stranger standing before her, chewing pizza. She had a perfect figure for the jeans and black tee shirt she was wearing. Tolstoy liked her, he was closing his eyes in contentment.

"I'm here with Bernice," I motioned over my shoulder. "We're friends of Sharon's. We were looking for him. We came here to feed him. Where did you find him?"

"I heard him me-owing behind the door, he sounded so lonely. Sharon left me a key, I live in the apartment upstairs. I took him upstairs with me. When I heard you come in, I thought that Sharon was back." She petted Tolstoy softly, he really liked her, I didn't blame him; she was beautiful. Bernice walked up, wiping her mouth with a napkin.

"Oh, you must be Cindy. I'm Bernice. This is my boss, Mr. Gomez."

"Pleased to meet you, Sharon talks a lot about you." She had a beautiful smile.

Bernice took Tolstoy from her, "Thank you for looking after him, did you feed him?"

"I tried to give him some tuna, but he wouldn't eat it."

"He eats nothing but dry food. Thanks, Cindy." A polite dismissal.

Maybe Cindy was hungry, "Would you like some pizza?" I asked.

"No, thank you. I have somebody upstairs." Lucky somebody, "Nice to have met you, see you later."

"So long."

"She's nice," I said.

"You were gawking at her."

"Was I?"

"Ha, ha, that's rich. I thought you said that beauty was phony."

"Your boss, Mr. Gomez."

"Let's finish the pizza."

"I've had enough, I want a drink." Beauty is devastating.

We sat on the sofa in the dark and drank the bourbon. The light from the kitchen was enough to let us see what we wanted to see. We had decided to spend the night but nothing had been said. We touched finger tips and tried to tell each other how we felt. We wanted to give each other something, to fall deeply in love, but we were afraid.

Her eyes were dark blue like the night pressing against the window. When we have gone, no one will know that we had walked here. There will be no trace. The happiness we wanted was broken, the pieces lay around our feet. We wondered if bourbon was enough to console us.

Tolstoy slept on the Guatemalan rug. The room was warm and yet cool, later we would have to turn on the floor furnace.

Was Sheila home? Why was I worried? I didn't know how drastically my life was changing. Bernice said that she didn't care if Murray was home or not. Women feel entitled to their vindictiveness.

The bourbon kicked in--we were kissing--brief, soft kisses. Eye delving into eye. This was all--there was nothing more. We were cut loose, rolling in the surf. Free.

"Guess who I called this morning?" I whispered.

"Who?"

"Clara."

"The queen?"

"Yes."

Whispering.

"What is this about Clara. Are you in love with her?"

"I'm in love with you."

"And Clara?"

"I don't know. She is sustained by something I don't understand. A dream, maybe. But she's not a dreamer, she's very practical."

"You made her up, she exists in your mind."

"She's real, I talked to her."

"That's not what I mean."

"Yes, I know, but the others, Ronnie and Philip--they responded to her."

"She exists in their minds, too."

"What is she?"

"A queen, isn't that what your book is about?"

"Yes, but a real queen. The story is true."

"Of course it's true--a real queen."

"Bernice?"

"Yes?"

"How do you know this--that she's a real queen?"

"You told me the story."

"How does the story end?"

"I don't know. You will have to write it."

"We're drunk."

"Very."

"Did I tell you that I have an appointment with Clara?"

"No."

"Tomorrow, at two o'clock. Would you come with me?"

"No. You have to go alone."

"Will you wait for me."

"Yes."

"Let's go to bed."

"All right."

In the morning she awoke with the thought of her possible pregnancy. She tried to think of the consequences, but she could not speculate clearly. She was numbed by all that had happened. She found Bobby in the kitchen drinking bourbon; he seemed more in a fog than ever. He was showered and shaved, ready to make his visit to Clara, the queen. He became slightly maudlin when he left, pleading, she thought, that she wait for him. "Of course, I'll wait for you, why are you worried about that?"

"I don't know, I don't know what's going to happen to me--to us. You do understand why I must see Clara, don't you?"

"Go, I will be here waiting for you, don't worry." She brushed a kiss across his cheek at the door, and stood for a long minute after he drove off, staring at the empty street.

I can't stand here and get depressed, she thought and went into the kitchen to make coffee.

She sat on the sofa to drink her coffee, and thought of Murray. She wanted to be free of him, the thought of dealing with him for a divorce annoyed her. She wanted to simply cancel him out of her life as if he were a cracked cup which she had finally decided to throw away. "If Bobby and I were to marry . . . ," she thought, rubbing her stomach and wondering if she was carrying his child. "We might have to get married. What have I gotten into?" She decided that she must get dressed and leave, but where to? She could think of nothing but the supermarket, a place where people were gathered, conducting the ordinary business of living from day to day. She would buy groceries and plan a meal. The thought of doing something so ordinary pleased her so much that she wondered about the sheer mystery of life itself. She showered, dressed, combed her hair and left, full of a strange exuberance. She remembered that Bobby had taken her car; she would have to walk. She began to think of walking as something special. Was it, she thought, that I have forgotten what it means to simply live in the world? The spring's soft sunlight glowed yellow-green in the new grass and foliage; the sky was cloudless. She walked along looking at everything, like a stranger from an alien planet. What had caused this rebirth, she did not know. She smiled and gave a cheery hello to an old lady sitting on her front porch.

At the supermarket, she was surprised to find it crowded and noisy. Wives accompanied by their husbands wheeled their carts about with almost reckless abandonment. They snatched at the merchandise with a furiousness which she did not understand. What is this, she thought, is the city under siege? She suddenly realized that these people were not angry or frightened but excited. This was the Monday before Mardi Gras. She had forgotten. Anger rose within her, she had come here to be charmed by daily life, and began to resent the intrusion of the festivities of this holiday which drove these people out of their normal routines. She was not ready for Mardi Gras, her life was not in order. How could she partake of such a bizarre thing as Mardi Gras? Her own life had become bizarre. She left her cart, got in an express line and bought a package of cigarettes. She walked back to the apartment and found Sharon's sleek little Porsch parked out front.

Sharon was sitting on the sofa petting Tolstoy. The huge cat was crouching and closing his eyes. Sharon looked up at Bernice and smiled as if she had been expecting her.

"Some of my friends are coming down from Canada, so I had to come back." Sharon told her.

"You must have known that I needed you," said Bernice impulsively. The sight of Sharon made her realize how alone she had been in her new troubles. Sharon, another woman and her friend, was someone to whom she could pour out her feelings. She wanted to go to Sharon and embrace her, but she knew that Sharon was never spontaneous.

Bernice made a little gesture of confusion with her hands, "Oh, Sharon, my life is such a mess."

Sharon, who was looking down at her cat, looked up alertly; a bare kind of concern shown in her swift smallish eyes. Bernice threw her head around. She was near tears.

"You better sit down and tell me about it." Sharon said with hardly a perceptible change, pushing Tolstoy off of the sofa; she patted the cushion, inviting Bernice to sit. "What's wrong?"

Bernice sat down, still holding back tears. "Murray and I are separated . . . and I am almost sure that I'm pregnant by another man." She pushed her fist into the cushion.

"Who is the man?" Sharon asked calmly.

"It's my boss, a married man."

"When did this happen?"

"Last night--here. I hope you don't mind."

"Of course not. Last night? Then you're only guessing that you're pregnant."

"I think I was ovulating."

"How do you feel about your boss--his name is Gomez, isn't it?"

"I don't know, I like him--I think that we needed each other. He told me that his wife is having an affair. I don't know if he would marry me if I'm pregnant."

"Do you want to marry him?"

"He's forty-eight years old, I don't know. It would be very complicated. He's not free to get married."

"Where is he now, did he go home?"

"He took my car to meet someone, he's coming back later this afternoon. I wasn't expecting you until Wednesday."

"He's not living with his wife?"

"Yes, he is. She doesn't know where he is. We've been very careless."

She told Sharon the whole story. Sharon patted her hand. "It's bad, Bernice, but not that bad. You will just have to work things out slowly. Breaking up is very depressing." It was what she expected from Sharon: the bare truth.

They went out to a nearby Italian restaurant for a pizza. Back at the apartment, they napped for an hour. Sharon produced a joint and they smoked. letting the quiet spring light steal away the hours. Bernice was lulled into vacancy in spite of herself.

They sat on the porch. Bernice told Sharon about Bobby's book, about Clara, the queen. She told the story with a surprising interest of her own. She seemed to want to convince Sharon that Clara was a very special person.

Darkness came and Bernice began looking down the street for the Toyota.

Part Four

Chapter 1

. . . . at length found myself, as the shades of the evening drew on, within view of the Melancholy House of Usher. I know not how it was--but, with the first glimpse of the building, a sense of insufferable gloom pervaded my spirit. I say insufferable; for the feeling was unrelieved by any of that half-pleasurable, because poetic, sentiment with which the mind usually received even the sternest natural images of the desolate or terrible. I looked upon the scene before me--upon the mere house, and the simple landscape features . . . .

Edgar Allen Poe, <u>Fall of the House of Usher</u>

The Toyota handled like a dream. It braced on its narrow tires, taking the curves without rock of chassis or squeak of rubber. The levee grass was still brown from the February frost. There was a high wind, which could have been read in the grass if it had been longer and limberer. There were no clouds in the sky where this wind would have been detected either. I knew it only from the whistling noise it made battering the butterfly window. The little Toyota was steady in its onslaught.

Everything was manor this and manor that, Manor Castle, Manor Oak, Manor Fountainbleu. Brick container walls, arching into an entrance with a sign, fake gold-leaf on fake carved wood: Manor Heights. Big brick homes, all in a row, different, but the same. Swiss Chalet, Tudor Gothic, Spanish Baroque, Tara Hall, different but the same. The Lower Coast was gone; the Algerines had moved down river to live with the nutria and muskrats. Houstonians were much more comfortable over there. For them, New Orleans consisted of the French Quarter and Manor Heights, a blend of the old and the new. Two little tow-headed kids were riding their bicycles ahead of me. If I stuck my head out of the window and called them boogalees, what would they think? He called you what? Must be a French word, he didn't know you were from Houston. Oh, yes, I did.

I heard a tug tooting on the river, something else tooted, a shriller, steamier blast: the ferryboat. Heavy traffic.

I looked respectful enough. We took the precaution of hanging up our clothes. I raked my face with Sharon's pink razor, dull and more suited for limbs, but I have a light beard anyway. I used Sharon's toothbrush, one of the two, I hope it was the guest brush, they were equally worn. I nixed the deodorant, a brand exclusively for women.

I should have called Sheila. What I was doing might push things off the edge. The foundation was cracking. I had bourbon for breakfast. Bernice made a face. I asked her how she felt. She said that she was only worried about Sharon coming back today. She was not expected back until Wednesday, but Bernice had a feeling. Sharon was visiting her rich aunt and uncle in Ocean Springs on the Mississippi Gulf Coast. Sharon's parents were rich, lived in New Orleans. Sharon was rich, she had an inheritance from her grandfather. Rich kids are not the same today. She's too old to "come out." Too old to be a Mardi Gras queen, divorced and tarnished. Mardi Gras queens are ideally virgins and teenagers.

We slept late. Eleven thirty. Don't wake up with the sun in your bed, says an old Southern proverb, nothing will go right, all day. This day was right and wrong. The rest of the bourbon was on the seat next to me. There was a double left. It was a little early for the appointment. In a minute or two, I was going to pull over, climb up the levee, drink the bourbon, and look at the river. I was not going to think about what I was doing. I couldn't afford to think. Thinking killed the buzz.

It was strange. I could have gone home and continued my old life. The day was very ordinary, and I was a very ordinary person. The sorcerer within me slept. I felt it this morning, when I opened my eyes. Bernice was the usual woman sleeping beside me in the usual way. The spirit had lain down, bored with its striving and plummeting. I had traded one ordinary life for another. I could have left a note on the pillow. Good-bye, I have gone home. Last night was wonderful, but I am an ordinary man not suited for the wonders of life. Find someone who has spark and fire, a gift for excitement. I am only able to find a little charm in this world. If I drink, I can prolong it for a day or two, but I am not a heavy drinker. I will never drive myself to a tragic end. You will grow old and worn with me. I cannot bite, slash, murder, or rape, and therefore I am poor at love. I will only whimper and use up dull days, I will tire you out with my dullness. I don't want life or death, but some vague thing which is neither.

Maybe I had time for a little nap on the levee. It was only one o'clock, or so.

The wind was strong. I sat on the riverside slope. There were more freighters anchored there than I could count. I sipped bourbon. The wind drove the water into myriad ripples. A wake from a tug came coursing through the current and washed onto the muddy bank. It had little force left and the sandy clay drank it up.

I just lay back, closed my eyes and let the wind blow my head clear.

Sparrows, warblers and buntings dropped into the ocean waves, exhausted. They drowned; the great waves swallowed them up. The few that made it to the shore sat, unable to move, their eyes bright with fatigue. I was stepping on them, smashing them to bloody smears. I could not help myself, I tried to find clear sand, but the little birds were everywhere. Philip was on the dune. He was yelling, waving his arms. "Up here, up here!" Was it really Philip? He was bearded. There was no way to avoid stepping on the birds, they would not move. I ran with all my strength to the dune, Philip helped me up. "Look what you have done," he said. The little birds were smashed and bleeding below, one of them was struggling with his last strength. "I couldn't help it, they were everywhere."

Bernice was with Philip. She was hugging him around the waist, pressing her head on his chest. When I reached out to touch her, she shied, clinging closer to Philip. She was frightened.

"Don't touch her, look at your hands," Philip told me sternly. There was nothing wrong with my hands. No blood.

Bernice and I walked down the dune away from Philip, "What are you doing with Philip?" "I am his mistress." I had lost her, and I was crying. "Don't you have any pity for me. I am lost." "Philip is my man." "Your man, you're a little slut." She walked on ignoring me. We were both naked. The thought of Philip touching her pierced me with great sorrow. The clouds were suddenly very black. A great wind moved them across the sky. It was terrible, the clouds were trembling and growing darker. The wind washed the clouds like a roaring surf. The wind blew my hair, it came out by the roots and flew away. It was a dream, I was dreaming. The wind was blowing my hair. Someone was standing there. Who was it?

"Bobby?"

When my eyes focused I could see it was Clara. Where the hell was the bottle?

What did she think? Sleeping on the levee, an empty bottle of bourbon?

I sat up, smoothing my hair.

There was the bottle, no point in disclaiming it. The wind blew her skirt into a flutter; she caught the flapping part and sat down beside me--beside the bottle, really.

"I dozed off, I must look like a wreck." She looked pleased of see me, and not at all surprised at having found me stretched out on the levee beside an empty bottle of bourbon.

I picked up the bottle, presenting it, it must have appeared, for her examination, an ancient pot discovered on a dig, in need of identification and labeling, "What can I say."

"Did you drink all of it?"

"Would you believe that I had only one drink, it was left from last night?"

"You don't look drunk, I believe you."

"May I explain all of this to you? I'm so embarrassed. I'm really not a wino, but I couldn't blame you if you thought so. I was a little early--for our appointment. So I decided to come up here to take a look at the river. It's such a beautiful day. I needed to kill some time. Well, the bottle was in the car from last night with one drink left in it. So I took it along. I'm getting in deeper, deeper, aren't you going to help me out." She looked so calm, so amused, so reassuring. Seeing her after so many years--I was no longer embarrassed, or interested in explaining these unusual circumstances to her. I was touched by how warmly she was feeling towards me. We were old friends who had not seen each other for years. I was now out of the fog of waking from a disturbing dream, and realized how remiss I had been in not greeting my old friend, "How wonderful it is to see you, Clara. Forgive me for all of this fumbling." I embraced her and kissed her on the mouth. The world was so bright. In spite of the frightful dream, the nap had refreshed me. My senses were very keen. I swallowed a lump in my throat. There was a rush of wings, of old images of past years fluttering in my breast. The wind struck my cheek, and the sun beamed a radiant screen across the water; the freighters looked spectral and powerful. A new world. Something had broken loose within me. Was there a tear in my eye, or was it the sting of the swift wind?

Clara was holding my hand, pressing it, "Wonderful to see you, too, Bobby." Her eyes were as moist as mine, "Let's not sit here and cry. Come on, I want to show you the house."

There is something so strange about the passage of time: an increment and transformation of things left in the interval of years, grown rich by the process of fermentation, when they were assumed to have been idle, losing their color and strength. Clara and I were never so warm to each other then. The warmth we were feeling was a dividend.

"While I slept, I dreamt of the wind. The river is really a dreaming place, isn't it?"

"Yes, I walk up here every day. When it rains, I sit out on my verandah."

I wanted to ask her if she walked on the levee with her father.

"What do you do with yourself these days?"

"Not very much. I guess I am one of these people who is easily satisfied. I see a few friends. I think about old friends like you and Sheila sometimes. Mother and I run over to Dallas once or twice a year to visit relatives and do a little business. Mother still has property there."

"Your mother lives with you?"

"Yes, but she's in Dallas now. She likes to get out of town for Mardi Gras."

I laughed.

"Why are you laughing?"

"I'm sorry. Aren't more and more people getting out of town for Mardi Gras? Have you noticed that? It's a private joke with me . . . "

I was going to explain the irony to her, but the house came into view.

On the far side of her property, an arched brick entrance, Empire Estates. Beyond the container wall, peeking through the foliage of a large elm tree I could see what looked to be a turret outfitted with narrow aluminum windows. On this side of her property there was, mercifully, an open field, fenced in and used as a pasture for horses. The horses were quietly grazing, munching on some kind of winter grass which was a brilliant green. Maison Maurice gave nothing away to Empire Estates, the sham gold-leaf sign looked ludicrous, the turret worse than that. It was a sin without hope of forgiveness: an incongruity born of barbarism. But Clara was not sentimental about her house. Some of us wish to preserve the past as a talisman against a grave suspicion that our own lives are empty and worthless, paltry and mean, a daily punishment for our impotence to seize something of worth in each passing moment. Clara was an anomaly. The continuity of her life was broken by her father's death, and for all those years between, she held the severed end of that thread until she could tie it to its other end. A true eccentric. Had she not grasped by dint of sheer innocence the meaning of succession, the way that history must repeat itself uniquely, the way to redeem the lost years of our lives, a deliverance from the limbo of anonymity?

We sat in the orchard gazebo. Nothing seemed to have changed since that night in 1957. The fruit trees were full size and leafless, their bare limbs studded with rust-colored buds. The avocado trees, Mr. Sol Ulysses' *piece de resistance*, had unfortunately been killed by the freeze of 1960, the year of her coronation. The temperature plummeted to ten degrees; it burst water pipes, killed the lovely camphor trees brought to the city during the Cotton Exposition of 1885--a death blow to this tropical city.

Clara was smoking, the cigarettes and Zippo lay on the gazebo bench between us. A few pale blue clouds appeared in the sky. A still, bird-song afternoon. It was about three-thirty.

She told me why she and Ronnie parted ways. Clara made no mystery of her life. No hidden demons lurked in dark places. Ronnie moved in the bristling, glamorous world of high finances. Money of such astronomical sums to make simple tendering trivial. She lived in a world where dollars and cents are bartered for bacon and eggs, food for our daily sustenance. He came home one day and asked her for a divorce. She was sorry that her usefulness to him had ended. But she was hurt and needed two years to recover. Clara was still a fine figure of a woman, and she was too straightforward not to have given herself in passion. She miscarried, and Ronnie refused to put her through the ordeal of pregnancy again. As a Catholic woman she wanted children. She would marry again, if . . . It is remarkable how unaware she was of her eccentricity.

Her hand groped for a cigarette, and I did the service. We all serviced her, and she accepted it. The hinge of the Zippo was so worn that its pin would soon break. One Zippo had replaced another, they were a constant connecting chain in her life, unless Zippos were more durable than I could imagine. Was this the same Zippo with which Ronnie lit her cigarettes in 1951? Its steel had worn through to the brass. It was just possible.

She was in time and out of it, no wonder Ronnie, who was in his own way as straightforward as she, did not understand her.

We discussed the possibility of an article in *Dixie*. She couldn't imagine that anyone would be interested. Shouldn't the article be about Philip, and her coronation but a curious turning point in a brilliant political career. But it was not just her coronation but her eccentric plan to rebuild her father's house which was the turning point in the life of Ronnie Hingle, the man who many people in this city thought was leading us into the future. She was right. It was not the subject for an article in *Dixie*, it was universal, the subject for a novel. Did I dare tell her that I had thought about writing such a novel?

Bernice was waiting for me at Sharon's apartment. Sheila was waiting for me. All of our friends were expected tomorrow. What could Sheila tell them, if I was not there to greet them on Mardi Gras?

We sat on the long Victorian sofa facing the piano. Clara offered me a brandy, and made a little joke about my drinking. I accepted the brandy, an amber drink for the calm asylum of this room. As I sipped the brandy I imagined the soft blade snapping munching of the grazing horses, the maniac who dwelled in the turret tower of Empire Estates had been taken away, locked up in a cubicle cell and sedated.

"Who plays the piano these days?" I asked.

"I play some, but it is wasted on me; I don't play very well. It was a gift from Grandpa Hypolite. Clifford Duveneaux--you remember Clifford . . . "

"Yes, the jazz pianist. I thought his fame had carried him away from New Orleans. Doesn't he perform in Europe?"

"All over the world. He comes to visit me with his friends whenever he is in town. He flatters me, but at least the piano gets some proper use."

"Clifford reminds me of something that I must confess to you. The night of your housewarming in 1957, when Clifford was playing the piano, I was out on the verandah. I had slipped out to look at the stars. You came out to smoke, and we talked, do you remember?"

"Yes, I remember that."

"I was watching you before I spoke, it wasn't polite to spy on you, but you seemed to be in a world of your own. You reminded me of a character in a book. I thought that it would be nice to write a novel about you and your house. It came to me as I watched you smoking and looking out into the night. You know what kind of idling fool I am sometimes."

"It wouldn't make a very interesting book, I'm too normal; characters in books should be eccentric. You're still feeling guilty about not recognizing me at the Beaux Arts Ball, aren't you? You shouldn't, it only proves what an ordinary person I am. But I am glad that you came to visit, it's very thoughtful, you don't have to pretend that you want to write articles or books about me."

"I just didn't expect to see you at a Mardi Gras ball, and you weren't in costume. Now that doesn't make any sense at all, does it? If you were in costume, I would have an excuse. By the way, how did you recognize me, I have changed some, haven't I, and I was in costume."

"It was easy, I recognized you at once. I told Dr. Meyers that it was you."

"Dr. Meyers?"

"You remember Dr. Meyers, don't you. He was the one who invited me to the ball."

"Yes, I remember him, he taught at Tulane. He must be very old."

"Eighty-three and still going strong. I can't keep up with him and Mother. Those two may be a case." A case. The expression didn't suit her.

"You mean . . . ?"

"I wouldn't be a bit surprised."

"Was your mother at the ball?"

"Yes."

"In costume?"

"Dante and Beatrice, she and Dr. Meyers." I saw them!

"I saw them, the costumes were beautiful."

I might have been losing my memory, the present became blurred, the distant past, vivid, the first sign of senility.

Bernice was waiting.

Evening was falling. I switched on the head lights. They cast their eerie yellow marks on shadowy River Road. Castle Manor. The mystery of chiaroscuro helped the houses, they looked almost authentic.

What was I doing in Algiers, the last frontier of this old city, driving a stranger's car as day departed? Why did I call Bernice a stranger? She and I were both strangers in my strange, new life. Why did I visit Clara in her great empty house; was I not confused enough, and now--after seeing her--more confused than ever, trying to find my way back to Sharon's apartment and Bernice?

Who is Clara--really--and what is it exactly that I want from her? I invited her to the apartment for Mardi Gras. She declined, Mardi Gras was too much for her. I wasn't going to be there myself.

Last night when I went out to get the bourbon, I called Sheila, but she wasn't home. I found Jules' number in the directory. I recognized his voice when he answered.

"Jules, this is Bobby Gomez."

"Bobby, what a pleasant surprise."

"Is Sheila there?"

"Sheila?"

"My wife."

Silence.

"Is she there?" I had taken two slugs of bourbon from the bottle.

"Are you all right, Bobby?" Smooth sonavabitch.

"Yes, I'm all right, will you call Sheila to the phone, please?"

"Just a moment, Bobby . . . "

Long silence.

"Hello--Bobby?"

"Sheila, are you coming home?"

"What's wrong with you, are you drunk? I'm over here having a drink with Jules and a few friends, I'll be home, is something wrong?"

"No, nothing wrong. I'm sorry I disturbed you. It sounds mighty quiet for a party."

"It's not a party, just a few people having a drink. Bobby, are you drunk?"

"No, just sleepy. Have a good time, good-bye."

"Bobby . . . "

It eased my conscience. There was still, if you wanted to be technical, no real evidence. I did not actually see them kiss at the Old Absinthe Bar. And even if they had, it might have been simply the affection of old friends who bumped into each other. But I was not fooling myself. Why didn't I call back and ask for a divorce?

Bernice's friend Sharon had gotten back, she and Bernice were sitting on the front porch with Tolstoy, they smiled as I approached, I couldn't tell if it was a smile of pleasure or of ridicule--but why would they ridicule me? Sharon had small, greenish eyes, a fleshy Irish face and a strong, shapeless body; her eyes had no warmth. I thought immediately that she was homosexual, that she had been in therapy since puberty and had both boy friends and girl friends before and after her marriage. She wore blue jeans, raveled on the bottom and a white tee shirt. Her breasts sagged like those of a woman in her late thirties, but her face was immature and coarse. My suspicion was that she and Bernice had been lovers, and still were. I could tell immediately that Bernice had told her everything.

She was stroking Tolstoy, whose black fur shone in the failng light. I smiled down on her when she looked up.

"That Tolstoy is a wonderful cat." I said. "He is the biggest cat I have ever seen. Do you give him vitamins to make his fur shine?"

"He's a good boy." she continued petting him with strong, long strokes.

Bernice gave me no clue when I looked at her.

"How was Clara?" She asked, "I told Sharon about her and she thinks her story would make a terrific novel." Sharon looked up at me with a perfunctory smile. Her little eyes did not reveal that she had heard a romantic tale. I was crushed that Bernice had told her. Where would Bernice and I spend the night? I felt old and out of place. Was I expected to leave so that these two could be alone?

Night was coming. Tolstoy peered at me with his golden eyes. He was my last remaining friend.

"Have you changed your mind about Mardi Gras?" I asked Sharon.

"Some friends from Montreal have decided to come down. I'm going to show them around."

Rich kids from Canada. What do you say we call Sharon and buzz down for Mardi Gras.

Bernice looked settled in, I should leave. I was stranded without transportation.

"Sharon has to pick up her friends at the airport."

"They're coming tonight?" I inquired.

"Eight-thirty, I better be on my way." She picked up Tolstoy and started inside, "Good night."

"I'll call you later this week," Bernice shouted.

"That was quick. Sharon doesn't fool around," I said idly.

"That's why I like her, no frills. Isn't she nice?"

"Yeah, she's nice. Very unpretentious. What now?"

"I don't know." My sweet, lost Bernice again.

"We can't go home. I don't want to go home. What about you?"

"Why don't we go to my place. Murray moved out."

"He may decide to come back."

"No chance."

"I don't know. What did you tell Sharon?"

"About Clara?"

"About us."

"Not much. She's my best friend."

"Let's go somewhere and eat, we'll talk things over----Bernice?"

"Yes?"

"Will you stick by me tonight?"

"We're in the same boat."

"That's right. What are we going to do?"

"I don't know."

Chapter 2

*W*e had a roast beef po-boy at Tall-T. Bernice, I discovered, liked the place. We had an argument. Perhaps she was right. Tall-T and the Napoleon House were really the same place, at different times.

"What did you and Clara talk about?" she asked me, back in her apartment.

"Old times."

"Did you tell her about the book?"

"No. Bernice, you don't seem to be worried about this situation."

We were sitting on an Early American sofa. I was surprised that Murray, an architect, would select Early American. There was also an oval corded rug and a spinning-machine lamp on the end table.

"I'm past worried. Murray and I will get a divorce, and that will be that."

"That's not what I mean. What about you and me?"

"You're married."

"If I get a divorce?"

"Would you?"

"I don't know."

"That's what I thought. Let's not talk about it tonight." She got up and went off in search of something.

"What are you looking for?"

"Cigarettes."

"You don't smoke."

"Sometimes I do."

"Are you nervous?"

"No. I just feel like smoking. Yes. I guess I am nervous. You're making me nervous."

"Why am *I* making you nervous? What have I done? That's a fine thing to say."

"I don't know what you want from me. Where the hell are those cigarettes?"

"I don't want anything from you. Do you want me to go out and get you some cigarettes?"

"No. That's all right. There are some here somewhere; unless Murray took them."

"It doesn't look like Murray took very much."

"He took his clothes. This is all my furniture. I bought it before we were married. Except for the record player, he'll probably come back for that. It's his pride and joy."

I went out to get her some cigarettes and a bottle of bourbon. We couldn't make love unless we were drunk. I had to wait in line. A drive-in all-night grocery. It was packed with college kids, buying beer and bottles of wine. There was excitement in the air. The kids were jostling each other, not a care in the world, ready for a big day tomorrow. It occurred to me that they were not much younger than Bernice. Parties were busting loose, these kids were cranking things up. They were smoking pot, getting high, lacing their high with wine and beer. Maybe I was getting the wrong kind of cigarettes. What an idiot I was. I knew what Sharon kept in her pots. Pot for the pots. Did Murray smoke pot? Of course he did. I was going to check out his record collection when I got back. Not a Beethoven in the bunch I'd bet. I couldn't believe what a fool I'd been.

I opened the bourbon right there in the parking area. Three college boys cheered me on. "You got it, baby." They held up their clenched fists and kicked the Toyota's tires. It was friendly, I couldn't take offense. I had a drink on them. "That's right, I've got it." *What* do I have?

Bernice had her legs up, half-reclined, her head resting on the back of the sofa.

"You look relaxed."

"What took so long?"

"I met some of your friends. I had a drink with them. Here are your cigarettes, hope they are the right kind."

"*My friends.* Who?"

"Just a joke. Want a drink?"

"Did you meet any of my friends?"

"I said it was a joke, how about that drink?"

"O.K."

I sat down with my bourbon, I was already feeling much better.

"Bernice, do you have any pot in the apartment?"

"What?"

"Pot, grass, marijuana. Do you have any?"

"Why do you want to know?"

"Do you have any?"

"Yes."

"Did you smoke any while I was gone?"

"What's wrong with you?"

"Did you?"

"No."

"I think you did. You look dreamy."

"You're wrong. Sharon and I smoked before you came, but I am down now."

"Would you teach me how to smoke?"

"You're in a funny mood. You're drunk."

"A little. What about it, will you teach me?"

"If you insist."

"I insist. What does it do? Pot?"

"It relaxes you. If it's good stuff, you get into things. Little things."

"That's what I want. To get into things. Little things. Big things puzzle me."

She told me that nothing usually happened the first time, it took a couple of times, that I wasn't holding it down in my lungs long enough.

But something *did* happen.

"Clara is so eccentric. It's so unbelievable."

"Eccentric? I thought you admired her."

"I do. She has made such a special life for herself. She doesn't know how unique she is. She thinks she's normal. She's done amazing things without realizing it."

"I don't understand."

"Without her, Philip would not be a Senator."

"Philip?"

"Senator Rotolo. Her coronation had him elected."

"You didn't tell me about that. Was he the councilman running for office?"

"Yes."

"You can't write about that. You'll get sued for sure."

"And Ronnie. He was down and out. Flunked out of Tulane, no place to go. Where would he be without her? She doesn't know what she's done."

"You're exaggerating, aren't you?"

"I don't think so. Do you know what got me the editor's job on *Dixie*? That cover story in *Time*. I can't prove it, but they called me in shortly after that and offered me the job."

"It all sounds very accidental to me. All of that would have happened anyway. Don't you think?"

"Maybe. She gave us faith."

"You're crazy. Faith. People make their own breaks."

"They're given opportunities, they must have faith, also."

"What is faith?"

"I don't know. It's believing in something strong enough to make sacrifices for it."

"You sound like a nun."

"I'm not a Catholic anymore, if that's what you mean. I'm giving serious thought to getting a divorce. That would tear me with the Church."

"Are you serious?"

"Sheila and I mean nothing to each other, if we ever did. I have no faith, I don't believe in anything anymore."

"What does Clara believe in?"

"I don't know. That's what fascinates me about her. She is sustained, and I don't know by what."

"She lives in a dream world. Lots of people live in a dream world, there's nothing different about that. She's neurotic."

"Maybe you're right."

"Let's make love again."

"All right. That's something to believe in. Maybe it's the only thing."

Tomorrow was Mardi Gras. Wednesday, the day after, was Ash Wednesday, which begins Lent; forty days of Penance. This old city believes in nothing. It has no faith in anything.

Chapter 3

I misjudged Murray. He was into classical music. I played the *Moonlight Sonata*. I didn't want to wake Bernice up, so I turned the volume down. Why was I not sleeping? I had had bourbon, pot, love, everything. What time was it? Three o'clock, four o'clock? It was Mardi Gras. At daybreak I would go out for donuts, an old tradition in New Orleans.

I had lain awake in bed with my eyes wide opened. There was no peace, I could not stop my mind, and yet it was empty. There was nothing for me to think. I stared into the black emptiness. Was I going crazy, broken loose and floating out into empty space? Was this what it was like to go crazy? Nothing, nothing to think, nothing to feel? I got up to feel my body moving. I walked around the room in the dark. If Bernice would have woken up, she would have thought that I was a maniac, circling around and around. Gone crazy, walking around and around, wringing my hands. Thank God she didn't wake up. I sat down on the sofa to calm myself. It didn't help. The same vacuum surrounded me. Nothing. Nothing.

Then I remembered . . . I was going to look through Murray's records.

The music had no magic. I failed Beethoven. He poured his heart into his music, and I sat there feeling nothing. It could be any set of sounds, the ratcheting, raucous hum of a chain saw, the click of two bricks set together . . .

Then I must have fallen asleep. What a merciful thing sleep is. I had many dreams. Everyone was there: Philip, Ronnie, Clara, Bernice, Sheila, everyone. We were in different houses, in places familiar and strange. There was a battle, a train speeding through the night, a flight above billowing clouds, and love. A woman, I was in love with, she had dark, wonderful eyes, she kissed me and told me that she loved no other. She was everything I ever wanted. The sun shone through the window, I was sitting up on the sofa. It was Mardi Gras.

When was it? 1952 or 1953. Sheila and I dressed up as Groucho and Harpo. We thought it was very original. I was Groucho. For Sheila, Harpo was easy, a curly wig and she was nearly there. We were still single, it must have been 1952. Bessie got something to make my mustache and eyebrows stick. I had a cigar that was nearly a foot long. I went about the Rosenberg house in the Groucho crouch, wheedling the cigar. Sheila wore one of Bernie's old raincoats, she had a Harpo horn; I don't remember where we got it.

Bernie came in with four dozen donuts. It was very early, not even eight o'clock. Mama Gomez and I had gotten up at five o'clock to catch the streetcar. The streetcar and the bus we transferred to were nearly empty except for a couple of old timers, night watchmen on their way home. It was a beautiful spring morning. I remember being very happy. Mama Gomez was very excited about going to the Rosenberg's for Mardi Gras.

Philip and Mary Ann came over dressed as clowns. Their costumes were beautiful. Satin. White with red polka dots. We tried to get Mary Ann to wear a big plastic red nose, but she refused. When we insisted and chased her, she locked herself in the bathroom. She came out and Mama Gomez protected her, swatting us with an old issue of *Harper's* magazine. "Leave that girl alone, you boys."

Even Bernie began to act uncivilized, he ate seven jelly donuts, belched and patted his flat stomach. Seven donuts and not a sign of a bulge. He washed the donuts down with a double martini, and Bessie warned him about getting drunk. As usual, Bessie was holding things together.

We all had martinis. Mama Gomez took one sip and handed hers to Philip. "Put some sugar in it, Philip." He did; everybody screamed at him and gagged. But we passed it around for a sample sip. Nasty, revolting.

Philip, Mary Ann, Sheila and I started out on foot, the only way to travel on Mardi Gras. We pulled a nifty little cart loaded with an ice chest full of beer and ham sandwiches wrapped in plastic bags. The sandwiches got soggy, and we threw them away.

We planned to meet Mama Gomez, Bessie and Bernie at Lee Circle to watch the Rex parade together. Bernie was going to drive the Fiat through all the side streets and get as close as he could. Such rendezvous' were sheer folly. "See you at Lee Circle," yelled we youngsters, and off we went.

At St. Charles and Napoleon Avenues we saw a woman dressed in a costume of playing cards strung together yelling angrily at a man who was encased in a huge die (pl. dice, seven come eleven). He was drunk, sitting on the curb. She lashed him with beads, "This your idea of fun, I'm going home." No one interfered.

Philip was a target for all the hairy legged transvestites. They flirted outrageously with him. One of them kissed him on the cheek; Philip pretended to swoon and offered his lover a beer. "I'm a lady, I don't drink." He was belting bourbon straight from the bottle.

There were many servicemen; soldiers, sailors, marines, fly-guys, a reminder that we were at war again in Korea. An unheroic war that was teaching us to be bitter about sacrificing our youth. The aura of the great war had faded.

We ran into Ronnie at Lee Circle. People were packed like sardines on the banquette around the circle, pedestrian traffic was flowing in both directions, we were being bumped around; someone knocked the ice chest off of the cart. We decided to move away from the monument to get some breathing room. We were all eager to talk to the quiet, pretty girl with Ronnie. We knew at once that it was Clara. There had been so much speculation about her.

Ronnie and Clara were not in costumes. We formed a circle, and Ronnie introduced us. The conversation was pleasant and reserved in sharp contrast to the bombast around us. Clara answered all of our questions, she seemed not unpleasantly surprised that she was the object of so much curiosity. She got quite a grilling, but took it in the friendly spirit in which it was given.

Why had I forgotten this meeting. Or was it the first? We saw her next in Algiers at her house. I must sit down with pencil and paper and make out a chronology. But who could I use to corroborate the facts? I had lost touch with Ronnie, Philip, and now Sheila. Clara herself was the only one, but she would suspect that I was serious about writing the book. It is a real story and cannot be written, except as my memoirs for posthumous publication, a painful autobiography.

I had reached the first real crisis in my life. I had an ordinary life with ordinary successes and ordinary failures. I was satisfied. What happened? Had I been avoiding all of these years, the excesses and tragedies which marked Alvin Harris' life, my real father, whose story I am so fond of telling? I could write his story in a book, no one would care. I could claim it as fiction, and no one would be the wiser. I would be wiser. Is tragedy the fountainhead of wisdom?

Bernice found me in he kitchen scribbling on the back of an envelope which I had picked out of her waste paper basket.

"What are you doing. What time is it?"

"It's Mardi Gras. I'm making out a chronology."

"A what?"

"A chronology. A list of events in their proper order of time."

"Did you make coffee?"

"No. I'm having bourbon. Make some coffee, when I finish with the chronology, I'll go out and get some donuts. We have to have donuts for breakfast. It's Mardi Gras."

She sat down, stretched, rubbed her eyes, and began to focus on the maniac writing furiously on an old envelope. One side was already filled up and the other side was going fast.

"Shouldn't you be thinking about going home?"

"I've been thinking about it. Are you trying to get rid or me?"

"No. But didn't you tell me that you and Sheila are having company today? Won't everyone be wondering where you are?"

"Are there any more envelopes?" I got up and searched through the waste paper basket.

"I think you've flipped out. Come here and talk to me. Let's decide what you are going to do. Sheila must know that you are with me. I'm worried. How did we get in this mess?"

I found another envelope; a big legal-sized one, and I started back to work.

"Bobby, stop! That can wait, whatever it is that you're doing. *Talk* to me."

I stopped writing and looked up at her. I was not going crazy, but I didn't know what I was doing. I could not explain to her why I was writing a chronology of my life. I knew that I should stop and talk to her. I should go home to be with Sheila, to greet our guests. No one would know that we were having problems. It was Mardi Gras, the day would pass rapidly, and in the morning we could discuss the chaos our lives had come to.

"Wouldn't you like some donuts for breakfast? It's an old tradition, " I offered.

"No, I wouldn't like some donuts. I don't like donuts, not even on Mardi Gras. Let's discuss what you are going to do."

"I'll have to go home. Isn't that obvious?"

"I'm glad that you realize it. Why don't you take a quick shower and get dressed, and I'll drop you off."

"What are you going to do? It's Mardi Gras, you can't stay here all alone."

"Don't worry about me, I'll manage. I'll go over to Sharon's, there'll be something going over there."

"Is Sharon straight?"

"What? Is she straight?"

"Sexually."

"What a cynical thing to say. Of course she's straight, she was married, wasn't she."

"That doesn't prove anything."

"What has gotten into you?"

"You're right. I shouldn't have said that, it was cynical. My brain must be scrambled. Forgive me."

"I forgive you. Now get your shower. By the way, neither one of us went to work yesterday. Do you realize that?"

"I called Tom and told him that we were on an assignment." I was lying. I had completely forgotten. Now I was going to be fired.

"Get your shower."

"Wait. I have a better idea. Why don't we go over to Clara's and spend the day with her. She's all alone, her mother is in Dallas."

"Don't be ridiculous, get your shower."

"I think that it's a great idea. What's wrong with it? Don't you want to meet Clara?"

"I'd love to meet Clara, but not today."

"Clara is all alone in that big house. What sustains her?"

"You're not going to start that again. Get your shower."

"Now I understand, you only pretended to be interested in my book about Clara. You're just like Sheila. She always pretended to be interested in my big ideas."

"How much have you had to drink?"

"How much have you had to drink?"

"Quite a bit. I went out last night and got another bottle. Would you like a drink?" The bottle was on the table, and it was only half full.

"No, I wouldn't like a drink. I better make some coffee. You're going to need it."

"How about a joint? You said you were going to teach me to smoke."

"Come on, Bobby. Get in that shower."

"O.K., I will. Just have one drink with me. There is one thing we have left to do."

"What's that?"

"A declaration of love. A written declaration of love." I scrawled it out on the envelope. I love Bernice. Signed Bobby. I love Bobby. Blank for signature, "Here, sign."

"O.K.," she signed.

"Now for the drink."

"Must we?"

"Just a short one. A symbol." I slugged a big drink and passed the bottle to her. She sipped and set the bottle down.

"Now, will you get your shower?"

"In a minute." I slugged another drink.

"Bobby." A sweet, low tone of warning. Another slug.

"I'm getting very sleepy. Maybe if I had a little nap . . ." Another slug and I got up and headed for the bedroom.

Nothing could be done with me, except to let me fall across the bed and sleep it off.

*B*obby slept as if he was dead. She became angry that he had gotten drunk and fallen apart on her. She didn't need a drunken man. She controlled the urge to wake him roughly and send him on his way. She realized, too, that his wife, Sheila, must know that he was with her. Her anger turned into frustrated helplessness. And then the phone rang. It startled her, but she picked up the receiver without hesitation. It was Sheila.

"Hello, Bernice."

"Yes, Sheila?"

"Is Bobby over there with you?"

"Yes, I . . . "

"I thought so. He really shouldn't be over there giving you trouble. You've been through enough already." She seemed very calm, her voice was motherly and intimately conspiratorial. Here we are, we two women, with a problem child on our hands.

Bernice was too relieved to resent this presumption. "He's had too much to drink, he's sleeping it off."

"I'm very sorry, Bernice, I'd come over and pick him up, but I have guests."

"He's dead to the world. Why don't I let him sleep it off. I'll give him some coffee and drive him over myself." She could hear loud voices in the background.

"If you would, I would appreciate it. How are you and Murray working things out?"

"Murray is gone, we're getting a divorce."

"Oh, I didn't know, I'm sorry. Are you managing?"

As condescending as this woman was, Bernice was at her mercy. Your husband spent the night with me, and has drunk himself into unconsciousness. He is this minute sleeping in my bed.

"I'm upset, of course, but I think that I will survive."

"I am sure that you will." The background noise seemed to get louder. Bernice heard a laughing woman call to Sheila, "Tell him to get his tail over here . . . ," and the woman's voice was suddenly muffled out. Sheila had cupped her hand over the phone.

"You better get back to your party. I'll get Bobby over as soon as I can. I hope you don't think . . . "

"I don't think anything, but you're right; it's getting very crowded in here. When Bobby wakes up, please bring him over. I'll talk to you later, Bernice. I'm sorry you've had this trouble." She was pitching her voice over the noise. "I have to go. Thank you, good-bye."

"Good-bye."

Was that, Bernice thought, an example of mature tact? The audacity of that woman, how cleverly she had swept this whole mess under the rug. Bernice was made to feel like a child, and yet she could not shake the feeling that Sheila was shallow and phony. Was that how marriages survived? One rose above their personal feelings, ignored their vulnerability, put the broken pieces back together, and put up a show of imperturbability. She felt petty and adolescent. What right did she have to run to Bobby? He was weak like her, unable to face up. Weaknesses like theirs tore down the structure of society; it was people like Sheila who held things together. Even Sheila's affair seemed not to skirt the boundaries of good conventionality. She was discreet, balancing her marriage, her affair, and her career. There was no need to be destructive in your pursuit of pleasure. She and Bobby were selfish and indulgent. Sheila's maturity loomed large, and yet Bernice knew that this woman was insensitive and faithless. She felt it but could not explain it. Her own life had broken into pieces, and she despaired of putting it back together again.

A tangle of excited voices and traffic sounds came to her from the streets. The city was celebrating. She was sitting alone and confused in her broken home on a day set aside for simple joy. Life goes on; but the lesson, whether grim or wise, was escaping her. She had to think things out and decide what to do.

She poured a cup of coffee, seated herself comfortably on the sofa and lit a cigarette. The cup of coffee felt warm in her hands as she gently gripped it. Warmth and tenderness pervaded her, and her eyes filled with tears. A large drop rolled slowly down her cheek. It hung on the ridge of her upper lip. She whispered, "The baby, my baby." Her nose began to run, and she began to wish with all of her heart that she was pregnant. She wiped her nose and smiled. "What a fool am I, what a foolish woman."

She looked down at the cigarette and thought of Clara, and she became, it seemed, privy to another secret. Wasn't that Clara's secret, being a fool, a foolish woman? I sit here, she thought, all alone in my house like Clara: we are the same.

She went into the bedroom and got the telephone directory. Bobby was sleeping on his side, curled up like a child. She passed her hand gently over his hair. She wanted to tell him that she loved him, and that she wanted to have his child.

She looked up Clara's number in the directory. It was listed under Duplantier, as she suspected. Was this a bit of feminine arrogance on Clara's part? Not Clara, thought Bernice, it would not have occurred to her to defy Ronnie. Perhaps Ronnie himself suggested that she drop his name, one Mrs. Hingle was enough.

Bernice smiled broadly and almost laughed out loud in spite of herself--how the hell would I know--I don't know any of these people! Nevertheless, she was preparing to call Clara on official business. It was business, wasn't it? Yes, it *was* business she concluded and actually giggled. She was about to call a perfect stranger on Mardi Gras and had not the slightest idea why.

She dialed the number and as the phone rang she suddenly felt panic--what am I going to tell her? The phone rang four times, and she was relieved. She was not home, wasn't that what I wanted to know--if Clara was sitting home all alone on Mardi Gras day? Well, she wasn't, she was out on the streets like any ordinary person would be on Mardi Gras. The phone was still ringing. What did Bobby think Clara was--a fixed sentinel in time, sitting in her big house all alone and waiting, waiting--always waiting? A voice said hello. She heard it distinctly--the voice of a person who was waiting. And she was waiting yet in that long second in which Bernice was frozen by the sound of her voice.

"Yes, hello--Clara, Miss Clara Duplantier?"

Chapter 4

*W*hen Bernice told Clara good-bye and hung up she had a brief moment of shock at what she had done. She wondered if she had been caught up in Bobby's illusion about Clara.

She went to the window to look out. The day was brilliant. Two little girls dressed as clowns were on the banquette tossing beads to one another. They were no more than four or five. Their costumes shimmered in the springtime sun. They tossed and caught their beads, jumping and screaming with glee. She heard their mother calling to them to be careful not to run in the street. The street seemed otherwise deserted on this Mardi Gras morning. The maskers and revelers had followed the parades up St. Charles Avenue to Canal Street which was by now thronged with pushing and shoving crowds. She and the little clown-girls had been left behind. All of this conspired, she thought--the deserted street, the private miniature celebration of the little girls, the brief sweetness of the new spring. Was there some lesson to be learned from this carefully arranged retreat? But she was in no mood to be taught lessons, nor did she know why she had called this woman, Bobby's fictional queen-saint. It was the silliest thing she had ever done. She smiled, combed through her hair with her fingers and lit a cigarette. She became possessed by a scientific coolness. It all fits nicely into place, doesn't it? Ronnie, Philip--people that she didn't even know--meeting Clara in their most crucial hour of need. And Bobby, Clara's appearance to him, dreamer that he is, was almost elaborately mystical--self-induced mystification. All I need now is spiritualism.

Sounds of loud laughter, hoots and happy screams erupted from the street. An old pick-up truck decorated with tattered streamers of crepe paper and swirls of spray paint had stopped in front of the little clown-girls. It was loaded with a happy, drunken band of maskers. They were tossing beads and doubloons to the little girls. One of the

343

maskers spotted Bernice at the window and threw her a pair of beads. The beads clattered against the glass panes and fell onto the porch. Bernice smiled broadly and waved. The maskers waved back as the truck went rumbling off.

Suddenly Bernice could not wait for Bobby to wake up.

Chapter 5

*W*hen I awoke, the sun shone strongly through the window. I
had dreamed many dreams but could not remember any of
them. I had dreamed deeply, where memory was primitive, the
recalling and reassembling of fundamental elements. By rights, I
should have had a headache and that strong, beaming sun should
have been blinding me, but I had the clear head and sweet eyes of a
nursery babe. Bernice was wiping my forehead with a wet cloth. She
was humming a little tune. A lullaby.

"How long did I sleep?"

"About three hours."

"Is that all? It seemed like centuries."

"How do you feel?"

"Wonderful. Rested."

"Would you like some coffee? I just made some."

"That would be nice."

"Wait. I'll get you some. Black?"

"Yes, thank you."

I propped up on one elbow and drank the coffee. As I sipped
slowly, I made a plan for my life. Everything was so simple and clear.
It was as if I had awakened from a torrid fever, sweating and looking
upon the light of a new day, a new life. I spent last night in the grips
of a crisis.

"What were you doing while I was asleep?"

"I was on the phone."

"Who were you talking to, Sharon? What is Sharon doing?
Did she meet her friends form Canada? I think I like Sharon. I'm
sorry I said that ugly thing about her."

"Sheila called."

"She did. What did she say?"

"She wanted to know if you were coming home."

"Was that all? How did she sound?"

"She was very calm. We talked a little while about my divorce. She asked about Murray."

"Who's over there? A crowd?"

"She said the place was packed. I could hear a lot of people talking and yelling."

"Was she mad? At me?"

"She didn't sound mad. And I called somebody else."

"Murray?"

"No. He's probably at his mother's house."

"Are you bitter about him leaving?"

"No. I haven't given him a thought all day. Don't you want to know who I called?"

"Is it such a mystery?"

"I think that you are going to be surprised."

"I think I know."

"Who?"

"Clara."

"How did you guess? I didn't think you would ever guess."

"I don't know, it just came to me. Why did you do that?"

"I wanted to know if she was real. You could have been lying to me. Not really lying but testing an idea."

"How did you find her number?"

"It's in the directory."

"Wasn't that enough to convince you that she was real?"

"No. The fact that someone named Clara Duplantier is living on the River Road in Algiers doesn't prove that she lived the life you told me she lived. There's almost a half column of Duplantiers in the directory. It crossed my mind that you may have flipped open the directory, closed your eyes, and picked out a name at random. That wouldn't be an outlandish way for a writer to find a name for a character in a book. So I called her, that was the only way I could be sure."

"I told you that she was married to Ronnie Hingle. And you know that he is real. You could have gone to the library where they have bound copies of old *Time* issues."

"I don't know why I called her."

"I think I do. I'm just surprised."

"You were the one who told me her story, why should you be surprised?"

"Was she home?"

"Yes."

"That proved nothing. Maybe your suspicion was right, the whole story is a sham; I made it up. Do you know who Jean Lafitte was?"

"The Buccaneer."

"That's right. Do you know that there are no authentic facts about his life? Everyone makes up their own story about him. None of it's true."

"That's not the case with Clara."

"What makes you so sure?"

"I talked with her, and I am going to visit her."

"Why?"

"I don't know, I shouldn't have to explain that to you."

"Did she give you directions, the house is hard to find."

"I'll find my way."

"I'm sure you will. I should be getting home, don't you think?"

"What are you going to do? You and Sheila?"

"I don't know. I'll find out when I talk to her. We have been married a long time, but a divorce is not out of the question, not even at our age."

"Get your shower, I'll press your clothes."

"O.K."

"One more thing."

"What?"

"Are you going to write Clara's story?"

"How could I? It's a real story. I'll be sued."

Chapter 6

*B*ernice was able to drop me off as close as Esplanade and Rampart. We had gone around by way of Carrollton Avenue to City Park which seemed utterly deserted except for a young couple we saw strolling near the lagoon; they were not in costume and were probably avoiding Mardi Gras. Bernice and I smiled.

The revelers along Esplanade walked swiftly and their numbers increased as we drew closer to the Quarter. The traffic increased, also, and finally we were bumper to bumper. As we inched along, I noticed that some of the maskers were already moving against the flow, going home. They seemed tired. I felt very fresh myself, clean and rested. I sat upright. Bernice seemed to share my peacefulness. Whatever we were going to do about each other would have to wait until I talked to Sheila.

"Are you all right?" Bernice asked me as I opened the door.

"Me? I'm fine--thanks to you. Look at me, do I look like I've been drinking all night?"

"You look great."

"Yes, I do."

I leaned over and kissed her on the cheek, "I'll see you tomorrow morning, my dear--don't be late."

There was no use closing the door. Some came through the bathroom. Others stuck their heads in, wondering why the door was closed. It was not right for a room to be closed off when a party was in full swing. Who closed this door, they seemed to say, what's going on in here? A woman I did not recognize was very blunt: "Who closed this door?"

"I'm talking to my wife, do you mind?"

"Are you Bobby? Where have you been?"

"Now that's none of your goddamn business, is it? I don't even know who the hell you are."

"Jesus Christ, what kind of party is this?" She slammed the door.

"Who the hell is that? One of the gang from D.C.?"

"She's a friend of Margaret's."

"And who's the asshole drunk on the bed?"

"A friend of Louis', I don't remember his name. I don't think that you're in any condition to talk."

"Yes, I am. Look at how fresh I look. I've had a shower, and I'm cold sober. Look, Sheila, I don't think I have to explain about Bernice. And you don't have to explain about Jules."

"What about Jules? What have you made over that?"

"Please, Sheila. I know that you have been seeing him. I'm not going to throw a jealous fit, I just want to say something to you, will you listen?"

"Tomorrow will be better, don't you think?"

The drunk on the bed was rousing himself. He asked for an aspirin, holding his head and moaning.

"Are you sure he's Louis' friend? He doesn't look like a Cajun to me."

"Don't be ugly."

"Sheila, I want a divorce."

Sheila looked at me very sternly. Fiercely. "Why did you have to say that here, in front of him? Don't you have any sense of decency?"

"He's nothing but a drunken Cajun, he doesn't know what the hell is going on."

"I think this conversation is over."

"Did you hear what I said? That's the important thing."

"Yes, I heard what you said. But I don't want to discuss it. Not here, and not now."

"We can't wait until tomorrow. We may forget."

"Are you going crazy?"

"Look at me, Sheila, do I look like I'm going crazy? Have you ever seen me calmer?"

I went into the bathroom, rinsed out the toothbrush glass, got the bottle of aspirins, and took them to the drunk.

When he looked up at me I could tell that he was a very decent sort. He took two aspirins from the bottle and washed them down with the water. He looked up at me, suddenly very alert.

"Why do you want to get a divorce?"

"That was a private conversation."

"I couldn't help overhearing. Don't get a divorce, you'll be making a terrible mistake."

"You don't know us, how can you say that, and it's none of your business anyway."

"I got a divorce last month. It was the worst thing that ever happened to me."

"I can't believe this," said Sheila. She headed for the door.

"Sheila, wait. Please, don't go," I yelled.

"I'm not going to stand here while you discuss our private business with a stranger."

"Please stay. I want to hear what he has to say."

"Hear what he has to say!" She opened the door to leave, but I closed it again, as gently as I could.

"Sheila, please stay and listen." The drunk was looking at us with tears in his eyes.

"Please . . . " he started, but could not continue. He sobbed. Sheila and I watched him cry. When he gained control he looked up at us.

"It really is none of my business. It's just that I'm so lost--and hurt. My wife and I thought that we were finished, that we no longer loved each other." He shed more tears. "I'm so lonely."

Sheila spoke first to him. "Why don't you ask her to take you back?"

"She wouldn't, I wouldn't ask her. It's over. It's best this way." He dried his tears with his hands and got up to leave. Sheila and I parted, making room for him. He closed the door softly behind himself.

Chapter 7

*B*ernice came in Wednesday with ashes on her forehead. I asked her if she was going back to Church. I didn't even know if she had fallen away, as Sheila and I had, long ago. "No," she said, "I was never religious, and I don't feel religious today. I was walking past the church, and I saw people going in. I had forgotten that it was Ash Wednesday. I followed them in to see what kind of service there was, I assumed it was Mass. I didn't intend to stay. When I saw the priest giving ashes I went up and knelt down, it didn't take long. I felt comforted somehow when he smeared the ashes on my forehead and mumbled the words; I wanted to see if I could believe. I couldn't, I don't think that I can ever believe again."

"Why didn't you wipe the ashes off," I asked.

"I thought I had, are they still there?"

"Yes," I said and wiped them away with my handkerchief.

We worked hard. There was a lot of catching up to do. I told Bernice that Sheila and I were talking about getting a divorce. She said that she was sorry. Tom Mahoney, my assistant, called in sick on both days. He needed the rest.

I teased Bernice about her appointment with Clara.

"Are you going to see her because you believe that story about her being a queen?"

She smiled, "Clara sounded like a very nice person on the phone, but my visit won't be social; I am going to interview her for a story, and I was going to ask you to help me. Would you?"

"Do you want to be a journalist?"

"Maybe."

"Sure I'll help you. I think it's a great idea, you've been a secretary long enough."

I gave her one of my notepads and a couple of pencils before she left.

Chapter 8

*B*ernice met Bobby on a new basis; she became his assistant, taking initiatives, working by his side, filling in for Tom Mahoney who called in sick. They felt a new companionship and went about their business, working hard and efficiently.

They sent out for sandwiches and had lunch in the office to save time. On Thursday as they sat quietly munching on their sandwiches, Bobby told her that he had asked Sheila for a divorce.

"What did she say?" Bernice inquired.

"She refused to discuss it."

"What are you going to do?"

"I don't know. What are you going to do?"

"About what?"

"Everything."

She wondered again if she was pregnant, but because this was only her speculation she said nothing about it.

Kenny MacDermott stuck his head in the office door and made some crude joke about them having lunch together. They smiled wearily at each other. Everything must wait, Bernice thought; and it came to her that everything was waiting somehow on her visit to Clara. She had to smile to herself. What had this strange woman come to mean to her? Clara had come into her life in the same curious way that she had come into the lives of all the others. Was it now her turn to have her life transformed? Bobby was looking over at her, his face ringed with a wry smile. "Why are you smiling?" she asked.

"You were in deep thought, and I thought it was very becoming."

She smiled herself, "I have the strangest feeling you knew exactly what I was thinking."

"No, I didn't," he said with quiet conviction.

"Are you sure?"

"I'm sure."

As she left the office, night had not yet fallen; the days grew longer. She walked to the garage to get the Toyota. Many people were walking the streets at this hour--office workers like herself, late shoppers. As she passed the Monteleone Hotel the doorman was loading a family of late Mardi Gras tourists into an airport limousine; they had the dejected, subdued look of travelers headed home. The clerks and shoppers also looked dejected. Two elderly ladies were standing on a corner; the evening sun raked a harsh light across their aging faces. They wore flower print dresses and nets over their blue tinted hair--a pair of bookends--but it was clear that they were friends and not sisters. She noticed that their shopping bags were nearly empty. Some dread feeling had gotten ahold of Bernice; she suddenly wanted to cry.

She drove to the library and parked in the rear parking lot. The night was moonless and clear--stars twinkled everywhere. A fresh, chilled breeze blew, and she huddled in her blouse.

The library seemed deserted; several librarians sat behind the counter on high stools, conversing in low voices, they seemed listless. A stout, dark haired woman got up to assist her. She wore no make up, and Bernice wondered if she was married. When Bernice looked at her hand she was surprised to see a wide wedding band on her left hand. Bernice explained that she was looking for an old issue of Time magazine, and was led back into the stacks. The librarian pulled a volume from the shelf and handed it to her and left. Bernice stood frozen for a moment. Yes, this was the right volume--1960, October-December. Finally she carried the unopened volume into the reading room and placed it before her on the table. She was tingling with excitement. But she hesitated, absently gripping the volume. A long minute passed, and she opened the volume and began turning the pages with trembling fingers.

And there she was: Clara, the queen of New Orleans. Nothing unexpected, though, all very accurately anticipated--a pretty, sober girl, placid in her prettiness. Nothing unexpected, and yet Bernice was thrilled. She pored over the photograph. She drank of it thirstily. She could not get enough of looking at it.

She flipped quickly to the article, to the other photographs, shots of the ceremony and parade. In four of them Clara was a mere blur in the general spectacle. In the fifth, she was closely framed and smiling, but the same serene Clara, no fissure in her composure, no breakdown in her placidity, no chink of woe-begone self consciousness. The article was as Bobby had said: smugly flip and amused.

That evening she and her mother went to the couturier for a final fitting of her gown and train. Her mother worried and fretted over every detail. The object was to fashion a gown without the rhinestone glitter of a Mardi Gras queen. Lovely folds of dark mauve silk and white satin trim looped down in the full skirt, the bodice fitted tightly around her waist and breast, falling off her shoulders, a tiara of large winey garnets shone with subtle tenebrous light out of her chestnut hair. The effect was replete with richness. There were rehearsals of the coronation ceremony, ending with her presentation to the citizens of the ninth ward in front of the church. The old priest resided over these rehearsals. Prayers were recited to invoke the blessings of the Holy Spirit. The old priest explained that although her authority was not real in a constitutional sense, its purpose was to bond the community in the ninth ward, a bond of charity to respect each other and care for those who need help. This authority, the priest said, was real. The ceremony would culminate with the lifting of her arms to heaven and out to the congregation when he would come forward to sprinkle holy water over all, uniting them in God's love. In the final rehearsal the priest sprinkled real holy water over the small gathering of reporters and well-wishers, everyone was very quiet as the droplets fell on their hair, cheeks and hands, it seemed more water than anyone imagined. Bobby Gomez, the Picayune *reporter was so moved that he blessed himself with the sign of the cross, and felt his own warm tears roll down his cheeks. He was embarrassed, but looked left and right to notice everyone wiping away tears. They all smiled at their strong feelings, especially the reporters from around the state who were suppose to be objective. Many offered lame excuses for of these tears----everyone cries at weddings.*

Then came the day of the coronation. Clara was quite resigned by now. Ready to be a queen, knowing that when it was over she could return to herself, that is, to being herself- the ordinary person she always thought herself to be. But no one was prepared for the sight of her when she emerged from the limousine in front of the church. Everyone froze--even the news photographers. She turned calmly to face them, not a waver of nervousness, perfectly at ease in her grandness--her majesty, thought Robert Gomez,--thinking that there was some real quality of queenliness that was in addition to the circumstances and the dress and everyone's anticipation. Clara had done this, he thought, added something like solemnity with her strange quietude. Only when Philip spoke to her with his buoyant enthusiasm did the crowd begin milling and chattering again. But the effect she had on them was memorable. Notes that Bobby Gomez had jotted down at that moment reminded him later of the moment, a moment that once it had passed, seemed to pass in oblivion. He wondered if this had really been the reaction, or one that he had imagined. But try as he may he could not erase the image of Clara's queenliness. For him, she would always be that becalmed, pure vision of peacefulness. This image of Clara as queen became sequestered in a kind of tabernacle of his mind.

There were two things about her one-day reign over the ninth ward that continued to puzzle Clara. One was the feeling she had as she mounted her throne on the float, a feeling that continued throughout the parade around St. Roch park. She thought she was going to feel awkward and embarrassed, but instead, she felt not only comfortable but fulfilled. The other thing concerned the doubloons embossed with her image, that she had thought would render her almost helplessly self-conscious, but again she was wrong; holding one of the coins in her hand, she felt flushed with a sense of pride, whether for herself or her family--her father and grandfather--she didn't know.

Bernice felt a fierce need to possess this issue, and went to the librarian to ask if she could borrow it. The librarian told her it was a reference book and suggested that she use the Xerox. But Bernice persisted. She identified herself as a reporter for *Dixie-Roto* and explained that the article was needed for purposes of reproduction. Finally the librarian relented and made her sign for it.

She drove home in the clear, chilled night with the volume on the seat next to her, wondering about Clara, trying to recall her voice.

She slept fitfully that night, getting up several times to use the bathroom. In the morning she got up and dressed quickly. As she put on her make-up, she noticed how pale she had become. She was too nervous for breakfast or even coffee. She checked the things she needed, her note-pad, two sharpened pencils, the bound volume of *Time*. She picked up the phone to call Bobby, but changed her mind and left. By nine o'clock she was on the bridge. A great trailer truck stacked with heavy steel had slowed the traffic and as the long line inched along Bernice looked far down the river. Even the most distant things could be seen clearly. The traffic was heavy, freighters and rigs shimmered in the brilliant sunlight, the muddy water appeared golden.

Near the top, the traffic completely stopped, and the view almost took her breath away. She was suddenly tempted to step out of the car onto the raised walkway where she could see everything. Goose pimples raised on her arm. How thrilling she thought it would be to step over the railing onto the edge and lean forward into the wind, like a Viking ship ornament, letting it blow her hair free. I could leap into the open arms of space she thought, it would not be so bad, it might even be glorious. She laughed nervously.

The car in front of her pulled off and she pressed the accelerator to follow it, tears streaming down her cheeks. The Toyota came down the curving cloverleaf spinning along a subdivision boulevard, past sparkling new brick cottages with emerald green lawns. On the empty parkway, little magnolia saplings had recently been staked out. The subdivision gave way to a stretch of empty lots, overgrown with weeds and wild flowers. Street signs were either missing or obscured by young trees which had sprung up along the edges of the lots. She slowed down on every corner, looking for her turn, but it was confusing and she feared getting lost. She drove on, sticking her head out of the window. Her street, when she finally came to it, was little more than a road, only the street sign reassured her; the road was bedded with white clam shells and meandered through thickly wooded lots. She was lost she almost frantically concluded when the little shell road suddenly led onto a freshly paved street lined with newly constructed, unoccupied brick houses. But the new street abruptly ended after two blocks, and the shell road took up again through woods. Far ahead, however, through the trees, she saw the levee, and she knew she was not lost.

She turned onto the River Road. The levee was in springtime bloom with clover and buttercups. Ragged little clouds appeared, drifting south but were no threat to the clarity of the day. She followed the curving road, relieved. Bustling river sounds floated over the levee. The wind blew in on her, she breathed deeply to smell Spring.

The man sat at the kitchen table with his hands around his cup of coffee, his eyes fixed on its contents and although he appeared calm and composed, terror had frozen his thin body. His wife stood near the stove, screaming at him. She held two dishes in her hand. She stopped screaming and desperately fought back her tears. She screamed again and dashed the dishes to the floor.

"Answer me--answer me!"

She pulled open the cabinet doors seizing more dishes, crashing them against the wall. But the man still stared at his coffee and in truth could not have moved or spoken if he wanted to. His body was leaden.

His wife moved again to the cabinet. Her body was strong and agile, she moved with the swiftness and power of an athlete; she began slinging dishes in a frenzy, determined to empty the cabinet.

The other person present was the daughter. She sat at the table with her father. She also sat motionless but it was willful determination and not fear that held her. She stared boldly at her frenzied mother, inviting eye contact. Such boldness belied her frailness. She looked several years younger than her fifteen years. She waited until her mother had thrown the last dish and nurtured her willfulness in the ensuing silence, her callow face animated with arrogance. She arched her eyebrow and lifted her chin and spoke to her mother.

"Are you finished?" The question shot through the stilled air like a bullet, but her mother had no answer for it, she seemed crumbling and nearly fallen amid all the broken china. The daughter met her pleading gaze with renewed defiance as if to repeat the question in silence. The mother murmured almost inaudibly, trying to pronounce her daughter's name, but she had little strength left, she slipped to the floor onto the broken china and began to cry. The daughter looked down at her with an absurd expression of childish triumph. The struggle was ended, and it seemed to the daughter that she had won the battle.

It wasn't until years later that the daughter realized how ridiculous was this illusion of victory. Everyone had lost, especially herself.

Bernice came out of her reverie, startled by the recognition of a street name. She struggled to recall the daydream. It had been vivid, but it was gone, only its bare outline remained. She shook herself to wakefulness; she must now pay close attention for she was nearing her destination. She felt her breath quicken and her heart pound. She turned another curve and the woods thickened. As far as she could see to the next wide curve, there was more wilderness. Three crows flew across the road and lit in a tall cottonwood. Had she gone too far? But she resisted the temptation to turn around, and beyond the next curve, the woods gave way to a clearing and she spotted a street sign ahead.

The streets now followed the right sequence. An arched brick entrance to a new subdivision appeared, its name carved on a rustic shingle, hanging from cast iron chains: Belaire Estates. The houses were replicas of European villas, half-timbered chalets, French chateaux with mansard roofs, etc.

She focused on the great foreshortened curve ahead where the road disappeared behind the mounting levee. Somewhere beyond that curve was Maison Maurice, Clara's house. She pushed forward in her seat, bringing her hands up higher on the steering wheel. A nerve in her cheek twitched erratically; her palms moistened. The road barely straightened out when the big house came into view just beyond a little pasture with grazing horses. It was huge--magnificent. She braked the Toyota, her breath quickened, and a sudden, swift wind blew in on her, disarraying her hair.

"Damn," she said, using one hand to push it back in place, and in the process, nearly missed the driveway. She turned the wheel sharply, sending white shells skidding onto the lawn. She had arrived, but why in such a huff? She got her hair brush out of the bag and brushed her hair, using the rear view mirror.

"There," she said, "I'm ready to meet Clara." But she stalled a few more seconds, her heart pounding away. She waited, almost trembling. Finally she got out of the car and took deep breaths, and started shakily towards the house.

She slowly mounted the stairway onto the verandah, halting before the entrance, where her distorted image wiggled out at her from the beveled glass paneling. No light shone in the breezeway within. She listened, hoping for something to stir. Not a sound; the whole house seemed dark and hushed--if she didn't know better? Why was she standing here looking and listening so attentively? She stepped cautiously and heavily across the verandah to the door; the floor boards creaked beneath her feet. She pulled the old fashioned pull-bell twice, hearing its clang muffled within. Seconds passed. She moved her head and thought she saw a movement in the breezeway, but it was only her reflection. She looked at her watch; it was six minutes passed eleven. She watched the sweep hand until it came full circle. She pulled the bell again, three times. This time she waited two minutes by her sweep hand. She began to feel annoyance, was she being stood up? She pulled forcefully on the bell, four, five, six times. That should be enough for Clara to hear if she was home. But five more minutes passed, and there was no answer--no sound but the song of a mockingbird singing somewhere beyond the pasture in the tall trees. Her annoyance turned into a dull sense of disappointment. She tried to think if she had gotten the day or time wrong. She couldn't have. What can be the explanation? Her watch said eleven-twenty. She was clearly being stood up, and she was disappointed as anyone would be. If this was the usual kind of disappointment one should feel . . . this feeling of being emptied out. It was more like desperation--or despair.

But wait, was Clara back in the fruit orchard? Of course! She felt her heart pounding again. She turned quickly and descended the stairway. She walked swiftly up the driveway. A new source of energy was carrying her along. The orchard had grown up (she knew so well this house and everything about it); it was in new bloom, and its beauty gave her pause. But she hesitated only for a moment. she spotted the gazebo; it was half-hidden among peach blossoms. There's where she must be--smoking no doubt with the Zippo lying on the bench beside her. She walked quickly down the brick pathway, but she could see very clearly that the gazebo was empty. This was the final blow. There was not a soul anywhere; she had been deceived. There was no Clara. It was a joke.

She reeled with the oppressiveness of her disappointment, her mind clouding with the old fears for her survival. She felt struck by a blow; she started to walk back to the car. An unwanted feeling of grim resignation possessed her. She would get back in her car and drive off. She would forget Clara, whoever Clara was. At her car, she stood frozen, waiting for some reason before opening her door--something was nagging her. Had she missed something, or more precisely, was she missing something? The faraway voice finally worked through the fog of her stunned brain. What was it? It was her name--someone was calling her name. She attended very carefully and began to hear it quite clearly. Someone was calling her, but from where? Where--where? Then she knew, it was from the levee. She turned quickly and looked up, there was a figure in white, waving to her. She knew immediately--it was Clara!

Chapter 9

I was all alone Friday. Tom was still recovering, but the work was all caught up, and in my idleness I grew anxious, for, in spite of my resolve, Sheila and I had been avoiding each other and had not discussed our problems.

I called her at her office and suggested that we have dinner at Galatoire's. It seemed like a good idea--there would be an opportunity to talk and she agreed. But it wasn't a good idea. We had dinner and cocktails, but no talk. The martinis only gave us an appetite, we ate ravenously. We were full and sleepy and went home to bed.

In the morning Bernice called.

Sheila and I were having coffee at our little breakfast table when the phone rang. It startled us for we had become very tense, pretending as we were that nothing was wrong, and putting off the moment when we would at last speak of our trouble. Sheila answered the phone and greeted Bernice as an old friend. I was amazed and became very nervous for I knew that Sheila in spite of her brave front must have thought it strange if not brazen for Bernice to call. And yet, she seemed friendly and calm. Perhaps I had made too much over what had happened. Was the worst over? Would we now settle back into our old lives? I thought frantically that I now knew why Bernice was calling. She was going back to Murray, and she was calling to tell me that she was resigning--and she was sorry for what happened. She would probably also wish me luck or something equally as corny. I was instantly depressed. Sheila finally handed me the phone. She had turned to face me, holding me a moment with her eyes.

"It's for you," she said. I watched her walk into her room. I was frozen, everything had moved to the edge. I had lost control of my life and worst--didn't care.

"Bobby," Bernice began, her voice full of edginess.

"If you want to talk to me," I said, interrupting her, "then meet me at Tall-T. I'll be there at one o'clock."

"It's not necessary." I would not let her tell me what she wanted to tell me.

"One o'clock, I'll see you then. O.K.--say O.K."

"O.K., but . . . "

"I'll see you at one o'clock."

*T*all-T was closed, the door was locked. I knocked on the door summoning a youth. It was opening time I indicated to him, pointing to my watch. He hesitated, but let me in when I shoved my watch against the glass door. I took a table by a window, where I could watch for Bernice (if she came), dodging other youths who bustled around readying the place for the afternoon rush. I grabbed one on his way through and ordered a bourbon. He looked at me as if I were a nuisance and would have rushed off had I not held on to his arm. "I'm a paying customer," I said, "will I have to call the manager to get a drink?" He smiled, "I am the manager, sir, and I will be happy to get you a drink."

I left the apartment without so much as telling Sheila good-bye. She was in the bedroom staring vacantly down at her jewelry box. It was not like Sheila (my dear, proud Sheila) to be so defeated as I thought she looked. Surely, I would have gone in to her if I had believed this, but I evidently didn't believe, or didn't see. I didn't know. I left.

What was the urgency of seeing Bernice? Would I plead with her not to go back to Murray? Try to force some statement of love? This was her idea, I remembered, she wanted to talk to me. Did she simply want to tell me of her visit with Clara, what they talked about? What does anyone talk to Clara about, that strange, lonely woman?

Through the window, out on the wide parkway here on Carrollton Avenue, I could see the azaleas; they were blooming. The sky was so clear it quivered, blue beyond imagining; the day brimmed with life. Closer to me along the borders of the banquette, the young crepe-myrtle trees oozed tiny waxen leaves. It was a sight so vivid as to be banal. The colors--pink, fuschia, violet, yellow-green made me giddy, and reminded me of the liturgical vestments worn by Catholic priests. It was Lent; I had forgotten. I am still a Catholic, though it has been a long time since I fasted for Lent. I used to enjoy that little bit of monastic life, munching on a lunch of hard boiled eggs in my office and dropping in on the noontime Stations of the Cross at the Jesuit Church on Baronne Street to share my faith with perfect strangers: shoppers, business men, lawyers, stockbrokers.

Sheila and I were hurt and lost, but had a new respect for one another. Perhaps it was the old respect. We were no longer comfortable roommates, but we were also too old to fight. Everything had settled down, and I feared the worst: that Bernice would not show up and Sheila was home packing to leave me. But even if this was not true, the prospects were not good. Would I talk to Bernice and go home to Sheila and my old life, for whatever it was, simply go on?

A solitary, whacked-out robin hopped around among the azaleas. Either he had arrived early, or had been left behind; in either case he was a lonely fellow. I should have been lonely myself, sitting in an empty college bar with only the hustling youths for company: they completely ignored me. But the goofy beauty of this day would not allow it; my thoughts were only the briefest, sweetest kind.

I picked up the bourbon, the wrong drink on this day. I wasn't going to let myself sink any deeper into this transparency. I gripped the glass and closed my eyes, not wanting to see, but I could not stop myself--I did see, very clearly. A young man was walking on the levee slowly, distractedly, not seeming to notice the young girl seated beyond; it was late day and the low sun, beaming across the wide river, burned them to dark silhouettes. They were barely distinguishable but I could tell--he was not Ronnie, or the girl, Clara; they were strangers. Someone touched my shoulder, I opened my eyes and they were gone.

"Is something wrong, sir?" It was the youthful manager.

"No, I'm fine, I was resting my eyes."

"Is the bourbon all right, you haven't touched it?"

"It's fine," I said, smiling. I lifted the glass and took my first sip, and looked out of the window at the parkway which was now crowded with a multitude of robins, and Bernice was pulling up to the curb in the Toyota.

Chapter 10

J have a new secretary, Bernice has been assigned to the society
page. She is doing very well, considering her background and her
interest in literature, she has read very little and never written
anything more serious than a friendly letter. She and Murray have
settled everything between them and completed their divorce. She
claims now that she will never marry again for love or money. I
understood by this that she was not bitter but subdued. I went over to
visit her yesterday; she looked very determined clicking away at her
terminal. The dividends of her job, she told me, were contacts she
was making with local celebrities. The writing has improved, also, she
proudly reported.

A brief friendship had flared up between Bernice and Sheila.
While I was at Tall-T trying to collect myself, Bernice called Sheila,
and they opened up to each other. Exactly what they talked about I
don't know. I asked Sheila, and she told me the conversation was
about things in general.

"That covers a great deal," I said, not meaning to be sarcastic.
Sheila began to walk away, and I was going to drop the subject.
But she spoke again, without stopping, turning her head slightly
towards me.

"She thought she was pregnant." It was thrown over her
shoulder, with the slyest cast of her eye..

"Pregnant?" I said, too low and too late, and was left to choke
on the tantalizing possibilities. Bernice had not talked to me at
Tall-T about motherhood or our future, hers and mine. She spoke
instead of her visit with Clara about which she was very excited. I
remember how she was pitching her voice over the noise because the
place was filling up fast with students. She had placed a briefcase on
the table, and as she talked she clutched it protectively.

"Is that a new briefcase?" I asked.

"Yes, it is," she said, smiling with great satisfaction. She slid the briefcase over and hugged it.

"What's in it?"

"Something," she said, pressing it to her breast.

"Are you going to let me read it?"

"Maybe."

"How did you find Clara?"

"She's fine," she said, opening the briefcase and taking out a file folder. She carefully handed it to me.

"What is it?"

"Read," she sweetly commanded over the noise.

I opened the folder and came face to face with Clara--on the cover of *Time*--queenly in her youthful reserve, framed by a purple and gold scrolled escutcheon, against a field of tiny New Orleanians living it up Mardi Gras style. The cover had been neatly torn away from the magazine.

"Where did you get this?" I asked.

"I borrowed it from the library."

"Stole it, you mean."

"Whatever. Read the article."

I read."The lady I visited today was once a queen and now she lives in a beautiful house in Algiers on the historic old River Road. It is a world apart: and of another time, as is the lady herself."

It went on like this, so simple and sincere, from her heart. Perfect for *Dixie*.

"It's good," I said, trying to hide the tender feelings her writing had aroused in me. But it was true, I felt redeemed. I had thought so cynically of Clara living alone in her father's house, her sanctuary really, barricaded against life--the definitively lonely woman, miraculously undeveloped, savoring in some hidden recesses of her mind the tragedy of her father's untimely death. And that old house of hers, she had not restored it for the usual reasons. The South is even today full of ladies who restore such houses, which is no more corrupt than wearing Paris originals or driving luxury cars. Clara, though, I thought grimly, had made her father's house a cenotaph. Looking again at her picture on the cover of *Time*, I began to penetrate the image of this imperiously sober, aloof woman, beyond the thick wall that protected her womanhood, into the inner sanctum of a perfectly realized femininity, engendered by her sacred bond with Maurice, that eternal man--forever handsome, charming and youthful.

"It's good? Is that all you have to say?" Bernice asked, reaching across to seize my hands.

"It's good enough to be published. We'll run it next week. But I think you should get Clara's permission."

"She's already given it."

Epilogue

Epilogue

The French Quarter, Monday, July 19, 1990

The rain has stopped, and the sky is again filled with the white bosomy clouds of summer. Water seeps in patios, between bricks and flagstones, and drips idly from balcony floors and roof eaves. The sun beams, twirling the hanging pots of fern on my balcony, burning what's left of the rainwater on the street into vapors of steam. The hot, moist air, unable to stir, rises to merge with the clouds as the wet morning slides quietly into the cauldron of afternoon.

The usual July storm it was--lightening and thunder exploding so violently that I thought the window panes would shatter. And rain-- deluging, blurring vision, pouring off roofs tops and flooding the narrow streets, bumping and hurtling down the old caste iron gutter pipes of this old building. But over so quickly that in the searing silence that follows, I hardly remember from where I sit on my Victorian settee how cheered I was by the furious, fluttering music of so much water decending from the heavens.

The streets are empty. Everyone is inside--alone again--thinking and remembering. Everyone but Sheila, who is out, as she usually is on Saturday, keeping in touch. I should do as much. Four years ago I left the paper and can now report that retirement is more challenging than I could have imagined. My days and weeks pass seamlessly--piling up lost time which, sooner or later I know I will have to account for. It is hard to believe how very busy I use to be, putting together *Dixie Roto*, that long-gone, old-fashion little magazine, and lately, even harder to believe how happy I thought I was going to be without *Dixie* and its grimy little problems--no more deadlines, no more late-night phone calls, no more editing.

Dixie is gone, replaced by a snappy Saturday serendipity tabloid and a nationally syndicated Sunday pullout magazine. We had gone out together. Everything, in fact, at the *Picayune* and the world has turned over, since that first day of my retirement when I went happily to the supermarket in the morning for empty boxes to pack the accumulations of twenty-five years from my desk and file cabinets. It was one of those rare Crescent City days when the world seemed to be smiling at me, a lucid May morning, smelling of the new Spring, sunny and dry. What could go wrong I was thinking ; it was 1986, two years beyond Orwell's entitled year of prophecy and as yet, throughout this USA of ours, everyone was free, the eager multitude still on the rampage; hadn't old George, for all of his wisdom, gotten it wrong? No one could control them, least of all here, where Big Brother would be drown out by the loud murmur of novena prayers.

It wasn't until I entered my office, that I realized how the spring weather had fooled me. Most of the furniture had been removed and the nearly empty room loomed cavernous. An unsettling spirit lurked as my foot-falls resounded like echoing thuds and I felt sudden alarm at my own shadows darting on the bare walls.

I had some inkling of the ordeal that leaving would be, but I had promised myself that I was going to take all of it in stride, not be sad and especially not nostalgic, and as I filled up my boxes, I was holding the line, forestalling the gloom that slowly gathered around me. And I might have succeeded if I had not found this nearly crushed folder buried at the bottom of my file cabinet, rising like an ancient scroll from some deep well of my past. It was bent and battered and sprinkled generously with tiny black nuggets of roach dung, its label and edges chewed by those vile creatures into a random kind of manila lace; but I recognized it immediately. Inside were two familiar, delicately nibbled clippings, so brown and brittle that I hesitated to handle them--news stories bearing my byline, dated 1960. The remaining item of heavier stock was a famous cover of Dixie, creased neatly into quadrants. which I unfolded stiffly, revealing a faded picture of Clara as a ninth ward queen from a reproduction of an original *Time* magazine cover. The *Time* cover was dated 1960 and the two-page feature article within, 1984, with a byline by Bernice Waguespack. I was reminded that I had wanted to fashion a novel about Clara until Sheila reminded me that writing a novel about a real, living person is possibly libelous and otherwise a lunatic idea that had more to do with my fear of getting old than with any authentic literary ambition.

Ah me, Clara, I whispered--where are you now?

But now I have another problem. Bernice called me last week and told me that she had gotten married again, this time to an ex-priest, a situation I found impossible to imagine. Her husband writes for the *Picayune* and asked her to arrange an appointment with me. I asked why--I thought surely he wanted to ask me of all of my fond memories with *Dixie*. But she said he wanted to ask me about Clara.

"Why does he want to do that?"

"Because I told him that you know something about Clara that nobody else knows, and he's really interested in doing her story. Do it as a favor to me, this is his first big assignment. "

I agreed--how could I resist meeting Bernice's new husband--a priest? I told her, though--chastely of course--that my involvement would end there. Not that I, who had so wisely forsaken my endless wonderment about Clara and her strange powers, had any curiosity about why an ex-priest, turned journalist, was making inquiries about her.

Sheila greeted the news of this interview with a patronizing smile, as I knew she would. Lately whenever Sheila and I talk of Clara, she reminds me that Clara is very much alive--a very nice, normal lady, she says, an old friend we should visit soon. Sheila's right, and I let it go at that--what would be the point of me resurrecting my obsession with Clara, surely not, I argued, to exorcize the spirit that Sheila claimed still haunted me of all the blank pages I never wrote about her--or to dispel what I once so extravagantly believed Clara meant to me and my friends, or more simply to sort out the Clara I knew from the one I thought I knew--or the Clara that was from the Clara that quite possibly never was, and to be finally done with her!

I can relate now to Sheila's great satisfaction that Bernice's husband, Paul Arceneaux or Father Arceneaux or whatever he calls himself now, my interviewer, has come and gone in the wake of another explosive thunder storm and I have fallen victim to exactly what she warned me against.

I had waited anxiously on my settee for his arrival with the rain pounding, wondering if he would be late because of the storm. But I needn't have worried because almost exactly on the appointed minute came the raucous sound of the buzzer downstairs, ungluing me from the settee to hurriedly check my condition in the full-length mirror in the hallway. It was too late--I had lost my chance--all morning I had tried to pick up the phone to cancel. I thought depressingly that he might do something really embarrassing such as presenting me with some phony award--a silver cup--or invite me to a reunion banquet to reminisce with other old-timers--janitors, night watchmen, guys from down in the pressroom.

I buzzed to release the downstairs lock as the rain ceased and sun rays broke through the clouds and streamed through the French windows. I heard my interviewer trudge heavily up the stairs, and waited an uncertain moment before opening the door to greet him--a tall young man with raincoat and dripping umbrella, carrying a large leather case and portfolio. He had thick, black curly hair and a boyish smile, though for all of that, could have been as old as forty-five. I had never before laid eyes on him.

"Mr. Arceneaux--Paul, is it? Come in--give me your umbrella. Are you soaked?"

"Yes--No, well, not much, thank you,"

"Can I take that case, it looks heavy. And your raincoat." He put the case down and shed his raincoat, which I hung up in the closet with his umbrella.

"Thank you. Well!" he exclaimed, giving himself a shake. "It came down so fast, but I think it cooled things off, for a while anyway."

"I'm Bobby Gomez." I offered, extending my hand. "Please sit down."

"Thanks." He replied carrying the case with him to the sofa and smiling broadly, "Well, it's so nice to finally meet you--Bobby." On the balcony, the sun shone on Sheila's splendid potted plants, sparkling them to green luminosity.

"What is that?" I inquired of the bulky, scuffed case, covered with venerable 1950's ersatz leather. It smelled musty and mildewed.

"A tape recorder."

"That's a real antique," I joked, nudging it with my shoe. He had set it down nearer to me than to him, which struck me as strange. "Somehow, it looks familiar."

"It should."

"What do you mean?"

"I salvaged it from the *Picayune's* basement; it was tagged with your name. You don't remember it?"

"No, are you sure it was my name?"

"Yes, but I don't think it was ever used. Bernice said that you had trouble operating it--because you were too traditional."

"How is Bernice?"

"She's fine and sends her best wishes. We're sorry we didn't invite you to the--no one was--because of the circumstances."

"Leaving the priesthood, you mean?

"Yes,"

"What has Bernice told you about me?"

"That you got her started at the paper, and--about the affair she had with you." I dropped my eyes and I think he did too.

"Is that all--not that it isn't enough?" I said bitterly, unbelieving that he had actually said what he did.

"No," he said soberly, clearing his throat. "She said you helped her when she needed it. I didn't mean to make you uncomfortable. She also said that you tell good stories."

"I don't think I'll tell you that story."

"I've already heard it, it's not the one I want to hear?"

"Yes, I know. What do you want to know about Clara---about her picture on the cover of *Time*?"

"That's part of it."

"And about my obsession with her--isn't that what Bernice told you?"

"Something like that."

"Did she also tell you I'm a frustrated writer and whatever I told her about Clara can't be trusted because I probably invented it? Besides Bernice could have told you what you want to know, she was the one who wrote the story for *Dixie*."

"Yes, I know--in 1984?"

"That's right. Then you've read it?'

"I did."

"What else is there to tell?"

"Your version of the story. That's why I brought the tape recorder--with extra tapes."

I smiled, "You're joking?"

"Not at all. Bernice and I discussed it, she said you would enjoy putting it all on tape for the record."

"I don't think you understand, it wouldn't be just Clara's story, it would be the story of what happened to all of us when we were young and didn't know what was go;ing to happen to us.."

"A time in which you think Clara played a key role?

"Yes, I thought that to be the case--once."

"What exactly did Clara do that made you believe this?"

"Nothing--like I said."

"But it's true that you thought she inspired you and your friends?"

"Yes, I guess so, but I didn't think that until much later, when my life wasn't going very well and I was looking for something that could explain what makes people successful and happy.

"So you invoked Clara to console yourself?

"I didn't think of it that way. But maybe I did. Maybe I thought of her as--I don't know--a kind of presence. You ought to know about appealing to saints, being a priest."

"An ex-priest. And I don't know what a saint is anymore, if I ever did. I just want the story."

"Just kidding. Sometimes I don't know if Clara was even good for herself. Her life was empty if you think about it."

"That picture of her on the cover of *Time* does not look like someone whose life was empty. She looks fulfilled in every way."

"Yes, if you don't know how her picture came to be on the cover of *Time*, but that's a long story, and what's in it for me to try to remember all of that." I gazed out of the window as I spoke; when I turned back, he was closing his note pad--apparently to end the interview."

"But don't get me wrong." I quickly resumed, not wanting him to give up on me." I think it would be very interesting to try to remember what I can about Clara, which won't be much more than you know now."

"Good," he concluded, slapping his pad and rising. "I'll leave the tape recorder here with you, with extra tapes, and in a couple of weeks I'll come back. But you're not under any obligation. If you use it, fine, but if you don't, that's all right, too. Where is my coat and umbrella?"

For some reason I couldn't move and had to helplessly watch him get his coat and umbrella from the closet and leave--just like that, with me stuck to the settee, eyes aglow, dredging up old memories for my old tape recorder.

Why did I agree to do this? After all, what do I really know about Clara--that strange lonely woman, living in her father's big, empty house? The very thought of it fills me with--I can't even say what.

Outside of my window, dark clouds gather again over the quaint and still sodden grandeur of the Quarter's rickety houses, among which Sheila and I have chosen to live in our success. Another storm approachs and I begin to ponder, drifting far away, listening to the steamy summer drone on, growing mold and sprouting wild fern in alleyways, patios and graveyards.

I turned on the tape-recorder ......

The text of this book is set in Arrus BT Roman
with Ribbon 131 for titling and initial caps.

It is printed on 55# Booktext Natural at 360 PPI.